Praise for the novels of
New York Times bestselling author
Brenda Joyce

"Merging depth of history with romance
is nothing new for the multitalented author,
but here she also brings in an intensity of political history
that is both fascinating and detailed."
—*RT Book Reviews* on *Seduction*

"Joyce excels at creating twists and turns
in her characters' personal lives."
—*Publishers Weekly*

"Another first-rate Regency, featuring multidimensional
protagonists and sweeping drama… Joyce's tight plot and
vivid cast combine for a romance that's just about perfect."
—*Publishers Weekly,* starred review, on *The Perfect Bride*

"Truly a stirring story with wonderfully etched characters,
Joyce's latest is Regency romance at its best."
—*Booklist* on *The Perfect Bride*

"Romance veteran Joyce brings her keen sense of humor
and storytelling prowess to bear on her witty,
fully formed characters."
—*Publishers Weekly* on *A Lady at Last*

"Joyce's characters carry considerable emotional weight,
which keeps this hefty entry absorbing,
and her fast-paced story keeps the pages turning."
—*Publishers Weekly* on *The Stolen Bride*

BRENDA JOYCE

Persuasion

HARLEQUIN®
entertain, enrich, inspire™

PB
Joyce,
Dreams

Recycling programs
for this product may
not exist in your area.

ISBN-13: 978-0-373-77692-4

PERSUASION

Copyright © 2012 by Brenda Joyce Dreams Unlimited, Inc.

Persuasion

PROLOGUE

La Prison de la Luxembourg, Paris, France
March, 1794

THEY WERE FINALLY COMING for him.

His heart lurched with fear. He could not breathe. Slowly, filled with tension, he turned to stare into the dark corridor. He heard soft, steady footfalls approaching.

He knew he needed his wits. He walked over to the front of the cell and grasped the ice-cold iron bars there. The footfalls were louder now.

His insides shrank. The fear was cloying. Would he live to see another day?

The cell stank. Whoever had inhabited it before him, they had urinated, defecated and vomited within its confines. There was dried blood on the floors and the pallet, upon which he refused to lie. The cell's previous inhabitants had been beaten, tortured. Of course they had—they had been enemies of *la Patrie*.

Even the air flowing into the cell from its single, barred window was fetid. La Place de la Révolution was just meters below the prison's walls. Hundreds—no, thousands—had been sent to the guillotine there. The blood of the guilty—and the innocent—tainted the very air.

He could hear their voices now.

He inhaled, sick with fear.

Ninety-six days had passed since he had been ambushed outside the offices where he clerked at the Commune. Ambushed, shackled, a hood thrown over his head. "Traitor," a familiar voice had spat as he was heaved onto the bed of a wagon. An hour later, the hood had been ripped from his head and he had found himself standing in the midst of this cell. He was being accused, the guard said, of crimes against the Republic. And everyone knew what that meant....

He had never seen the man who had spoken, yet he was fairly certain that he was Jean Lafleur, one of the most radical officials of the city's government.

Images danced in his head. His two sons were small, handsome, innocent boys. He had been very careful, but not careful enough, when he had left France in order to visit his sons. They had been in London. It had been William's birthday. He had missed him—and John— terribly. He hadn't stayed in London very long; he hadn't dared linger, for fear of discovery. No one, outside of the family, had known he was in town. But with his departure hanging over him, it had been a bittersweet reunion.

And from the moment he had returned to French shores, he had felt that he was being watched. He had never caught anyone following him, but he was certain he was being pursued. Like most Frenchmen and women, he had begun to live in constant fear. Every shadow made him jump. At night, he would awaken, thinking he had heard that dreaded knock upon his door. When they knocked at midnight, it meant they were coming for you....

As they were coming for him now. The footsteps had become louder.

He inhaled, fighting his panic. If they sensed his fear,

it would be over. His fear would be the equivalent of a confession—for them. For that was how it was now in Paris, and even in the countryside.

He seized the cell bars. His time had just run out. Either he would be added to the *Liste Générale des Condamnés,* and he would await trial and then execution for his crimes, or he would walk out of the prison, a free man....

Finding courage was the hardest act of his life.

The light of a torch was ahead. It approached, illuminating the dank stone walls of the prison. And finally, he saw the outlines of the men. They were silent.

His heart thundered. Otherwise, he did not move.

The prison guard came into view, leering with anticipation, as if he knew his fate already. He recognized the Jacobin who was behind him. It was the rabidly radical, brutally violent Hébertiste Jean Lafleur as he had suspected.

Tall and thin, his visage pale, Lafleur came up to the bars of his cell. *"Bonjour, Jourdan. Comment allez-vous, aujourd'hui?"* He grinned, delighting in the moment.

"Il va bien," he said smoothly—all is well. When he did not beg for mercy or declare his innocence, Lafleur's smile vanished and his stare sharpened.

"Is that all you have to say? You are a traitor, Jourdan. Confess to your crimes and we will make certain your trial is swift. I will even make certain your head comes off first." He grinned again.

If it ever came to that, he hoped he would be the first to the guillotine—no one wanted to stand there for hours and hours, in shackles, watching the ghastly executions while awaiting one's own fate. "Then the loss would be yours." He could barely believe how calm he sounded.

Lafleur stared. "Why aren't you declaring your innocence?"

"Will it help my cause?"

"No."

"I did not think so."

"You are the Viscomte Jourdan's third son, and your redemption has been a lie. You do not love *la Patrie*—you spy! Your family is dead, and you will soon join them at the gates of purgatory."

"There is a new spymaster in London."

Lafleur's eyes widened in surprise. "What ploy is this?"

"You must know that my family has financed the merchants in Lyons for years, and that we have extensive relations with the British."

The radical Jacobin studied him. "You vanished from Paris for a month. You went to London?"

"Yes, I did."

"So you confess?"

"I confess to having business affairs in London that I had to attend, Lafleur. Look around you. Everyone in Paris is starving. The *assignat* is worthless. Yet I always have bread on my table."

"Smuggling is a crime." But Lafleur's eyes glittered.

Finally, he let his mouth soften and he shrugged. The black market in Paris was vast and untouchable. It was not going to end, not now, not ever.

"What can you get me?" Lafleur demanded softly. His black gaze was unwavering now.

"Didn't you hear me?"

"Are we speaking about bread and gold—or the new spymaster?"

Very softly, he said, "I have more than business relations in that country. The Earl of St. Just is my cousin, and if you have properly researched my family, you would have realized that."

He felt Lafleur's mind racing.

"St. Just is very well placed in London's highest circles. I think that he would be thrilled to learn that one of his relations has survived the destruction of the city. I even think he would welcome me with open arms into his home."

Lafleur still stared. "This is a trick," he finally said. "You would never come back!"

He slowly smiled. "I suppose that is possible," he said. "I suppose I might never come back. Or I could be the *Enragé* I claim to be, as loyal to *la Liberté* as you are, and I could return with the kind of information very few of Carnot's spies could ever attain—priceless information to help us win the war."

Lafleur's gaze was unwavering.

He did not bother to point out that the gains to be made if he did as he said—move within the highest echelons of Tory London and return to *la République* with classified information—far outweighed the risk that he might vanish from France never to return.

"I cannot make this kind of decision by myself," Lafleur finally said. "I will bring you before *le Comité*, Jourdan, and if you convince them of your worth, you will be spared."

He did not move.

Lafleur left.

And Simon Grenville collapsed upon the pallet on the floor.

CHAPTER ONE

Greystone Manor, Cornwall
April 4, 1794

GRENVILLE'S WIFE WAS DEAD.

Amelia Greystone stared at her brother, not even seeing him, a stack of plates in her hands.

"Did you hear what I said?" Lucas asked, his gray eyes filled with concern. "Lady Grenville died last night giving birth to an infant daughter."

His wife was dead.

Amelia was paralyzed. There was news every day about the war or the violence in France—all of it awful, all of it shocking. But she had not expected this.

How could Lady Grenville be dead? She was so elegant, so beautiful—and too young to die!

Amelia could barely think. Lady Grenville had never set foot in St. Just Hall since their marriage ten years ago, and neither had her husband. Then she had appeared in January at the earl's ancestral home with her household and two sons—and a child obviously on the way. St. Just had not been with her.

Cornwall was a godforsaken place in general, but even worse in January. The region was frigidly cold and inhospitable in the midst of winter, when gale winds blew, and vicious storms swept the coast.

Who would come to the farthest end of the country

in winter to give birth to a child? Her appearance had been so terribly strange.

Amelia had been as surprised as everyone else in the parish to hear that the countess was in residence, and when she had received an invitation to tea, she hadn't even considered refusing. She had been very curious to meet Elizabeth Grenville, and not just because they were neighbors. She had wondered what the Countess of St. Just was like.

And she had been exactly what Amelia was expecting—blonde and beautiful, gracious, elegant and so very genteel. She had been perfect for the dark, brooding earl. Elizabeth Grenville was everything that Amelia Greystone was not.

And because Amelia had buried the past so long ago—a decade ago, in fact—she hadn't once made the comparison. But now, as she stood there reeling in shock, she wondered suddenly if she had wished to inspect and interview the woman Grenville had decided to marry—the woman he had chosen instead of her.

Amelia trembled, holding the plates tightly to her chest. If she wasn't careful, she would remember the past! She refused to believe that she had really wished to meet Lady Grenville in order to decide what she was like. She was horrified by the comprehension.

She had liked Elizabeth Grenville. And her own affair with Grenville had ended a decade ago.

She had dismissed it from her mind then. She did not want to go back in time now.

But suddenly she felt as if she were sixteen years old, young and beautiful, naive and trusting, and oh so vulnerable. It was as if she were in Simon Grenville's powerful arms, awaiting his declaration of love and his marriage proposal.

She was stricken, but it was too late. A floodgate in her mind had opened. The heady images flashed—they were on the ground on a picnic blanket, they were in the maze behind the hall, they were in his carriage. He was kissing her wildly and she was kissing him back, and they were both in the throes of a very dangerous, mindless passion...

She inhaled, shaken by the sudden, jarring memory of that long-ago summer. He hadn't ever been sincere. He hadn't ever been courting her. She was sensible enough to know that now. Yet she had expected an offer of marriage from him and the betrayal had been devastating.

Why would Lady Grenville's terrible death cause her to remember a time in her life when she had been so young and so foolish? She hadn't given that summer a single thought in years, not even when she had been in Lady Grenville's salon, sipping tea and discussing the war.

But Grenville was a widower now....

Lucas seized the pile of plates she was holding, jerking her back to reality. She simply stared at him, horrified by her last thought and afraid of what it might mean.

"Amelia?" he asked with concern.

She mustn't think about the past. She did not know why those foolish memories had arisen, but she was a woman of twenty-six years now. That flirtation had to be forgotten. She hadn't wanted to ever recall that encounter—or any other like it—again. That was why she had dismissed the affair from her mind all those years ago, when he had left Cornwall without a word, upon the heels of the tragic accident that had killed his brother.

It all had to be forgotten.

And it was forgotten! There had been heartache, of

course, and grief, but she had moved on with her life. She had turned all of her attention to Momma, who was addled, her brothers and sister and the estate. She had genuinely managed to forget about him and their affair for an entire decade. She was a busy woman, with strained circumstances and onerous responsibilities. He had moved on, as well. He had married and had children.

And there were no regrets. Her family had needed her. It had been her duty to take care of them all, ever since she was a child, when Papa had abandoned them. But then the revolution had come, the war had begun, and everything had changed.

"You were about to drop the plates!" Lucas exclaimed. "Are you ill? You have turned as white as a sheet!"

She shivered. She certainly felt ill. But she was not going to allow the past, which was dead and buried, to affect her now. "This is terrible, a tragedy."

His golden hair pulled casually back in a queue, Lucas studied her. He had only just walked in the door, having come from London—or so he claimed. He was tall and dashing in his emerald-velvet coat, his fawn breeches and stockings, as he spoke, "Come now, Amelia, why are you upset?"

She managed a tight smile. Why was she upset? This wasn't about Grenville. A young, beautiful mother had died, leaving behind three small children. "She died giving birth to a third child, Lucas. And there are two small boys. I met her in February. She was as beautiful, as gracious, as elegant as everyone claimed." It had been obvious from the moment she had walked into the salon why Grenville had chosen her. He was dark and powerful, she was fair and lighthearted. They had made the perfect aristocratic couple. "I was very impressed with her kindness and her hospitality. She was clever, too. We had an amusing conversation. This is a shame."

"It is a shame. I am very sorry for those children and for St. Just."

Amelia felt some of her composure returning. And while Grenville's dark image seemed to haunt her now, her common sense returned. Lady Grenville was dead, leaving behind three small children. Her neighbors needed her condolences now, and possibly her help.

"Those poor boys—that poor infant! I feel so terribly for them!"

"It will be a rough patch," Lucas agreed. He gave her an odd look. "One never gets accustomed to the young dying."

She knew he was thinking about the war; she knew all about his wartime activities. But she kept thinking about those poor children now—which felt better, safer, than thinking about Grenville. She took the plates from Lucas and began setting the table grimly. She was so saddened for the children. Grenville was probably grieving, as well, but she did not want to consider him or his feelings, even if he was her neighbor.

She put the last plate down on the rather ancient dining-room table and stared at the highly polished, scarred wood. So much time had gone by. Once, she had been in love, but she certainly didn't love Grenville now. Surely she could do what was right.

In fact, she hadn't seen Simon Grenville in ten years. She probably wouldn't even recognize him now. He was probably overweight. His hair might be graying. He would not be a dashing young rake, capable of making her heart race with a single, heavy look.

And he would hardly recognize her. She was still slender—too slender, in fact—and petite, but her looks had faded as all looks were prone to do. Although older gentlemen still glanced at her occasionally, she was hardly as pretty as she had once been.

She felt some small relief. That terrible attraction which had once raged would not burn now. And she would not be intimidated by him, as she had once been. After all, she was older and wiser now, too. She might be an impoverished gentlewoman, but what she lacked in means she made up for in character. Life had made her a strong and resolute woman.

So when she did see Grenville, she must offer her condolences, just as she would to any neighbor suffering from such a tragedy.

Amelia felt slightly better. There was some small relief. That silly memory had been just that — silly.

"I am sure the family is reeling," Lucas was saying quietly. "She was certainly too young to die. St. Just must be in shock."

Amelia looked up carefully. Lucas was right. Grenville had to have loved his beautiful wife very much. She cleared her throat. "You have taken me by surprise, Lucas, as you always do! I was hardly expecting you, and you step in the door, with such stunning news."

He put his arm around her. "I am sorry. I heard about Lady Grenville when I stopped in Penzance to change carriages."

"I am very concerned about the children. We must help the family in every way that we can." She meant her every word. She never turned her back on anyone in need.

He smiled slightly. "Now that is the sister I know and love. Of course you are concerned. I am sure Grenville will make the appropriate arrangements for everyone, once he can think clearly."

She stared thoughtfully. Grenville was undoubtedly
in shock. Now, deliberately, she kept his dark, handsome image at bay—remembering that he was likely
fat and gray. "Yes, of course he will." She surveyed the
cheerfully set table. It wasn't easy making up a table, not
when their circumstances were so pinched. The gardens
were not yet in bloom, so the centerpiece was a tall silver candelabra, left over from better times. An ancient
sideboard was the only piece of furniture in the room,
and their best china was displayed there. Their hall was
as sparsely furnished. "Luncheon will be ready in a few
more minutes. Will you go upstairs and get Momma?"

"Of course. And you did not have to go to this trouble."

"I am thrilled when you are home. Of course we will
dine as if we are an ordinary family."

His smile was wry. "There are few ordinary families
left, Amelia, not in these times."

Her small smile faded. Lucas had just walked in the
door moments ago, and she hadn't seen him in a month
or more. There were shadows under his eyes and a small
scar on his cheekbone, which hadn't been there before.
She was afraid to ask how he'd gotten it, and even more
afraid to ask where. He was still a dangerously handsome man, but the revolution in France and the war had
entirely changed their lives.

Before the French monarchy had fallen, they had all
lived simple lives. Lucas had spent his time managing
the estate, his biggest concern increasing the productiv-
ity of their mine and quarry. Jack, who was a year her
junior, had been just another Cornish smuggler, laughing about outracing the Revenue Men. And her younger
sister, Julianne, had spent her every spare moment innocently in the library, reading everything she could

and honing her Jacobin sympathies. Greystone Manor had been a busy, happy home. Although the small estate depended almost entirely upon an iron quarry and tin mine for its income, they managed well enough. Amelia had an entire family to take care of—including her mother. The only thing that the war hadn't changed was that Momma remained entirely senile.

John Greystone, her father, had left the family when Amelia was only seven years old, and Momma had begun losing her grip on reality shortly thereafter. Amelia had instinctively stepped into the breach, helping with the household, making shopping lists and planning menus, and even ordering their few servants about. And mostly she had cared for Julianne, then a toddler. Their uncle, Sebastian Warlock, had sent a forcman to manage the estate, but Lucas had taken over those duties before he was even fifteen. Theirs had been an unusual household, but it had been a busy and familial one, filled with love and laughter, no matter the financial strain.

The house was nearly empty now. Julianne had fallen in love with the Earl of Bedford when he had been deposited at the manor by their brothers, while at death's door. Of course, she hadn't known who he was—he had seemed to be a French army officer at the time. It had been a very rocky road—he had been a spy for Pitt and she had been a Jacobin sympathizer. It was still rather amazing, but she had recently eloped with Bedford, and she had just given birth to their daughter in London, where they lived. Amelia shook her head, bemused. Her radical sister was now the Countess of Bedford—and madly in love with her Tory husband.

Her brothers' lives had changed because of the war, as well. Lucas was rarely at Greystone Manor now. Because they were but two years apart in age, and because they had taken over the roles of their parents, they were close. Amelia was his confidante, although he did not tell her every detail of his affairs. Lucas had not been able to sit idly by while the revolution swept over France. Some time ago, Lucas had secretly offered his services up to the War Office. Even before the Terror began sweeping France, there had been a flood of émigrés fleeing the revolutionaries—fleeing for their lives. Lucas had spent the past two years "extracting" émigrés from the shores of France.

It was a dangerous activity. If Lucas were ever caught by the French authorities, he would be instantly arrested and sent to the guillotine. Amelia was proud of him, but she was also so afraid for him.

She worried about Lucas all of the time, of course. He was the anchor of the family—its patriarch. But she worried about Jack even more. Jack was fearless. He was reckless. He acted as if he thought himself to be immortal. Before the war, he had been a simple Cornish smuggler—one of the dozens making such a living, and following in the footsteps of too many of his ancestors to count. Now Jack was making a fortune from the smuggling of various goods between the countries at war. No game could be more dangerous. Jack had been outwitting and outrunning the Royal Navy for years. Before the war, a prison sentence had awaited him if he were ever captured. Now, however, he would be accused of treason if the British authorities caught him defying the blockade of France. Treason was a hanging offense.

And from time to time, Jack aided Lucas in smuggling people across the channel.

Amelia was grateful that, at least, Julianne was comfortably settled and preoccupied with her husband and daughter. She met Lucas's probing regard. "I worry about you and I worry about Jack. At least I don't have to worry about Julianne now."

He smiled. "On that point I agree. She is well cared for and out of all danger."

"If only the war would end! If only there was good news!" Amelia shook her head, thinking how Lady Grenville had died, leaving behind an innocent newborn daughter and two small boys. "I can't imagine what it would be like, to live without war."

"We are fortunate we do not live in France." He wasn't smiling now.

"Please, I cannot listen to another horrible story. The rumors are bad enough."

"I was not going to burden you with one. You do not need to know the details of how the innocent in France suffer. If we are fortunate, our armies will defeat the French this spring. We are poised to invade Flanders, Amelia. We have strong positions from Ypres to the Meuse River, and I think Coburg, the Austrian, is a good general." He was quiet for a moment. "If we win the war, the Republic will fall. And that will be liberation for us all."

"I am praying we will win," she said, but she was still thinking about the Countess of St. Just and the children she had left behind.

Lucas took her elbow. When he spoke, his tone was low, as if he did not want to be overheard, although there was no one except Garrett, the servant, to really overhear them. "I came home because I am worried. Did you hear what happened at Squire Penwaithe's?"

She met his gaze, tensing. "Of course I did. Everyone heard. Three French sailors—deserters—appeared at his front door, asking for food. The squire gave them a meal. Afterward, they held the family at gunpoint and looted the house."

"Fortunately they were apprehended the next day and no one was hurt." Lucas was grim.

Amelia was well aware of what he was thinking. She was living in such isolation with their mother and their one servant. Garrett happened to have been a sergeant in the British infantry, and was adept with weapons. Still, Greystone Manor was at one of the farthest southwestern points of Cornwall. Its isolation was one reason the parish had been such a haven for smugglers over the centuries. It was a very short run from Sennen Cove, which was just below the house, to Brest, in France.

Those deserters could have shown up at her door, Amelia thought.

A headache had begun. Suddenly tired of worrying, Amelia rubbed her temples. At least the gun closet was full—and being a Cornish woman, she knew very well how to load and fire a musket, a carbine and a pistol.

"I think you and Momma should spend the spring in London," Lucas said flatly. "There is plenty of room at Warlock's Cavendish Square flat, and you will be able to visit with Julianne frequently." He smiled, but it did not reach his eyes.

She had just spent a month in London with her sister, after her niece's birth. They were close, and it had been a wonderful, almost peaceful, interlude. Amelia began to consider leaving her home temporarily. Maybe Lucas was right. "It is not a bad idea, but what about the manor? Will we simply close it up? And what about Farmer Richards? You know he pays me the rents, now that you are always gone."

"I can make arrangements to have the rents collected.

I feel I would be negligent in my familial duty, Amelia, if I did not remove you and Momma to safer ground."

He was right, Amelia realized. "It will take some time to make the proper arrangements," she said.

"Try to close up this house as swiftly as possible," he returned. "I have to go back to London, and I will do so after the funeral. When you are ready to join me, I will either come for you myself, or send Jack or a driver."

Amelia nodded, but now, all she could think about was the impending funeral. "Lucas, do you know when they will hold the funeral?"

"I heard that they will have a service at the St. Just chapel on Sunday, but she will be buried in the family mausoleum in London."

She tensed. It was already Friday! And there was Grenville, with his dark eyes and dark hair, assailing her in her mind's eye another time. She wet her lips. "I have to attend. So do you."

"Yes. We can go together."

She looked at him, her heart lurching. She could not stop her thoughts. On Sunday she would see Simon for the first time in ten years.

AMELIA SAT WITH LUCAS and Momma in their carriage, clutching her gloved hands tightly together. She could not believe the amount of tension within her. She could barely breathe.

It was noon on Sunday. In another half an hour, the service for Elizabeth Grenville would begin.

St. Just Hall was in sight.

It was a huge manor that was entirely out of place in Cornwall. Built of pale stone, the central part of the house was three stories high, with four huge alabaster columns gracing the entrance. A lower, two-story wing was on the landward side, with sloping slate roofs. At the farthest end was the chapel, replete with its own courtyard, columns gracing the facade and corner towers abutting the adjacent entry.

Tall, black leafless trees surrounded the house. The grounds were equally barren from the long winter, but in May, the gardens would start to bloom. By the summer, the grounds would be a canvas of rioting color, the trees lush and green, the maze of hedges behind the house almost impossible to escape.

Amelia knew all of that firsthand.

She must not remember being lost in that maze now. She must not remember being breathless and giddy, and then Simon had turned the corner, sweeping her into his arms…

She shut off her thoughts, shaken, as their carriage moved up the graveled drive, following two dozen other vehicles. The entire parish would turn out for Lady Grenville's funeral. Farmers would stand side by side with squires.

And in a few more minutes, she would see Grenville again.

"Is it a ball?" Momma asked excitedly. "Oh, darling, are we going to a ball?"

Lucas patted her hand. "Momma, it is I, Lucas, and, no, we are attending the funeral for Lady Grenville."

Momma was a tiny, gray-haired woman, even smaller than Amelia. She stared blankly at Lucas. Amelia was no longer saddened by her condition. She was so rarely coherent these days. As she often did, Momma thought herself a young debutante again, and that Lucas was either their father or one of her previous beaux.

Amelia stared out of her carriage window as Momma sat between her and Lucas. She had done her best, these past two days, to focus on the tasks at hand. She had a huge list to get through if she were to close up the manor and remove herself and Momma to town. She had already written Julianne, apprising her of the current events. She had begun to pack up linens, store preserves and put away their winter clothing, and organize what they would need for a season in town. Keeping busy had been a relief. From time to time she had worried about Lady Grenville's children, but she had managed not to think about St. Just, not even once—but his dark, handsome face continually lurked in the back of her mind.

There was no denying her anxiety now. She was riddled with tension and she could barely breathe. Yet it was absurd. So what if they came face-to-face again after all these years? He was not going to recognize her, and if he did, he would not even recall their foolish flirtation—she was certain.

But images from that long-ago affair kept trying to creep into her whirling thoughts as her carriage moved forward. The urge to indulge in those memories had begun the moment she had arisen at dawn.

Amelia knew that she must keep her wits about her. But she had begun to remember how crushed she had truly been when she had learned that he had left Cornwall. Not only hadn't he said goodbye, he hadn't even left a note.

She was beginning to remember the weeks of heartache and grief; the nights she had cried herself to sleep.

She had to behave with pride and dignity now. She had to remember that they were neighbors, and nothing more. She hugged herself.

"Are you all right?" Lucas's grim voice cut into her thoughts.

She didn't try to force a smile. "I am glad we are here.

I hope I have a moment to meet the children before the service begins. They are my most pressing concern."

"Children do not attend balls," Momma said firmly.

Amelia smiled at her. "Of course they don't." She turned back to Lucas.

He said, "You seem very tense."

"I have been so preoccupied with getting everything done before we leave for town," she lied. "I feel as if I am on pins and needles." She smiled at Momma. "Won't it be wonderful, to go back to town?"

Momma's eyes widened. "Are we going to town?" She was delighted.

Amelia took her hand and squeezed it. "Yes, we are, as soon as we can be ready."

Lucas's stare seemed skeptical. "You know, if you are thinking about the past, no one would blame you."

She choked as she released her mother's hand. "I beg your pardon?"

"It was long ago, but I haven't forgotten how he played you." His gaze narrowed. "He broke your heart, Amelia."

"I was sixteen!" she gasped. Lucas clearly hadn't forgotten a thing. "That was ten years ago!"

"Yes, it was. And he hasn't been back in all that time, not even once, so I imagine you might be somewhat nervous. Are you?"

She flushed. Lucas knew her so well, and while she did not keep secrets from him, he hardly had to know that she was foolishly anxious now. "Lucas, I forgot the past a long time ago."

"Good." He was firm. "I am glad to hear that!" He added, "I've never said anything, but I've seen him now and then, in town. It has been cordial. There did not seem a point in holding a grudge, not after so many years."

She whispered, "You are right—there is no point in

holding any kind of grudge. Our lives took different paths." She hadn't realized that Lucas had socialized with Grenville, but he was in London often now, so of course their paths would eventually cross. She almost wanted to ask him how Simon was, and how he had changed. But she knew better. She smiled a bit, instead.

He stared for another moment, searching her gaze with his own. "Well, something is keeping him. My understanding is that he has yet to arrive at St. Just Hall."

Amelia was disbelieving. "That is impossible. Wherever he was when Lady Grenville passed, it has been three days. He would certainly be here by now!"

Lucas looked away as their carriage finally halted, not far from the chapel's courtyard. "The roads are bad at this time of year, but I would agree, he should be here by now."

She stared blankly. "Surely they will not hold the funeral without St. Just?"

"Everyone in the parish has turned out."

Amelia looked out of her window. The grounds were cluttered with coaches and carriages of all descriptions. Grenville had to have arranged for the funeral. Only he could postpone it. But if he were not present, how could he do that?

"My God," she whispered, distraught, "he might miss his own wife's funeral!"

"Let us hope he arrives at any moment." Lucas alighted, then turned to help Momma down. He held out his hand for Amelia. Still shocked, Amelia stepped down carefully. Maybe they would not meet that day after all. Was she relieved? If she did not know better, she would almost think that she almost felt disappointed.

A somberly dressed crowd was streaming into the chapel's courtyard, on foot. Amelia paused and glanced

sharply around. It was a gray, bleak, blustery day and
she shivered, in spite of the wool coat she wore. It had
been ten years since she had been at the hall, but nothing had changed. The house remained as imposing and
stately as ever.

As they left the drive, intending to follow everyone
else inside, her low heels sank into the ground. The
lawns were thawing and somewhat muddy. Lucas steered
her to the stone path leading toward the chapel's courtyard.

Was the rest of the family already inside? Amelia
wondered.

She glanced back toward the palatial front entrance
of the house and faltered. A slender man and a plump,
gray-haired woman were just coming down the front
steps with two small boys.

Those were Grenville's sons, she thought instantly,
oddly shaken.

She did not move. They were both dark-haired, and
dressed in dark, somber little jackets, breeches and pale
stockings. One boy was about eight, the other perhaps
four or five. The smaller boy held his older brother's
hand tightly. Now she realized that the governess carried
the infant, bundled in a heavy white blanket.

She hadn't met the boys the day that she had had tea
with their mother. As they came closer, she realized
that both boys so resembled their father—they would
grow up to be handsome men. Her heart lurched. The
younger boy was crying, while his older brother was
trying so hard to be stoic. Both children were clearly
grief-stricken.

Amelia's heart broke. "Take Momma inside. I will be
right back," she said, and not waiting for Lucas to answer, she started determinedly toward them.

She hurried toward the two adults and the children, giving the gentleman a firm smile. "I am Miss Amelia Greystone, Lady Grenville's neighbor. What a tragic day."

The gentleman had tears in his eyes. Although well dressed, it was obvious he was a servant of some sort and a foreigner. "I am Signor Antonio Barelli, Miss Greystone, the boys' tutor. And this is Mrs. Murdock, the governess. This is Lord William and Master John."

Amelia quickly shook hands with the tutor and Mrs. Murdock, who was also near tears. But she did not blame them; she imagined that Lady Grenville had been well loved. And then she smiled at William, the older boy, realizing that Grenville had named his heir after his deceased older brother. "I am very sorry for your loss, William. I met your mother recently and I liked her very much. She was a great lady."

William nodded solemnly, his mouth downturned. "We saw you when you called, Miss Greystone. Sometimes we watch callers arrive from an upstairs window."

"That must be amusing," Amelia said, smiling.

"Yes, it can be. This is my little brother, John." But William did not smile in return.

She smiled at John and squatted. "And how old are you, John?"

John looked at her, his face wet with tears, but his eyes were wide with curiosity. "Four," he finally said.

"Four!" she exclaimed. "I thought you were eight, at least!"

"I am eight," William said seriously. Then his gaze narrowed skeptically. "How old did you think I was?"

"Ten or eleven." Amelia smiled. "I see you are taking good care of your brother, as you should do. Your mother would be so proud of you."

He nodded solemnly, and glanced at Mrs. Murdock. "We have a sister now. She doesn't have a name yet."

Amelia smiled at him. "That is not unusual." She laid her hand on his head; his hair was silky soft, like his father's. She started, removing her hand. "I am here to help, in any way that I can. I am less than an hour away by coach."

"That is kind of you," William said, sounding very much like a grown-up.

Amelia smiled at him again, patted John on the shoulder and turned to the governess. The older woman, who was heavyset and gray-haired, was beginning to cry, tears slipping down her ruddy cheeks. Amelia dearly hoped she would discipline herself—the children needed her now. "And how is the baby faring?"

Mrs. Murdock inhaled. "She has been fussing ever since…ever since… I cannot get her to nurse properly, Miss Greystone. I am at a loss!" she cried, clearly panicked.

Amelia stepped closer to look at the sleeping infant. Mrs. Murdock moved an edge of the blanket away, and Amelia saw a fair-haired child, who was clearly the image of her blonde mother. "She is beautiful."

"Isn't she the exact image of Lady Grenville? God rest her soul. Oh, dear! I was only recently employed, Miss Greystone. I am entirely new here! We are all at a loss—and we have no housekeeper."

Amelia started. "What?"

"Mrs. Delaney was with Lady Grenville for many years, but she fell ill and died just after I was hired around Christmastime. Lady Grenville has been managing this household ever since, Miss Greystone. She meant to hire a new housekeeper, but no one met with her approval. Now no one is running this home!"

Amelia realized that the house must be in chaos, indeed. "I am sure his lordship will hire a new housekeeper immediately," she said.

"But he isn't even here!" Mrs. Murdock cried, and more tears fell.

"He is never in residence," Signor Barelli said with some disapproval, a tremor in his tone. "We last saw him in November—briefly. Is he going to come? Why isn't he here now? Where could he possibly be?"

Amelia was dismayed. She repeated what Lucas had said earlier. "He will be here at any moment. The roads are terrible at this time of year. Is he coming from London?"

"We don't know where he is. He usually claims he is in the north, at one of his great estates there."

Amelia wondered at the use of the word *claim*. What did the tutor mean?

"Father came home for my birthday," William said gravely, but with some pride. "Even though he is preoccupied with the estate."

Amelia was certain the boy was parroting his father. She could not absorb such a surprising state of affairs. There was no housekeeper; St. Just was never in residence; no one knew, precisely, where he was now. What did this mean?

John began to cry again. William took his hand. "He is coming home," William said fiercely and insistently. But he batted back tears with his lashes furiously.

Amelia looked at him and realized he would be exactly like his father—he certainly was in charge now. Before she could reassure him and tell him that St. Just would arrive at any moment and repair the household immediately, she heard the sound of an approaching carriage.

And she had not a doubt as to who it was before William even cried out. Slowly, she turned.

The huge black coach was thundering up the drive. Six magnificent black carriage horses were in the traces. The driver was in St. Just's royal-blue-and-gold livery, as were the two footmen standing on the rear fender. She realized she was holding her breath. St. Just had returned, after all.

The six-in-hand came around the circular drive at a near gallop. Passing the chapel, the coachman braked, shouting, "Whoa!" As the team came to a halt, not far from where they stood, gravel sprayed.

Amelia's heart was thundering. Her cheeks felt as if they were on fire. Simon Grenville was home.

Both footmen leaped to the ground and rushed to open Grenville's door for him. The Earl of St. Just stepped out.

Her mind went blank.

Clad impeccably in a dark brown velvet jacket with some embroidery, black breeches, white stockings and black shoes, he started toward their group. He was tall—perhaps an inch or two over six feet—and broad-shouldered, and he remained small of hip. Amelia glimpsed his high cheekbones, his strong jaw and that chiseled mouth. Her heart slammed.

He hadn't changed at all.

He was as handsome as she remembered. If he was gray, she wouldn't know—he wore a dark wig, in a somewhat redder shade than his natural hair, beneath a bicorne hat.

Amelia felt paralyzed. She stared, incapable of looking at anyone other than Grenville, who had eyes only for his sons.

In fact, it was as if he hadn't seen her. But she had

known he wouldn't remember her. So she could look openly at him. He was even more devastatingly handsome now that he was thirty, she somehow thought, in despair. He was even more commanding in appearance.

And the memories begged to be let loose. She fought them.

Grenville's strides were long and hard. His gaze unwavering, he reached the boys and pulled them both into his arms. John wept. William clung.

Amelia trembled, aware that she was an intruder. He hadn't looked at her—acknowledged her—recognized her. She should be relieved—this was the scenario she had envisioned—but she felt dismayed.

Grenville did not move, not for a long moment, as he embraced both of his sons. He kept his head bowed over them so she could not see his face. She wanted to leave, because this was such an intense familial reunion, but she was afraid to attract his attention.

And she heard him inhale, raggedly. Grenville straightened and released the boys, taking both of their hands. She had the oddest sense that he was afraid to let them go.

Finally, the earl nodded at the nurse and tutor. Both murmured, "My lord," their heads bowed.

Amelia wanted to disappear. He would glance at her at any moment—unless he meant to ignore her. Her heart kept thundering. She hoped he wouldn't hear it. She desperately hoped he wouldn't notice her, either.

But Grenville turned and looked directly at her.

She froze as their gazes met.

His dark gaze seemed to widen and then it locked with hers. Time seemed to stop. All noise seemed to vanish. There was only her deafening heartbeat, his surprise and the intense look they shared.

In that moment, Amelia realized that he had recognized her after all.

He didn't speak. Yet he didn't have to. Somehow, she felt the pain and anguish coursing through him. It was immense. In that moment, she knew he needed her as never before.

She lifted her hand toward him.

Grenville abruptly glanced at his sons. "It's too cold to linger outside." He put an arm around each boy and started forward. They entered the courtyard and vanished.

She inhaled, reeling.

He had recognized her.

And then she realized that he hadn't looked at his infant daughter a single time.

CHAPTER TWO

SIMON STARED BLINDLY AHEAD. He was seated in the first row of the chapel with his sons, but he was in a state of disbelief. Was he really back in Cornwall? Was he actually attending his wife's funeral?

Simon realized that his fists were clenched. He was staring at the reverend, who droned on and on about Elizabeth, but he hardly saw him and he did not hear him. Three days ago he had been in Paris, posing as Henri Jourdan, a Jacobin; three days ago he had been standing amongst the bloodthirsty crowd at La Place de la Révolution, witnessing dozens of executions. The very last one had been his friend, Danton, who had become a voice of moderation amongst the insane. Watching him lose his head had been a test of his loyalty. Lafleur had been with him. So he had applauded each beheading, and somehow, he hadn't become physically sick.

He wasn't in Paris now. He wasn't in France. He was in Cornwall, a place he hadn't meant to ever return to, and he felt dazed and disoriented. The last time he had been in Cornwall, his brother had died. The last time he had been in that chapel, he had been attending Will's funeral!

And maybe that was a part of the reason why he felt so ill. Still, the stench of blood was everywhere, as if it had followed him from Paris. It was even inside the chapel. But he smelled blood everywhere, all of the time—in his rooms, on his clothes, on his servants—he smelled blood even when he slept.

But then, death was everywhere. After all, he was attending his wife's funeral!

And he almost laughed, bitterly. Death had been following him for a very long time, so he should not be dazed, confused or surprised. His brother had died on these moors. Elizabeth had died in that house. He had spent the past year in Paris, where the Terror reigned. How ironic it all was. How fitting.

Simon turned and looked at the rapt crowd, who was devouring the reverend's every word—as if Elizabeth's death genuinely mattered, as if she were not one more innocent, lost amongst thousands. They were all strangers, he realized grimly, not friends and neighbors. He had nothing in common with any one of them, except for his nationality. He was an outsider now, the stranger in their midst....

He faced the pulpit again. He should try to listen, he should attempt to focus. Elizabeth was dead, and she had been his wife. The disbelief was almost stronger now. In his mind's eye, he could see inside that coffin. But Elizabeth did not lie inside; his brother did.

His tension escalated. He had left the parish within days of Will's tragic death. And if Elizabeth hadn't died at St. Just Hall, he wouldn't have returned.

God, he hated Cornwall!

Not for the first time, he wished that Will hadn't died. But he no longer railed against fate. He knew better. He had learned firsthand that the good and the innocent were always the first to die, which was why fate had just claimed his wife.

He closed his eyes and gave up. His mind ran free. Tears briefly burned his closed lids.

Why hadn't he been the one to die?

Will should have been the earl; Elizabeth should have been his wife!

Simon opened his eyes carefully, shaken by such thoughts. He did not know if he was still grieving for his older brother, who had died tragically in a riding accident so many years ago, or if he were grieving for those executed by the Terror, or even if he grieved for his wife, whom he hadn't really known. But he knew he must control his mind. It was Elizabeth, his wife, who was in that coffin. It was Elizabeth who was being eulogized. It was Elizabeth he should be thinking of—for the sake of his sons—until he went back to London to begin the dirty work of playing war games.

But he just couldn't do it. He could not concentrate on his dead wife. The ghosts that had been haunting him for weeks, months and years began to form before him, becoming the faces of his friends and neighbors in the crowd, and they were the faces of every man, woman and child he had seen in chains or guillotined. Those faces accused him of hypocrisy and cowardice, of ruthless self-survival, of his failure as a man, a husband, a brother.

He closed his eyes, as if that action might send those ghosts away, but it did not.

Simon wondered if he was finally losing his mind. He looked across the chapel and out the light stained-glass windows. The moors stretched endlessly away. No sight had ever been as ugly. He knew he must stop his thoughts. He had his sons to think of now, to care for.

And the minister was still speaking but Simon didn't hear a word he was saying. The image slammed over him and he could not move. He had been with the two grooms when they had found his brother lying on the hard rocky ground. He had been on his back, faceup, eyes open, the moonlight spilling over his handsome features.

All he could see was his dead brother now.

It was as if he had just found Will on the moors; it was as if the past had become the present.

Simon realized a tear was sliding down his face. There was so much heartache, so much pain. Would he mourn his brother all over again? He hadn't ever wanted to go back to the place in time!

Or was he finally mourning Elizabeth? Or even Danton? He hadn't allowed himself to grieve for anyone, ever. He didn't know, and he didn't care, but he was crying now. He felt the tears streaming helplessly down his face.

He realized he was staring through tears at the open coffin. He saw Elizabeth, so perfectly beautiful, even in death, but he also saw Will. His brother had been as golden, as perfect, as beautiful, in death. Elizabeth had been an angel, Will had been a hero.

There were so many memories rushing at him now, all vivid and painful. In some, he was with his brother, whom he had respected, admired and loved. In others, he was with his wife, whom he had tolerated but hadn't loved.

This was the reason he had not come back to this goddamned place, he thought, in sudden anguish. Will should be alive today. He had been gallant, charming and honorable. He would have been a great earl; he would have admired and loved Elizabeth. Will would not have sold out to the radicals.

Simon suddenly thought how prophetic his father had been. On numerous occasions, the earl had faulted him for his utter lack of character. Will was the perfect son, but Simon was not. Simon was the shameless one. He was reckless, inept and irresponsible, with no sense of honor or duty.

And he was the dishonorable one. For even now, he had two letters in his pocket, proving his absolute disloyalty. One was from Pitt's secret spymaster, Warlock, the other from his French master, Lafleur. Even Will would be ashamed of him now.

"Papa?"

It took Simon a moment to realize that his son had spoken to him. He managed to smile grimly at him. His cheeks felt wet. He did not want the boys to see. He knew John and William needed reassurance. "It will be all right."

"You're hurting me," John whispered.

Simon realized he was holding his hand, far too tightly. He loosened his death grip.

He heard Reverend Collins saying, "One of the kindest, most compassionate of ladies, forever giving to others, never taking for herself."

He wondered if it were true, he wondered if his wife had been a generous and kind woman. If she had had those qualities, he hadn't ever noticed. And now, it was too late.

He felt so sick now, perhaps from the addition of guilt to the rest of his roiling feelings.

Thump.

Someone had dropped his Bible.

Simon froze.

He did not see the reverend now. Instead, Danton stood on the red-stained steps of the guillotine, shouting his last words defiantly to the crowd, which chanted in return, *"À la guillotine! À la guillotine!"*

Simon saw the huge blade come down. Yet he knew it was impossible, that no blade was in the chapel. He laughed loudly. There was no mirth in the sound, and even he heard the hysteria and fear there.

But William tightened his grip on his hand, jerking him back to reality, and he looked down. William looked up at him with stricken concern. John seemed ready to cry again.

"And she will be sorely missed by her loving husband, by her devoted sons, by her grieving family and friends..." Reverend Collins cried.

He forced himself to become still. He fought the nausea, the grief. The boys would miss their mother, even if he would not. His sons needed her, the earldom needed her.

The ghosts of the innocent whirled in his mind and around him, becoming the crowd, and now, amongst them, he saw his wife and he saw his brother. He could not stand it.

He stood. "I will be right back," he said.

And as he pushed into the aisle and down the nave, praying he would not become sick until he went outside, her baby wailed.

He could not believe it. As he rushed toward the door, he found them in the last row. He looked at the child in the nurse's arms, briefly. Then he saw Amelia Greystone, and their gazes locked.

A moment later he was outside behind the chapel, on his knees, vomiting.

THE SERVICE WAS FINALLY OVER. And just in time, Amelia thought grimly, because the newborn had begun to fuss rather loudly and Mrs. Murdock seemed incapable of quieting her. A number of guests had turned to glance toward the crying baby. Had Grenville actually glared at his own daughter?

Her tension knew no bounds. It had been impossible to keep her gaze from his broad shoulders during the service. He had recognized her.

Amelia had never been as shaken.

But the crowd was beginning to arise. "We should slip out before the other guests," Amelia suggested. "The child is certainly hungry." But her eyes were on the front of the chapel. Grenville's two sons were seated in the front row by themselves. Grenville had left a few minutes ago, before the eulogy was over. How could he leave his children like that? Had he been that distraught?

When he had rushed up the nave, he had looked right at her. He had been terribly pale, as if he was about to become sick.

She shouldn't care, but she did.

"She misses her mother," Mrs. Murdock said. Tears began to slide down her face. "That is why she is so fussy."

Amelia hesitated. The governess had managed to control herself throughout the service, and she could not blame her for crying now. A funeral was overwhelming under the best of circumstances, and Elizabeth dying so young was the worst of events. But the infant had never known her mother. "Where is Signor Barelli? I don't know if St. Just will return. I think I should get the boys."

"I saw him leave before his lordship did," Mrs. Murdock said, rocking the child. "He adored Lady Grenville. I believe Signor Barelli was too distraught to stay. He was ready to weep!"

Amelia decided that Grenville had been too distraught to remain for the end of the service, as well. "Wait a moment," she said, and she hurried past the guests, most of whom were now leaving their seats. She knew them all, and she nodded at those she passed. "William? John? We are going back to the house. I am going to help Mrs. Murdock settle your sister. Afterward, I was wondering if you might give me a tour of your rooms?" She smiled.

Both boys stared at her, stricken. John said tearfully, "Where is Papa?" But he held out his hand.

Amelia took it, her heart surging. "He is grieving for your mother," she said softly. How wonderful the small boy's hand felt in hers. "I believe he went outside because he needed a moment alone."

John nodded, but William gave her an odd look, as if he wished to say something but knew better. Amelia took his hand as well, leading them toward the governess. "Signor Barelli has already left. I am sure he is waiting for you at the house."

"We are not having lessons today," William said firmly. Then, "I should like to see Father."

Amelia nodded at Mrs. Murdock. The infant was whimpering, as the governess rocked to hush her. The guests ahead of them stepped aside, clearly understanding their need to leave quickly. Amelia smiled at everyone as they passed. "Thank you, Mrs. Harrod," she said. "Thank you, Squire Penwaithe, for coming today. Hello, Millie. Hello, George. Apparently refreshments will be served shortly in the great hall." Mrs. Murdock had said as much, but now she wondered if Grenville would even bother to greet his guests.

Her neighbors smiled at her. Millie, a dairymaid, cried, "What a beautiful baby!"

As they left the chapel, Amelia glanced around and realized she was searching for Grenville. By now, he would have returned to the house, but he was not in sight. It had begun to drizzle. The infant started to cry again, this time very loudly.

Amelia took the wailing baby from the governess. "May I? Perhaps I can be of help." She cradled her close to her chest. It was too cold for the baby to be outside.

"I do hope so. I don't think she likes me. She knows I am not her natural mother," Mrs. Murdock exclaimed.

Amelia kept an impassive expression, inwardly sighing. She wished the governess would cease making such disturbing declarations, at least in front of the boys. Then she looked down at the beautiful baby, and she smiled. Her heart warmed. Oh, the little girl was such an angel! "Hush, sweetheart. We are going inside now. No child your age should have to attend a funeral." She realized she was somewhat angry. The baby should have remained in her nursery, safe and warm; surely she could sense the distress and sorrow in the chapel. But no one had advised Mrs. Murdock. After all, there was no housekeeper, and Grenville had only returned moments before the service had started.

How could he be so negligent?

The infant hiccupped and looked at her. Then she smiled.

Amelia cried out, delighted. "She is smiling! Oh, how pretty she is!"

"Do you have any of your own?" Mrs. Murdock asked.

Amelia felt some of her pleasure vanish. She was too old to marry, and she would never have a child of her own. The knowledge caused some sadness, but she wasn't about to indulge in self-pity. "No, I do not." She looked up and saw Lucas and her mother approaching.

Lucas's mouth softened. "I wondered how long it would take you to put the babe in your arms." He spoke with affection.

"Oh, what a beautiful child," Momma said. "Is she your first?"

Amelia sighed. Momma didn't recognize her, but that was hardly unusual. She introduced her brother and mother to the governess, then turned to Lucas. "Could you take Momma home and then send the carriage back? I am going to stay for a bit. I want to settle the baby and the boys."

His gaze narrowed. "I know you are merely being kind, but is that wise?"

She did not have a clue as to what he might mean.

He took her arm and steered her a short distance away from the boys. "Grenville seemed rather unhinged." There was warning in his tone.

"What on earth does that mean? Of course he is grief-stricken. But I am not attending St. Just." She kept her voice to a whisper. "He is so distraught he left his sons by themselves. Let me get everyone settled, Lucas. I simply must help out."

He shook his head, but he smiled. "Then you can expect Garrett back in two hours." His smile faded. "I hope you do not regret this, Amelia."

Her heart lurched. "Why would I regret helping those small boys? Or this beautiful child?"

He kissed her cheek and they returned to the group. Momma was babbling on about a debut, and Amelia winced as Lucas gently led her away. Mrs. Murdock gave her a wide-eyed look as they started toward the house. "Momma is addled," Amelia said softly. "It is rare, indeed, when she is coherent and cognizant of her surroundings."

"I am so sorry," Mrs. Murdock said.

The huge rosewood door was ahead, set back within the temple entrance of the house. Amelia felt herself tense. It had been ten years since she had set foot within the house.

And suddenly she recalled darting into the library, with Simon in pursuit. She had been laughing, and they had wound up on the sofa in a passionate embrace.

She hesitated inside the high-ceilinged entry hall, a circular room with marble floors, gilded furniture and crystal chandeliers. Did she genuinely wish to go inside?

"Will you really come upstairs?" William asked, jerking her back into the present.

Her heart leaped oddly. It almost felt dangerous, being in Grenville's house. But she smiled, rocking the infant gently. The children needed her; she had no doubt. "Do you want me to come upstairs?"

"I am happy to show you our suite of rooms," William said gravely, sounding like an adult.

"I have a soldier," John announced with pride. "He's a Prussian infant."

Amelia smiled as William said, taking John's hand, "He's a Prussian infantryman. You can show Miss Greystone all of your soldiers, if she so wishes." He looked at Amelia, and she saw the eagerness in his eyes.

"I cannot wait," she said, smiling. And for the first time since she met him, William smiled back.

THE BABY HAD finally fallen asleep after nursing hungrily, while still in Amelia's arms. Amelia had no wish to let her go, but she could hardly linger with Elizabeth's child now. Smiling but saddened, Amelia stood and laid the sleeping infant in her crib, a beautiful affair furnished with white eyelet coverlets. As she covered her tiny body with a white patchwork quilt, she said softly, "She needs a name."

"You are so good with children!" Mrs. Murdock exclaimed. "I have never seen her nurse as greedily, and the boys adore you when you have only just met!"

Amelia smiled. The boys were playing with the toy soldiers in their rooms. John had shown her every single solider that he had. "She was hungry."

"No, she loves you already!" The governess sobered. "There has been too much turmoil in this household. I so wish you were not leaving us."

Amelia started. "I have my own family to attend," she said, but she wondered if Mrs. Murdock was right. Had the grief and upheaval in the house affected the infant? How could it not? But at least the blue-and-white nursery was a quiet sanctuary for the child. Clearly, Elizabeth had been hoping for another boy.

Mrs. Murdock sat down in a large blue-striped chair. "I am surprised that you do not have children of your own, Miss Greystone."

Amelia felt herself tense. Of course there was dismay, after taking care of that beautiful baby. "I am not married, Mrs. Murdock, and as you have seen, I have my mother to take care of."

"You could certainly take care of her and a husband," Mrs. Murdock said. She seemed far too curious for comfort. "You are so pretty, if you do not mind my saying so. How could you be unwed?"

An image of Grenville, so dark and handsome, his stare impossibly direct, came immediately to mind.

Why had he looked at her that way?

And what could she say? That she had fallen foolishly in love with St. Just a decade ago, only to have her heart broken? There had been a few offers afterward, but none had interested her. Very carefully, she said, "There was someone once, long ago. He was not serious, and I was too young to realize it."

"The cad!" Mrs. Murdock cried.

"Let us leave the subject for now. What's done is done, after all." She smiled firmly. "I am glad the boys are playing. I am glad they ate—and I am glad the baby nursed and quieted down. I imagine she will sleep for some time."

"Thank you so much for your help," Mrs. Murdock said, standing. But she seemed anxious. "Are you leaving?"

"I have to go."

She grimaced. "What should I do if he comes here?"

It took Amelia a moment to understand. "Do you mean, if Grenville comes to see his child?"

She wrung her hands. "Maybe he won't come. He doesn't seem to like this child."

"He will love this child, as he does his sons!" Amelia exclaimed, entirely distressed by such an unfounded accusation.

"He frightens me!"

Amelia started, "Mrs. Murdock, he is your employer and the Earl of St. Just. I suppose he is somewhat intimidating—"

The governess cut her off. "He frightens all of us. He frightened her ladyship!"

Amelia stiffened with displeasure. "Mrs. Murdock, I must object to such a discussion. I am sure that Lady Grenville held his lordship in the highest regard, and it was a mutual matter!"

"She changed whenever he was home. She was a happy woman—except when he was in residence. She worried about his returning. She told me how much she worried—she told me that she always seemed to displease him!"

Amelia sat abruptly down. Could this be possible?

Could their marriage have been so strained? "I cannot abide gossip," she finally said. She realized that she wished to defend Grenville. How could he have been displeased with such a wife?

"I am hardly gossiping. I heard them shouting at one another in November—when he returned for Lord William's birthday. They argued last summer, when he suddenly appeared in town, surprising her so. And she left, within days of his arrival, she was that distraught. She did not want to be in residence with him, Miss Greystone, you may be sure of that. I do not think he cared very much for her, but she was afraid of him, I witnessed that firsthand!"

Amelia's mind was racing. There was utter confusion. Had Elizabeth Grenville left town because her husband had arrived? Had she wished to avoid him? Had she been afraid of him? But why?

Hadn't Mrs. Murdock claimed that Grenville was rarely in residence? She hadn't wanted to believe that. Had there been another woman? She found herself wondering. Why else would he stay away?

As if on the same tangent, Mrs. Murdock lowered her voice. "Lady Grenville never knew where he was. Oh, she told me so herself many times, when she wished to write him and ask him for advice and guidance! Apparently when he stated he was going to the country, he never did. He would claim to be at someone's estate, but he was never there. It is so odd, don't you think?"

It certainly sounded as if there was another woman, Amelia thought grimly. But why should she be surprised? Hadn't he treated her with utter disrespect?

"But perhaps it was all for the best, since he frightened her so with his dark moods and strange ramblings,"

Mrs. Murdock said flatly. "We have wondered if he is a bit mad."

Amelia stood, angered now. But she spoke with calm. "Grenville isn't a madman. In fact, I do not think it helpful for you to even suggest such a thing!"

"Oh, I did not mean to make you angry. But I am worried about being alone in this house with him!"

"Then you must rein in your thoughts," Amelia said, quietly furious. "Grenville will hardly murder you in your sleep. I imagine he will be in to see his child within moments." She tried to soften. "Mrs. Murdock, the man I saw in that chapel was grieving. He was distraught. Perhaps he loved Lady Grenville, in his own way, and you simply misconstrued the nature of their relationship. After all, he would be very preoccupied with his affairs of state. Perhaps, now that she is deceased, you should give his lordship the benefit of the doubt." Amelia firmly believed that this was all a huge misunderstanding. How could Grenville have not loved his wife?

"He walks in his sleep," Mrs. Murdock said defensively. "Lady Grenville hated it."

Amelia stared, speechlessly.

"She decided to move the entire household to Cornwall— when she had never once set foot in this house. How odd is that? Do you think she wanted to escape him, by coming here? That is what we all think!"

"I truly doubt she was fleeing her own husband," Amelia said grimly. The gossip was too unsettling!

"Why else would she come to Cornwall in her condition—in the winter?" Mrs. Murdock nodded. "It was a very troubled marriage, Miss Greystone."

Amelia looked down at the sleeping newborn. She didn't know what to think. "I don't think you should raise your concerns with anyone else, Mrs. Murdock.

Especially not now, with the household in mourning. Such suspicions and doubts no longer matter."

"You are right," Mrs. Murdock said. "I wonder what he will do now? His sons—his daughter—need their father. I imagine he will take us with him, wherever he goes." She seemed unhappy.

"You should hope that is the case, as it would be best for the children." Amelia was firm. But she returned to the crib and stared down at the sleeping baby. He hadn't looked at his beautiful daughter, not even once. She had a distinct feeling of dread. Something was certainly wrong. Maybe Mrs. Murdock hadn't been exaggerating, as she hoped.

"Thank you so much for being so kind," Mrs. Murdock cried. "Could you possibly call on us?"

Amelia slowly faced her. The nurse was in a state. Tears filled her eyes. She missed her mistress, Amelia thought, and she was afraid of Grenville. And how would Grenville manage? Even if his marriage had been strained, surely he was grieving now. She had seen the anguish in his eyes. "I am at Greystone Manor, a half hour's ride away if astride. If I can be of further help, send a groom with a message."

Mrs. Murdock thanked her profusely.

It was time to leave. Picking up her coat, Amelia went to the boys' rooms to say goodbye, and to promise to visit soon. At least they seemed to have forgotten their grief for the moment, she thought, watching them play with the tiny soldiers. But she was very disturbed as she went down the corridor. She almost wished that she had never had such a conversation with Mrs. Murdock.

As she started downstairs, her tension spiraled impossibly. She did not know where Grenville was. Hopefully he was with his guests and she would slip out of his house unnoticed. They day had been far too trying. She was not up to exchanging greetings now.

She hurried past the second landing, which she believed housed his apartments. Her tension had increased. It was foolish, but she almost seemed to feel his presence, nearby.

As she started down the last flight of stairs, she realized that someone was coming up them. It was a man, his head down, and she recognized him before he looked up and saw her.

She faltered. Her heart slammed.

Grenville halted three or four steps below her, glancing up.

Instantly his gaze locked with hers.

Dread began. How could this be happening? And she knew that her dismay was written all over her face; she wondered if he could hear her thundering heartbeat. But his expression was impossible to read. If he was surprised to see her, she could not tell. And if he was consumed with grief, it was not obvious. His face was a mask of dispassion.

And they were alone on the stairs. She felt trapped.

But then, strangely, his eyes began to gleam.

Her panic intensified. "Good afternoon, my lord. I am so sorry for your loss." She tried to smile politely and failed. "What a terrible tragedy! Lady Grenville was a kind and gracious woman. She was far too young to pass this way, leaving behind such beautiful children!" Was she speaking in a nervous rush? It seemed that way. "I hope to help, in any way that I can!" she added desperately.

His dark gaze never shifted from her face. "Hello, Amelia."

She froze. She had not expected such an informal—

and intimate—form of address. It was highly inappropriate for him to call her Amelia. But he had called her
by her given name all summer long....

"I hadn't expected to see you here." His tone remained
flat and calm.

She could not breathe properly. "I would never fail to
attend Lady Grenville's funeral."

"Of course not." His gaze slipped to her mouth. Amelia realized what he was doing and she was shocked.
Then he looked directly at her hands.

She had yet to don her gloves. Instinctively, she
hugged her coat to her chest, hiding her hands. Had
he been remarking her lack of rings? Surely he hadn't
been searching for a wedding band. But why else would
he look at her hands? "I had better go. Lucas must be
waiting." And without considering the fact that he was
a rather large man, and it would not be easy to pass by
him, she impulsively started down the stairs. She had
to escape him.

But Grenville grasped the railing, blocking her way.
Amelia crashed into the barrier provided by his strong
arm.

Incapable of breathing normally, Amelia looked from
his velvet-clad arm, locked against her waist, to his hand,
which firmly gripped the banister. He was barring her
way. Then she slowly looked up into his eyes.

"What were you doing upstairs in my house?" he
asked without emotion. But his gaze was unwavering
upon her face.

She wanted him to remove his arm—for now, she was
actually trapped. She stared into his dark eyes. "I put
your daughter to sleep. She is very beautiful," she said
tersely, wishing she dared to look away.

His mouth finally seemed to soften. His gaze lowered.

Thick, black lashes fanned against his high cheekbones. Amelia could feel him thinking, carefully, deliberately. But he did not move and he did not release the railing. He finally said, "You still babble when you are nervous."

Her heart kept thundering. What kind of comment was that? She finally managed, "You are blocking my way."

He looked up, still using his arm as a barrier to prevent her from going downstairs. "I beg your pardon." Finally, almost reluctantly, he released the banister. But he did not move aside. His body took up most of the space of the stairwell.

Amelia didn't move. She wanted to go, she truly did, but she felt so paralyzed. "I hope I am not intruding. Mrs. Murdock seemed to need my help."

"I am making you nervous."

She trembled. What could she say when he was right? "It has been a very trying day—for everyone!"

"Yes, it has been a very trying day for us all." His regard flickered, but it still remained unwavering upon her. "I see that you remain as kind and compassionate as ever."

That was another odd statement to make, she thought nervously. It was as if he remembered her very well. "Mrs. Murdock was so very attached to Lady Grenville. She is distraught. And the boys were distraught. They are playing in their rooms now."

"Then I am grateful." His gaze narrowed. "Mrs. Murdock?"

"The nurse," she cried, realizing he hadn't had a clue as to whom she was discussing.

"Ah, yes, Elizabeth's hire…"

His tone seemed wry and she could not get a sense as to what he was thinking or feeling now. He had even looked away. His words seemed to hang upon the air. Did he want to talk about his wife? He probably needed to talk about her. She wanted to flee, but how could she? He had been so very upset in the church.

He suddenly said, "She is afraid of me."

Amelia inhaled, realizing that he was referring to the nurse. "Yes, I think she is."

He glanced directly at her and their gazes met.

"That will change," Amelia managed, "I am sure of it."

"Yes, you would be certain."

Was he amused by her optimism? "Now that you will be in residence, she will become accustomed to you," Amelia said quickly. When his eyes widened, she flushed. "I met Lady Grenville. And I meant it when I said I am so sorry. She was so gracious and so beautiful!"

His stare had sharpened. His mouth seemed hard. "Yes, I suppose she was very beautiful."

And Amelia realized he had spoken reluctantly, as if he had no wish to praise or discuss his deceased wife. Had Mrs. Murdock been right? Surely he was grieving for Elizabeth! "She invited me for tea. It was a lovely afternoon."

"I am sure it was."

And Amelia realized that she knew him well enough to know that he did not mean his words. Feeling helpless and very confused, she stared back. They had had an unhappy marriage, she somehow thought.

"I am truly sorry," she whispered, at a loss. "If there is anything I can do to help you now, in such a difficult time, you must ask." She felt her heart lurch. His stare had become unnerving.

"You haven't changed at all."

She could not comprehend him. His wife was dead. It was Elizabeth they must discuss.

"You rescued the babe, and perhaps even the nurse. Now you wish to comfort me in my time of grief." His eyes flickered oddly. "In spite of the past."

Her heart slammed. They must never discuss the past! How could he even raise it? "We are neighbors," she cried, flustered. And surely he had noticed that she was ten years older now. "I must go! Garrett, my driver, is surely waiting. I must prepare supper!" Knowing she sounded as frantic as she felt, she started forward but he grasped the banister and blocked her way again.

"I am not trying to frighten you, Amelia."

The pressure of his arm against her ribs was unnerving. "What are you doing? You cannot call me Amelia!"

"I am curious.... It has been a long time, yet here you are. You could have decided not to attend my wife's service."

She did not know what to do—she wanted to flee! He was obviously determined to remind her of the past—and it was so dishonorable to do so. She was acutely aware of him. "Of course I would attend Lady Grenville's service. I really must go, Grenville."

He released the banister, watching her carefully.

Feeling almost like a mouse in a lion's den, she hesitated. Then she blurted, "And you should visit the boys—they wish to see you—and your daughter."

His closed expression never changed. "Will you meddle in my personal affairs?"

Had she been meddling? "Of course not."

His stare was oddly watchful. "I do not think I mind very much if you do."

His tone was wry, but was it also suggestive? She

froze, debating telling him that she was merely being a good neighbor.

He added, so softly she had to strain to hear, "You aren't wearing a ring."

She had been right. He had looked at her hands earlier for a sign of whether she was married or not. But why would he do such a thing?

He made a harsh, mirthless sound. As he reached into the interior pocket of his brown-velvet jacket, removing a silver flask, his gaze moved slowly over her features, one by one. Amelia was rigid. His look was somehow suggestive. "You are being kind and I am being rude. Barring your way. Asking impertinent questions. Failing to offer you a proper drink." He took a draught from the flask. "The lady and the beast." He smiled slowly. "Would you care to have a drink, Amelia? Would you care to have a drink…with me?"

The panic returned, full-blown. What was he doing? She was certain he was not inebriated. "I cannot have a drink with you," she gasped.

His mouth curled. He tipped the flask again, taking a longer draught this time. "Somehow, I did not think you would join me."

She inhaled. "I do not imbibe in the afternoon."

And suddenly he smiled with some humor. "So you do imbibe?"

Her heart slammed and raced. He had one dimple on his right cheek, and she had forgotten how devastatingly good-looking and seductive he was when he smiled. "I take a brandy before bed," she said, sharply and defensively.

His smile vanished.

She was afraid of what he might be thinking. "It helps me to sleep," she added quickly.

Those thick lashes had lowered again. He put the silver flask back into his pocket. "You remain sensible and direct. Intelligent and bold. You haven't changed." He spoke reflectively, staring down at the steps he stood upon. "I, on the other hand, have become an entirely different person."

Couldn't he see that ten years had changed her—making her a wiser, stronger and older woman?

He finally looked up, his gaze bland. "Thank you for coming today. I am sure Elizabeth appreciates it—God rest her blessed soul." He nodded curtly. Then, before she could move, he brushed past her up the stairs and was gone.

Amelia collapsed against the wall. She began to shake. What had just happened?

She realized she was straining to hear his footsteps above her, fading away.

Amelia seized the banister for support and rushed downstairs, fleeing Simon Grenville.

CHAPTER THREE

AMELIA STARED UP at her night-darkened ceiling.

She lay on her back, unmoving. Her temples throbbed. She had a terrible migraine, and her entire body was stiff with tension.

What was she going to do?

She had replayed her encounter with Grenville over and over in her mind, his dark, handsome image engraved there. He hadn't forgotten her. And he had made it very clear that he hadn't forgotten their affair, either.

Despair claimed her.

She closed her eyes tightly. She had left two windows slightly ajar, as she loved the tangy ocean air, and both shutters were gently rapping on the walls. The tide was high at night, and there was always a stiff breeze. But the melodic sound was not soothing.

She had been so unnerved during their encounter. It made no sense, none at all. Worse, she was still unnerved.

Did she dare consider the possibility that she still found him darkly attractive, and dangerously seductive?

How could she have ever imagined, even for a moment, that he would have become fat and gray and unrecognizable?

She almost laughed, but without mirth. Amelia opened her eyes, her fists clenched. She did not know what to do! But she did know that he had to be grieving.

Lady Grenville had been an extraordinary woman, and he could not be indifferent to her death. Hadn't she seen his anguish upon first meeting him, when he had just arrived at St. Just Hall? And there had been no mistaking it when he had rushed from the chapel, before the funeral service was even over.

And what about his poor, motherless children?

When she had left, the baby had been soundly asleep and the boys had been playing. She knew that there would be stark moments of grief still. But they were children. The little girl hadn't ever known her mother, and the boys would eventually adjust, as children were wont to do.

But the next few days and weeks would be difficult for them—for everyone.

Of course she wanted to help, if she could. But did she want to help Grenville?

Grenville's smoldering gaze was in her mind. Was he even now alone in his apartments, grieving openly for Elizabeth?

She had the inappropriate urge to reach out to him, and somehow offer him condolences, or even comfort.

Oh, what was wrong with her! He had betrayed her! She must not allow herself any attraction at all. He did not deserve her concern or her compassion!

But she was compassionate by nature. And she did not believe in grudges.

She had buried the past long ago. She had moved on.

But the affair no longer felt like ancient history. It felt as if they had met yesterday.

I believe you were trying to purchase this.

Amelia stiffened, recalling the seductive murmur of his voice exactly. They had met at the village market. Amelia's neighbor was preoccupied with her newborn infant, and Amelia had taken her three-year-old daughter for a walk amongst the vendors, to give the taxed mother a chance to do her shopping. The little girl was desolate, as she had lost her doll. Hand in hand, they had wandered amongst the merchants, until Amelia had espied a vendor hawking ribbons and buttons. They had oohed and aahed over a red ribbon, and Amelia had tried to negotiate a better price with the merchant for it. She really had no change to spare for a ribbon for the child.

"This is now yours."

The man standing behind her spoke in soft, seductive, masculine tones. Amelia had slowly turned, her heart racing. When she looked into a pair of nearly black eyes, the entire fair—its merchants and the crowd of villagers around her—had seemed to disappear. She found herself staring at a dark, devastatingly handsome man, perhaps five years older than she was.

He had smiled slowly, revealing a single dimple, holding the red ribbon out. "I insist." And he had bowed.

In that moment, she had realized he was a nobleman, and a wealthy one. He was dressed as casually as a country squire, in a hacking coat, breeches and boots meant for riding, but she sensed his authority immediately. "I don't believe it proper, sir, to accept a gift from a stranger." She had meant to be proper, but she heard how flustered she sounded.

Amusement filled his eyes. "You are correct. Therefore, we must rectify the matter immediately. I would like an introduction."

Her heart had slammed. "We can hardly introduce ourselves," she managed to answer, flushing.

"Why not? I am Grenville, Simon Grenville. And I wish to make your acquaintance."

Rather helplessly, perhaps already smitten, she had

taken the ribbon. Simon Grenville, the Earl of St. Just's younger son, had called on her the very next day.

And Amelia had felt as if she were a princess in a fairy tale. He had driven up to Greystone Manor in a handsome coach pulled by two magnificent horses, taking her for a picnic on the cliffs. From the moment she had stepped inside his carriage, an attraction had raged between them. He had kissed her that very afternoon— and she had kissed him back.

Lucas had quickly forbidden him from calling upon her. Amelia had pleaded with him to change his mind, but he had refused. He had insisted that he was protecting her—that Grenville was a rake and a rogue. But Simon hadn't cared. He had laughed in Lucas's face. A secret rendezvous had followed. They had met in the village and he had taken her to stroll in the magnificent rose gardens at St. Just Hall, where another heated encounter had ensued....

Lucas had gone away to attend the quarry or the mine, she could not recall, assuming she would obey him. But she hadn't. Simon had called on her almost every day, taking her for carriage rides, for walks, to tea and even shopping.

She had fallen deeply in love before the week was out.

Amelia could not stand such memories. Her body was on fire, as if she wished to be with him still. She sat up, throwing the covers aside, oblivious to the chill in the air. Amelia slid her bare feet to the floor. She had been such a fool. She had been a lamb, hunted by a wolf. Oh, she knew that now. He had never had a single serious intention toward her, otherwise he wouldn't have left as he had.

Thank God she had never succumbed to temptation; thank God she had never let him completely seduce her.

"I am desperate to be with you," he had murmured, breathing hard.

They were in one another's arms, in the gazebo that was behind the house. He had just given her so much pleasure. She was flushed and exhilarated—and she desperately wanted to consummate their affair. "I am desperate, too," she had returned, meaning it. "But I can't, Simon, you know I cannot...."

She wanted to be innocent on their wedding night. She wanted to give him her virginity then.

His stare had darkened, but he hadn't said a word, and she wondered when he would ask her to marry him—when, not if he would do so. She had no doubt that his intentions were honorable. She knew he loved her as she loved him.

Simon had been courting her for six weeks. Then one day, the stableman hurried to the manor and announced that William Grenville was dead. He had been found on the cliffs, his neck broken, obviously having fallen from his horse. The family was in mourning.

Amelia had been stunned. She had met Will several times, and he had been everything the earl's heir should be—noble, upright, handsome, charming. And Simon adored him, she knew that, as well. He spoke of him often, and so highly.

She had rushed to St. Just Hall to tell Simon in person how sorry she was. But the family was not receiving; she had written a hasty note and left it with a servant.

He did not reply. A few days later there was more stunning news—the family had left Cornwall. And Simon had left with them.

He did not write.

And he did not return.

Amelia realized she was standing by the open window, her feet bare, in just a nightgown. Somehow, a tear had arisen and was slipping down her cheek. She shivered.

He hadn't ever truly loved her. His behavior that summer was entirely reprehensible. She wiped the tear away. Impossibly, she felt raw and bruised. Was she still hurt, after all these years?

And in that moment, she recalled her father. He had been a rake and a rogue, she knew that now, although she had not known it when she was a child. Amelia had adored her handsome, dashing father, and he had loved Amelia. He had said so, time and again. He had taken her with him when he made his rounds of the tenant farms, and lavishly praised her for every small accomplishment. And then one day, he was gone. He had left her mother and his children for the gaming halls and fallen women of Amsterdam and Paris.

Amelia had been seven years old when Papa had left them. She had been certain he would come back. It had taken her years to realize that he wasn't ever returning.

But she had known almost immediately that Simon was never coming back. He had left without a word, he hadn't really loved her.

Papa's betrayal had bewildered her. Simon's betrayal was crushing.

A year later, he had married the Lambert heiress. She had not been surprised....

Amelia stared out to sea. From where she stood, she could see the night-clad, shimmering waters of the Atlantic Ocean. Only a very naive, very young, very innocent girl would have ever believed, even for a moment, that St. Just's son, heir or not, would ever be genuinely interested in her. She could blame him for pursuing her and nearly seducing her, but she had only herself to blame for the folly of falling in love, and then having her heart broken.

Well, there was good news. She wasn't a trusting young girl anymore. She knew better. Grenville was not for her. He might arouse her and attract her, but it was not to be. He was grieving now; he had lost his wife. She was his neighbor, nothing more. If she could help his children, she was happy to do so. She even wished to help him, for the past was forgiven. But there would not be anything personal between them.

She had learned her lesson a very long time ago.

Amelia did not feel better. There was simply too much tension within her—and too many unanswered questions.

THEY WERE COMING FOR HIM.

He heard the soft, steady footfalls and he was terrified. He clutched the bars of his cell, certain that there would be no escape this time. He had been caught. He was on the list of the damned. He was going to the guillotine....

And ghastly images flashed, of the innocents he had seen kneeling before the guillotine, some in hysterics, others silent and stoic, and then of his friend, just days ago, who had told the crowd as he marched up those bloody stairs, "Don't forget to show my head to the people!" The bloodthirsty crowd had cheered but he had wanted to weep, except he did not dare, as Lafleur was with him, watching him closely for a sign of weakness....

He cried out, because Will was there, going up those soaking wet steps. He screamed.

The huge iron blade came down. Blood rained, filling his vision, as the child wailed.

Simon Grenville sat bolt upright, panting and covered with sweat. He was on the sofa in the sitting room of his private apartments, not standing with the roaring crowd at La Place de la Révolution—a place Will had never been!

Simon groaned, his temples hammering, as the child wailed even louder. He realized his face was covered with tears and he used his sleeve to wipe his cheeks. Then he rushed to the chamber pot to vomit helplessly, mostly the scotch whiskey he'd been drinking since the funeral yesterday.

When would the nightmares stop? He had been incarcerated for three months and six days; he had been released in time to attend Danton's trial, as he had prepared to leave Paris for London. In the last year, Georges Danton had become a moderate and a voice of reason, but that had only incited Robespierre, and it had, in the end, ensured his bloody death.

He did not want to recall standing helplessly in the crowd, pretending to applaud the execution, when he was so sickened he could barely prevent himself from retching.

Afterward, the Jacobin had bought him a glass of wine at a nearby inn, telling him how pleased he was that "Henri Jourdan" was departing for London. The timing could not be better, he said. The Allied line ran west to east from Ypres to Valenciennes and then to the Meuse River, Namur and Trier. The French were expecting an invasion of Belgium, soon. And Lafleur had slipped a list into his hand. "These are your London contacts."

Simon had gone back to his flat for the very last time—only to find one of Warlock's couriers there. For one moment, he had thought he had been uncovered, but instead, he had been told that his wife was dead....

Simon stood unsteadily—he was still very foxed. And that suited him very well. He walked over to a handsome sideboard and poured another scotch. The baby kept crying and he cursed.

He had enough problems without that damned child. He hated that bastard, but not as much as he hated himself.

But he had escaped the guillotine. How many French political prisoners could claim that?

He thought of his relations in Lyons, none of whom he'd ever met, all of whom were now deceased, a part of the vengeance wreaked upon Lyons when *le Comité* had ordered the rebel city destroyed. His cousin, the true Henri Jourdan, was among the dead.

He was acutely aware he was on a tightrope.

One misstep and he would fall, either into the clutches of his French masters or those of Warlock.

The Earl of St. Just was well-known. When he met with his Jacobin contacts, he would have to be very careful that no one would recognize him. He would have to manage some sort of disguise—a growth of beard, his natural hair, impoverished clothes. Perhaps he could even use chalk or lime to add a false scar to his face.

His stomach churned anew. If Lafleur ever learned he was Simon Grenville, not Henri Jourdan, he would be in imminent danger—and so would his sons.

He had no delusions about the lengths to which the radicals would go. He had seen children sent to the guillotine, because their fathers were disloyal to *La Patrie*. Last fall, an assassin had tried to murder Bedford, right outside his own house. In January, an attempt had been made on the War Secretary, as he was getting into his carriage outside of the Parliament. There were émigrés in Britain now who were in hiding, fearing for their lives. Why should he think his sons safe?

Everyone knew that London was filled with agents and spies, and soon it would have another one.

The reach of the Terror was vast. The vengeful serpent was inside Great Britain now.

Simon downed half the whiskey. He did not know how long he could play this double-edged game without losing his own head. Lafleur wanted information about the Allied war effort as swiftly as possible—before the anticipated invasion of Flanders. And that meant he would have to return to London immediately, as he would not learn any valuable state secrets in Cornwall.

But he was a patriot. He had to be very careful not to give away any information that was truly important for the Allied war effort. And at the very same time, Warlock wanted him to uncover what French secrets he could. He might even want Simon to return to Paris. It was a tightrope, indeed. But in the end, he would do what he had to do—because he was determined to protect his sons. He would give up the state for them; he would die for them if need be.

The baby cried again.

And he simply snapped. He threw the glass at the wall, where it shattered. Damn Elizabeth, for leaving him with her bastard! And then he covered his face with his hands.

And he began to cry. He wept for his sons, because they had loved their mother and they needed her still. He wept for Danton and all of his relations who had been victims of *le Razor*. He wept for those he did not know—rebels and royalists, nobles and priests, old men, women and children…the rich and the poor, for these days, it was guilt by suspicion or just association, and

the poor wound up without their heads as well, when
they were as innocent as his sons…. And he supposed
he even cried for that damned bastard child, because she
had nothing and no one at all—just like him.

And then he laughed through his tears. The bastard
had Amelia Greystone.

Why had she come to the service, damn it! Why had
she barged into his home? Why hadn't she changed at
all? Damn her! So much had changed. He had changed.
He didn't even recognize himself anymore!

He cursed Amelia again and again, because he lived
in darkness and fear, and he knew that there was no way
out and that the light she offered was an illusion.

"AMELIA, DEAR, WHY are you packing up my clothing?"

Two days had passed since the funeral. Amelia had
never been as preoccupied. As she prepared to close
up the house, her mind kept straying from the tasks at
hand. Frankly, she had been worrying about Grenville's
children ever since the funeral. She was going to have
to call upon them and make certain that all was well.

She smiled at Momma, who was lucid now. They
were standing in the center of her small, bare bedchamber, a single window looking out over the muddy front
lawns. "We are going to spend the spring in town," she
said cheerfully. But she wasn't truly cheerful. She realized she was reluctant to leave Cornwall now. She would
not be able to offer comfort to those children if she were
miles and miles away.

Garrett's heavy footfall sounded in the corridor outside of Momma's bedchamber. Amelia paused as the
heavyset manservant appeared on the threshold of the
room. "You have a caller, Miss Greystone. It is Mrs.
Murdock, from St. Just Hall."

Amelia's heart lurched. "Momma, wait here! Is anything wrong?" she cried, already dashing past the Scot and racing down the hall.

"She seems rather distressed," Garrett called after her. He did not follow her as he knew his duty well; Momma was almost never left alone.

The gray-haired governess was pacing in the great hall, back and forth past the two red-velvet chairs that faced the vast stone hearth. A huge tapestry was hanging on an adjacent wall, over a long, narrow wooden bench with carved legs. The floors were stone, and covered with old rugs. But a new, very beautiful, gleaming piano was in one corner of the room, surrounded by six equally new chairs with gilded legs and gold seats. The instrument and the chairs were a gift from the dowager Countess of Bedford, recently given to Julianne.

Mrs. Murdock did not have anyone with her.

Amelia realized she had secretly hoped that the governess had brought the baby. She dearly wished to see and hold her again. But her disappointment was foolish. The child hardly needed to drive through the chilly Cornish countryside.

"Good day, Mrs. Murdock. This is such a pleasant surprise," she began, when she wished to demand if anything was amiss.

Mrs. Murdock hurried toward her as Amelia left the stairs, and tears quickly arose. "Oh, Miss Greystone, I am at a loss, we all are!" she cried. She seized Amelia's hands.

"What has happened?" Amelia said with dread.

"St. Just Hall is in a state," she declared, her second chin wobbling. "We cannot get on!"

Amelia put her arm around her and realized she was

trembling, she was that agitated. "Come, sit down and tell me what is wrong," she said soothingly.

"The baby cries day in and day out. She is hardly nursing now! The boys have decided to do as they please—they are running wild! They will not attend the classroom, they defy Signor Barelli, they are running about the grounds, as ill-mannered as street urchins. Yesterday Lord William took a hack out—by himself— and he was gone for hours and hours! And we could not find John—as it turned out, he had gone into the attics and hid!" She started to cry. "If they did not need me so, I would leave such a horrid place."

She hadn't said a word about Grenville. "The boys are surely grieving. They are good boys, I saw that, they will soon stop misbehaving." Amelia meant her every word.

"They miss their mother, we all do!" She choked on a sob.

Amelia clasped her shoulder. "And his lordship?"

Mrs. Murdock stopped crying. A moment passed before she said, "The earl has locked himself in his rooms."

Amelia tensed. "What do you mean?"

"He has not come out of his apartments since the funeral, Miss Greystone."

AN HOUR LATER, AMELIA FOLLOWED Mrs. Murdock into St. Just Hall, shaking the rain from her coat. It was so silent inside the marble-floored foyer that she could have heard a pin drop. Outside, the rain beat down on the windows and the roof. For that, she was somewhat thankful, as it drowned out the sound of her thundering heart.

Keeping her voice low, she said, "Where are the children?"

"When I left, they had both gone outdoors. Of course, it is raining now."

If the boys were still outside, they would become terribly ill. A liveried manservant appeared and Amelia handed him her soaking wet coat. "What is your name, sir?" she asked firmly.

"Lloyd," he said, bowing.

"Are the boys within?"

"Yes, madam, they came in an hour ago, when it began to rain."

"Where were they?"

"I suspect they were in the stables—they were covered with hay, and they both had an odor."

At least they were safely within. She glanced at Mrs. Murdock, who was apparently awaiting her lead. Amelia cleared her throat. Her heart raced even more swiftly. "And his lordship?"

A look of dismay flitted across the servant's face. "He remains inside his rooms, madam."

She inhaled nervously and said, "Tell him Miss Greystone has called."

Lloyd hesitated, as if considering an objection. Amelia nodded with encouragement and he left. Suddenly Mrs. Murdock said, "I will send for tea." She fled.

Amelia realized that they were all fearful of Grenville. Mrs. Murdock had not exaggerated, then. She began to pace. How could he lock himself in his rooms? On the drive over, Mrs. Murdock had revealed an astonishing and disturbing fact: he had not seen his children since the funeral, either.

That was so very wrong. It was selfish!

The servant appeared several moments later. He flushed and said, "I do not believe his lordship is receiving, Miss Greystone."

"What did he say?"

"He did not answer the door."

Amelia hesitated. If he would not come downstairs to speak with her, she would have to go upstairs to speak to him. Filled with trepidation, she fought for courage and looked at Lloyd. "Take me to his rooms."

Blanching, the servant nodded and led her into the corridor and up the stairs.

They paused before a heavy teakwood door. Lloyd was even paler now, and Amelia hoped Grenville wouldn't dismiss him for his audacity in bringing her to his rooms. She whispered, "Perhaps you should go."

He fled.

Her heart slammed. But there was no choice, so she lifted her hand and knocked sharply on his door.

There was no response. She rapped on the door again.

When only silence greeted her efforts, she took a fist and pounded on the door. "Grenville! Open up!"

There was still no response, although she thought she heard a footstep. "Grenville!" She pounded on the door several times. "It is Amelia Greystone. I wish to—"

And the door was flung open.

Amelia did not finish her sentence. Simon stood before her, clad only in an unbuttoned shirt and his breeches. Half of his very muscular chest was revealed. He wore no stockings, no shoes. There was a great deal of bearded growth upon his face, and his hair was loose. Dark and nearly black, it reached his shoulders.

He stared at her unpleasantly.

She did not know what she had expected, but she had not expected him to greet her in such a disheveled state. And now she smelled the whiskey. "Grenville... Thank you for coming to the door," she stammered.

His mouth began to curl. His eyes darkened. "Amelia. Have you come to save my soul?" He laughed softly. "I must warn you, I cannot be saved, not even by you."

Amelia did not move. His dark eyes were smoldering; she recognized the look. Worse, her own heart was rioting. And she was briefly speechless.

What could he possibly be thinking?

He was smiling seductively. "You are wet. Come in... if you dare."

She had heard that tone before. Did he intend to flirt? Or worse, seduce her?

His smile widened. "Surely I am not frightening you?"

She fought for her composure. She had come to see him because his household was in a state, and there was no one in charge. His children needed him. They had to be cared for!

Some sanity returned. He had never looked as dangerous, or as dissipated—he had been drinking, excessively. They were facing one another over the threshold of his sitting room. She finally glanced inside. It was in a horrific condition. The pillows that belonged on the sofa were on the floor. Drinking glasses, some empty, some partly full, were on the various tabletops. A lamp was on the floor, broken in pieces. So was a mirror.

Several of the decanters on the sideboard were empty. There were empty wine bottles there, as well. There was also a dark red stain on the pale blue wall by the fireplace. And finally, she saw broken glass on the floor.

He was inebriated—and he had been in a rage. Obviously he had broken the lamp, the mirror and God only knew what else. "What can you be thinking?" she cried, overcome with genuine concern.

His eyes widened but she was already shoving past him. Then she turned and slammed his door. She did not want any of his staff to see the condition his rooms were in, or worse, the condition he was in.

"Let me guess," he said in that purr again. "You wish to be alone with me."

She trembled, wishing he would cease flirting. "Hardly!" she snapped. "I do hope you are proud of yourself." She marched to the scattered pillows, retrieved them, and tidied up the sofa. But even as angry as she was becoming, her heart was racing wildly. She did not like being alone with him like this. He was far too masculine—far too intriguing.

"What are you doing?"

She knelt and began collecting glass, using her skirts as an apron. "I am tidying up, Grenville." She decided not to look his way. Maybe he would close his shirt.

"There are maids who clean this house."

She refused to turn, but the image of him, more unclothed than not, remained fresh and graphic in her mind. "I don't want anyone to see your rooms like this." She stood and went to the trash can and emptied her skirt into it. Then she knelt to begin picking up the shards of the broken mirror.

The next thing she knew, he was clasping her shoulders as he knelt behind her and her body was spooned into his. "You are not a housemaid, Amelia, you are my guest," he murmured.

Amelia couldn't move. Her mind became utterly blank. His body was large and male, hard and strong, and she felt tiny, pressed against him as she was. Her heart was rioting so wildly that she could not breathe.

"Amelia," he said softly, and she felt his lips against her cheek.

"Release me!" she cried, struggling to stand and get free.

"I thought you liked it when I held you," he whispered into her ear. He did not release her; he did not allow her to stand.

Impossibly, desire flamed. She felt the urgency in every part of her body, in every fiber of her being. "You are intoxicated," she accused.

"Yes, I am. And I had forgotten just how tiny and beautiful you are, and how perfectly you fit in my arms."

Panic gave her unusual strength—or he was done toying with her. Amelia wrenched free. She leaped to her feet as he slowly stood to tower over her. She faced him, defiantly. "What can you possibly be thinking?" she cried.

"I am thinking that you are so pretty, and that we are alone." He was amused. "You are blushing."

"I am old!" What had he been doing? Had he tried to embrace her? Had she felt his mouth on her cheek?

Had he kissed her?

She backed away. Coming into his rooms had been a mistake, she realized that now. "Do not touch me again!" she warned.

His dark eyes gleamed. "You entered at your own risk."

"What does that mean?"

"It means you know as well as I do that I am not to be trusted."

She did not know what to say. He had just made a very direct reference to his courtship of her—and his betrayal. She stood there with her backside against the sideboard, trying to regain her breath. His hands fisted and found his hips. He stared at her, unsmiling, unmoving. She despaired, because now she had the vast opportunity to ogle the hard planes of his chest, the angles of his ribs and to notice that he did not have an ounce of fat upon him. He was leaner than he had been at the age of twenty-one. He was, undoubtedly, too thin.

"You are staring." He spoke flatly.

She jerked her gaze away, and saw the pieces of broken mirror, not far from his bare feet. "You are not properly dressed."

"Surely my bare legs do not bother you…Amelia?"

She glanced up and their gazes met. His smile was twisted, his dark gaze filled with speculation. "You have seen far more than my bare calves," he said.

"That was uncalled for!" she cried, aghast. Now she recalled unbuttoning his shirt in a fit of passion, and running her hands over those hard muscles.

"I never claimed to be a gentleman." But he reached for the sides of his shirt, pulling them together. Never moving his gaze from her, he buttoned up his shirt. "Is that better?"

It wasn't better at all. She knew she must stop her memories from spilling over now. "There is broken glass everywhere. Your feet are bare." She spoke sharply.

Suddenly sober, he said, "A shard of glass cannot hurt me."

She saw numerous cuts on his feet. She jerked her gaze up. "Your foot is already bleeding, Grenville." This was safer ground.

He made a derisive sound. "You are worried about a few tiny scratches?"

She was worried, but not about those cuts! "You do not want to get an infection," she tried.

"Men die every day." He was hard, harsh and angry. "From bayonets, powder, cannon, the Blade… And you are worried about a few little pieces of glass." He laughed, but the sound was frightening.

She stared, hugging herself. He was talking about

the war and the revolution, but why? Most Britons had
been affected in some way by the wars, and the average
citizen read about the war on an almost daily basis. War
stories abounded in every inn and tavern, and rumors
ran rampant—the threat of invasion, the reach of the
Terror, the possible fall of the Republic. But Grenville
sounded almost personally involved. "Have you been to
war?" she heard herself ask. "Have you been to France?"

He suddenly turned away. Not looking at her, he
walked over to the low table before the gold sofa and
picked up a glass of scotch. As if he hadn't heard her, he
studied it. He finally said, "I do not like drinking alone.
Is it late? I seem to recall that you enjoy a glass of brandy
before bedtime. If I broke the decanter of brandy, there
are plenty of bottles downstairs." He looked at her and
stared. His regard was challenging and very, very dark.

The terrible tension returned. "It is midday, Grenville." She prayed he wasn't flirting with her.

Sipping, he studied her over the rim of his glass.
"Simon. Join me anyway. Drinking alone is an abhor-
rent habit. Despicable, truly."

She was not about to have a drink with him, especially not now, like this. "Do you frequently drink
alone?"

"All of the time." He saluted her with his glass.

What had happened to him? Why wasn't he comforting his children? Why had he avoided his marriage, if
Mrs. Murdock were right?

"Ah, I see you are feeling sorry for me." His eyes
gleamed and Amelia realized he was pleased.

"You are grieving. Of course I am feeling sorry for
you."

His smile vanished. "It is not what you think." He
tossed off the rest of his drink and strode over to the

sideboard, coming precariously close to walking over shattered glass as he did so.

She cried out. "Grenville, be careful!"

"I don't care about the damned glass!"

She froze, because he had suddenly shouted at her and there was so much fury in his tone. It was as if lightning had ripped apart the sky, out of the blue. She stared, aghast, as he braced both arms against the sideboard.

She had the frightening urge to rush over to him and clasp his shoulder and ask him what was wrong. She wet her lips and said, "Are you all right?"

"No." He poured another scotch, his movements stiff with anger. Then he slowly turned and faced her. "Why are you here?"

She hesitated. "You haven't come out of your rooms in days. You haven't seen your children."

"No, I have not." He made a mocking sound. "And you are here to rescue me from myself?"

"Yes."

"Ah, we are being honest now." His gaze darkened.

"When did you become so dark—so cynical—so unhappy?" she asked.

He started. And she saw the wave of anger as it came. He drained that drink, too, and slammed it down. "Has it ever occurred to you that being here—alone with me—is dangerous?"

She trembled. "Yes, it has."

"I do not feel like being rescued. You should go."

"I don't think I should leave you when you are in such a state."

He folded his arms across his broad chest and began to smile. "I was wrong. You have changed. The child I once knew was so terribly pliant. She was putty in my hands. I am facing a stubborn and annoying woman now."

His words stabbed through her. "You are hurt, so you are lashing out."

He laughed coldly at her. "Think as you will."

Amelia watched him pour another drink, wanting to take it away. "I know you are grieving. Your children are grieving, as well. But grief doesn't give you the right to behave as if you are a spoiled child."

His eyes widened. "You dare to berate me?"

"Someone must set you upside down on your ear!" she cried in frustration.

He set the glass down hard, and this time, the drink was untouched. "You were never entirely intimidated by me. Even when you were sixteen, and as naive and as innocent as a newborn babe, you had the courage I find lacking in most women and most men."

She was rigid. "I do not intend to discuss the past."

"But you did hold me in some awe. Are you still awed?" His tone was mocking, but his gaze was hard and unwavering.

"Grenville, you could awe no one just now."

"This is truly intriguing. I look at you and I see glimpses of that trusting, sweet girl—but then I find myself facing a sharp-tongued harridan."

She flushed. "Insult me if it makes you feel better! But I do not want to discuss the past."

"Why not? It is there, looming between us, as if an elephant in this chamber."

"What happened is over, and I have forgotten all about it."

"Liar." She started in dismay as he added softly, "You are the one who came here uninvited, into my rooms, seeking to rescue me.... A man who did not know you as well would draw but one conclusion."

She knew her face flamed. He said, "Do you wish to pick up where we left off?"

She cried out, close to marching over to him and striking him. "You know me better than that! How can you be so rude when you know I have come here to help?"

"Yes, I do know you well.... You are meddling out of kindness. The other day it was rather endearing. Today, however, I cannot decide if I mind or not."

"Someone has to meddle, Grenville—you are hardly a bachelor, free to indulge yourself. You have a family to think of. You have duties toward them."

"Ah, yes, duty—a subject of which you are inordinately fond. Who better to lecture me? Do you still take care of your mother exclusively? Julianne was far too preoccupied with her books and lectures, if I recall, to be of any help."

"She is my mother. Of course I take care of her. And Julianne is married now to the Earl of Bedford."

He started. "Little Julianne married Dominic Paget?"

"Yes, she did. And they have a child."

He smiled and shook his head. "Well, your mother is a noble cause, to be sure—but time passes swiftly, Amelia, and you remain unwed."

She crossed her arms defensively. "I am very content." She did not know how they had gotten onto such a personal topic. "Your children need you. And that is why I am here. That is the only reason I am here."

His smile was filled with skepticism. "I think you are here for several reasons." He sipped from his glass. "I think that you are a woman of compassion, and you currently harbor a great deal of compassion for me."

He wasn't as foxed as she had thought. "You are grieving. You have lost your wife. Of course I feel sympathy for you. You have not seen your children since the funeral. It is time to sober up, Grenville."

His lashes lowered and she could feel him thinking. "Send up for supper. I will stop drinking if you join me." And he smiled at her. "I am enjoying your company, Amelia."

She was in disbelief. "First you flirt, then you fly into several rages, and now you are bribing me in order to have me dine with you?"

"Why not?"

Trembling, she finally marched to him. His brows lifted. She snatched the glass from his hand, spilling whiskey on them both. He seemed amused, which only angered her even further. Flushing, she cried tersely, "I will not be bribed. If you want to behave like a common drunk, then so be it. I know you are grieving for Elizabeth, but your grief does not entitle you to this bout of self-destruction, not when your children are in this house."

"I am not grieving for Elizabeth," he said flatly.

She knew she had misheard. "I beg your pardon?"

His face had become dark with anger again. "I hardly knew her. She was a stranger. I am sorry she is deceased, as my sons adored her. And she certainly did not deserve to die at the age of twenty-seven. But let us cease all pretense. I am not grieving for her."

Was it true, then, what the nurse had said? That the marriage had been troubled?

He was staring. "You seem so surprised."

She did not know what to say to him now. Finally, "Perhaps you are not being entirely honest with yourself. She was gracious, elegant, beautiful—"

He laughed harshly then, interrupting her. "I am being entirely honest, Amelia."

She hesitated because he was so obviously anguished. She did not know what to believe or think. "This is a terrible time," she finally said. "How can I help?"

He slowly smiled, and his dark eyes smoldered. Suddenly he brushed some hair from her face, and his fingertips fluttered over her jaw and cheek. Desire fisted and Amelia froze.

Very seductively, he said, "I need you, Amelia. I have always needed you."

For one more moment, she could not move. The urge to go into his arms was overwhelming. Simon needed her. She believed that.

"And somehow," he said, slowly reaching for her, "I think that you need me, too." His hand closed over her wrist.

In another moment, if she did not defy him, he would pull her into his embrace! He was poised to do so—and he was watching her so carefully. Amelia braced against him but did not move away. There was no denying the wild attraction that she still felt for him.

But it didn't matter. She must never allow him any liberties again! Still, the panic she had felt earlier was far less intense now.

"Isn't that why you are here? To comfort me?" He leaned closer, still holding her arm.

Amelia felt as if she were in a whirlwind of mixed emotions—confusion, fear, panic, but also a fierce, complicated desire.

"Please let me go," she whispered, and tears arose. She wasn't sure what they signified.

He started, and released her.

She managed, "I am here to help if I can, but not in the way that you suggest."

He shook his head. "I did not think so." Then he walked past her to the sofa and collapsed upon it.

Amelia realized she was trembling, taut with tension and desire. She closed her eyes, seeking some small degree of composure.

And then she took a breath and opened her eyes. Simon hadn't moved.

He lay on his back, one arm over his head, and she realized that he had fallen into a deep, drunken stupor.

Amelia stared, shaken to the core of her being. A long moment passed. Then she found a throw and covered him with it.

CHAPTER FOUR

AMELIA HESITATED, POISED to go up the front steps of St. Just Hall.

It was the next afternoon, and the sun was trying to break through the overcast skies. Small buds had appeared on the tall black trees surrounding the house. Even the lawns seemed to be turning a bit green. Spring was on its way, but she was not cheered.

She had not been able to sleep at all last night. That terrible encounter with Grenville had replayed over and over in her mind. His image had haunted her, at times mocking, at times anguished, and so terribly seductive.

He was grieving and angry, and an attraction still raged between them. She did not know what to do.

She had gone to visit the children after leaving him sleeping in his rooms. The boys had been thrilled to see her, but she had instantly noticed how out-of-sorts they were. John had broken a china horse model and showed no remorse. William had scribbled blackly in one of his schoolbooks. The boys had been smiling and happy to see her, but she knew they were suffering over the loss of their mother and that their misbehavior was a cry for help.

She had gone to visit the little girl, too. Mrs. Murdock had been out, which had been a relief of sorts, and a housemaid had allowed her to hold and feed the infant. Afterward, she had thought about checking upon Grenville. Instead, she had decided that the wisest course of action was to flee his house.

But she had worried about him and his children ever since.

"I will give the mare water, miss," the groom said, interrupting her thoughts.

Amelia half turned. A stableman had taken hold of the mare in the traces of the curricle she had used to drive over. She thanked him, summoned up her courage—no easy task—and started up the steps to the house.

Was she afraid of him? She was far more nervous now than she had been yesterday. Or was it her own reaction to him that frightened her?

In any case, she prayed he was doing better that day. She hoped, fervently, that she had imagined the attraction that had arisen between them yesterday. And if she had not, she must fight her own feelings.

A wiser woman would have stayed away, she thought, knocking nervously on the front door. But he had been so devastated yesterday. Ignoring his pain was simply impossible.

A liveried doorman allowed her inside, and a moment later, Lloyd had entered the front hall. Amelia smiled brightly and falsely at him as she removed her coat. "Good afternoon. I was hoping to call upon his lordship." Their gazes met and held. She continued to sound cheerful. "Is he up and about today?"

"He has just come downstairs," Lloyd said. "But he was very adamant, Miss Greystone, he is not receiving callers today."

Her relief was instantaneous and huge. Grenville had come out of his rooms! She was so thankful. Surely she did not need to seek him out, if that was the case. She could simply return home—that would be so much safer than actually calling upon him! "Then I should go. But first, how are the children?"

Lloyd's eyes flickered with concern. "Lord William seems very distraught today, Miss Greystone. This morning he locked himself in his rooms, and it took Signor Barelli several hours to convince him to come out."

Her relief vanished. She would expect such behavior of John, not his older brother. "And where was his lordship at the time?"

"He had yet to come down, Miss Greystone. I do not believe he has been told of the incident."

Her tension spiraled. "But he has seen the children since coming down?"

Lloyd shook his head. "I do not believe he has seen the children since the funeral, Miss Greystone."

Amelia stared at him, appalled. Then, "How is he?"

Lloyd lowered his voice. "I do not believe he is feeling very well today."

And she knew she could not leave yet. "Where is he?"

Lloyd was alarmed. "He is dining, Miss Greystone, but he was very specific—"

"I will manage his lordship," she said, hurrying into the corridor. Determination filled her. He was probably suffering from the effects of his binge. Well, no matter how poorly he felt, it was time for him to step up and be a father to his children.

If she remembered correctly, the dining chamber was a vast room paneled in dark wood with a timbered ceiling, several oil paintings on the walls and a long oak table with two dozen stately burgundy-velvet chairs. Two ebony doors guarded the chamber. Both were closed. A liveried servant stood outside the doors, as still and unblinking as a statue. Amelia did not hesitate and she did not knock. She pushed open both doors and stepped over the threshold.

Grenville sat at the head of the long table at the other end of the room, facing the doors. The table was set beautifully with linen and crystal for one. Tall white candles formed a centerpiece. He was eating, seeming preoccupied, when she barged inside.

He looked up; she halted. Staring from across the great room, he laid his utensils down.

Amelia hesitated, then turned and closed the doors. The ensuing conversation should probably remain private. She hoped that cornering him now was not a huge mistake.

Turning, she was aware of some dread—was she baiting the lion yet again in his den? It certainly felt that way. She started grimly forward, straining to make out his expression.

Grenville continued to stare as she approached. Only a short distance separated them when he finally laid a gold cloth napkin on the table and stood up. "You could not stay away, I see." He did not smile.

She paused when two chairs separated them, grasping the back of one. He did not look well. He had shaved, but there were shadows under his bloodshot eyes. He was pale, in spite of his olive complexion. He was impeccably dressed in a navy blue coat, his shirt frothing lace at the throat and cuffs, his breeches fawn, his stockings white. But his hair had been pulled carelessly back into a queue. He looked as if he had spent a very long night carousing, which, for all intents and purposes, he had. "I remain concerned about the children."

"But your concern does not extend to me?"

She decided to ignore the taunt. "Are you feeling better today?"

"I feel exactly the way I look—like hell."

She bit back a smile. "One must pay the piper," she said tartly.

"Hmm, I think you are pleased to see me suffering so."

"You could hardly think that you would escape the consequences of such a binge unscathed?" She lifted her brows. "But I am not pleased if you are feeling ill."

"I do not believe," he said slowly, his gaze unwavering upon her face, "that I was thinking at all."

A silence fell. No, he had not been thinking, he had been feeling—he had been angry and grief-stricken. He had also been very, very suggestive. Amelia glanced away, finally breaking the stare they shared.

He gestured at the chair she was grasping. Amelia saw the gesture from the corner of her eye and shook her head, glancing at him again. "I am not staying long."

"Ah, yes, your mother awaits."

She tensed. Had there been mockery in his tone? But clearly, he remembered their encounter.

Abruptly, he said, "Why are you here…Amelia?"

Her heart lurched. He did not sound pleased. "I told you, I wish to make certain the children are well. And, yes, some concern extends to you."

"I am touched."

She stared closely at him, but if he was mocking her now, she could not tell. His expression was hard.

"I was just thinking about you," he said, staring down at the edge of the table. Then he looked up, his gaze dark. "I was thinking about the encounter we shared last night."

There was so much tension, of course there was. Amelia waited, uncertain of where he meant to go.

His gaze held hers. "My recollection is patchy. But I believe I owe you an apology."

She inhaled. Hopefully he did not recall very much! "You do."

"Was I very rude?"

She hesitated, because he had been far more than rude—he had been bold, he had referred to their past affair several times, and he had been entirely seductive. "It doesn't matter, your apology is accepted." She was final.

But he was not. "I tried to seduce you."

She stiffened, wondering if she could deny it.

"I happen to remember holding you in my arms. Did I seduce you?" he asked, almost casually.

She exhaled. He did not remember the extent of their exchange? "No, you did not."

He glanced aside, and she had no clue as to what he was thinking. Then, very softly, his gaze frighteningly direct again, he said, "But we kissed."

She was almost speechless now. She wasn't sure whether his mouth had brushed her cheek, but that wasn't what he meant. Then she whispered, "No, Simon, we did not kiss."

His eyes widened.

She was surprised by his surprise. And there was so much tension in the room, between them, that it was hard to breathe. Or was all the tension coming from her? "I'd like to see the children," she said, hoping to rapidly change the subject.

"Are you certain?" he asked, as if he hadn't heard her.

She bit her lip. "Yes, I am certain." She knew she must end this subject now. "You were entirely foxed. I do not believe you were responsible for most of your behavior. You said some strange things as well, which I did not understand."

"Such as?" He came around his chair toward her.

Oh, she did not want to be trapped in that small space between the table and the wall! She hoped he would not reach out and touch her! Of course, she could simply turn and run down the length of the table and out of the room—which was exactly what she felt like doing. Instead, she did not move.

"Such as?" he said again, but his tone was demanding, and he stood within reach of her.

What she would not do was tell him that he had wanted to discuss the past, that he had raised the subject several times. "You sounded as if you had been to France, or had been involved in the war."

He made a dismissive sound. "Really? I have not been abroad in years. What else did I say?"

"We talked about Lady Grenville."

His gaze sharpened. "Ah, yes. I vaguely recall telling you that I was not fond of my wife."

She clasped her hands and said, unhappily, "You claimed you were not grieving for her but I did not believe you."

He made a mocking sound. "Of course, you would think the best of me."

"What does that mean?"

"You always believed in me. Your faith was unshakable."

He wished to discuss the past again? She was incredulous. "I believe," she said carefully, "that you love your children and you loved your wife, although perhaps not in a conventional way."

"As I said, your faith is unshakable. Apparently I was being entirely truthful with you last night. I am not grieving for Lady Grenville. I hardly wished her ill, but I cannot grieve for a woman I barely knew."

"How is that even possible?" Amelia gasped. "You shared children and she was so beautiful and so gracious!"

"It was her duty to bear my sons," he pointed out, rather darkly. "Just as it was my duty to marry her and beget an heir."

She felt her eyes widen. It hadn't been a love match. It didn't even sound as if he had had a choice. Was all the terrible gossip true? She didn't dare ask. She said softly, "I am so sorry. You both deserved more."

Grenville was clearly incredulous. "You are sorry that I did not love my wife? That she did not love me? That I am not brokenhearted? You would wish me well?"

"Yes—no!" Then, blushing and aware of it, she cried, "I would not wish anyone ill." She stopped. They were fast approaching dangerous ground—today would be an even worse time to venture onto the subject of their past. She quickly said, hoping to divert him, "If you are not grieving for Lady Grenville, then there is another cause for your anguish. I had forgotten that the last time you were in residence, your brother died."

His face hardened. "That was a decade ago."

She almost pointed out that he seemed to remember their affair well, so surely he recalled that tragedy, as well. "I am sorry that you had to return under these painful circumstances."

"I think I believe you," he said. "Only you would continue to care, to have concern and even compassion for me." He shook his head. "The question becomes, how is it possible that you would still have faith in me?"

She hated this tangent! But apparently, he would not be diverted. "I am not a cynic," she managed to respond. And did she still have faith in him? Grenville was a man of honor, a man of duty, a man of character—even if he had behaved so callously with her. She did believe it, God help her.

"I have found, Amelia, that in this life the cynics are usually right."

"Then I am sorry for you," she snapped.

"And I fear for you—for one day, you will learn such a lesson."

"No. I will remain an optimist, and I will continue to have faith in my friends and neighbors." She meant it.

He was staring intensely. "I wonder what I will have to do this time to shake that faith."

What did that mean? She cried, "There will not be another time!"

"Ah, so now we get to the gist of the matter."

"I am only here out of concern for the children."

"Liar!" He smiled dangerously now. "Do you think I have not noticed that every time I mention the past, or even refer to it with a vague innuendo, you become rather undone?"

She hugged herself. "Well, that is because last night you were relentless! And even today, it is as if you wish to remind me of the past, when I have forgotten it entirely!" There, the fighting gloves were off.

He slowly said, his eyes gleaming, "You do know that you have just raised a red flag at a bull?"

What did that mean? "Have you been imbibing today?"

"No, I have not. But do not baldly lie to my face! Do not tell me that you have forgotten the past, when the one thing I do recall is that last night I held you in my arms, and you were trembling." He had raised his voice. His dark eyes flashed.

And she found herself lying, instinctively. "You were

frightening—at times you erupted in anger—I had never seen you in such a state!"

"And even now—" he pointed at her "—you are trembling, and we both know why."

She cried out. But he was right—desire was coursing through her veins.

And he became dismissive. "You should stay away from this house. You should stay away from me. You should give up your goddamned faith. Because you are still an innocent, and I am not referring to your status as a woman. You are an innocent at heart, and do not deny it. You do not have a clue as to what transpires in the world, outside of your precious Cornwall! You do not have a clue that life is really only about death—that death is everywhere, and that nobility is for fools!" His eyes blazed.

She cringed. "What has happened to you?" She wanted to weep.

"You need to stay far away from me," he continued furiously. "Either that, or come here and suffer the consequences."

She gasped again. Did he mean that he would attempt a seduction, then and there?

"Do not look so surprised! I am a rogue, remember— a rake."

She did not know how to reply. But she was about to defend him, and she closed her mouth to stop herself from doing so.

He laughed. "God, you would defend me even now!"

She backed up and hit the dining-room wall. Finally she found her voice. "I will defend you, Grenville, when you have been unjustly and erroneously accused of some misdeed. But right now, I will not even attempt to excuse your atrocious behavior!" Was she shouting?

His eyes widened.

"You are obviously in a state of grief—do not deny it! Whether you are grieving over your wife, your brother, or someone else, the anguish is obvious. But your grief does not give you a carte blanche to treat me with utter disrespect!"

His mouth pursed, as if he fought to prevent himself from speaking.

She realized she was shaking. "I am genuinely concerned for your children, and, yes, for you. If you choose to think I harbor some ancient flame, then so be it. I am not going to try to change your mind. However, I must say something, and you will not like it. Your selfish behavior must cease."

Grenville was motionless. But he was listening to her, his gaze narrow.

"Go see your sons. Go see your newborn daughter! They need you, Grenville. And then do something to repair this household!" She was most definitely shouting at the Earl of St. Just, but she could not recall ever having been as angry.

He finally said, "Are you finished?"

"Yes, I have said what needed to be said." She lifted her chin defiantly. "And I am going to check in on the children before I go—unless you object." She dared to meet his gaze, wondering if he was about to forbid her from associating with his children. If he did, she would not blame him. She would not be surprised if he ordered her forthright from his house.

His face impossible to read, he said calmly, "I believe they will be pleased to see you."

Relief almost swamped her. Amelia quickly turned and rushed down the length of the dining hall, beginning to realize what she had done. She had just scolded

Grenville. She had just shouted at him. She had berated him at the top of her lungs.

She had, in fact, behaved exactly like the harridan he had accused her of being.

And in the hall, she glanced back at him.

The Earl of St. Just hadn't moved, not a single muscle. He was staring, and if he despised her now, she could not tell.

AMELIA REALIZED SHE WAS flushed and perspiring as she reached the classroom door. Worse, her heart would not stop racing.

She should not care if Grenville despised her now. Someone had to set him down and stop him from continuing his selfish and self-destructive behavior.

Signor Barelli rushed to the threshold of the room. He had been seated at one of the three desks in the room, reading. John was on the floor, playing with dominoes. William stood at the window, gazing outside, a fishing rod in his hand.

So much for their lessons, she thought.

"I am so pleased to see you," the Italian cried. He was clearly distraught as he lowered his voice and said, "They will not do the reading I have assigned them."

John leaped up and rushed into her arms. Amelia hugged him as William walked over, his dark face set. "Hello," she said, as cheerfully as possible. "Aren't we fortunate? It has stopped raining and tomorrow promises to be a glorious day."

"Good, I will go riding," William said, far too decisively for a boy his age.

"I will go riding, too," John said, beaming at her. "Can you come with us? Please?"

Amelia glanced at the tutor. "I would love to go riding with you, but I do not have a hack. However," she said, before they could protest, "if you both settle down and begin your assignments, I will ask your father permission to take you on a picnic on the weekend—after all your assignments are done."

William's sullen expression had vanished. "Picnics are for the summertime," he said.

"I want to go on a picnic!" John shouted, jumping up and down.

"This will be a special picnic," Amelia told William. "And if the weather permits, we will even bring your sister."

John began dancing around the room. Amelia realized he was entirely out of bounds. William said seriously, "I'd like that. But Father is locked in his rooms."

Amelia took his hand. "No, he is downstairs, dining."

Such a poignant look of hope flared across the small boy's face that she went still. The best medicine for these children would be their father, she was certain. And she wondered if she dared take them downstairs, then and there, and reunite the family.

Signor Barelli said, "Thank the lord he has come out of his apartments. They miss him dearly, Miss Greystone."

Did she dare?

"I want Papa," John cried, pouting. His gaze was moist with tears.

If she went through with this, he would throw her out of the house, once and for all. But did it matter? She held out her other hand. "Come, John. We are going to call on your father."

John's eyes widened and he ran to her, giving her his hand.

Amelia prayed she was not making a mistake. She

turned to Barelli. "I think they need a moment with their father before they resume their lessons."

"I think you are right," he said with relief.

Amelia smiled at both boys, holding their hands, and they went into the corridor. As they started down the hall, the nursery door opened and Mrs. Murdock came out, her eyes wide. "I thought I heard your voice, Miss Greystone," she said, smiling. "Oh, I am so glad you have called!"

Amelia paused to greet her. "I am taking the boys downstairs. It is high time they chatted with their father. How is the baby?"

"She has just awoken."

Amelia looked past Mrs. Murdock. From where she stood, she could see into a part of the crib. The infant lay on her back, her hands and feet in the air. She was gazing at a toy suspended over the crib.

He had yet to see his newborn daughter, she thought with unease. Did she dare bring the baby down, as well?

"Why don't you take her and join us? His lordship hasn't seen her yet, has he?"

Mrs. Murdock seemed to grasp the significance of what they were doing. She paled. "Only that one time, when he first arrived from London."

But he hadn't even looked at the baby then, Amelia thought. "He will fall in love with her," Amelia said, speaking her thoughts aloud.

Mrs. Murdock smiled and retrieved the baby. The group then went downstairs. Amelia led them toward the dining hall, her heart pounding. The moment everyone was settled, she would make her escape; she hardly needed another word with Grenville now.

The servant was outside the dining room, unmoving. Both doors remained open. John screamed, "Papa!" He

released her hand and ran into the dining room. William
let her go and followed.

Grenville had been seated at the far end of the table,
reading a news journal. He stood up, incredulous. Then,
as John barreled into him, she saw the smile break over
his face. As he embraced his son, lifting him up and
whirling him about in a sign of sheer joy, Amelia felt
faint with relief.

He so loved the boys.

He set John down and hugged William, hard. When
he released him and straightened, he was still smiling.

"I broke my horse," John told him.

"Miss Greystone wants to take us on a picnic," William said eagerly. "Can we go, Father?"

"Can we? Can we?" John cried, hopping up and down.

His hand on William's shoulder, Grenville turned and
looked at her. Then his gaze moved behind her to Mrs.
Murdock, who carried the baby. A chilling expression
crossed his face.

Alarm began. He did not want to see his daughter.

He hadn't looked at her at the funeral.

But he quickly turned to both boys. "We will discuss
the possibility of a picnic after you tell me all about your
lessons." And as both boys tried to speak at once, explaining why they had not been doing their lessons, he
glanced up at Amelia.

His face dark, he said, "I will see the child another
time." And he moved, putting his back between them
and his sons.

No action could have been as clear. They had been
dismissed.

Amelia took Mrs. Murdock's arm in disbelief. As
they stepped into the hallway, the governess looked at
her, wide-eyed.

He would not look at his own child, she thought, torn between anger and sorrow. How could he be so callous, so cold?

"Oh, Miss Greystone," Mrs. Murdock whispered. "I know you despise gossip, but I fear that this time, the gossip is true."

Amelia stared at her, then quickly turned and closed the dining-room doors. A terrible thought had occurred to her. "He blames this poor baby for his wife's death," she managed to say.

"I do not think that is the case," Mrs. Murdock said unevenly.

"If you have another explanation, I should like to hear it!"

"The child isn't his."

CHAPTER FIVE

SOMEONE WAS KNOCKING on the door.

He could not imagine who was there, in the middle of the night. The knocking became louder. It became insistent.

And suddenly he knew who was at his front door and he sat up. Terror consumed him.

"St. Just! Open up! We know who you are and what you have done!" a man shouted.

They had discovered his identity, they knew he was playing both sides against one another, they meant to seize him, imprison him and return him to France!

The memories—of women begging for the lives of their children, grown men weeping, of Danton so courageously standing before the guillotine, addressing the crowd—whirled and rioted in his mind.

Thump. Aahhhh! Thump. Aahhhhh!

He was going to be sick. He could not stand that sound, followed by those cheers....

He looked down and saw the blood covering his body. Panic claimed him.

And then he realized he was gripping the cold iron bars of his cell. He had already been returned to France—he was back in that prison—that place of no escape!

Except the knocking was even louder now.

Simon gasped, sitting bolt upright. Bright sunlight

blinded him and he blinked. He was sitting on a magnificent gold-and-white brocade sofa, in a gold library,
and it was the arm of the couch he held, not iron bars.
He was drenched in sweat, not blood. A liveried servant
was at the door of the library, with his luncheon tray.

He was in his home at St. Just Hall, not in a prison
in France.

He slumped against the back of the sofa, gasping for
breath. Would these nightmares never cease? They were
becoming worse and worse. Not a night went by that he
did not dream of being seized, imprisoned and sent to the
guillotine. He had begun to avoid going to bed—he had
begun to sleep as few hours as possible—all in the desperate hope of avoiding these terribly vivid nightmares.

But he wasn't in Paris now. Warlock meant to send
him back, and he would probably have to go, but until
then he was safe—as safe as someone in his position
could possibly be.

He closed his eyes, willing away the last remnants of
terror and fear. And as he tried to regain his composure,
so many jumbled-up pieces of his life assailed him. He
saw his brother, Will, smiling at him as they stood on
the beach, preparing to dive through the waves into the
ocean; he recalled the stoic look on Elizabeth's face as
he slipped her wedding ring onto her finger; he remembered holding William as a newborn infant, his heart
swelling with love....

And then there was Amelia Greystone, looking at him
with utter horror when he would not allow that governess to bring Elizabeth's bastard into the dining room.

He had never expected to see Amelia again. But she
had come to the funeral—and he had recognized her
immediately.

His heart lurched. For he recalled Amelia looking at

him when he had been poised to kiss her, the other day when he had been so foxed, her eyes filled with both desire and fear.

She was afraid of the attraction they still had for one another.

His head ached terribly now. He flung one arm across his forehead. Could he really blame her? The attraction he felt for her seemed, impossibly, more furious than ever. And that frightened him, as well. "Johnson, set the tray upon my desk, thank you very much."

He did not look at the servant as he obeyed. He knew his thoughts were becoming dangerous. But he could not turn them off.

Instead, he recalled Amelia standing on the threshold of the dining room with his sons, holding each of their hands.

He would never forget the sight of her with his two sons. And damn it, he did not want to—it was a small pleasure in his hellish life.

She had come to Elizabeth's funeral, she had helped his children in their time of grief and she had even attempted to rescue him. But then, that was Amelia Greystone—she had always been the most compassionate woman he knew.

When it came to meddling, no one surpassed Amelia. But she interfered out of concern. How could he tell her not to intervene, especially when it came to the boys? But her meddling could be dangerous—very dangerous—and she did not have a clue.

Sebastian Warlock was her uncle. He was also Simon's British spymaster. Simon had been involved in Warlock's war games for almost two years, so he knew Sebastian. The spymaster would never allow his niece near the truth, Simon was certain.

However, Amelia was astute. And then there were
her brothers. He did not know either one well, but he did
know that Lucas was very involved in the war, and he
also knew that, from time to time, Jack aided the émigrés fleeing France. Still, he doubted her brothers would
ever endanger her by revealing any of their activities to
her. And he was relieved.

He wasn't certain he liked such a reaction on his part,
just as he wasn't certain how he should feel about his
raging desire for her.

Simon leaned back against the pillows on the sofa,
ignoring his luncheon—he had no appetite. He was torn.
He knew he must not think about her, yet he was helpless not to. It was as if she had returned to his life with
a vengeance.

She always saw the good in everyone—even him—
when no one else did. Even after what he had done to her,
even after leaving her the way that he had, she believed
in him. And she wanted to comfort him now.

He stared out at the gray, barren moors. He wished
life had dealt them both a different hand, but it had not.
By the time Will had been laid in his coffin, he had
known their relationship was over. The moment Will
had been flung from his horse, breaking his neck, their
relationship had ended. For in that single devastating
instant, he had become the earl's heir. And he hadn't
thought twice about leaving Cornwall without a word.

But even then, he hadn't realized that his duties were
a small price to pay in the larger scheme of things. He
hadn't known that, one day, he would be nothing but a
pawn in the midst of war and revolution, his neck hanging in the balance, his sons' lives at stake.

And in that moment, as he contemplated the danger
he had put his children in, he knew he must forget about

Amelia Greystone. He was well aware that he wished to make love to her, the way he hadn't been able to ten years ago. He was aware that his passion was far stronger now than before. But he wouldn't toy with her, and not because he had hurt her once and he wasn't selfish enough to do so again. His life was far too dangerous. She must never become seriously involved with him.

He stood and walked over to his desk. It was time to forget about Amelia. If she called again, he would make certain he did not receive her. He supposed he could allow her to see the children. His sons adored her already.

Elizabeth was already on her way to London to be laid to rest in the family mausoleum there. Her death had been a brief respite from the war and his role in it. But the truth was, Jourdan had to make an appearance in town very soon.

The night he had left Paris, Lafleur had been clear. If Simon did not prove his loyalty to the *Enragé* and the rest of *le Comité,* they would hunt him down like a rabid dog.

He had to return to London and begin digging for intelligence immediately. He needed the kind of information that would appease his French masters, but not jeopardize the Allied war effort.

And he had yet to speak with Warlock. When he had left Paris, he had gone directly to Le Havre, finding a smuggler to take him to Dover, then hired a coach to take him the rest of the way to St. Just. There had been no opportunity to meet with and brief Warlock in a passing tavern.

He did not know what Warlock knew about his past months in Paris, or how much he would reveal to him. But he would not underestimate Sebastian. Warlock probably knew he had been imprisoned for ninety-six days. He would want to know how he had gotten out of prison. If he claimed he had escaped, Warlock would demand to know how he had managed such a feat. If he said he had been freed, Warlock would become immediately suspicious. He was going to have to tread very carefully with the man who had enticed him into this web of intrigue.

And Warlock would also expect Simon to return to his place in the Commune, in order to relay more intelligence to the British—just as Lafleur wanted information now, before the Allied invasion of Flanders.

He picked up a glass of wine, suddenly furious—no, enraged. There was no control. In that moment, he wanted to break apart every furnishing in the room. If Amelia returned, daring to meddle in his life, there would be consequences to pay! She would not be safe from him. He would prove to her and to himself that he was a selfish bastard and seduce her the moment she walked through his door....

He had never felt as desperate. It crossed his mind that in her arms, the world and the war would cease to exist. In her arms, there would be pleasure, light, laughter and love....

Simon suddenly flung the glass at the wall. It shattered.

Trembling, he sat down, staring at the covered plates on his luncheon tray. His temper was becoming worse, too.

He took several deep breaths, but Amelia's image remained, as did those of his sons. And he cradled his forehead in his hands.

He had to return to London. And he had a terrible

decision to make. Would it be safer to leave the boys in Cornwall? Or should he take them with him to town?

He knew immediately that they had to be close; that he would live in constant panic if he left them in Cornwall, fearing for their safety with his every waking breath. If his subterfuge were uncovered, they would be in dire danger.

He pushed the tray back and leaned back in his chair. He was about to return to London. His activities would be dangerous. He would come and go at all hours—and especially in the dark hours of the night. Obviously he needed to hire a housekeeper, but it would have to be someone with great intelligence, with strength of character and common sense. It would have to be someone he could trust.

Signor Barelli had no spine. The governess, whose name he could not recall, had been Elizabeth's hire. Every time he had glimpsed her, she had been in tears. Clearly, she was a hysterical woman.

Elizabeth had run his household and, more importantly, overseen the boys' upbringing, and she had done it well. The old housekeeper, who had passed away some months ago, had deferred to Lady Grenville. Elizabeth had been far more than a beautiful countess; she had been a housekeeper and a mother.

And instantly, he recalled Amelia standing on the threshold of the dining room, the boys on each side of her, holding hands.

Amelia, who was alone at Greystone Manor, caring for her addled mother and claiming she was content.

AMELIA FINISHED DUSTING the piano that the dowager Countess of Bedford had purchased for her sister. She straightened and eyed the instrument, which gleamed.

Because the great hall was barely furnished—two crimson chairs were placed before the huge stone hearth, and there was a bench along one stone wall—they had placed six cheerful red-damask chairs around the piano. Before Julianne had eloped with Bedford, she would play for hours at a time, and their neighbors had often come to sit and listen. The Comte D'Archand, an émigré, had begun the habit of bringing his violin and joining Julianne. Amelia recalled the hall being filled with music and conversation, warmth and laughter.

Just then, Amelia felt so very alone. As it had been for months on end, the manor was stunningly silent.

She was not going to recall being in Grenville's presence—or his arms.

She dusted the top of the grand piano again. Momma was upstairs, sleeping. Garrett was outside, walking the property with the herd dogs. Lucas had left for London days ago, and she did not know where Jack was. Hopefully, he was on the high seas, outracing His Majesty's Royal Navy.

Momma wasn't good company, unfortunately. Neither was the taciturn Scot. In a way, the house might as well have been entirely empty.

She wished Nadine D'Archand were in the parish. She had become good friends with the Comte's eldest daughter during the winter, but Nadine had gone back to town with her family. The Frenchwoman was not fond of the country. Amelia suspected she was also involved in the war effort. She was rabidly anti-Jacobin, and always current on the latest revolutionary developments.

Grenville's image tugged at her, strongly. So did an image of his beautiful infant daughter. It would be so easy to surrender to her thoughts. In fact, the pair was just about all she could think of!

Very grimly, she began dusting the closest window-sill, never mind that she had already done so. She did not know how to reconcile father and daughter, but she was determined to do just that. Grenville had many faults, obviously, but he was a good father—and a loving one. Every time she saw him with his sons, she was impressed. For how long would he turn his back on his daughter? She had spent a sleepless night, trying to decide how she might bring Grenville to his senses.

As for Mrs. Murdock's absurd ramblings, she would not entertain them. That kind of gossip was sordid, indeed, and she did not believe it for a moment! Of course the babe was his!

She had cleaned the entire house thoroughly. She doubted there was a speck of dust or particle of dirt anywhere. The kitchens were so clean that they did not look as if they had been used. Momma's bags were packed. Her own belongings would take less than an hour to prepare for travel, as she was a simple woman with few possessions.

"Amelia."

She froze at the sound of Grenville's voice. Incredulous, certain she had hallucinated, she turned.

She hadn't imagined him. The Earl of St. Just stood on the threshold of the great room, clad in a copper velvet coat, beige breeches and paler stockings. He wore his hair naturally, but pulled back, under a bicorne hat. His brows lifted as he looked at her. She was in her oldest housedress and an apron, holding a feather duster.

She flushed. "You simply walked in?"

"I knocked three times. I even called out. No one heard me." His gaze had narrowed. "Why are you cleaning the house?"

"I hardly have a staff of maids to do so for me," she

said tartly. But her heart was racing wildly. Why on earth was Grenville calling?

"That is unacceptable," he said flatly, looking past her at the great room. "Nothing has changed, I see, except that you have let your staff go."

A decade ago, there had been a maid to clean the house. She was rigid. "I prefer not to discuss the matter of whether or not I have any help in my home."

He gave her a dark look. "May I come in? My intention is not to make you uncomfortable."

"You are doing just that," she said tersely.

Slowly, he smiled. "Perhaps it is my presence, not the topic of conversation, that is so disturbing?"

She bit her lip. He was correct. She hated being caught in such dishabille, as if a mere domestic, and her heart was pounding wildly in response to his powerful presence. "Had I known you meant to call, I would have prepared tea," she said tartly.

He smiled, and the smile lightened his eyes. "I would love to have tea with you." She was dismayed, as she had nothing to offer him as an additional refreshment. He added, "But as that would require you to light a fire and boil water, steep the bags, set a tray and deprive me, in general, of your company for some time, I will decline the offer."

Her relief was immediate. He knew, she thought. He was being kind.

His gaze searched hers, half of a smile remaining.

Ten years ago, he had also been kind. He had brought her too many gifts to count when calling or shopping. When she had worried about Momma, he had listened. When she had complained about Julianne, who was wont to shirk her duties, he had advised her. When she had been angry with Lucas, for his stance against them, he had been calm and sensible. Mostly, though, she had been grateful that he had always pretended that he did not notice the vast difference of economy and class which existed between them.

"I am being rude. I do not mind making tea," she said slowly. What was he doing there?

"I had tea before I left the house. However, I will sit with you if you wish to take some."

She shook her head, relieved all over again. "Please. Come in."

He smiled briefly at her and walked into the great hall. "Is Lucas here?" he asked.

"Lucas left for town, immediately after the funeral."

He seemed to accept that. He laid his hand on the piano. "This is new."

"The dowager Countess of Bedford bought it for Julianne."

"That was nice of her."

Would they go around and around like this, being excessively polite with one another? Amelia asked, very carefully, "So is this simply a neighborly social call?"

"No, it is not." He faced her, seeming chagrined. "I wish to apologize a second time."

She started. "For your behavior yesterday?"

"Yes. I was a boor, once again. But I can claim, in self-defense, that I was feeling rather poorly."

She smiled. "You do realize that I also owe you an apology?"

And he smiled. "I will not accept it."

"Why ever not?" she cried.

"Because I needed to be set down. You were right. My behavior had been entirely selfish and self-serving."

Amelia was in disbelief.

"You are gaping," he said mildly.

And his tone was so pleasant that her heart slammed. Desire, running just beneath the surface, crested. I still love him, she thought, and in that instant, she was horrified. Shocked by such a treacherous thought, Amelia turned away. She was not in love with Grenville. It was impossible.

"Amelia? Have I upset you?"

His tone continued to be mild and pleasant. She whirled and forced a smile. "Of course not. How are the children faring?"

She saw his expression close, but he said, calmly, "The boys seem to be doing a bit better. When we return to London, I am going to purchase a Connemara pony for John. I am fond of the breed," he added. "William wishes to enter his first fencing tourney. He has been fencing for some time. I am also buying him his own yacht."

When was he returning to London? And why was she so utterly dismayed? "I am sure they will be thrilled with such gifts." She hesitated.

"You disapprove."

"Spoiling them won't bring back their mother."

"No, it will not." His gaze met hers and held it.

She did not blame him for wanting to shower the boys with gifts. But what about his daughter? "Have you named her yet?"

"No." His tone was hard. He turned his back on her and paced slowly. He paused before the pair of crimson chairs. "I thought the mine was doing well, and iron is very profitable ore."

He was changing the subject. But his daughter needed a name—and a father! She was shocked. "You know how successfully Lucas manages the estate. I believe the mine and quarry are doing very well. But these are difficult times. It would be foolish to spend our income, especially with prices so inflated by the war."

He faced her. "The house needs maintenance, Amelia, whether we are at war or not."

He was right, but that was not the subject she wished to digress upon. "Simon, I remain concerned about your children."

He walked back over to her, and took the duster from her. Their hands brushed and she shivered. He did not seem to notice the minimal contact, and she watched in some despair as he laid the duster in a corner by one window. "I will never be accustomed to seeing you houseclean."

"Someone must do it."

His gaze moved over her features, far too slowly. He said, casually, "I would like to make you an offer, Amelia—a proposition, so to speak—but I do not want you to be insulted."

She stared in surprise—she had not expected such a declaration. An oddly enigmatic expression was on Grenville's face, and she could not discern his thoughts or feelings. What could he possibly suggest?

And suddenly she had the wild notion that he meant to ask her to be his mistress.

A dozen heated images flashed through her mind.

Would she dare accept such a proposal?

"I need a housekeeper," he said, slowly.

"I beg your pardon?" she said, barely able to speak.

"I am in rather desperate need of a housekeeper. I am constantly in the north, where I have some very large, successful estates, and I intend to keep my sons in London—town is best for them. They hardly need to travel as frequently as I do. Elizabeth actually managed the household. She was very involved in both boys' daily activities. I need someone to manage the household as she did, and supervise their daily care."

Amelia was reeling. He wanted to hire her as his housekeeper.

And she had assumed he wanted her in his bed!

"I need someone I can trust, Amelia."

She managed to meet his dark, steady gaze. She felt as if he had just stabbed her in the heart. My God, she was almost insulted.

Yet she should not be insulted to be asked to be a highly placed, well-paid housekeeper. She was an impoverished gentlewoman. The position was low, but not entirely beneath her. She certainly needed the income.

But she was insulted. Terribly so!

"Are you going to refuse me?" he asked, very carefully.

She felt her cheeks flame. "I can hardly accept such an offer."

"I meant it when I said I do not mean to insult you."

She folded her arms. "I have my own home—my own family—to manage!"

"I have heard that Lucas is removing you and your mother to town, and that you are closing up this house. Of course, I have room for your mother in my Mayfair home."

All she could think of was Simon, taking her into his arms. "I do not think I can accept," she said.

"Amelia, I need your help," he said swiftly. "My boys need someone like you in their life. Even that child—she has no one. And if it eases your mind, I travel frequently to my various estates, so we will hardly be in residence together—or, at least not often." His stare was intense.

"What does that mean?"

"It means that even I am in some doubt as to my trustworthiness. We both know how I have behaved around you. Is that why you are hesitating? I hold you in the highest regard—I always have."

And she wanted to cry, "You left without a word." Shocked at the sudden return of that old heartbreak, she stared.

"You and your mother will lack for naught. You will be in town—and you will have every opportunity to visit your sister and brother. I do not expect you to behave as the usual housekeeper. We will plan a schedule, one that suits your every need," he said firmly. "I am not going to be denied."

And Amelia knew he was not going to let her refuse. And she also realized exactly what his offer meant—a lucrative position in London, where she would not have to worry about the war, or enemy soldiers, or spies or assassins. She would not have to worry about a French invasion. There would be no worry about putting the next meal on the table. Her only worry would be just how to care for his children.

But there was far more to worry about than that. How would she manage her own confusion in regards to the past that they shared? And what about the attraction that simmered between them?

But Momma would be safe. And the boys needed her. His daughter needed her!

"I see you are, finally, intrigued." A hard light filled his eyes.

"Yes, I am intrigued. Your children—all three of them—have intrigued me from the moment we met."

His smile vanished. "I am aware of that."

"She is your daughter, Grenville. Why haven't you named her? You have seen her, haven't you? How can you not have fallen absolutely in love with her?"

He looked mutely at her, folding his arms across his chest. He finally said, "I do not love her and I do not care what she is named."

"You do not love her!"

He inhaled. "You will learn the truth sooner or later. She is not mine."

Amelia cried out. The gossip was true? She prayed not! "Surely that is not true—surely you do not believe such a thing!"

"The bastard is not mine."

She was stricken with dismay. "You cannot be certain," she began.

And he gave her a dark look. "Oh, I am certain! She cannot be mine, Amelia. It is impossible."

And Amelia began to understand.

With an expression of revulsion, he said, "I haven't been in Elizabeth's bed since John was conceived."

Amelia could barely believe what he was telling her. He hadn't had relations with his wife in years! She could not look away from his dark, blazing regard.

"Well?" he demanded.

She whispered, "I'll do it."

And his smile was hard and satisfied.

CHAPTER SIX

"OH, ARE WE FINALLY stopping for the evening?" Mrs. Murdock cried hopefully.

Amelia held the baby in her arms, helping her to nurse from a teat. She was seated beside her mother, facing the governess and Garrett in the smaller of the three passenger vehicles they were taking to town. Grenville and his sons were in the coach just ahead of them. Signor Barelli, Lloyd and the cook were in another carriage. Their belongings followed in two wagons.

They had been traveling since shortly after sunrise, and it was almost dark now. It had taken Grenville three days to prepare his household for the journey to London; in that time, Amelia had stayed as far from St. Just Hall as possible. From the moment she had agreed to become his housekeeper, she had been filled with confusion and uncertainty.

Only a very foolish woman would think that taking this position was a good idea. The past remained a divisive issue looming between them. Even if he retreated into formality and never acknowledged their history again, could she do the same thing?

Momma, however, was thrilled to be undertaking the adventure. She had been quite lucid for the past few days. Amelia had explained the situation to her— Momma chose to believe that they would be the Earl of St. Just's guests for the season. "He must be court-ing you, Amelia, to extend such an invitation!" she had cried.

Amelia had decided not to answer.

Now, she held the baby close and strained to glance out of her window. A cheerful inn with white stucco walls was ahead, smoke coming from both red chim-neys. They had reached the outskirts of Bodmin, and the oak trees were huge and green, with ivy creeping over the inn's whitewashed walls. Roses spilled over the wood fence in the courtyard; sheep milled about an adjacent field, crisscrossed with stone walls. The set-ting sun stained the sky with its mauve fingers. It was so picturesque, but Amelia was not charmed.

In another moment, she and Grenville would be face-to-face. There was no denying that the prospect affected her greatly. Her position as his housekeeper felt awk-ward and unnatural.

She had not seen him since he had called on her at Greystone Manor, except briefly that morning. In the past three days, he had sent her lists and a note which apprised her of their intended departure date. There had been no word about her new role as housekeeper, when she had expected to have several conversations about her employment. She supposed they would sit down in his library upon reaching London, to hash out the details then.

He had sent their coach to the manor to pick her, Momma and Garrett up at dawn that morning. They had met with St. Just and the rest of his entourage on the highway outside of Penzance. He had alighted from his coach, but his greeting had been polite and perfunc-tory. Then he had vanished back into his coach and the convoy had set off for London. Amelia had been shaken by the encounter.

Had she expected more? She sighed. Formality would be the best recourse for them both, even if it somehow bothered her. But she was his housekeeper now.

She smiled at Mrs. Murdock. "It has been a very long, very tiring day. I imagine everyone is ready for a hot meal and bed." She refrained from rubbing her hip, which ached. She wondered what would happen now. Would he take the boys and vanish into the inn and their rooms? That would probably be for the best, too.

"My back cannot withstand the constant jarring," Mrs. Murdock complained, shifting in her seat. "I cannot wait to go to sleep. But we are fortunate that Lucille is such a good traveler."

Amelia smiled at the baby. They had dared to name her. She had so desperately needed a name—they couldn't keep referring to her as the child or the baby—and apparently Lady Grenville had liked Lucille. "She is a wonderful companion." She clasped her tiny, downy head. "At this rate, we will probably be in London late tomorrow, unless we lose a wheel or some such thing," Amelia said. Traveling from Land's End to London in two days was practically unthinkable, especially for such a convoy. It felt as if Grenville was in a rush to get to town, but she could not imagine why.

She saw the door of Grenville's huge black coach opening. Her heart slammed. He stepped out, his great coat swinging about his narrow hips and long legs, his handsome face set in an impassive expression.

A pang went through her. Her body dared to tighten. He was a magnificent, attractive man. Would it always be this way? she wondered miserably. Would she always look at him and have this yearning? But what, precisely, did she yearn for?

She was afraid to answer her own question; she knew she must leave it alone!

But she was so drawn to him. Even following his huge coach with their smaller carriage, she was acutely aware that he was just a few horse lengths ahead of them. A part of her anticipated their next encounter, no matter how she tried to be oblivious to the fact that it would most definitely occur, and soon. If she counted the minutes—the seconds—to their every exchange, how would she manage as his housekeeper? And to think that she had thought, even if for a moment, that he wanted her to be his mistress!

How laughable that was!

Maybe, if she remained as formal as possible, if she did her best to forget the past—and his behavior in his rooms after the funeral—she would be able to successfully adopt the role of housekeeper. Maybe her yearning would fade away and die. She must focus on the reasons she had accepted the position. His sons needed her and she already loved both boys. And this poor child—Lady Grenville's bastard—needed her! She loved the baby, too. Who wouldn't love such an adorable infant?

But he hadn't slept with his wife in years.

She closed her eyes tightly for a moment. What did that mean, exactly? If only he hadn't told her such a thing.

She looked down at the infant, who had finished nursing and was yawning widely. She smiled a little. It meant that his marriage had been as troubled, as strained and loveless as the governess had described.

Her heart lurched. When they had been in the midst

of their mad flirtation, he hadn't been able to keep his hands to himself. If she knew one thing, it was that Simon Grenville was a very passionate and virile man.

After the funeral, he had tried to seduce her. What should she make of that equation, Amelia wondered. He had avoided his wife—but he had tried to kiss her.

That did not mean he had kept a torch burning for her, she told herself with as much conviction as she could muster. To even consider such a notion was dangerous! Surely she didn't want him to want her still? How awkward that would be.

If he desired her that way, he would not have asked her to become his housekeeper. He would have seduced her or asked her to become his mistress.

"Would you hand off the child to the governess and help Signor Barelli settle the boys?"

She stiffened at the sound of Grenville's soft, commanding voice and met his gaze through her carriage window. He opened her door, unsmiling. She vaguely heard a footman crying out in dismay as he did so.

Biting her lip, aware that her heart was racing, Amelia handed the baby to Mrs. Murdock. He was being so very formal and distant now. What she had to do was navigate her way through this difficult new beginning; she was his housekeeper, not the woman he was courting, and certainly not his mistress.

But Grenville took her hand without her offering it. Aware of his grasp, Amelia stepped down. He released her and gestured toward the front door of the inn, where William and John were racing about as if playing tag, the two of them shouting happily. Two small, yapping dogs had appeared and were chasing the boys. A heavyset man in a coat and breeches stepped out, smiling jovially. Amelia assumed him to be the innkeeper.

The sight of the boys relieved her. She was thrilled that they were in such good spirits.

And Grenville seemed pleased, too, for he watched his sons, and he smiled. Her heart turned over, hard.

Then he faced her, the smile gone. "I hope you are not the worse for wear. I apologize for the day being overly long."

Amelia suddenly wished he would shed the facade of employer. "I am young and fit." She smiled. "I hardly mind traveling for twelve hours straight, but Mrs. Murdock has indicated that her back is bothering her."

"We did stop to change horses," he said, turning to look at the boys again.

"Yes, we did. But I am a bit concerned about her, Grenville." She knew she sounded tart, but surely he had some concern for the middle-aged governess, too.

He faced her abruptly. "I do not care about the governess. I am asking you how you are." His gaze held hers. "I do not wish to put you out, Amelia."

She did not expect him to resort to the pretense of addressing her as Miss Greystone, that would be absurd, but he was not acting like her employer now. And she was relieved, when she should not be. "I am fine." She smiled ruefully. "But I admit to being tired. And hungry." They had brought lunch baskets with them, but she was ravenous now.

"Tomorrow will be as long a day," he said tersely. "Can you manage?"

She wondered if there was some urgency on his part. "Of course I can manage."

"And your mother?" He glanced past her.

Garrett had helped Momma out, and they were coming toward them. Amelia faced Grenville. "Momma is thrilled to be returning to town. She spent half of the trip sleeping."

He nodded. "Then I am relieved." He touched her elbow and she started. He dropped his hand and gestured at the inn. Her heart racing, Amelia preceded him.

"How have the boys fared today?" she asked.

"They traveled well." He hesitated and she met his gaze determinedly. He said, "It has been enjoyable for me, traveling with them." The moment he spoke, his expression closed. She had the feeling he regretted sharing his feelings with her.

She wanted to ask why he had so rarely been in residence with his family. She wanted to ask if he had despised his wife so greatly that he had chosen to stay away from the children because of her. "I imagine they have been as pleased to spend this time with you," she said softly, aware that no housekeeper would ever make such a remark.

At first, she thought he would not answer. Then he said carefully, "Yes, they have regaled me with stories of their exploits over the past year."

She halted, touching his coat sleeve. His gaze widened, shooting to hers. But she could not remain in her new role now. "Lady Grenville's death was a tragedy. But you deserve the opportunity to be a father to your sons. Maybe some good will come from her death. Maybe it will strengthen your relationship."

His face hardened. "They need their mother, Amelia."

"Of course they do." She hesitated. "I know I am only your housekeeper, but I will do my best to help them overcome their loss."

It was a moment before he spoke. "I know you will. That is why I asked you to take this position." He paused. "Am I being too hard on everyone, rushing back to London this way?"

She was so surprised by the tentative nature of his tone, and the doubt he was evincing. "Unless there is an emergency, it would be far more pleasant for everyone to go halfway tomorrow, and make the journey in three days."

He inhaled rather raggedly.

There was an emergency, she thought, in surprise. "Simon—Grenville—if you need to get back to town, maybe you should go on ahead."

"No." He was flat. "Tomorrow you will travel with us. Leave the child with Mrs. Murdock, your mother with the Scot. They can take two more days to travel, but we will be in London by midnight."

She did not understand. But she had seen a frightening light in his eyes, and she also thought she had seen the shadow of fear flit through his gaze. What was going on? Why couldn't he go on alone, if he was in such a rush? "The boys could travel with me and my group," she began carefully.

"No!" The single word was an explosion. "My sons remain with me—you will join us tomorrow. It is for the best."

He started toward the inn without her. Something was very wrong, but she had no idea what could be frightening him, if fear was what she was witnessing.

Suddenly he halted, and turned back to her. He smiled grimly at her. "I apologize for the outburst."

"It's all right."

"No, it's not. I am trying very hard to be thoughtful

and polite. I am trying to behave as an employer might. However, we were friends once, and I do not think your position can change that. As importantly, I value your wisdom and advice."

Her heart soared. She did not mind his reference to their past, not when he had made it in such a respectful manner. But she kept to the matter at hand. "Then, if you can, you might explain to me what is actually happening, so I could truly advise you."

His stare became blank. "Nothing is happening. My sons have lost their mother. They must remain with me. And I have pressing business matters to attend to in town." He shrugged.

She did not know if she should believe him, but why would he lie about his children? And what he had just said made sense. There was really no way to fault the explanation.

But she did not like the look that she had seen in his eyes. Nor had she mistaken the tension within him.

"Papa!" John came running up. "I am hungry!"

Amelia smiled at him and tousled his hair. Then she glanced up at Grenville. She was thrilled their old friendship might return, despite her position as housekeeper.

"I am also starved," he said, smiling at his son. "Could you politely ask Mr. Hayes to have supper trays sent up to our rooms?"

John nodded and ran off.

"I imagine they will be asleep within moments of lying down, never mind that they seem so filled with energy now." Grenville's smile faded.

He was worried, Amelia realized. And she was afraid he was worried about more than his sons surviving the ordeal of their mother's death. "Yes, I imagine so."

They had reached the front doors of the inn. The inn-keeper came down the steps, beaming. "Good day, my lord. I have been expecting you. Your rooms are ready." He glanced at Amelia and she knew he couldn't decide if she was a servant, a relative or the earl's guest.

"Thank you, Mr. Hayes. I am appreciative. This is Miss Greystone. Did my son ask for supper trays?"

"Yes, he did, my lord, and you will have them within a half an hour. May I show you to your rooms?"

"I think that is a good idea." Grenville looked at her. "You do not mind sharing a room, with your mother?"

"I prefer it that way," she said.

"Good. I will see you at sunrise, then." He hesitated, his gaze intense upon her face. "Amelia, make no mistake, I am very appreciative that you are here with my family."

And she realized that Grenville needed her, too.

London, April 19, 1794

SHE HAD NEVER BEEN to Grenville's London home. Amelia slowly moved around the extraordinary, lavishly furnished bedroom she had been given. The upper halves of the walls were painted pale green, the lower halves were molded wood, painted white. The white ceiling boasted mauve and green starburst plastering. The canopied bed had green floral curtains, the coverlets a paisley. Most of the furniture was gilded, and fine Aubusson rugs were underfoot. The fireplace was white plaster, with a huge gilded clock atop it.

It was well past midnight. They had arrived in town just an hour earlier. A handful of staff had greeted them, and Grenville had told her he would get the boys to bed

himself. He had ordered a housemaid to show her upstairs, and she had been taken to this bedchamber.

The maid had made a mistake. She was not Grenville's guest; she was his housekeeper. Tomorrow she
would be given lodging appropriate for a servant.

*We were friends once, and I do not think your posi-
tion can change that.*

Still dressed for travel in a pale blue jacket and skirt,
Amelia sat down on a white ottoman. His implication
had been clear—that they remained friends of a sort.

But there was a fine line between them now, she
thought. On the one hand, she was in his employ; on
the other, they shared a past and some affection for one
another. A great many challenges faced them.

She had certainly just passed the longest day of her
life. If she had been a mere housekeeper, it would not
have felt that way! She wished for a brandy, but had
already surmised that no decanter graced any table in
the room.

The coach had been too small for them both. She had
sat facing Grenville, with William beside her. In hind-
sight, facing him had probably been worse than being
seated beside him. She had spent almost eighteen hours
trying not to meet his gaze, determined not to feel his
presence or experience any attraction to him.

But she had looked at him, repeatedly, although she
had pretended to read for most of the trip. The boys and
their father had kept up a nearly constant conversation,
except when the boys had napped. They had discussed
their studies—William excelled at languages, and was
taking both French and German; their hobbies—John
was apparently an excellent horseman, even at his young
age; what they would do upon arriving in London—both

boys wanted to go to the circus; and some recent world events. They had stopped three times, briefly, to change horses and answer nature's call.

Amelia had been fascinated by every exchange. The boys adored Simon; he adored them. How was it possible that he had not been in residence over the years? Had Mrs. Murdock been exaggerating?

Every now and then, as she had stolen a glance at him over the edge of her book, it had been impossible not to marvel at how handsome and noble he was. But he had caught her in the act, more often than not. When their gazes met, he had looked away, as she had. But the tension between them remained.

She stared at the beautiful room. It seemed obvious to her during the journey that he had been determined to treat her as his housekeeper, just as she had been determined to remain in that role. It had been difficult and awkward. She wasn't sure why he had slipped into the informality of friendship last night. She supposed that it was probably best that they tried to remain in the roles of employer and employee, as much as was possible. But she also knew that when he needed her, she would gladly return to being his friend.

The day had been the most trying of her life, she decided, sighing. She was so glad it was over. But one fact was glaring—she was not immune to her employer. His presence overwhelmed her.

She slowly got up. In any case, she could brood about it at another time. They had just arrived in town, and she had been hired to manage his household and help in the raising of his sons. She had so much to do!

She was tired—exhausted—but she knew she wouldn't sleep. The house was mostly empty; two maids, a manservant, the boys and Grenville were its only occupants. But by tomorrow evening that would change.

Rooms had to be aired. Menus had to be planned, meals served. Cook would not arrive in time to make even the evening meal, so she would have to make breakfast, lunch and supper herself. She did not mind. She wanted something to do!

Given the fact that she had an entire household to organize, with very little help, would she be able to see to the boys, as well? She began to worry. It would not hurt to take the boys on some kind of exciting outing, if she could. Or could she enlist Grenville to do so while she worked on the tasks necessary to getting the household up and running?

She paced. She already missed Lucille terribly. She was worried about her. She hoped Mrs. Murdock had kept her calm and content while traveling. She was so afraid the baby had fretted—and missed her. But not having the infant there tomorrow would allow her more freedom to take care of the rest of her responsibilities.

She needed a quill and parchment. She had so many lists to make, and while she was searching for writing instruments, she would also find herself a drink. She longed to sneak a peek at the boys, but as they were in the family wing of the house—where Grenville slept— that was not a good idea. She decided she must avoid that part of the house, at least for now, and especially at such a late hour.

His image assailed her, but not as he had been during their journey that day. Instead, she recalled him as he had been in the days after the funeral, locked in his rooms. His hair was down, he was more unclothed than clothed, and his smile was so very suggestive....

Her heart lurched and she shoved the recollection aside. That encounter must be forgotten! Determined, Amelia hurried across the room. As she did, she glimpsed her reflection in the mirror.

Her traveling ensemble was a sensible outfit, one she'd worn a hundred times. She would hardly turn heads in the robin's-egg blue jacket and skirt. She'd already removed the simple beret, trimmed with ribbon, that she had been wearing. Her honey-colored hair had been teased and pulled back, one long coil hanging over her shoulder.

For one moment she stared at her reflection. Her cheeks were rosy, her gray eyes bright. It was as if she'd just taken a brisk walk upon the moors. But she wasn't flushed from walking. Attraction to her employer had done that. She did not look plain now. She did not look like an aging spinster....

Then she dismissed her thoughts. It didn't matter how she looked. She was not in Grenville's home to parade before him. Besides, it was very late. She wasn't going to run into anyone, and not Grenville—or she certainly hoped not.

Taking a candle in its holder, Amelia left the sanctuary of her temporary room.

She was not accustomed to the house. She had been led inside an imposing entry hall, with high ceilings and marble floors, then ushered into the south wing of the house. Grenville and the boys had gone off in the opposite direction. Every door she had passed on her way up to this guest chamber on the second floor had been closed. Now, she traversed a mostly dark hall, a single pair of wall sconces boasting lit candles. The stairwell was dark. The candle she held barely helped her see.

She made her way down the stairs carefully. The hall below was better lit and she followed it, intending to return to the entry hall. From there, she would surely find a salon with a *secretaire* and a bar cart. Or perhaps she would find the library.

But a pair of handsome doors was just ahead, wide open. She could tell from the glow that a fire was burning in the hearth. She faltered. Only one person could be within that room, at this hour.

Grenville stepped abruptly onto the chamber's threshold, holding a glass of wine in his hand.

Their gazes met. Amelia felt her heart surge.

"I heard footsteps." He lifted his glass as if toasting her, but his thick lashes lowered. She had not a clue as to what he was thinking, or if he was displeased to find her wandering about his home at such an hour.

He had shed his jacket and waistcoat. He wore only a beautiful lawn shirt with cascading lace lapels and cuffs, fawn-colored breeches and stockings and shoes. His hair remained tied back loosely, with many hanks falling about his shoulders. He slowly looked up. His gaze was unwavering upon her.

"I can't sleep. I want to make a list. I have so much to do tomorrow." How hoarse she sounded!

He stepped aside. "Only you would wish to make up lists at one in the morning."

She hesitated. It was very late. Friends or not, she should not walk into that room—they should not be alone together. "Is that a criticism?"

"Hardly. It might even be a compliment."

Their gazes met again. He looked away first. "Would you like a drink? It is bedtime, Amelia."

His tone wasn't exactly suggestive. Yet it wasn't entirely formal, either. "I am your housekeeper," she heard herself say. "Perhaps we should set our friendship aside entirely, now that we are in London?"

He shrugged, glancing at her. "Is that what you really wish to do?"

She was afraid to answer.

Suddenly his regard was intent. "I don't think we can set our friendship aside, even if we wish to. And we have had a long day." He turned and walked into the room, which was a library. Two walls were filled with bookshelves. Another wall was painted burgundy, and boasted a black-marble fireplace. The fourth wall boasted windows and doors that led to the gardens outside—or so she assumed. Amelia watched him set his glass down on a handsome side table, where several bottles of wine graced a silver tray. He poured a second glass.

He was right, she thought. They could pretend many things, but the truth would always be between them. The past would always be there, too. She wondered if traveling together had also disturbed him. "I suppose we must stumble about, finding our way as employer and housekeeper."

He turned and smiled. "Yes, I think so. But I do not mind making up the rules as we go. Besides, I would like to have a drink with you."

He was so calm, while she was filled with tension. Worse, his smile had made her heart somersault. She knew that she should take the writing materials she needed and go back to her room. She felt more attracted to him than ever before. "I'd like that, too."

"Do you mind red? It is an exceptional French claret.

But if you wish for white, I have a fine Burgundy in the house."

She slowly walked inside, against all of her better judgment. Her heart drummed. "Thank you." She took the glass from him, and took a much-needed sip. Then, as she realized she was standing much too close to him, she walked about the room, pretending to inspect it. "I expected you to be asleep by now." She tried to sound casual, but their late-night glass of wine did not feel casual, and one glance in his direction told her that he was staring.

"I rarely sleep at this hour."

She was surprised, facing him, some distance between them now. "Why not?"

He picked up his glass, settling his lean hip against the table. "Like you, I have trouble sleeping. There is always something to brood about."

She realized she was noticing how his breeches molded his hips and thighs; she jerked her gaze away. "I assume the boys are sleeping?"

"John was asleep before his head even hit the pillow." Grenville smiled. "William was asleep a moment later. They are exhausted." He seemed to carefully note the distance she had put between them—the length of the sofa, at least.

She said, "I have so much to do tomorrow. I have an entire house to familiarize myself with and to organize. But the boys need direction. Do you have any interest in taking them for an afternoon outing?"

His stare moved slowly over her features. "You need not build Rome in a day."

When he looked at her mouth—as if he were thinking very illicit thoughts—it was difficult to think clearly. "You and your sons must be fed, at the very least."

"We will manage."

"I happen to be an excellent cook."

His eyes widened. He set his glass down so hard as he stood up that red wine spilled over its rim. "Absolutely not!"

Why would he object to her cooking for him and his children? "Grenville, you must eat. At sunrise, I will send a maid out for fresh eggs and bread. I can make excellent eggs and sausages—"

"Absolutely not!" he repeated, seeming aghast.

She hugged her glass to her chest. His gaze slammed to her hands—her breasts—and lifted.

"Amelia, you are not an ordinary servant. I will not treat you as if you were one. You may supervise breakfast—and lunch and supper—but you make certain one of the housemaids cooks our meals. And if neither maid can manage that, we will adjourn to the St. James Hotel." He was final.

Should she be flattered? she wondered. "I really don't mind, but I see that you have made up your mind."

"I have." He stared. "And as you are both my guest and in my employ, you will do as I wish."

She felt like pointing out to him that she could not be both his guest and his housekeeper, just as she could not be both his friend and servant. But he had been explicit—he intended to make the rules of their relationship. "Very well. In any case, tomorrow will be a busy day. I appreciate the fact that you do not expect me to build Rome in a single day. However, I intend to try."

He did not smile.

She wet her lips. "Are you all right? Is something wrong? I was trying to make a jest."

He simply picked up his drink and began to slowly pace. "I cannot take the boys out tomorrow. I have a great deal to do myself," he said.

"Then I will make the time to do so. Simon—" she hesitated "—is something bothering you?"

He faced her, eyes wide. "You call me Simon now?"

She trembled. "Grenville, then. I sense that something is amiss, although I may be imagining it. If something is wrong, I would like to help."

"Of course you would." His stare was hard. "I hope I have not made a mistake, Amelia, asking you to join us here in London."

He was having regrets, she thought, stunned. "I know that this is awkward, but the children need me. I am glad to help. I am glad to be here. Even if you hadn't asked me to become your housekeeper, I would do what I could to help you and the children."

He paused for a long moment. "Your determination— compassion—loyalty—they all amaze me."

"In time, we will both become accustomed to our new relationship," she said, still not believing it herself.

He raised a brow, clearly skeptical. Then he drained his wine. "You deserve more than to be embroiled in my life."

She was so surprised by his words. "I want to be here. Otherwise, I would have rejected your offer."

"I hope you do not come to regret the decision you have made."

"You are confusing me," she heard herself say. "I know you are in mourning, Simon, but sometimes I won- der if it is only the crisis of Lady Grenville's death that is affecting you." When he did not respond, she tensed. "Last night, I realized you were worried about something. I thought it was the boys. But you were in a terrible rush to return to town. And your expression is so dire. What is bothering you?"

"If I have frightened you, I am sorry." His smile was tight. "Nothing is wrong. I am overwhelmed, that is all." He set his glass down and walked over to the desk.

She stared, wishing he would be honest with her.

"I forgot. You have come downstairs not to enjoy my morbid company, but for writing utensils."

As he opened the desk drawer, something banged twice, very suddenly. It banged again.

Amelia assumed it was a shutter, banging against the house. But Grenville withdrew a pistol from the drawer and rushed around the desk.

"What are you doing?" Amelia cried, shocked.

He glanced at her, his eyes blazing. His expression was savage. "Stay here!"

She gasped, following him to the threshold of the room. "Simon!"

"Someone is at the door," he told her, his face hard and set. "I said, stay here!"

"Simon—it was a shutter!" she cried.

"Do not move from this room!" Giving her a frightening look, he rushed into the hall.

Amelia was stunned. She was certain the banging had been a loose shutter, not someone knocking on the door. And even if someone were at the door at midnight, it was probably a neighbor in distress. She followed Simon into the hall, hurrying toward the entry.

The front door was open. Simon stood there, holding the pistol, gazing out into the dark, cloudy night. Suddenly he pulled the door closed and locked it. Then he turned. Their eyes met.

"You were right."

Amelia realized that there was sweat upon his brow, trickling down his temple. And she saw him tremble.

Why would he think it necessary to go to the door with a loaded gun? She walked over to him. "Are you all right?" she asked softly.

He didn't hear her. She saw a faraway look in his eyes. It was haunted; worse, it was fearful. "Simon!" She clasped his arm.

He jerked and glanced at her. The faraway look vanished. "I told you to stay in the library." He was furious now.

She studied him, taken aback. "Who did you expect to see at this hour?"

His expression tightened. "No one," he finally said.

And Amelia knew he was lying.

CHAPTER SEVEN

AMELIA CLOSED THE BIN beneath the large table in the center of the kitchen. "And we also need onions," she said to the maid, a slender girl with freckles and red hair.

Jane nodded, but she made no move to put on her cloak or leave.

Amelia had just given her an extensive list of the foodstuffs that she would need to make a satisfactory breakfast for Grenville and his sons. Not that she would cook their meal. She didn't see the point in defying Grenville, especially when the issue seemed so silly. Jane's aunt would be arriving shortly; she was an excellent cook, or so the maid claimed, and she was eager to help in these circumstances.

"And please, do hurry. It is almost seven," Amelia added, rather impatiently. When Jane began to slowly don her wool cloak, Amelia said, "Now, shoo!"

Jane started and rushed from the kitchens.

Perspiring, Amelia sighed. The maid was very shy, and possibly dim-witted. She certainly hoped the rest of the staff was more energetic. Noticing a speck upon the island table, she reached for a rag and wiped it off. Although the table was used for the preparation of meals and the cleaning of pots, pans and utensils, the oak surface was highly waxed and gleaming. Every surface in the kitchen—from the stove to the ovens to the sinks—was spotlessly clean.

The kitchens were vast, and boasted every possible convenience. A woman could always tell the nature of a household by its kitchens. Amelia was pleased and impressed.

She had learned that Lambert Hall had been a part of Lady Grenville's dowry. She did not have to ask to know that Grenville would not care less about modernizing his kitchens. This room, and all of its equipment, was the work of his wife.

It also had a door which let out onto the street, which was very convenient for the receipt of deliveries and groceries. Jane had left the door ajar and Amelia went to close it, glancing outside at the deserted London street. A single carriage was moving down the tree-lined block. Handsome homes with shady drives faced her on the adjacent side. It was a very posh neighborhood, indeed.

Lambert Hall took up most of the block. The gardens formed an interior courtyard of sorts, the house shaped in a U around it. It was very early, but Amelia had been up since five. She had explored the house as thoroughly as possible, given the fact that she felt very rushed and had a huge list of tasks to get through. She had discovered the staff's sleeping quarters upstairs, on the third floor, in the wing of the house where she had slept last night. The rooms belonging to Signor Barelli, Mrs. Murdock and the rest of the servants were being aired and refreshed by the other housemaid.

She had discovered three salons downstairs, in the central part of the house. The west wing of the house boasted a music room and a ballroom, the east side the dining room and the library. Every room was magnificently furnished. Royalty would be comfortable here.

The only rooms she hadn't explored were those belonging to Grenville and his sons. The family's apartments took up the entire second floor of the west wing. She had refused to set foot there.

Nor would she even think about the conversation they had had last night, the drink they had shared—or Grenville's odd reaction to the banging shutter. She did not have time to worry about the loaded gun he kept in his desk, apparently expecting an intruder he might have to shoot.

Grenville and the boys remained abed, but she imagined they would all be up shortly. A sterling tray was already set with biscuits and jams, and water was boiling on the stove. At least the family would have a small repast when they awoke.

She had already set the dining-room table, but she left the kitchens to inspect the table one last time.

The dining room was a long chamber with pale blue walls and dark gold damask draperies. A crystal chandelier was overhead. The table could seat two-dozen guests. The delicate, bone-colored chairs had elaborately scrolled backs, the seats upholstered in blue and gold.

She had set the table with gold-striped linens, Waterford glasses and gilded flatware. White roses and lilies from the hothouse behind the gardens formed a beautiful centerpiece.

Grenville would be pleased, she thought, smiling.

And then a movement outside caught her eye.

Amelia quickly moved to the window. A man was crossing the gardens.

He had obviously just entered from the street, and he was approaching the house!

For one moment, she watched, her mind spinning. Were the gates not locked? Or were they kept open, so anyone could enter? Was he trespassing? She could not imagine why someone was in the gardens.

She noted that he was tall and lean, his hair white. His coat was royal-blue, and he wore breeches with white stockings.

He was most definitely hurrying toward the house!

"Harold!" she cried, rushing out of the dining room. She ran into the library, directly to Grenville's desk. The pistol was in the drawer there, as it had been last night.

"Miss Greystone?"

She whirled at the sound of Harold's voice. He was a young man of perhaps eighteen, who did odd chores around the house and helped in the kitchens. "Have you seen St. Just? There is someone outside—I think a stranger means to sneak into this house!"

Harold paled. "His lordship remains upstairs, abed. Should I go rouse him?"

"Damn," Amelia cried. By the time Harold returned with Grenville, the intruder would be inside. "Do we have a neighbor who would call at such an early hour— by way of the gardens?"

"I know of no such neighbor, Miss Greystone," Harold said, wide-eyed. "Who would call at seven in the morning? Besides, who knows that his lordship has even returned to town?"

The man was an intruder! "Come with me. And grab a knife—no, seize that poker, in case you have to use it."

Of course, there could be a simple explanation, but she would not give the stranger the benefit of the doubt, not in these times of war. Amelia rushed from the library, not bothering to wait for Harold, but she heard him following her. She wished that there had been time to genuinely become familiar with the house. She didn't know which rooms had doors leading outside onto the gardens.

The doors to every chamber had been opened that

morning, however. They rushed past the largest salon,
a gold-and-red room, leaving the center of the house.
She continued past the music room. Then she thought
the better of it and about-faced, crashed into Harold. She
seized him and dragged him with her into the small, airy
room. A piano and harp was in its center. Two dozen
gold chairs surrounded it. Behind the instruments was a
pair of glass doors that opened onto a small brick patio
and the gardens.

Panting, she halted at the doors. The gardens would
soon be spectacular—blooms were emerging everywhere. But she did not see a gentleman in a white wig
and blue jacket. "He is already inside."

"I should get his lordship." Harold was terse.

Amelia wondered where the gun closet was. "Follow
me," she said. And as she left the music room and turned
right, she saw Grenville approaching.

His eyes widened. "What are you doing? Why do
you have my gun?"

"There is an intruder in the house!" she cried, trembling with relief.

He reached her, removing the gun from her hands.
"You are shaking!" He put his arm around her. "Amelia—
what are you saying?"

"I was checking on the dining room when I saw a
man in the gardens—heading for this side of the house!
But he is gone now—he must be inside," she cried. She
looked at Grenville. What was he doing wandering about
the west wing on the ground floor?

He handed Harold the gun. "Take care, it is primed,"
he said. Then he took both of her hands in his and smiled.
"I think you are imagining things. I have been making a
cursory inspection of the house, Amelia. I went through

every room in this wing. I did not see anyone. Are you sure you saw someone outside?"

She stared at him in sudden confusion. "Yes, I saw a bulky man with white hair. He was on the far side of the gardens, by the street, and he was heading toward the house."

Grenville did not seem alarmed. "Harold, please put the pistol back in the middle drawer of my desk in the library. And you may put that poker back, as well." He put his arm around her. "What did you intend to do, if you found an intruder? Do you know how to fire a pistol?"

"I most certainly know how to fire a pistol—I am an excellent marksman," she cried. "We should search the house, Simon. I saw someone outside."

He studied her for a moment, then nodded. Taking her arm, they went to the threshold of the ballroom. The doors were closed. Grenville pushed them open.

Amelia stared into a huge room with gleaming wood floors, red walls and gilded columns. Above her head, there were four magnificent crystal chandeliers. An entire wall of French doors opened onto a large flagstone patio, which overlooked the gardens. "This room is stunning," she said. She had never been to a ball, but she could easily imagine the room overflowing with guests in silks and brocades, diamonds and rubies.

"There hasn't been a ball here since Elizabeth and I were engaged."

His tone was odd.

Distracted, Amelia looked up at him. Had they had an engagement ball, then?

He grimaced. "I haven't thought about that night in a decade."

She realized the memories were not pleasant. They were standing side by side, so closely that her skirts brushed his thighs and hips. She did not move away. Instead, she studied him. He lowered his gaze and stared back at her.

Her heart raced. Nothing had changed since the previous evening. Neither the specter of an intruder or the vast list of tasks she must get through could diminish his effect upon her. "There is no intruder," she said softly.

"No. There is no intruder."

"I did see someone in the gardens, Simon."

"Perhaps you did. But he is gone now. I am an early riser. I will keep an eye out tomorrow, and instruct the staff, when they arrive, to do so, as well."

His body was hard and warm, dwarfing hers. Amelia knew she should put some distance between them, but she couldn't seem to force herself to do so. "Why aren't you alarmed?"

"Because I can't imagine why a thief would attempt to steal into this house when the entire household is awakening." He did not move away from her, either.

She realized he was right. A thief would break in at night, when everyone was asleep. "If I am correct, and a man was in your gardens, then he was not a thief."

Grenville's brows lifted.

"This is a time of war, Grenville. There are stories I could tell you," she said, thinking of Julianne's husband, who had been one of Pitt's spies.

"Are you suggesting that you could tell me war stories?" He smiled, as if amused.

"Julianne became quite a radical—she was a huge Jacobin supporter, until she fell in love with Bedford." She decided that now was not the time to fill in the rest of the blanks. "You must have heard about the French deserters who showed up in St. Just parish at Squire Penwaithe's."

"I did. Are you also suggesting that a spy—or a Frenchman—was in my gardens?"

"All I am saying is that you must keep the gates locked, and that anything is possible." She was firm.

"I will keep that in mind," he murmured. He gave her a very odd and thoughtful look, indeed. "Did you sleep at all last night?"

She slowly shook her head. "I slept fitfully. My mind kept turning over all I wish to do. I have been up since five. But, I am usually up at six," she added, suddenly feeling foolish. She was such a sensible woman, but she was rambling. She hoped Grenville did not think her a hysterical ninny.

"I can see that you are going to try to build Rome in a single day," he said softly, but his mouth was curving slightly.

"I meant it when I said I intended to try." She smiled back.

"Harold heard me call you Amelia."

She started.

He touched her cheek, very suddenly. "I am sorry you were frightened." He dropped his hand. "I am going to rouse the boys, if they are not up already."

And before she could respond, Grenville had turned and was striding away, leaving her standing there outside of his magnificent ballroom, aware of that insistent yearning again.

HYDE PARK WAS MAGNIFICENT in the spring. Daffodils were blooming, the lawns were emerald-green, and the elms and oaks were thick with new foliage. The sky was perfectly blue. No clouds marred it. The sun was bright and strong. It was a perfect day.

Or was it?

Simon sat the dark bay Thoroughbred hunter he had recently purchased through an agent. The mare excelled at the hunt, and was fearless when it came to jumping high hedges and wide stone walls. He had heard that she would take an "in and out" without the slightest hesitation. He looked forward to their first hunt.

Now, though, he kept a loose rein, allowing her to walk slowly along the riding path.

The park was very busy that day. Other gentlemen were on the path, astride their mounts, and at least a half a dozen open carriages were in sight, filled with gentlewomen in their afternoon finery. Pedestrians abounded, too, the ladies with parasols. King Charles spaniels were afoot. One gent walked a mastiff. He was recognized by everyone and greeted warmly. He responded in turn with a brief nod or a curt "hello."

He did not mean to be abrupt, but his mood was hardly light. Jourdan's contact had failed to show.

He had left the house before five that morning, in disguise, to meet the Jacobin. But no one had been waiting for him at the cobbler's shop on Darby Lane.

That failure meant one thing. His contact had either been imprisoned or he had been killed.

And either scenario was threatening to him. If Pitt's agents were onto Latleur's men, they might eventually uncover his masquerade.

But there was more. Amelia had almost caught him returning home.

His heart lurched. He would not make that mistake again. The next time he went out as his French cousin, he would make sure to change his clothing before he came within sight of his house. As it was, he had shed the white wig and the blue coat the moment he had entered the ballroom. He had left the items behind a love seat.

After Amelia had returned to her duties in the house, he had fetched the items and burned them.

He hated deceiving Amelia.

But she could never learn the truth.

He could not tell her he had been sent to France to spy for Pitt and his cronies, and that he had been deeply embedded in the revolutionary government in Paris. Nor could he tell her that he had made a terrible mistake. He could not tell her that he played both sides, and that he did not know how the game would end. He would never tell her that he would sell out his own country—if he had to—to protect his sons.

She would never understand his offering his talents and services to the Jacobins. She would think him a coward—and rightly so.

God, she would finally despise him!

His heart raced. She continued to admire him. He was experienced enough to realize that. But if she ever learned the truth, she would finally lose her faith in him.

Oddly, he so needed her faith!

If she ever learned the truth, she would be in danger. He desperately hoped that he had not put her in danger already, by bringing her to London with him. But she was only the housekeeper. No one would ever guess that they shared a past, that they had almost become lovers once, or that they were friends. No one could possibly know that he needed her as a friend and wanted her in his bed. No one would ever know that she held a very significant place in his life.

Except he had addressed her as Amelia that morning, in front of the young servant. It had been a terrible slip of the tongue.

Servants gossiped. He was going to have to be much more careful.

And he thought of the simple breakfast she had served, the table set as if for a state dinner. She had gone to so much trouble, and she had been so pleased to seat him and his boys at the table.

At eleven, she had insisted upon serving an elaborate meal of eggs, sausages, ham and too many side dishes to count. How had she managed that? He still did not know. But when he had looked at her, wondering if she had defied him and if she had been in the kitchens, cooking like a servant, she had smiled sweetly and denied it.

There had been another slip. He had asked her if she wished to sit with them. He hadn't considered the invitation or what it meant—noblemen did not invite housekeepers to dine—and she had swiftly refused.

It would have been natural for her to have joined them at the table. Her role as a housekeeper was not natural at all. He was going to have to be as careful in his own home now as he was outside of it. He was going to have to start to consider Amelia as a part of the dangerous game he played—in order to keep her out of jeopardy.

It had been hard, keeping his attention on his sons and his plate. He had kept watching her coming and going instead.

He realized that, in spite of these vast burdens, he was almost smiling, and just then, some of the weight lifted from his shoulders. His sons needed her. So he had made the right choice.

"I see that you are in a good disposition today."

Simon started at the sound of Sebastian Warlock's slightly amused tone. He had been so preoccupied that he had not seen the spymaster approach, astride his black gelding. "Hello, Warlock. You are deluded. I am never in a good disposition—or haven't you heard?"

Warlock's mouth curled. He was a tall, taciturn man

with an open disdain for fashion. He was somberly clad
as usual, in a black-velvet coat, dark breeches and riding boots. His dark hair was pulled back and he wore
a bicorne hat. He was darkly handsome, and the ladies
passing by gave him a second glance.

"I believe I saw you smiling. Not that I blame you.
The fresh air must be invigorating—after Paris."

Was that a jab? Simon wondered. Was he referring to
Simon's incarceration? Simon had no intention of men-
tioning it, for if the spymaster did not know he had been
imprisoned, it would be for the best. It would be harder
for Warlock to ever discover the extent of his duplicity.
On the other hand, the spymaster seemed to know everything. "I am enjoying my new mare and a perfectly
pleasing spring day."

"Let's tether the horses," Warlock said, and it was not
a suggestion. He halted and dismounted.

Simon followed suit. They walked their mounts off
of the path and toward a grove of oak trees, where they
tied them to a branch. "I have missed town," Simon said,
simply making conversation.

"I can imagine that you have. I am very sorry for
your loss, Grenville."

He shrugged. "She was too young to die."

"They are always too young to die."

"Yes, they are." He knew they were both thinking of
the innocent victims of the war and the revolution. His
stomach curdled.

"I do not think a regime of terror can live on indefinitely." Warlock had begun to stroll toward a pond.
Simon followed. "Tyrants always fall."

"There are divisions within *le Comité* and within
the Commune," Simon said, referring to Robespierre's
governing committee and the Parisian city government.

"But no one is safe from suspicion. Everyone fears a knock on the door in the middle of the night." How calm he sounded!

"As you did?"

Simon tensed. "I would have been a fool not to fear being discovered."

Warlock halted, as did Simon. The hairs in his nape rose as Warlock said softly, "What do you have for me, Grenville?"

He knew, Simon thought, with a sinking sensation. He knew he had been imprisoned, and he was a brilliant man. If he hadn't figured out how Simon had gotten out of prison and then out of France, he soon would.

He knew he could not gamble now. There was a chance that Warlock did not know of his incarceration, but his every instinct told him that was not the case. Therefore, he must begin to reveal parts of the truth....

"I did not expect to ever return home," Simon said carefully.

"And I did not expect to ever see you again." Warlock stared.

"So you knew I was incarcerated?" He tried to forget that dark, dank prison cell, no easy task, when he dreamed so vividly of it every night.

"It is my business to know such things. You are one of my men. I was told on December 24 that you had been imprisoned four days earlier. I was dismayed."

Of course he was. "The moment I returned to France, at the end of November, I was certain I was being watched and followed," Simon said tersely.

"But you were imprisoned anyway."

"Yes. They seized me when I was least expecting it."

"How did you escape the guillotine?" Warlock asked, as if they were discussing a horse race.

"I used the relationship between Jourdan and St. Just to my advantage. I assured *les Enragés* that, as Jourdan, I would be welcome at my cousin's home in London. I told them that St. Just would take me into his home with open arms. 'Jourdan' would then be able to move about London's highest Tory circles without suspicion. I promised them that I would provide them with invaluable information." Simon realized he was sweating. He had just told Warlock almost everything—except that he did not know on which side he would end up.

Warlock was calm. "That was clever of you, Simon, damnably clever."

"One finds brilliance when one is about to lose one's head."

"And will you provide them with invaluable information?" Warlock asked.

"Of course I will!" He was sharp. "Otherwise they will hunt me down, Warlock, and murder me. Worse, they could realize who I really am and take revenge upon my sons."

Warlock was not affected by his outburst. "But of course, you will only give them information I approve."

"Of course," Simon lied. "I am many things, but I am a patriot."

"Yes, you are a patriot," Warlock said, as if musing. "Have you established Jourdan's presence here in London?"

"He has taken a room at the London Arms, and I am certain the innkeeper has seen him coming and going several times." It had been necessary to find a residence for his alter identity, as he could hardly claim that Jourdan was staying with St. Just.

"Good." Warlock smiled. "And your means of contacting Jourdan's cronies?"

He hardly wished to share such information with Warlock, so he lied. "I have yet to be given those instructions. They know I am at the Arms, and they are clever and cautious."

"Keep me posted, then. You do know that I need you back in Paris, sooner rather than later?"

He was ill. "I had assumed so."

"We must exploit the factions within *le Comité*," Warlock said matter-of-factly. "As you must know, there have been attempts to organize an opposition to Robespierre."

"You have other agents in place."

"I do, but I do not have anyone inside *le Comité*. Weren't you presented to them as Jourdan?"

He froze. Warlock knew that Lafleur had brought him before Robespierre and his committee. What else did he know?

"How hard would it be for you to speak personally with Robespierre? You are, Grenville, invaluable to me."

He wet his lips. "Of course I will do my duty, Warlock. But Elizabeth just passed. My sons need me now."

"I did not mean that you must return tomorrow. Besides, before you go, you must establish Jourdan's loyalty to *les Enragés*."

He was sweating even more profusely. So there would be a respite, if one could call playing both sides a respite. "They will be expecting information soon—before the Allied invasion of Flanders."

"And we will give them some tidbit to make them happy." Warlock's eyes glittered. He was, Simon thought with sudden fury, enjoying himself. And he knew beyond any doubt that Warlock would use him ruthlessly, to play out all of his spy games. He also knew that Warlock would realize the extent of his loyalty, sooner or later, if he were not very careful.

"I have children," he said harshly. "I have to prove my loyalty, Warlock, for my own reasons. I have to give them something genuine, without compromising our war effort."

"I know. And we will give them something of value, but we can also take from them, as well." Warlock's smile was hard. "You are far too well placed now, Grenville. You are caught squarely in the middle. You have the ear of everyone. It is almost perfect—I could have hardly arranged such a brilliant scenario, if I had wanted to."

Simon knew he meant his every word; he was thrilled that Simon was in such a terrible position. "I am happy to play your games—as long as my sons remain safe."

"I know that," Warlock said. "Let me chart out some options for us. But you will have a tasty morsel to give to our French friends before we invade Flanders. And by the time you return to France, Jourdan will be a revolutionary hero."

Simon did not move. Too much tension immobilized him. Warlock patted his shoulder and walked back to his horse. Simon stared after him.

Warlock was brilliant, but their interests were not one and the same. Simon would put the lives of his children first. Warlock would always put Great Britain first. He was going to have to outwit the spymaster in the end— for the sake of his children.

Warlock had mounted. He saluted him and cantered off. Weighed down by these games, Simon went to his own horse, untying the reins.

If Warlock had his way, he would go back to France within the next six months. He would love to help the Republic fall, but he would never survive. He would be found out. He suddenly knew it the way he knew that the sun would soon set and the moon would rise.

But if his sons were safe, would it matter? Could he keep them safe? For their safety was all that mattered.

If he did not return, the boys would have Amelia to watch out for them.

So there was some small consolation in this terrible world.

CHAPTER EIGHT

"Miss Greystone? Your mother has arrived. She is in the front hall with Mrs. Murdock. I see that supper is under way?"

Amelia was in the kitchen with Jane, Jane's aunt Maggie and Harold. Her sleeves were rolled up and she wore the same apron she had used all day. Just then, she was peering into the oven to check on the condition of four roasting guinea hens. But her heart leaped wildly when she heard Lloyd, and she whirled.

She felt how wide her smile was. Lucille was back! She had missed her so.

And of course she was always glad to see Momma.

She began to remove her apron. "Supper will be served in an hour, Lloyd. I hope you had a comfortable journey?"

He rushed into the kitchens. "It was very comfortable," he said, greeting Jane's aunt.

Amelia only meant to supervise the preparation of supper for Grenville and the boys, but the truth of the matter was that she enjoyed cooking, just as she had always enjoyed taking care of her family—just as she was enjoying taking care of Grenville's family. She knew she should not interfere, but she said to Maggie, "If you mix salt, pepper and thyme with the bread crumbs, it will make the bean casserole delicious."

Jane's aunt looked at her and said, "That is a wonderful idea, Miss Greystone."

Pleased that Maggie did not dispute her, she added, "And maybe we should take the hens out and let them rest for a while." She did not want them overcooked. She had already explained to Maggie how to make a cognac and raspberry glaze for the hens, to be served on the side, of course.

Maggie smiled at her and told Harold to remove the hens.

"I will be right back," Amelia said, her heart racing wildly. She had been anticipating this moment all day. She had missed Lucille so much it was as if she were her own daughter.

Her mother was with Garrett in the entry hall, her eyes wide as she took in the lavish surroundings. Mrs. Murdock was with them, Lucille in her arms. William and John had come downstairs to greet them. John was chatting eagerly with Signor Barelli, telling him about their outing that day to Piccadilly Circus, while William was looking carefully at his sister. "Is she smiling at me?" he asked.

Her heart turned over. Grenville had vanished that afternoon, and she had decided it was more important to take the boys for a stroll than to continue organizing the house. They had browsed in shop windows, purchased some sweets from the confectioner and sat for a while on a park bench, watching the elegant passersby. She had loved every moment spent with the boys.

She had to be careful, she thought, or she would fall in love with the boys and that little girl. After all, they were not her family and she was just a friend and a housekeeper. She knew the day of reckoning must come. She and Grenville had yet to sit down to discuss anything.

They had not discussed the boys' studies or their other activities; they had not discussed Lucille or her future.

"Momma!" Amelia cried, hurrying across the room. She hugged her. "You are finally here! How was your trip?"

"Oh, it was very pleasant, Amelia, but my, are we really staying here?" her mother cried, ogling the overhead chandelier. It was the size of a grand piano.

"Yes, we are really staying here." She smiled, glancing at Garrett. "Momma's room is on the second floor in that wing. It is yellow and white."

She had not discussed their accommodations with Grenville, so she had chosen a smaller guest bedroom at the end of the hall in the east wing for Momma. It adjoined another small bedchamber, which she would take for herself. Although hardly as luxurious as the room she had first been given, the chambers were much more comfortable than those in their own home.

"I cannot wait to see my room," Momma cried excitedly.

She was so lucid today, Amelia thought, turning to Mrs. Murdock. "How are you? How is the baby?"

Mrs. Murdock handed the infant to her. "She has been the perfect traveler, Miss Greystone. She has fussed a bit now and then, but mostly, she has slept."

Amelia cuddled Lucille to her bosom. The infant was wide-awake and she was gazing raptly at her with her big blue eyes. "Oh, I have missed her!" She rocked her and smiled. "I was worried. I am so glad to hear that the journey passed without incident."

"She is a little angel," Momma said.

Lloyd approached. "I want to thank you for organizing supper, Miss Greystone."

"It was my pleasure. If you do not mind, I would like

to oversee the family's meals on a daily basis." They both knew a housekeeper's duties did not necessarily include such supervision. Her duties could strictly pertain to the running of the house. "And every room in this house has been aired and cleaned. I think you will be pleased."

He looked relieved. "I am pleased, and I do not mind your preparing our daily menus. Lady Grenville did so herself. I will check on his lordship. He prefers to have a glass of wine before supper, in the library."

Was that where Grenville was? She hadn't seen him since that morning. Supper would soon be served and it would be very pleasing. She would dine with Momma separately, in their rooms. She would make certain the kitchens were spotless before she allowed the staff to retire for the night. But she wanted to spend some time with Lucille now. She hoped to feed her. She supposed that if she sat down, she would realize she was exhausted, but just then, she was acutely alert.

She looked down at the baby. She was already in love with the infant. But how could she not adore this tiny, motherless child?

Lucille had no mother, and she did not know who her father was. For all intents and purposes, it was Grenville. Many genteel homes had an illegitimate offspring or two within their midst. It was not uncommon for either the lord or the lady of the house to have had an affair and to wind up with the custody of his or her bastard; usually the other spouse pretended the child was his, when the whole world knew the truth. Did Grenville intend to raise Lucille as his own daughter? Did he intend to contact the father—if he even knew who that was? Had he even spared a thought to Lucille and her future?

He probably did not even know that she had been named.

She wondered if she dared take Lucille into the library with her, to introduce Grenville to her. She was afraid he might become angry if she dared to attempt to reconcile him to Elizabeth's daughter. But if Lucille were to remain in the house, he would have to meet her and accept her, at least as his wife's child. He certainly had a duty to her.

He would not throw her out of his home, would he? She refused to believe he would do anything that horrid.

She kissed Lucille's forehead, then she handed the baby back to Mrs. Murdock. "I am going to speak with his lordship. There are a number of matters we need to discuss, and I haven't had a spare moment all day."

Mrs. Murdock smiled. "The house feels as if it has been open for months and months. It's as if a happy, loving family lives here now. How odd!"

Amelia started.

Mrs. Murdock said, "It wasn't a very happy place when we left, Miss Greystone. It was dark and dismal. Everyone was worried and sad. She cried so frequently. So did John."

Amelia imagined that Lady Grenville had been beside herself, carrying another man's child and knowing that, sooner or later, she would have to face Grenville. That kind of tension would certainly affect the entire household. "This is a new beginning," she said firmly. "Lady Grenville's death is a tragedy. We are all sad that she has passed. But we must go forward, and eagerly. It is a new, bright day."

Mrs. Murdock smiled. "Yes, I am beginning to think so. Will you come up to feed her at seven?"

Her heart skipped. "I would not miss her feeding for the entire world!"

"I thought so." Mrs. Murdock gave her a knowing

look. "Good luck, dear," she said, as if she knew that Amelia meant to confront the lion in his den.

Amelia turned to both boys. "Will you go up with Signor Barelli? You must clean up before supper. Supper is at seven."

The Italian tutor told her he would make certain that they washed their hands and donned their coats. Amelia smiled, watching him herd the boys out.

She turned to her mother and Garrett. "I will be up shortly, Momma. Why don't you get rested before we dine? We will do so in your room. How lovely will that be?"

"Oh, I am so happy, Amelia, it is as if the past decades have never happened!" She hugged her daughter, hard.

Amelia sobered. She had always thought that her mother's losing touch had been a reaction to her father leaving them. She had always wondered if her mother simply could not deal with the pain of the present, and thus had to slip away into the past. "I am glad," she said, patting her back.

She watched Garrett lead her mother away. Then her smile faded. She was nervous, but that was absurd. Grenville was an adult. Surely by now, his feelings for Lucille had dissipated. After all, the child was the innocent victim in all of this.

The teakwood library doors were wide open, as they had been last night. And suddenly she recalled the drink they had shared. She had had no right to spend that time with him, alone and at such a late hour, whether they were friends or not.

As suddenly, she recalled his touching her cheek, very inappropriately, that morning, when they had failed to locate any intruder.

She felt her cheeks warm.

"Are you looking for me?"

She had paused on the threshold of the library. Now, she looked up.

Grenville sat at his desk, apparently reading from a sheaf of papers. He was staring at her, his gaze riveted and intense.

Her heart lurched wildly. Oh, she was not immune to him, and perhaps she never would be!

He wore a beautiful emerald-green coat with gold embroidery. His hair had been pulled carefully back. Lace frothed at his throat and over his hands. Rings glinted there; he wore an emerald on one hand, an onyx on the other. He was beautiful and masculine, and waves of authority and power emanated from him.

She suddenly felt so drab. She was in the same tired dress she had put on that morning, suitable for a day spent opening up a house that had been closed for several months. It was more gray than blue, made of heavy cotton. The elbows of her long sleeves were almost worn through, and there was a tear in the hem of her skirts. She wondered if her hair was coming down. She had arranged it into numerous braided coils.

I must look exactly like a housekeeper, she thought.

"Amelia?" He smiled slightly and stood. "I understand that you have been very busy today."

She came inside, noticing that he looked very tired. "I hope you will be pleased. We have aired every room. Most have been cleaned. And Jane's aunt has made a lavish meal. In fact, I am so impressed with her that I am hoping we might find a position for her in the kitchens."

"If you wish to hire her, then she is hired."

What did that mean? she wondered, trembling. "Do you wish for references?"

"No. If you think she will be a suitable addition to

the staff, then so be it. I have faith in your judgment," he said.

"I am flattered."

"It is not flattery. The house seems to be in perfect condition, Amelia, and you have been here for a single day."

She was thrilled by his praise—and by the warm look in his eyes. "It is hardly as if the house were falling down, or as if it had been closed up for years. A few of the rooms were musty, and the pantry was rather bare, that is all. Oh! I was wondering if you would mind if we refurbished the boys' bedchamber. The furnishings are suitable for John, but not for William. I think he would be pleased if the room were entirely redone."

He smiled. "I don't mind. You know, I saw the boys when I came in, and they could not stop talking about you."

"I took them for a walk today."

"I know. They adore you, Amelia."

She hesitated. "I am already so very fond of them."

Their gazes locked. He finally looked away and said, "They began to tell me about the smugglers of Sennen Cove."

She laughed. "I told them some tall tales of my ancestors' legendary exploits."

Smiling, he said, "John has declared that he wishes to be a smuggler."

"Oh, no!" she cried, but she was smiling, too.

"I am sure he will realize the folly of his ways when he is an adult."

"Jack has never realized the folly of his ways."

"How is Jack, by the way?"

She hesitated. "He has not changed, Simon."

He stared down at his desk. Then he looked up. "So

he continues to smuggle, in a time of war? If so, he must elude two navies, not one."

She twisted her hands. She so wanted to share her fears with him. "It is worse than that," she said softly. "Jack is running our blockade of France."

Grenville made a harsh sound. "If he is caught, he will hang! He is as reckless as ever. And how could he think to help the French republicans?"

"He is only thinking of the profit he is making," she said defensively. "He has also helped several émigré families reach British shores."

"I am glad to hear that." He left his desk. "Do you wish for a glass of wine or a sherry before supper? I am ready for a drink."

She felt so prim now. "Grenville, I can hardly imbibe at this hour."

He was pouring a glass of red wine. He gave her an amused look. "Of course not. Your day is not yet done. It is not bedtime."

She flushed. "I am sorry I ever told you that I sip a brandy before bed."

"I'm not."

Was he laughing? She hoped so. "When you smile like that, your eyes lighten and it is as if you have shed the weight of the world!"

"You are being fanciful," he said, scowling. "I am not carrying the weight of the world, Amelia, just that of a small earldom and my family."

Why had her comment upset him? Sometimes his behavior was so odd.

Grenville walked over to the sofa, gestured at her and sat. "Have you spoken with Lucas yet? Does he know you have taken up this position?"

Amelia sat down in an adjacent chair. "I haven't had

the chance to speak with Lucas. He wanted me to move to town, but I imagine he will be surprised when he learns that I am your housekeeper."

"Surprised or angry?"

Did he recall that Lucas had refused to allow him to call on her? It had been so long ago. "Lucas mentioned that he has seen you in town from time to time. He hardly seemed angry when he spoke of you." She had no intention of bring up the past.

He sipped his wine. "I am on somewhat friendly terms with your uncle, Amelia. Lucas often stays with Warlock when he is in town, so our paths have crossed."

Amelia hadn't realized that Grenville knew her uncle. Sebastian Warlock was not close to Amelia and her siblings, although they had met a few times. "It is a small world, then."

"Very."

"I think Lucas will be surprised when he learns of my decision to become your housekeeper, but in the end he will understand why I made such a choice."

He studied her. "We shall see. Are you sure you don't want a small sip of wine or sherry?"

She almost felt as if the devil were offering her a terrible temptation. "No, thank you. In fact, in a moment I must go upstairs. Actually, there are some matters I was hoping to discuss with you." Tension filled her. Somehow, she did not think they would discuss Lucille's future calmly. "The others have arrived, in case you did not hear the commotion in front of the house."

"I heard."

"We need to discuss Lucille, Grenville."

His gaze narrowed. "Lucille?" Abruptly, he stood.

She also rose, feeling defensive. "She has needed a name for the past ten days. You were very clear—you did

not care what she was named. Apparently Lady Grenville favored the name Lucille. Therefore, that is what
we have named her."

"And what will you do if Southland changes it?" His
eyes were hard.

"Who is Southland? Is that her father?"

"Yes, he is. Thomas Southland is the child's natural
father. I wrote him last week, telling him of the child's
birth."

Alarm began. She was afraid and dismayed. "What
do you mean, you wrote him? Do I know of him?"

"If you mean, is he a gentleman, the answer is yes.
Elizabeth chose her lovers with care." His face was entirely closed now. "I do not think she ever dallied with
a stable boy."

"That is a terrible thing to say!"

"Well, I could be wrong. For all I know, she slept with
my gardener." He suddenly finished his entire glass of
wine and set the glass down on a side table.

His wife had hurt him. Hadn't she? Why else would
he speak so disparagingly of the dead? "I am so sorry
that Lucille is not your daughter."

"I'm not. However, her birth is highly inconvenient."

"Simon, stop! You can't mean it—"

"I do mean it. She never told me she was with child,
Amelia. Warlock told me when it became obvious. I had
asked him to keep an eye on my sons, while I was in the
north. I didn't even know she was fleeing to Cornwall
to have the child. I don't know what she planned. Perhaps she meant to have the babe in secret, and then to
cast her off to a convent orphanage."

Amelia was aghast. "No mother would so such a
thing!"

"Ah, so you keep faith in a dead woman—my dead wife."

He was mocking her. "You are speaking very poorly of her."

"Yes, I am."

It wasn't her place to ask, but she blurted, "Why didn't you like her?"

"It was my duty to marry and beget heirs, not my duty to like her."

"But you could have chosen a different bride."

He raised a brow. "I chose to do as my father wished, Amelia. Perhaps I should have objected, but I did not— because I didn't really care. My marriage was going to be arranged for all the right reasons, one way or another." His smile was derisive. "But we took a mutual dislike to one another from the moment we were engaged."

"That doesn't make sense!"

"I am not my brother."

It took her a moment to comprehend him. "Elizabeth had wanted to marry William?" And she thought about how different the two brothers had been.

"They had met several times. A marriage between them had been discussed." He poured another glass of wine. "They made an attractive couple. I think they would have gotten on."

He was being so calm. She ached for him. His wife had wanted to marry his brother. How could that have not hurt him?

She wanted to touch him. She wanted to comfort him. Instead, she clasped her hands tightly together. "I am so genuinely sorry that you and Lady Grenville both suffered as you did. And even though it doesn't matter, I thought the two of you very well matched."

"You would."

She knew she could not delay any longer. She inhaled. "Simon, Lucille is an innocent child. She has done no wrong. She has lost her mother and she needs a father now."

"Then you should hope that Southland comes to retrieve her."

She was stricken by his cold response. "Is that what you have asked him to do?"

"Of course I have!" He snapped. "I have no desire to raise that bastard!"

Tears arose. She didn't even try to wipe them away. He was dead set against Lucille. She had to find composure, she had to think! "Did he know she was carrying his child?"

"I have no idea." He spoke very calmly now. "After all, she did not confide in me."

He was in so much pain, she thought, but he would never admit it.

"Stop looking at me with pity," he warned.

"I don't pity you."

"Like hell you don't."

Amelia gave up. She went to him and took one of his hands in both of her smaller ones. "You are hurt. You are wounded. It is understandable. But you are a good man! And when some time has passed, when your wounds are not so raw, I know you will feel differently about Lucille."

"Do you really think it wise to offer me comfort now?" he asked, his gaze suddenly bright.

Her heart was pounding. Did he think to turn this into a seduction? For one more moment, she held his hand. "You need comfort, Simon."

"Do you also think it wise to continue to call me Simon? Our love affair ended years ago."

She tensed and glanced at the open doors, but no one stood there.

"Yes, there is a house full of servants—and servants talk." He shrugged his hand free of hers abruptly. "This is dangerous ground, Amelia."

"Even you admitted that we are friends. Friends comfort one another, Grenville, in a time of need."

"Ah, so some common sense returns—it is Grenville again."

"What has made you so dark and so frightening? It cannot simply be marriage to a woman you did not love!"

"So I am dark and frightening now?"

"You have changed entirely!" she cried.

"Well, we finally agree upon something." He sauntered away from her and sank down on the sofa, almost slumping. He glanced up. "I asked you here because my sons need you. We both know you accepted this position because the boys lost their mother. I do not need you, Amelia. I do not need your comfort. But, if you keep offering it, you might become very sorry, indeed."

"Are you threatening me?" she cried, in disbelief.

"We both know an attraction remains." He shrugged.

He was so casual and complacent about it! He was right that an attraction remained and his boys needed her. But Simon was wrong about needing her. He was wounded, although she did not know how. Whatever had caused his wounds, it was far more than a failed marriage.

She thought about his terrible reaction to the banging shutter last night.

He eyed her from where he was sprawled on the sofa.

"Why do you keep a loaded pistol in that drawer?" she asked. "Why were you afraid of whomever you thought was at your door last night?"

He smiled, but it was a ruthless baring of his teeth. "London is filled with crooks, cheats and thieves."

"Oh, please! Thieves do not knock!"

"As you have noticed—and as I have pointed out—I have changed."

"You ran to the door with a loaded gun!" she cried, refusing to back down. "I am very worried about you, Simon. You have said some very strange things—you have behaved very oddly. If I can help, I wish to do so."

His stare was unwavering. "I am sorry, because I did not mean to frighten you last night. Life changes everyone, Amelia, and it has certainly changed me. I suppose my behavior is, at times, odd. You are already helping." He attempted a smile and failed. "My sons really do need you. You must focus your compassion upon them, not me."

In that moment, her determination to help him through whatever struggle he was in was fierce and consuming. She was so thankful she had taken up her position in his household. But she would have to be far less direct, if she wished to aid him.

"Are you scheming?" he asked softly, his gaze riveted upon her face.

She went to the sofa and very carefully sat down at one end. He was in its middle. "I wish to discuss the boys' schedule with you."

His regard moved over her features with care. "We can do so in the morning."

"Good. But perhaps we should finish discussing Lucille and her future."

His gaze wandered over her mouth, then returned to her eyes. "I hadn't realized we were discussing Lucille's future."

"Do you think Southland will come?" She fought the

tug of despair. It would be right if the infant were re-united with her natural father.

"I don't know. Perhaps not. He is a bachelor, with a reputation."

Her heart sank. "He will not come, then. A bachelor cannot possibly raise his illegitimate child!"

"Perhaps his parents might step forward. Amelia... are you dismayed or pleased?"

She clasped her hands in her lap, sitting erectly. "I want what is best for her."

"Yes, you probably do. But you have become far too fond of her already."

"How can anyone not fall in love with her?"

He pushed both feet to the floor, sitting up more correctly. "You are twenty-six years old. Yet you have never married, and you do not have children of your own."

"We are discussing Lucille."

"Yes, we are—and she is not your child, Amelia, nor is she mine. But it is glaringly obvious that you have sacrificed your life to the care of your failing mother."

"It is a sacrifice I am gladly making," she said, meaning it.

"But look at how happy you are, being here in my home, caring for my boys and Lucille."

She leaped to her feet. "I do not see the point you are making."

He sighed. "I am not sure that I was making a point. Perhaps, though, you should consider marriage. You surely need a family of your own."

"And then who would take care of you and your children?" she cried.

His gaze widened. "I don't know," he said slowly.

She realized how her comment had sounded and what

it had implied. She flushed. "I do not have any suitors, Grenville."

His expression was impossible to read.

She twisted her hands. "What will happen if Southland doesn't come?" she finally asked.

He sighed. "I am not completely without morals, or as irresponsible as is so commonly claimed. I will raise Elizabeth's bastard if I have to."

Her relief knew no bounds. "I knew you would do what is right. Thank you, Grenville."

"You are attached." His gaze narrowed.

"Yes, I am attached." And she thought about how much his entire family meant to her. For one more moment they stared at one another, and then she excused herself and fled.

THE KITCHENS WERE SPOTLESS. Amelia smiled at Jane, Maggie, Cook and Harold, wishing everyone good-night. She would see them at six the next morning.

"Thank you for your help today," Maggie said warmly, before leaving.

When everyone was gone, Amelia locked the kitchen door and bolted it. She felt very pleased. It had been a long but good day.

Lucille had been fed and was now sleeping. Amelia had taken some supper with her mother, and encouraged Momma to go to bed early, as she was so clearly tired from the journey. Before she had come downstairs, she had made certain her mother was getting into bed. She had also looked in on Lucille one last time. She thought about the infant's natural father, who very well might not come to claim her, and was saddened.

Her day was done. Her only regret, she thought, was that she could not go up and say good-night to the boys.

The one thing she knew she must not do was venture into Grenville's family rooms.

Amelia blew out the last candles and left the kitchen. Was she being a fool? Was she worried that, if she went upstairs in the west wing, he would seduce her? She knew better than to dally with her employer, past history or not. Still, she had wanted to offer him some comfort earlier. But he had immediately turned her attempt into something with sexual overtones. She would have to be careful about how she approached him in the future, she thought. When his behavior became suggestive like that, it unnerved her.

Her heart skipped. She must not become attached to Grenville. A friendship was tolerable, as long as her affection remained only that. She must focus her compassion on the children, as he had said.

She dismissed the nagging of worry, pausing in the foyer. The house was so quiet. She held a taper and she could see into the east wing, just slightly. The library doors were open and a fire blazed within the room, filling it with light.

Her heart turned over. She would love a drink, but tonight she should skip the nightcap, as Grenville was obviously up and about. The previous encounter with Grenville remained fresh on her mind. It felt dangerous to even think of venturing into his company. She should make certain a decanter and a glass were left in her room.

But she would have to slip by the library to go upstairs. If he noticed her, she would simply nod and increase her pace, she decided.

Amelia entered the hall. She glanced into the library, expecting to find him standing there. But he was not anywhere in the room.

As she looked within, she heard a harsh, guttural cry.

She faltered. The sound had been hoarse and either sexual or filled with pain.

"God help me," Simon cried.

She gasped, because his words were so clearly anguished. She rushed forward. When she crossed the library's threshold, she saw Simon lying prone on the couch. One arm was flung upwards, and he was asleep.

He was dreaming, she realized. He thrashed wildly and cried, "God, Danton, no!" His words were choked, as if on a sob.

He was in a terrible nightmare.

Amelia rushed forward without thinking. She set the candle down and knelt beside him, grasping his arm. "Simon, wake up. You are dreaming!"

"They are coming for me." His eyes flew open and he stared at her. Tears shimmered on his thick lashes. "I am next. I have been discovered."

He spoke so lucidly that she froze. What was he saying?

"I am going to be sick. There is too much blood! I cannot stand it, not anymore!" As he stared wildly at her, she realized he did not even see her.

"Simon!" She shook him. "Wake up. You are dreaming." She shook him harder still.

And his eyes widened. "Amelia?"

She sagged in relief, still holding on to his arm tightly. "It is all right," she soothed, as if to a child. "You were having a nightmare."

His gaze held hers. "Am I still dreaming?" he asked thickly. With his free hand, he reached out and suddenly she was pressed against his chest as she knelt beside him. Their faces were very close. "I do not mind being comforted now, Amelia," he murmured. "I do not mind at all."

His eyes were fixed on her mouth. He slid his other arm free and encircled her. "You should know better," he said softly, "than to awaken a sleeping man."

She knew she should wrench free, but she did not move. She was in Simon's arms. "You were having a terrible nightmare."

"Yes, I was, and I wonder, am I still dreaming?" He smiled slightly, shifting so his mouth was even closer to her face. Her breasts were crushed against his chest. "Are you comforting me in my dreams, sweet Amelia? If so, I do not wish to awaken."

She knew she had to protest. He was half asleep, but that made him even more dangerous. She meant to speak, she truly did, but he leaned closer and grazed her mouth with his.

She went still, her senses exploding with urgency. He made a harsh sound, then feathered her lips another time, and another. Amelia felt the pressure build. She needed him so!

One strong hand went to the back of her head, anchoring her, and his mouth became forceful, opening hers.

Amelia gave in. She kissed him back, heatedly, eagerly, frantically. And their tongues touched....

He suddenly pulled away from her, his eyes wide and completely lucid. "This is not a dream."

She knew her cheeks were red. Her entire body was on fire. She wanted him to kiss her, caress her, she wanted to explode. "No, it is not," she gasped.

For one more moment, he stared. "Damn it," he finally said. And he shoved away from her, throwing his legs over the couch, sitting up.

Amelia rocked back onto her calves, trembling.

Simon had kissed her and she had kissed him back.

He said roughly, "You are sitting on the floor."

She realized she was doing precisely that, and he was on the sofa, looking down at her. She glimpsed his strained breeches and knew she flushed even more. Amelia leaped to her feet. Her knees felt useless.

Simon stretched back against the sofa, throwing one arm over his eyes.

She covered her burning face with her hands. Now what? She heard him get up. She tensed as he walked past her.

She turned and watched him pour two brandies. He handed her one. "Thank you," she whispered, aware that she should leave, but she desperately needed that drink.

"You might want to think twice about surprising me while I sleep." His tone was calm, his gaze watchful.

She trembled, taking a huge draught of the brandy. It was delicious and she took another sip.

"That will not douse the fire," he said.

She took a third gulp. "I could not possibly leave you thrashing about on the sofa."

"Next time, you might think twice about it. I am not sure I will be as considerate."

She clutched the snifter very tightly. Next time—if there was a next time—he would not stop himself from making love to her. She knew she must not even consider the possibility that she would be in his arms again! "What on earth were you dreaming about?"

His gaze became vacant. "I don't recall."

"You called out someone's name. It sounded like Danton."

He shrugged, but he seemed wary now. "I don't know anyone by that name."

"You sounded anguished. You said there was too much blood!" Amelia cried.

Holding his drink, he walked away from her.

She followed him, determined. "What could you have possibly been dreaming about?"

"I don't know."

"You were not there when Elizabeth died, otherwise I would think the blood referred to her dying in childbirth."

"Leave it alone," he said sharply.

"How can I ignore your anguish?" she demanded, almost furious. "You said something about having been discovered. What does that mean?"

He looked at her, his face hard with anger. "I don't know! It was a damned dream! But you are probably right. I was probably dreaming about Elizabeth!"

"You said that they were coming for you!" she added, not believing him for a moment.

"God, you are like a damned terrier with a bone!" he cried.

"Who is haunting you? Who is coming for you? Is that why you keep that pistol in your drawer? Is someone pursuing you, Simon?"

"Damn it," he roared. "Damn it!" And he threw his glass at the wall.

She flinched, recoiling. The glass shattered and brandy stained the beautiful green fabric. "Leave well enough alone, Amelia."

She set her drink down carefully, shaken. She recalled the state of his rooms at St. Just Hall. "We are friends. You have said so yourself."

"Then I made a vast mistake. Right now, you are my housekeeper, and I am in the mood to dismiss you."

She ignored him. "Something is bothering you. You

were worried that first night on the road—I saw it in your eyes. I even felt it. For some reason, you were in a rush to get to town. You were gone all afternoon—you did not tell anyone where you were going, or when you would be back. What is going on, Simon? Is someone pursuing you? Are you in danger?"

He choked. "I am not in danger! Your imagination is excessive! And all because of a dream!"

"I would dismiss this incident if it were the only one," she said, never taking her gaze from him.

"I am hardly a child, to report to my elders," he said tersely.

"And what if there were an emergency and we needed to reach you? Be reasonable."

A long, interminable moment passed. He walked back to the sideboard and filled another snifter. He did not look at her as he spoke. "You are right. I should have told you how to reach me, in case there was a problem with the boys." He paced away to pause before the fire and stare at it.

She followed. She had noticed a tremor going through him. He was pretending calm. "What were you dreaming about? What has left you so shaken?"

"God, you are persistent. I don't recall, Amelia." His glance was brief and sharp, filled with warning.

She stepped forward, so they stood side by side. At this proximity, the fire in the hearth was too warm. "I only want to help. And maybe I could help, if I knew what is bothering you so much that you have nightmares about it. Has it ever occurred to you that your distress will affect the boys?"

"Everything I have done, everything I am doing, is for their sake!" he said harshly.

He was in a terrible predicament, she thought. Something had happened, or was happening, to distress him so. "Sometimes you almost sound as if you have been abroad, as if you have experienced the war firsthand."

He looked at her, wide-eyed. "What the hell would make you think that?"

She hesitated. "Lucas is involved in the war, Simon, secretly. And Bedford was once an agent for our country."

He paled. "I cannot believe you are telling me this. I do not think you know what you are speaking of."

"I am hardly a spinster, sitting at home in oblivion. When I first met Bedford, he was gravely wounded, and we thought he was a French army officer. He had been in France, spying for Pitt."

"So that is why you have such an imagination," he said, his eyes still wide.

"French deserters looted my neighbor's house. My best friend is an émigré. The war is a terrible fact of my life. I cannot help but wonder if it has somehow affected you."

"I am too busy managing this earldom to even think about the war."

"Then you are fortunate," she said. "Do you have such dreams often?"

He stared incredulously at her. "As I said, you are like a terrier with a bone. Will you ever give up?"

"Not in this instance, not when you are suffering, not when there are needy children in the house." She was final.

"I don't recall the damned dream, and I don't want to," he snapped. "But if you must know, I have nightmares frequently. All of the time, in fact! And next time you happen upon me in such a dream, I suggest you walk away. It is not your affair."

"I am making it my affair," she managed to answer. "Because I am worried about you and I care about the children."

"Then do so at your own risk. Because next time you interfere, I am going to take what I want."

"You are threatening me?" She was shocked.

"No. I am not threatening you, Amelia. I am making you a promise. Next time, I will satisfy my desires—and yours." And with that hard pronouncement, his eyes ablaze, he walked abruptly out.

Amelia rushed to the closest chair and sat down before her knees gave out. Then she began to fight the urge to cry. What was happening? Was Simon in danger?

And she realized that all she knew was that Simon was suffering, and it hurt her, too. Damn it, she would help him, if she could. But first, she had to find out what was going on.

CHAPTER NINE

AMELIA SMILED WITH EXCITEMENT as she alighted from the St. Just coach. Bedford House was a magnificent home just a few blocks from Lambert Hall; she had meant to walk, but Grenville had caught her going out and he had insisted she take the coach or one of his smaller carriages. Before she could argue, he had ordered the coach brought around. Then he had vanished into the library, closing both doors behind him.

Two days had passed. It was the first moment she had been able to spare to go visit her sister. She had been far too busy to call on Julianne. Nor had she sent her a note to tell her she had arrived in town. Instead, she had the house cleaned from top to bottom, the pantries filled to overflowing, the piano and harp tuned, the servants' uniforms laundered. She and Signor Barelli had spent an entire afternoon revising the boys' schedule of classes and activities. She had also spent three hours planning the boys' new bedroom decor. John and William had been moved into a guest bedroom; their bedroom was being painted a dark blue with white trim. Navy paisley fabrics had been chosen for their bedding, blue-and-white silks for two chairs, and a pale blue damask for their sofa. All the furniture was being refurbished that week.

She had also taken a few hours to shop for Lucille, who now had an adorable wardrobe of her own, most of the tiny clothes pink or yellow.

She had not seen Grenville except in passing. She felt certain he was avoiding her after the kiss they had shared. He probably felt the danger of their attraction, as she did. He probably knew, as she did, that they must keep their distance.

Any kind of intimacy was simply too dangerous.

When she did see him, he was polite and distant. He thanked her after every meal. Mostly, he was either locked in his library or he was out, attending various meetings. Last night he had gone to a supper party at Lord Dell's home. She had been awake when he had come in, and it had been well after midnight.

She did not want to question his whereabouts, but weekday dinner parties usually ended before two in the morning.

She realized then he had a mistress. All men of his stature did.

Oddly, she felt hurt, and not just by his dalliance, if that was what it was. She knew she should be relieved that they were playing the role of housekeeper and employer. Still, it was no easy task. Whenever their eyes met, she felt an instant tension, an immediate awareness, and she knew that he did, too. The moment their gazes met, Grenville would look aside.

She also noticed how tired he looked. Was he still sleeping poorly? Was he having nightmares? Was he in trouble, or even danger? He had been so evasive! Her worry knew no bounds.

Could he have been out so late for a purpose other than dallying with a lover?

She knew better than to ask how he was. The few times she had almost done so, he had immediately turned away, as if knowing where she wished to lead.

Now she kept a decanter in her bedchamber, so she

could take her brandy before bed without having to encounter him downstairs. Yet part of her really had no wish to avoid him. A part of her even missed his company! In any case, she knew she could not continue to avoid him indefinitely.

It was midafternoon and she had decided it was time to take care of herself. The boys were in their classroom with Signor Barelli—their first day back to their studies, a relief!—the shopping for the day had been done, lunch was over, Grenville was out, and supper was being prepared. Her duties for the moment were done. She missed and needed her sister.

But Amelia felt a tinge of guilt as she hurried to the front door of the palatial house. Momma always took a long nap after lunch and Amelia had encouraged her to do so that day. Amelia knew that Momma would wish to see Julianne—not that she would necessarily recognize her. But she desperately needed to speak privately with her sister now.

And before she had reached the front door, it flew open and Julianne was standing there.

"I saw the coach enter the drive," Julianne cried, smiling. "St. Just never calls. I knew it had to be you!" And Julianne pulled her into her arms.

Amelia embraced her back, hard. Then she took a long look at her sister. Once, Julianne had been a country gentlewoman with limited means. She had spent her days doing chores in a drab housedress, then reading in the library, or agitating for the Jacobins in France. Now she was every bit the countess she had become in her silks and jewels. "I barely recognize you," Amelia said, as she walked inside with her sister. "I don't know if I can become accustomed to your having become so elegant!"

Julianne was tall, willowy, with reddish-blond hair.

She was resplendent in a dark green brocade gown with striped gold silk underskirts. She wore an emerald pendant on a chain and emerald teardrop earrings. Her hair was curled and pulled back, to fall past her shoulders and down her back. She was wearing a very small headdress, with a gold headband.

The top of Amelia's head probably reached her chin. "Are you wearing rouge?" she asked teasingly, looking up at her.

"Just a touch on my lips. I am a very fallen woman." She almost snickered, smiling wickedly.

Amelia knew her sister had never been happier. "You are glowing. I have never seen you as radiant. How is my niece?"

"Jaquelyn is crawling everywhere!" Julianne laughed, looping their arms together. "I spend most of my time rushing after her as she vanishes beneath chairs and settees."

Amelia smiled, glancing around the high-ceilinged entry hall. Of course, she had been Julianne's guest for several weeks, just prior to and just after her sister had given birth. She was not a stranger to Bedford House. "Can I see her before I leave?"

"Of course you can. She is napping, but I will do the unthinkable and wake her up if I have to." Julianne's smile faded as she led her into an opulent salon with gold walls, gilded furniture and a vast array of seating arrangements. She released her arm and faced her. "Why are you wearing that horrid dress?"

Amelia hesitated. Julianne had insisted on lavishing funds on her for their family. Amelia had put every penny into a banking account.

Julianne gave her a dark look and smiled at the butler who had just appeared. "Gerard, would you please bring tea and those sinfully decadent chocolate pastries we had last night?"

He bowed and left.

Julianne faced her. "Forget the dress, then. I knew you wouldn't spend a penny of the funds I gave you. I am going to have to deliver some decent gowns to your door."

"I don't need new gowns, Julianne," Amelia said, although that was hardly true.

Julianne scowled. "You did it, didn't you? You really took up with St. Just?"

"I am his housekeeper," Amelia insisted.

"I very nearly swooned when I received your letter," Julianne cried. "I could not believe what I was reading. I could not believe that he had offered you a position as a common servant and that you had accepted!"

"Did you also read about his poor children and the state of his household? His wife has just passed away, Julianne!"

"He broke your heart."

Amelia froze.

"Yes, I am going to the gist of the matter. Forget that you are a gentlewoman, and your brother-in-law is Bedford and that you are no longer without means. He broke your heart. He played you for an entire summer, you expected an offer of marriage, and then he simply left. You may have forgotten, but I have not!" She was flushed with anger.

"I have forgiven him, Julianne," Amelia said. "And I am asking you to do the same."

"Like hell I will," Julianne cried, trembling. "How on earth could you forgive him? How can you manage his household? How can you care for his children?"

Amelia knew that Julianne's rage was a direct result

of the love she felt for her sister. But she sighed. She so needed her sister's advice, but if Julianne was this angry, her advice would not be worth very much. "They are suffering," she said softly.

"Has he seduced you?" Julianne demanded. "Is that what this is about?"

Amelia gasped in surprise. Before she could deny it, Gerard and a maid returned, wheeling in a cart filled with exotic pastries, a silver teapot and porcelain cups and saucers. Julianne managed to thank the servants. When they had left, Amelia said, "That is unfair."

"No, his leaving you was unfair!" Her gray eyes flashed. "His pursuit was unfair! The kisses you shared with him were unfair!"

Amelia sat down. Julianne was fiery and passionate. She would let her ramble on, until she calmed down. Eventually her sister would become reasonable, but she was sorry she had mentioned, all those years ago, that he had kissed her.

"So, is he still dark and handsome? Is he still dangerous and dashing?" Julianne asked, oddly accusing.

"He is still an attractive man," Amelia said, far more calmly than she felt. "But he has changed, Julianne, terribly. I am very worried about him."

"You are worried about him?" Julianne cried, aghast. She sat down beside Amelia, the tea forgotten. "You never answered my question. Oh, Amelia, he hurt you so—I don't want you ever hurt that way again—and he isn't good enough for you!"

Amelia chose her words with care, taking Julianne's hand. "First of all, he has not seduced me." She hoped she wasn't blushing. "I am his housekeeper. I cannot tell you enough how much his boys need me—how Lucille needs me. But... I am also his friend."

She choked. "Only you would find it in your heart to befriend him now!"

"He dearly needs a friend."

Julianne shook her head. "Is Lucille the baby?"

She nodded. "Julianne, Lucille isn't his daughter. She is Lady Grenville's bastard, and he is very angry about it!"

"Oh, dear!" Julianne cried, clearly forgetting her grudge against Grenville now.

"She is so beautiful and so innocent! I am in love with her already. She is one of the reasons I took the post. That poor infant has neither a father nor a mother, and I am so worried about her."

Julianne hugged her. "Of course you are. I cannot imagine how I would feel if Jaquelyn were being raised in some stranger's home. Oh, the one thing I have learned a great deal about is male pride. St. Just must be grieving, of course, for Lady Grenville—but he must be furious to be left with her bastard!"

Amelia debated keeping the truth from her sister, but she could not. "They did not have a good marriage. They did not care for one another."

A moment passed. "And how would you know that? You never heed gossip."

"He told me so himself."

Julianne paled and stood up. "He told you? And you believe him? I knew it. You have never gotten over him. That is why you never married. Amelia, you cannot be friends, after all that he has done!"

"You hardly know him, Julianne. You should not suggest that he is lying about his marriage, or that our friendship is false." Amelia stood, grim.

"I am going to look after you, Amelia, when you have always been the one to look after me. I believe I am a bit better acquainted with men than you are. He is playing you now, the way he played you ten years ago."

Amelia thought of how seductive Grenville could become, in the blink of an eye. If she allowed him liberties, he would not hesitate. Was Julianne right? Could he be playing her? She had believed him when he had declared that, in spite of everything, they were friends.

"I see you are uncertain," Julianne said. "You do know he has a miserable reputation."

She tensed. "If you are going to tell me that he is a ladies' man, I do not want to hear it."

"No, but he is a renowned recluse, Amelia. And everyone knows better than to invite him to supper, for he will most likely brood."

Amelia ached for Simon. "Then perhaps the changes I have seen in him began some time ago. He was not a recluse when we were young." She smiled, feeling sad. "He has become dark and anguished. I noticed the changes the moment I saw him at the funeral, before we even had a chance to speak." When Julianne was silent, she said, "Something is bothering him, but he will not tell me what it is."

"Perhaps he is simply afflicted with melancholia," Julianne said. "Did he recognize you, Amelia? Did he remember your affair?"

Amelia didn't hesitate. "When I heard that Lady Grenville had died and I knew we would see one another at the funeral, I was certain he would not even recognize me. But he remembered me, Julianne."

She started. "After all these years?"

"There is a connection, Julianne, that defies all common sense—that defies the past we shared." How calm she sounded, Amelia thought. "And that is why we are friends now."

"How can you be friends when you were in love with him once? You cannot ignore your past."

"I am his friend!" She seized her sister's arm, her heart pounding. "And as his friend, I will be present for him now, when he is suffering and troubled. Just as I will be present for the children. The truth is, I took the position because of the children, not because of Grenville. They need me desperately, Julianne."

Julianne studied her for a moment. "If those children need you, you will always put them first. I suppose I am slightly relieved. But, Amelia, has he tried to seduce you?"

She knew she must dissemble. But she hesitated, and then, as her sister's eyes widened, she whispered, "A terrible attraction remains. We are both fighting it."

Julianne threw her hands up in the air and paced. "I knew it! I am so frightened for you." She turned. "Let me guess. He is grieving and anguished and you want to comfort him."

Amelia trembled. Julianne was mostly right. "Please don't be frightened for me. He needs me, but I am not going to allow him any liberties." Just then, she thought of the kiss they had recently shared. "I am not a naive little fool still, Julianne."

"I think he is playing you for a fool!" she returned. "You have no experience, he is a man of the world. You cannot be attracted to him without loving him, I am certain. But trust me, for him it is only a matter of desire and lust."

She flinched. "Was it that way with Bedford?"

"Of course not—we fell in love!"

She was becoming angry with her sister. "I realize you remain furious with Grenville. And maybe he deserves your continued wrath. However, I think he should be given the benefit of the doubt. I am in his household now, and your warnings and suspicions will not change that."

Julianne moaned. "You are digging in."

"Yes, I am. But I need your help." Finally, she softened. She took her sister's hand. "I really do, Julianne. I need you as a sister, a friend and a confidante. Because St. Just and the children are depending upon me, and I must lean on you."

Julianne hugged her. "You can always count on me, you know that. And you can count on Dom, too."

Amelia hugged her back and stepped apart. "The boys are just beginning to recover from their mother's death. They are very needy now. In a way, I am a substitute for Elizabeth."

"Is that wise?"

"I don't know. But I care for them deeply, and they need someone to show their lessons to, to take them strolling, to tuck them into bed." She realized a tear had arisen. She wiped it away. "But it is Lucille I am so worried about. Lucille's father might not come for her. Grenville loathes the sight of her, yet he has said he will raise her if he must. I am determined to reconcile them if the child's father doesn't come."

"Why is there any doubt whether the babe's father will come for her?"

"He is a bachelor, Julianne. It's unlikely he will want to raise his child. Do you know Thomas Southland?"

"I think I have heard the name. I will ask Dominic about him."

"Thank you." Amelia took her hand and squeezed it.

Julianne said, more quietly, "Well, your mind is made up. I still do not think it wise for you to be so immersed in St. Just's family, to be so concerned for them. I am going to pray that you keep your distance from him, except as a housekeeper and a friend."

Amelia smiled slightly.

Julianne walked to the tea cart and put pastries on two plates. She handed one to Amelia, who set it aside on a small table by the sofa. Then she poured tea, handing Amelia a cup and saucer. Amelia thanked her.

Julianne sat beside her. "Have you really forgotten the past? Have you genuinely recovered from it?"

Amelia took a sip of her tea before setting the cup down. "I thought I had forgotten the past entirely, but the truth is, seeing him again brought every detail back. But I have reminded myself that the past is simply history."

"Have you talked about it?"

She froze. "Not precisely. There have been references on his part. I prefer to avoid the subject." She added, "We know that we share a history. But we are both determined not to repeat past mistakes." But was she deluding herself? Simon would eagerly seduce her if he could—she was almost certain.

"You are very brave."

"No, I am frightened. I meant it when I said Simon has changed and that he is deeply troubled. The other reason I have called, beyond simply seeing you, was because I desperately need your advice."

Julianne stared. "You are worried—and not about a seduction."

"I am very worried. His behavior has been so odd."

"How so?"

"He was in a terrible rush to return to London, doing so in two days, and he seemed afraid to leave his sons behind. They could have traveled at a more leisurely pace with Momma, Garrett and some other staff. Instead, he insisted the two small boys travel with him."

"Perhaps that was a reaction to Lady Grenville's sudden death?"

"No. After the funeral, he locked himself in his rooms. I was asked to intervene. He was inebriated, and he said the oddest things."

"Again, his wife just died. Good marriage or not, he was grieving for her, Amelia."

"He told me directly that he was not grieving for her, although he was sorry she had passed."

"That is a strange statement." Julianne seemed taken aback.

"He started to ramble and he was angry. He spoke of men dying every day—it almost sounded as if he were talking about the war."

Julianne paled. "Was he?"

"I don't know. But he keeps a pistol in his desk drawer, Julianne. He keeps it loaded."

When Julianne stared, Amelia added, "The night we arrived in town, a shutter came loose and started banging on the side of the house. There was nothing unusual about it, but Simon seized the pistol and ran to the front door as if he expected marauders to be there!"

"That is very odd," Julianne said, her eyes wider now.

"His behavior is so strange. I caught him in a nightmare the other day, Julianne. He said there was blood everywhere and he could not stand it. He also said, and I am quoting, 'They are coming for me.' When I asked him what he was dreaming about, he became very evasive, as if he did not recall. But I did not believe him. I know he recalled that dream."

"Elizabeth died in childbirth—maybe he was dreaming about her," Julianne said, but her tone was doubtful.

"I briefly considered that, but I am certain he was not dreaming about her."

"What could the statement 'They are coming for me' mean?" Julianne asked. "Is he being pursued? He is the Earl of St. Just!"

Amelia sat beside her. "I have no idea. But I can tell you he was very distraught upon awakening. It was a terrific nightmare! He did finally confess to having nightmares frequently."

"Dominic had nightmares when we first met."

Amelia felt her heart lurch with dread. "Julianne, do you think he has been to France, and has been in the war, somehow?"

"Why would I think that?" Julianne asked.

She swallowed and said, "He is friendly with Warlock."

Julianne had been taking a sip of tea. Instantly, she put her teacup down, and the saucer rattled. "We should not jump to conclusions."

"You rarely spoke of Sebastian, Julianne, when you returned home after Bedford left you and went back to France. But you made two things clear. First, that you did not like him at all, and second, that he was Bedford's spymaster."

"He was. Dom jumped through Warlock's every hoop. And I believe Warlock is still in the game of war and espionage, although I rarely cross paths with him now that Dominic is an ordinary civilian." She was sitting very rigidly.

"I am so worried!" Amelia cried. "Simon is never in residence with his family, Julianne. That is a hard, cold fact."

"So you are beginning to think he is in France when he is not with his household?"

"I hope that is not the case! He is probably at a northern estate—he has several large estates in the north."

"France is in a reign of terror. I know you are not half as political as I am, but you should know how dangerous it is to be in France, unless you are an *Enragé,* like Hébert and Tallien. Entire villages have been slaughtered, Amelia, when just a family or two dares to oppose the revolutionary regime. Guilt is by association! The cause I once supported is gone. It has been taken over by a group of insanely radical tyrants, not the least of whom is Robespierre. No one is allowed to dissent. Look at what happened to Georges Danton."

Amelia gasped. "He cried out a name in his nightmare—it sounded like Danton!"

Julianne was pale. "Danton was beheaded a few weeks ago. He was a Jacobin, Amelia, but he turned against Robespierre and paid the ultimate price for it."

"I must have misheard," Amelia said, her heart racing. "Simon would not be dreaming about a Jacobin who was recently guillotined!" But he had cried that there was so much blood and he could not stand it…. Amelia leaped up and began to pace.

"I cannot imagine St. Just being an agent, the way Dom was," Julianne said, her voice low. She stood. "He is a recluse, Amelia."

"I hope you are right, that he is a recluse suffering from a bad humor. Simon never talks politics. He does not seem at all interested in the war. I am undoubtedly making much ado about nothing," Amelia said. She really could not imagine Grenville in France, and if so, doing what? Spying, as Bedford had done? Commanding troops, as other British noblemen were doing? It made no sense! "Besides, he so loves his boys. I don't think he would put his life in danger in any way, not when they need him so."

Julianne put her arm around her. "Just because he has

bad dreams, we should not assume he is dreaming about the war. He could be dreaming about anything, Amelia. You do not know that you heard him cry out Georges Danton's name. And even if you did, perhaps they were friends before the war. Dom knew so many Frenchmen, most Englishmen do. But I am going to ask Dominic directly what he knows about St. Just."

"I think that is a good idea. Surely if Simon were involved in Warlock's schemes, Dominic would know." Amelia prayed Bedford would confirm that Simon was simply a reclusive Brit.

Julianne stared at her. "You keep calling him Simon."

She flushed. "It is a slip of the tongue."

"Is it?" Julianne crossed her arms. "Surely you do not call him Simon when you are asking him what his preference is for the next day's meals?"

"No, I do not." But she knew her color had increased.

"I am worried about you," Julianne said. "Be honest with me now. Do you still love him?"

Amelia felt her tension explode. "How can you ask me such a thing?"

"I can, and I am."

"I am fond of him and I am worried about him. That is all."

Julianne shook her head. "You still love him. You have never stopped loving him. No good can come of this, Amelia. He used you once—can't you see? He will only wind up using you again."

"Not if I am careful," she protested. But she realized she did not believe her own words.

Julianne gave her a pitying look.

AMELIA PEEKED INTO the dining room. Grenville sat at the head of the table, John on one side, William on the other. They were finishing up the main course—roasted venison with dumplings and *haricot verts*. The table was set with gold linens, gilded flatware and plates, white candles in brass candlesticks and a centerpiece of yellow roses. The boys were so handsome in their navy blue coats. Grenville was magnificent in a bronze dinner jacket, smiling at something John had just said.

Her heart lurched at the sight. She stared almost helplessly at the family scene.

Grenville's smile changed his entire face. John was laughing, too. Even William, who always tried to be so grown-up, was smiling now....

They were talking about a new yacht and a voyage up the river.

She stepped into the doorway and signaled the liveried servant who stood by the sideboard. Immediately he began to remove the family's dinner plates and scrape away stray crumbs from the table. Satisfied that not a morsel of food or even a piece of lint would mar the tidiness of the table, Amelia glanced up and met Grenville's eyes.

His smile faded. His gaze intensified. The look felt entirely significant. But Amelia somehow nodded politely at him and followed the waiter out of the room.

However, her heart continued to pound as she strode briskly after Peter into the kitchens. "Dessert is to be served," she declared.

What had that long, intense look meant?

Was she in danger of imminent seduction?

Was she already in love?

As a beautiful sterling platter filled with freshly baked pastries and tarts was bustled from the kitchens, she inhaled. The conversation she'd had that afternoon with Julianne remained etched upon her mind.

He was not involved in the war and the revolution, she was certain. He hardly ever glanced at the newspapers, when the headlines were screaming with news of France or a pronouncement made by Pitt or his war secretary, Windham. She hadn't ever seen a journal about the revolution and its effects upon society and Great Britain lying about the room. And he had never once mentioned the subject of war. Another person might think that odd—everyone talked about the war—but she did not. After all, Lady Grenville had died so recently and his hands were full.

He was having odd nightmares and he was troubled, but he was simply a recluse prone to dark moods. He had to be.

Julianne was right. She was deeply involved with his family. She was so concerned about them—about him. But he was not playing her. He was not using the recent tragedy to lure her more deeply into his web. That was a terrible thing to suggest!

The kettle was singing. Amelia filled a sterling teapot with the boiling water, despite Maggie's protestations. A servant took the tray with the pot and its cups and saucers from her. She followed him back to the dining room.

As she entered, she saw that both boys were devouring their desserts. Grenville's was untouched.

She happened to know that he did not care for sweets, but as the tea was served, she said, "Does the dessert displease you, my lord? Is there something else that we can bring you?"

He settled back in his chair, his gaze wandering slowly over her face. "Nothing displeases me at this moment." He smiled. "Thank you for another lovely meal."

She smiled back at him.

"That is all," he told the servant. The waiter bowed

and left the room. Grenville then looked at his sons. "You may be excused, if you wish."

Amelia tensed, realizing that if the boys left, they would be alone. And John and William jumped up, almost simultaneously. John rushed to her as William said, "Thank you, Father."

Amelia laid her hand on John's head as Grenville said, "You are welcome."

John grinned up at her. "You said you would tell us a story. Can you do so before we go to bed?"

She hesitated. Telling a story before their bedtime would require her to go upstairs, into the family's private rooms. She had only been upstairs in the west wing during daylight hours, as she obviously had to supervise the management of that part of the house. She had found the time to do so when Grenville was out.

"Do you wish to tell the boys a story, or to read them one?" Grenville asked.

His regard was that of a very satisfied man.

"I would love nothing more," she said, but her heart was slamming. Did she really want to venture upstairs at this hour? Yet wouldn't he go into the library, as was his habit?

"Amelia will be up shortly. Why don't you prepare for bed in the meanwhile," Grenville suggested.

The boys ran out, smiling. Amelia hesitated, certain he wished to be alone with her, and not certain that would be wise. "Do you wish to speak to me?" she asked, her heart racing. But she kept her voice calm.

"You never go upstairs," he said softly.

It was an accusation. She dared to meet his dark regard. "Those are private rooms. It does not seem the best recourse."

"I don't mind."

She was aware that he had consumed most of a bottle of red wine. "We have been attempting to maintain a certain formality."

"Is that what you would call it?" He seemed amused. "You have been avoiding me, ever since you caught me asleep on my library sofa, while I have been trying to decide if I can truly put the welfare of my children first."

What did that mean? There was no mistaking his reference to the kiss they had shared. "I am trying to fulfill my duties as a housekeeper. You have also avoided me, so clearly you are putting the children first!"

"I suppose I have been keeping a careful distance. But I have not forgotten that encounter." He shoved his teacup aside. "It would please me, Amelia, if you read to the boys at night. They need your attention, and their needs must come before mine."

She fought to remain composed. "Thank you. I would love to do so."

"Are you afraid that I will intrude upon you while you are with them?"

Before she could dissemble and deny it, he said, "I want you to be candid."

"Yes," she breathed.

He glanced down at the table. "Perhaps I wish to hear the story, too. Perhaps it is as simple as that."

She looked at him closely. He had been denied the company of his children for so long and he was desperate to be with his family. Maybe he simply wanted to join in another family moment.

Maybe he was lonely.

He suddenly stood up. "How did your visit with your sister go?"

She inhaled, shaken by her thoughts but determined

to include him during bedtime storytelling. "It was wonderful to see her."

He came around the table. "And does she approve of the position you have taken in my household?"

She would not tell him that her sister held a deep grudge against him. "She understands why I have taken it."

"I recall you being close. So she has forgotten the past? Or forgiven it?"

She did not want to lie. When she hesitated, he cried, "Oh, ho! So you have discussed the past—you have discussed me."

"I spent some time explaining the plight that all three children are in. She is very concerned for them, of course." Amelia was firm.

"So she has accepted your rationale for taking up this position?"

"Of course she has."

"Really? Because I do not believe that the Countess of Bedford has forgiven me for my transgressions. If she has, then I am impressed with your powers of persuasion." He smiled. "And have you complained about me? About my behavior?"

She started. "I would never do such a thing."

"So you did not tell her I behave oddly at times, as you put it? Or that you have found me having nightmares?"

She had thought he was referring to his sometimes bold and seductive behavior, but he was asking her if she had discussed his nightmares with Julianne. And she had done precisely that! "I did mention I am worried about you, that you seem troubled and that I am determined to help."

"Of course you did." He looked at her. "Did you share

your theory with her? That you think I am in some kind of danger?" He laughed.

Amelia did not smile. "Yes, I told her I think there is a reason you are very troubled, and that I wished I knew why."

"I am only troubled because my children have lost their mother," he said quite sharply.

Amelia was silent. She hoped he was being truthful with her—but she did not believe him.

"So what was the verdict, in the end? Does your sister believe you are doing the right thing, helping me and my children? Does she also think that I am troubled?"

Their gazes met and held. Was he asking her if Julianne was also suspicious of him? Could he be that astute? "Julianne thinks you are suffering from the loss of your wife," she said slowly.

He smiled, but not with mirth. "That would be a usual conclusion, would it not? This is a difficult time."

"Yes, it would be the conclusion most would draw."

He gave her a sidelong look. Then he said, "I cannot imagine that she is pleased with your being here, no matter the circumstances."

"She has accepted my decision."

His brows lifted. "I am certain the two of you had quite the row. Let us be frank, Amelia. If she knew the truth, she would drag you from this house."

Amelia felt herself flush. "If she knew you as I do—" she stopped.

His eyes were wide. "If she knew me the way you do, she would be somewhat fond of me?" He was amused. "Amelia, you are so unique."

"Julianne isn't being fair," Amelia said quickly. "She will come around."

"Ah, it is as I suspected. She does not approve of

your being here and she doesn't trust me where you are concerned. I cannot blame her. I hardly trust myself."

Amelia could not look away, her heart racing. If she were not careful, their encounter would turn romantic—she was certain of it. But then, didn't she fear that their every encounter would become romantic? "I trust you," she finally whispered, and a part of her trusted him with her entire being, even knowing that he would seduce her if he could.

"But you are afraid to go upstairs."

"Yes," she said breathlessly. "I am afraid to go up into your family's apartments."

He stared at her, his dark gaze smoldering. But he did not speak.

The silence became thick, and the tension crackled. Amelia wet her lips and said, "I think we are both behaving in a commendable manner, given the difficult circumstances in which we have found ourselves."

For one moment, she did not think he would answer her, but he did. "What I like best about you, Amelia," he said slowly, "is that you appear to be entirely prim and proper."

She knew she flushed, because they both knew she was neither prim nor proper at all.

"You are afraid to go upstairs and attend my children," he continued softly. "You are afraid to approach me in the library. You are afraid that, right now, I will come too close to you."

"Fine, yes, I am afraid!" she cried. "I trust myself even less than I trust you!"

And the moment she spoke, she realized she had just given him an opening.

He seized it. His eyes, already dark, smoldered. He

YOUR PARTICIPATION IS REQUESTED!

Dear Reader,

Since you are a lover of historical romance fiction – we would like to get to know you!

Inside you will find a short Reader's Survey. Sharing your answers with us will help our editorial staff understand who you are and what activities you enjoy.

To thank you for your participation, we would like to send you 2 books and 2 gifts – **ABSOLUTELY FREE!**

Enjoy your gifts with our appreciation,

Pam Powers

SEE INSIDE FOR READER'S SURVEY

YOUR READER'S SURVEY
"THANK YOU" FREE GIFTS INCLUDE:

▶ 2 Historical Romance books
▶ 2 lovely surprise gifts

PLEASE FILL IN THE CIRCLES COMPLETELY TO RESPOND

1) What type of fiction books do you enjoy reading? (Check all that apply)
○ Suspense/Thrillers   ○ Action/Adventure   ○ Modern-day Romances
○ Historical Romance   ○ Humour   ○ Paranormal Romance

2) What attracted you most to the last fiction book you purchased on impulse?
○ The Title   ○ The Cover   ○ The Author   ○ The Story

3) What is usually the greatest influencer when you <u>plan</u> to buy a book?
○ Advertising   ○ Referral   ○ Book Review

4) How often do you access the internet?
○ Daily   ○ Weekly   ○ Monthly   ○ Rarely or never.

5) How many NEW paperback fiction novels have you purchased in the past 3 months?
○ 0 - 2   ○ 3 - 6   ○ 7 or more

YES! I have completed the Reader's Survey. Please send me the 2 FREE books and 2 FREE gifts (gifts are worth about $10) for which I quality. I understand that I am under no obligation to purchase any books, as explained on the back of this card.

246/349 HDL FS9U

FIRST NAME	LAST NAME

ADDRESS

APT.#	CITY

STATE/PROV.	ZIP/POSTAL CODE

The Reader Service — Here's How It Works:

stepped forward and pulled her close. "That is good to hear."

"Is it?" she whispered, her heart surging, her hands closing on his muscular arms.

"It is very good to hear. Amelia. This is impossible." Urgency burning in his eyes, he kissed her.

Amelia closed her eyes and she did not move. Instead, she exulted in the growing pressure of his mouth on hers, in the waves of pleasure washing over her and building within her as he kissed her again and again. And finally, she kissed him back.

He opened. Her tongue moved deeply inside his mouth, twisting and mating with his.

Simon pulled away from her and slid his hand over her hair. "You are supposed to be my housekeeper," he said harshly. "But I cannot forget what you feel like in my arms."

"I know," she whispered, stunned by the burning desire. She was ready to do the unthinkable. She was ready to go upstairs and join him in his bed, and to hell with the consequences.

"If we become lovers, there is no going back," he said flatly.

She trembled. Being in his arms felt so right, but was she going to be both a mistress and a housekeeper?

What about her feelings? She was in love, wasn't she? What about her own standards, her morality? Her future?

He rubbed his knuckles over her cheek. "Amelia? This is not a good idea."

"I think the boys must be ready for their story now," she said breathlessly. But in a way, she wanted to cry.

He released her and she stepped away from the circle of his arms. But their stares never wavered. She hesitated. "You should join us, Simon."

His mouth curled but it was derisive. He dropped his gaze, but not before she saw the dark shadows flitting through his eyes. "I don't think so."

And he turned and walked into the library, closing both doors behind him.

CHAPTER TEN

SIMON HADN'T BEEN TO Bedford House in years. Although Dominic Paget, the Earl of Bedford, was no longer active in the war effort, he had once been deeply involved in the royalist insurgency in France. From the moment Simon had been lured into Warlock's web of intrigue, he had been told that it was prudent to feign indifference to men like Paget, Penrose and Greystone. Warlock had made certain that those elite agents were well aware of one another. It was a circle of the charmed, so to speak, or perhaps of the damned. In any case, Simon knew the identity of almost two dozen agents, most of whom were deeply embedded in France, gathering information for the War Office and now for the Alien Office, as well.

He had been recruited by Sebastian Warlock almost two years ago. The powers in Europe were in a panic over the anarchy in France, fearing the revolution would insidiously spread into their own countries. In Britain, it had been no different. In London's highest Tory circles, Pitt and his cronies huddled into the night, trying to comprehend the extent of the damage in France and if it could leak over into Britain and her allies. Everyone in the country with something to lose was afraid of the anarchy in France now.

It was no secret that Simon was fluent in French, Spanish, Italian and German, and that he also spoke a spattering of Russian. It was no secret that he was a Tory and a supporter of Pitt's, although not terribly active in political circles thus far. Mostly, it was no secret that he was in an unhappy marriage, and that he spent most of his time on his northern estates, avoiding his wife.

One foggy night in London, his friend Burke had invited him to White's. He had been introduced to Warlock then. A day later, Warlock had appeared at Lambert House, insisting he join him for lunch. And in the dark shadows of Sebastian's carriage, the shades drawn, he had been recruited to save his country from anarchy and revolution.

"You are never in town. You have the perfect alibi," Warlock had said.

Simon had not hesitated. His life had become an exile of sort, even if it was self-imposed. He had chosen to avoid Elizabeth, even if it meant giving up his relationship with his sons, because he could not stand the thought of a lifetime with her. Warlock's offer had been a means of escape. He had eagerly taken up the challenge of reinventing himself as a Frenchman and a Jacobin.

He knew Paget well and liked him immensely. As his coach approached Dominic Paget's home, he wondered if he dared resume the old friendship. He did not think it wise, not when he was playing both sides. But one call would not be too alarming. In any case, Paget could be a fountain of information.

Although his contact hadn't shown up the other morning, "Jourdan" had received a note earlier in the day, requesting a rendezvous. His new contact would be a man called Marcel. The Jacobin had suggested a midnight tryst in the public room of a tavern in the East End tomorrow night.

His heart drummed as he considered it. He would have to go, of course, and he was going to have to bring information he did not yet have. Jourdan had been in Britain for close to three weeks. After all, it did not matter that he was actually Simon Grenville, and that his wife had died, and that he had been in Cornwall, doing nothing except attend his children, until a week ago. He had thirty-six hours to acquire something for Lafleur and his French masters, and he was already sweating because of it.

When he had gone out the other morning, he had worn a white wig and shabby clothing, to protect his identity. In France, as Jourdan, he had changed colorful wigs frequently, wearing white only for a formal occasion. Lafleur had undoubtedly given Marcel a description of Jourdan—that he was tall, lean and prone to colorful wigs. All that was fine, but he might have to go even further, as far as a disguise went. Being in London as Jourdan was inherently dangerous. Too many people could recognize him.

He considered his options carefully.

Amelia had caught him returning to the house, but she hadn't recognized him from a distance. He felt a terrible tension.

He had brought her into his household because his children needed her. And if he were truly honest with himself, it was also because he needed her.

His heart leaped. He needed to see her every single day and know that she was caring for his children, her heart filled with affection for them. The sight of her with the boys warmed him impossibly.

Of course, he needed her in other ways, too. He looked forward to having a moment alone with her after supper, so they could converse. And he would not even try to deny that his body raged around her. When she was in his arms, he was torn between an insane need to be with her and the oddest feelings of safety, as if she were the harbor he so desperately needed in a world of storm-tossed seas.

But he hadn't considered the problems her presence in his home would generate. She got up early and went to sleep late. She had caught him in an act of subterfuge after dawn, when most gentlewomen were asleep. He was going to have to sneak out before midnight to meet Marcel, in disguise, and he doubted she would be asleep by then. He must somehow make certain she did not see him.

Could he somehow find a way to preoccupy her with the children, even at that late hour? What if she believed one of the boys to be ill? Or could he formulate some other distraction? He knew he must not trust that she would be soundly asleep in her bed while he was trying to steal out of the house.

She was already suspicious of him. She had every reason to wonder at his odd behavior and his terrible nightmares. Unfortunately, she knew too much about Lucas's activities. She even knew that Paget had once been a spy.

His coach stopped and he sighed. Amelia must never find out the truth.

His footman opened the door. Bedford House was square and three stories tall, with three towers, the central one serving as the entry hall. Roses and ivy crept along the stone walls surrounding the property. A fountain was in the center of the circular drive. Simon smiled slightly and stepped down from the coach. Nothing appeared to have changed since he had last called, several years ago.

A moment later he was being escorted through the magnificent house to Paget's library. He passed rooms with gilded furniture and brocade draperies. Masterpieces adorned the walls. A red runner was underfoot.

Dominic was expecting him, and the Earl of Bedford stepped away from his desk as Simon was shown inside a vast, wood-paneled, book-lined room.

"I was surprised but pleased to receive your note, Simon." Paget smiled, extending his hand.

Simon took it, marveling at how well Paget appeared. Like Simon, he preferred to go without a wig, and his dark hair was pulled back. He wore a sapphire-blue velvet coat, pale breeches and white stockings, with lace frothing from his cuffs, gold glinting from his hands. Simon had seen him for a moment last summer, and he had been haggard in appearance. The war did that to a spy. Now he seemed well rested and very content. The shadows that had been in his eyes—shadows of doubt, tension and fear, which Simon recognized—were gone. His smile reached his eyes.

"We are never in town at the same time, and I thought it opportune to call and congratulate you on both your marriage and the birth of your daughter," Simon said.

Dominic Paget's smile faded. "And I am so sorry for your loss, Simon."

Simon shrugged. "It is a tragedy. Elizabeth did not deserve to die."

Dominic said, "That will be all, Gerard." When the butler bowed and left, closing both doors, he turned and poured two cognacs.

Simon accepted the drink. "Thank you."

"These days, life is so damned uncertain. How are your children managing?"

Simon took a sip of the cognac, which was French and excellent. He absorbed the reference to the war, not quite ready to go there. "The boys seem to be adapting

better than I expected." He hesitated. He did not wish
to discuss Elizabeth's daughter. "I have your wife's sister to thank for that."

Mildly, Dominic said, "I have had an earful from
Julianne."

"And my ears are burning," Simon said, wondering
if he flushed.

Dominic eyed him. "Shall we sit?"

Simon took a seat on the sofa, as did his host.

"Is it true that you pursued Amelia some ten years
ago with illicit intentions?"

"We were both very young, and very passionate. But I
do not believe I ever had illicit intentions, no matter what
Lady Paget thinks. My admiration for Amelia knew no
bounds then, and that remains true. And now, of course,
I am deeply in her debt."

"You do know that, when push comes to shove, I must
obey my wife?"

Simon had to smile. Paget was not the kind of man
to obey anyone, yet he seemed eager to allow his wife
to rule the roost. "So the countess has the final say?"

"Of course she does." Paget smiled. "When she is
pleased, I am pleased."

He was entirely besotted, and it was rather charming,
Simon thought. "So if I fail to behave as a proper employer, I will pay for my transgressions—and you will
be lined up with Lady Paget to collect that payment?"

"I will always take her side. And Amelia is my sister-
in-law. I cannot say I know her well, and frankly, once
upon a time, she did not like me very much. Of course,
I did have very illicit intentions toward Julianne when
I first met her. But that is history." He sighed, but he
smiled.

Simon was intrigued, but he said, "My intentions

were never illicit. My respect for Amelia is even greater than my admiration for her."

Dominic's smile vanished. "You sound smitten."

And Simon knew he flushed now. "My children need her. They adore her. She is genuinely fond of them. I could not manage without her. This is entirely about the children."

"I imagine you could not manage without her, either," Dominic said slowly. "Hmm, this is rather interesting, I think."

"What is interesting? That I have become dependent on my housekeeper? That is probably a trait common to most bachelors and widowers."

"No, that you have become dependent on the woman you once pursued, whom you admire and respect immensely. Amelia is rather attractive, with all that dark blond hair and those startling gray eyes, if one can get past those drab gowns she favors."

He refused to take the bait, and he said nothing.

"Oh, ho!" Dominic laughed, delighted. "You still think her attractive!"

Stiffly, he said, "She is obviously a handsome woman, but frankly, I do not think about it."

"Very well, I will pretend to believe you." Seriously, he said, "I meant what I said earlier. We are friends, and I will always have your back, but not if it goes against my family. I adore my wife and Amelia is a part of my family. Make certain you remember that. Make certain you treat her with the respect she deserves."

Simon took another sip of his cognac. "That is my intention, Paget. Will I have the opportunity to become reacquainted with Lady Paget before I leave?" He did want to say hello, and if possible get past any ancient animosity, but he also wanted to know if she was at home.

"Julianne has gone to call on Amelia, actually, with Nadine D'Archand, an old and dear family friend." He stretched out his long legs. "You seem in rather good spirits, Grenville. How are you really?"

The tension was instantaneous. To cover it up, Simon sipped his drink while recrossing his legs. It was always wise to stay as close to the truth as possible. "Being home is almost like being in a different world. Everything is the same…. Nothing is the same."

Paget was considering. "You are in an entirely different world. I remember the feeling well. It is a feeling of being trapped. You are damned no matter what you do."

Simon jerked. He had no desire to discuss the dilemma he was in. But how right Paget was! "I am thrilled to be with my boys now."

"For how long?"

Simon set his drink down. "I imagine I will have a month, maybe two."

Dominic was grim. "When I was trapped in Warlock's world, I did not have children and I did not have Julianne. At the time I was engaged to Nadine, but I thought her dead. I cannot imagine how you do it, Simon. How the hell do you return to France—to Paris, of all places, where the Terror reigns? How do you leave your family behind?"

Simon did not stand. "I had relatives in Lyons. Did you know that? My maternal grandfather was French. Almost the entire town was executed for its opposition to the Republic—including all of my relations. I know all about the retribution *le Comité* is capable of." But he felt sick.

He was most definitely trapped. It was a fact—a feeling—he lived with every single day of his life.

"Death is everywhere, and no one grieves more than

I do, because I am as much a Frenchman as I am an Englishman," Dominic said. "But it is worse now than it was last summer, before Robespierre took power, so much worse. God knows, I should not tell you what to do. But let me tell you this much, I have never been happier, Simon. I am deeply in love with both my wife and my daughter. I used to have terrible nightmares. It feels like a miracle to awaken in the morning, with a smile on my face, looking forward to the day!"

"I am happy for you," Simon said, suddenly yearning for even a semblance of what Paget had. But he was trapped between Lafleur and Warlock, which Paget did not know—which he could never know. "One of the reasons I begged Amelia to take up as my housekeeper was that I knew she would take care of the children in my absence, the way their mother would."

He nodded. "So you will not contemplate getting out of the goddamned game."

"Warlock would never let me out, and you know it." He spoke mildly.

"He actually has a heart. It may be buried beneath extra thick skin, but it is there, trust me," Dominic said.

Simon shrugged. He'd believe Warlock had compassion when he saw it himself. But even if that were true, he could not get out without compromising his sons' safety—not unless he were dead. "We need to win this war. If the French are defeated, the Republic falls and the revolution ends."

"Did you hear the latest news? The French crossed our lines and have taken Menin and Courtrai. We will surely invade Flanders now."

Simon made certain his expression did not change when he was surprised. He hadn't heard. Lafleur needed information before the invasion. "I imagine we may al-

ready be on the march. Have you heard any details about
the impending invasion?"

"I have heard some gossip. There is an argument
amongst the Allied command over leadership. I have
also heard that Coburg has mustered some sixty thousand men. I doubt the French can raise as many troops,"
Dominic said.

"Do not be too sure. Times have changed since the
conscription became law last August," Simon said
bluntly. "I heard it projected before I left Paris that the
army would total one million troops by this fall."

Dominic paled.

"Hopefully they will not even come close to that number, but I myself have seen how rabid the common man
has become. The army offers mobility now that no one
could dream of before. Privates quickly become ser-
geants. Cobblers become generals. I am afraid."

Dominic clasped his shoulder grimly. "Think about
getting out now, while you can. Your children need you,
Simon."

Simon almost laughed. His entire raison d'être was
his sons. But he would not tell his friend that. "I will
get out when I can, but that time is not now." He looked
Paget in the eye. "I need something, Dom, something
that could save my life if I am ever uncovered after
I return to France." He realized he was sweating. He
doubted Paget had anything that valuable to impart, or
that he would give up such information if he had it, but
it was worth a try.

"I may have something for you," Dominic said
thoughtfully.

Hope flooding him, Simon just looked at him.

"There is a mole in the War Office."

Simon almost choked.

"Warlock knows. The mole is working closely with Windham. In fact, Warlock even knows who it is, and he has known for some time. He is being kept in place, and being carefully used against the French."

Simon was almost dazed. There was a French spy in the War Office.

He had just been given information that could save his life and those of his sons. If he ever told Lafleur that his man had been made, he would be trusted completely. But Warlock's clever game would be over.

He managed to speak. "I am not sure I should ask, but who is it?"

"I happen to know, because I helped uncover him. However, I believe that the fewer people who know the mole's identity, the better."

"You are right," Simon said, still shocked. But he had all the information he would ever need now—if he ever had to go so far as to betray his country. "Warlock is playing a dangerous game."

"Yes, he is, but no one is better at such subtlety and subterfuge."

"No one," Simon agreed. But he felt like he was lying, because just then he was the one up to his neck in deception and lies.

"AND FROM THAT MOMENT on, they lived happily ever after," Amelia said softly, her hands clasped in her lap. She had just told the boys an outrageously sensational but eventually happy story of a dark knight and his princess. The story had been filled with gypsies, thieves, sorcerers and even flying dragons.

William was hugging his knees to his chest as he sat in his bed. John was soundly asleep in the adjacent bed, a small smile on his handsome face. But it was past nine, and that was terribly late for a four-year-old child. "Did you make up that story, Miss Greystone?" William asked seriously.

Amelia approached and he scooted down under the blue covers. "I most certainly did," she said.

William yawned as she turned to pull the covers up high over John. "Prince Godfrey reminded me of Father."

Straightening, Amelia tensed. Her heart lurched. Simon had not joined them.

All day, it had been an act of sheer will not to think about last night. The kiss they shared had been haunting her throughout her duties. But so had her newfound comprehension that he was lonely. She felt certain she was right. Simon was lonely; he missed his family.

She wished that Simon had joined them for the telling of the tall tale she had just fabricated. But she had not been given an opportunity to ask him upstairs. In fact, there had been no casual conversation after supper at all, much less any sense of intimacy or any hint that he had ever thought about her in any way other than as his housekeeper. He had thanked her perfunctorily for the meal while arising. And then he had asked her if she was going to read to the children. She had replied that, yes, she intended to do so. He had nodded and left the dining room, abruptly ending the brief exchange.

She knew he would have enjoyed the past hour, no matter what had happened last night, but she also knew it was probably better this way.

She smiled at William now. "I suppose there were a few similarities between your father and the prince. After all, they are both very handsome men."

William started. "You think Father handsome?"

"Yes, I do. Now close your eyes and dream sweet dreams," Amelia said firmly.

But William surprised her by saying, "My mother did not think him handsome."

Amelia had just blown out one candle. She tensed. "I am sure she admired him, William," she managed to say.

"I don't know. She did not like him very much, and he did not like her." He was watchful.

Amelia felt her heart break. She returned to his bedside, and sat down on the edge of the mattress. "Sometimes, husbands and wives do not get along as well as they should. But sometimes they get along famously. It rather depends on the individuals, and their reasons for marrying in the first place."

"Did your parents like one another?" he asked.

She started. "The truth is, they did love one another, but my father had an obsession for gaming, William. He left us in the country, because he preferred the gaming halls of cities like Paris and Amsterdam. And in doing so, he hurt my mother terribly."

William nodded grimly. "Father leaves us all the time, but not to gamble. He has great estates in the north. One day, he has said he will take me with him when he goes."

Tears welled. "I know he cannot wait to take you with him." Impulsively, she kissed his cheek. "But you must be a bit older, I think. So in the meantime, you must excel at your lessons and make him proud." As she stood, she added, "But he is already terribly proud of you!"

William smiled at her. "I know."

Amelia smiled back and went around the bedroom to blow out every taper. But her temples throbbed. Simon should have been present for the boys' bedtime story. Tomorrow, she would make certain he joined them!

She paused to glance through the darkness at the

sleeping boys. Her heart surged with the affection she felt for them. Surely Simon was not risking his life out of some sense of patriotic duty, not when he had a great estate to run and William to groom as his heir.

She stepped out of the bedroom, leaving the door ajar. She went across the hall to the nursery, where Lucille was sleeping. She wanted to spend a few minutes with the infant, and then she would say good-night to her mother.

Mrs. Murdock was not present, and Amelia knew she had the habit of going down to the kitchens before bed to make tea with honey. Amelia sat in the chair that was stationed by the cradle.

Lucille was sleeping on her stomach, her thumb in her mouth. She was beautiful even in sleep, with her blond hair and plump cheeks. And her pink nightgown was adorable. Amelia stood and brushed her tiny back with her fingertips. The baby did not stir. How could Southland not come for her? How could Simon not take one look at her and fall madly in love?

Was Southland going to take her away?

Her heart lurched with dread. As far as she knew, he hadn't replied to Simon's letter. It had been three weeks. He could be traveling. Otherwise, it meant he intended to ignore the fact that he had sired a daughter.

Amelia wondered if she should suggest that Simon send a servant to Southland's London flat to find out if he was in town or not. She dreaded doing so, but Lucille belonged with her natural father, not Simon Grenville, and certainly not with her.

"I wish you were my daughter," she whispered, stroking the sleeping baby another time.

She knew she would be heartbroken when Southland came—if he came. And she knew she had to consider the possibility that he would not come. Simon had yet to acknowledge the baby. But if he held Lucille only once, he would surely begin to thaw toward her.

There was no time, she supposed, like the morrow.

Mrs. Murdock returned in her nightclothes, her gray hair sticking out of her nightcap like tiny wires. Amelia and the women exchanged whispered good-evenings. "Are the boys settled?" the governess asked.

"They are both soundly asleep. I will see you tomorrow." Amelia smiled and stepped out of the nursery.

Her gaze veered down the hall. The door to Simon's suite was at the end, not far from the stairs, and it was closed.

It was probably a quarter to ten by then. He surely remained in the library. In any case, she should swiftly cross the hall and go downstairs, before taking the east staircase to her bedroom. She should not wonder—or even care—where he was.

Amelia started down the corridor. But her pace did not increase as she approached his door—only her heart rate did. Instead, as if of their own volition, her steps slowed.

And she heard a movement from within his rooms, a thump of some sort, and her heart lurched wildly. He was in his apartments.

She hesitated, and then realized what she was doing— she was standing outside his door, straining to hear!

Just as she started forward, he cried out harshly.

The sound was rough, as if he had been hurt. Amelia seized the doorknob. "Grenville?"

"Damn you," he cried.

She froze, thinking he was cursing her. Sounding as if he choked on a sob, he cried, "Lafleur!"

He was dreaming. Amelia barged inside.

"Prêtez-moi!" he shouted.

He was speaking French!

She rushed through the suite. No lights were on in the sitting room. Directly ahead was the open door to his bedchamber. The king-size canopied bed was front and center. Of ebony wood, with red-and-gold hangings, it dominated the room. Several candles flickered from one bedside table and she saw Simon instantly.

He was on his back in the bed, asleep, one arm flung over his face. He had shed his coat, but was otherwise dressed. Clearly he had lain down for a moment.

He muttered something and thrashed out. Amelia hurried forward. She set her taper down and grasped his shoulder to shake him. "Simon."

And before the word was even out of her mouth he had seized her, thrown her down on the bed and had the barrel of a pistol grinding into her temple. His body covered hers.

Fear exploded as their gazes met. "Simon, it is I!"

His dark eyes were wide and burning with fury; his face was a mask of ruthless rage. *"Bâtard!"*

"Don't shoot," she gasped, terrified now. "Don't shoot! It is I—Amelia!"

And she saw the comprehension flood his gaze. "What the hell are you doing?" he demanded, and he shuddered, removing the gun from her temple.

She began to breathe, hard and fast, sweat pouring down her body. He was on his hands and knees above her. "I heard you crying out," she answered, gasping.

He sat up on the bed beside her, and set the gun in the drawer of the bedside table, which remained open. He had reacted so swiftly to her that she hadn't even seen him open it or seize the pistol. Amelia also sat up, and then she collapsed against the half-dozen pillows on his bed, trembling wildly.

Simon stared at her, as if torn between shock and revulsion. Their gazes locked.

He had drawn a gun on her. He slept with a pistol beside his bed.

She could not stop shaking. She could not look away from him. She was never going to forget the look she had just witnessed—the rage, the fury, the burning determination. If she had been a stranger, she would now be dead.

Oh, God.

But he was trembling, too. She saw that he was covered in perspiration. His lawn shirt clung to the hard planes and flat surface of his chest and torso. He was breathing hard, as if he had just been in a foot race.

"Are you all right?" he asked roughly.

She touched her temple, where he had jammed the pistol against it. Who had he thought her to be? "Is it loaded?"

He stared at her, not answering—which was answer enough.

She realized she was feeling ill. He slept with a loaded pistol by his bed; he was afraid of intruders in the middle of the night; he was afflicted with terrible nightmares.

If he was not involved in clandestine war activities, he was involved in something equally horrible.

"Did I hurt you?"

She flinched and met his dark, probing eyes. "Not very much."

He cursed. Then his regard moved from her eyes to her mouth and down her bodice to her waist. It instantly lifted. "Does...your head hurt?"

Amelia tensed impossibly—differently. She was in Simon's bed. "A little."

He stood up. "You shouldn't have come in here!" he exclaimed. "What the hell did you think you were doing? These are my private rooms!"

"You were having another nightmare. You sounded hurt!" she cried, shuddering. But she hugged herself. How did one get out of the middle of a king-size bed without looking like a coward—without evincing that she was afraid of being seduced? And then, how did she get past him?

He flushed. "We both know what happened the last time I had a dream and you dared to interfere."

She did not move from her position in the middle of his vast bed. She tried not to notice the way his shirt molded to his muscular chest and shoulders, how his breeches outlined his hard, powerful legs. Other than the candles that burned from the bedside table, the room was in darkness.

Amelia leaned forward, about to throw her legs over the side of the bed. His hand slammed down on the mattress by her hip, preventing her from moving. "You shouldn't have come in here."

She sank slowly back against the pillows. It was a moment before she spoke. "You were shouting in your sleep."

Still leaning toward her, his eyes blazed. "Was I?" Then his lashes lowered. She took a moment to notice the flush on his high cheekbones.

They lifted. A new light was smoldering there. "Did the boys enjoy the story?"

She ignored his question. "Who is Lafleur? You even spoke in French. What were you dreaming about?"

His expression never changed, although his mouth

curled slightly. "*La fleur* means the flower. I doubt you heard me speaking of flowers, Amelia."

"I think it was someone's name, like Danton."

His face hardened, but the slight curve of his lips never changed. He spoke very softly. And as he did, he leaned ever so slightly closer. "Damn it, Amelia, I hired you to take care of my children, not to pry." His gaze slithered over her bodice again.

She was wearing a drab gray gown with a rounded neckline and three-quarter sleeves. But she felt as if she were in an impossibly daring, low-cut evening dress, or worse, not wearing anything at all.

Amelia felt her cheeks flame. She knew she should get up and get out of that bed but she did not dare move. His arm and his body were in her way. "Were you dreaming about the war?"

For one moment, he stared, his gaze predatory. "Why would I dream about the war, when I don't give a damn what happens over there?"

"I am not sure I believe you," Amelia whispered, still hugging herself. Somewhere she heard Lucille crying.

"The infant is crying. Aren't you going to go help the nurse?"

"No. I am beginning to believe that you might care about the war after all. Simon, you can trust me."

He straightened, folding his arms across his chest. The gesture caused his biceps to bulge. An odd half smile formed on his face, but it was mirthless. His expression had a ruthless quality to it. "I think you should go tend the child. I do not care for this interrogation."

She tensed. "I would never interrogate you! But Julianne told me that Georges Danton was recently executed in Paris."

Surprise covered his face.

She had caught him, because it was a second before he rearranged his expression into passivity and indifference. And that told her he knew all about Danton's execution; he just hadn't expected her to know about it or even mention it.

"I don't know what you are talking about."

He was lying. "I think you know very well what I am talking of. I heard you crying out for Danton, just as I heard you cry out for another Frenchman named Lafleur!" She inhaled, praying for calm, because there was no mistaking the anger filling his eyes. "I want to help."

Fury turned his gaze black. He leaned over her again, one hand on each side of her hip. "You know how you can help. I believe I made myself very clear last time. You entered these premises—my private rooms—at your own risk."

She was trapped between him and the pillows piled against the headboard of the bed. His face was so close that she felt his warm breath on her skin. "You are changing the subject."

He slowly smiled, some of the fury in his eyes fading. "Am I? Because the only subject I am cognizant of is that there is a lovely woman in my room." His smile vanished. "Amelia, you are in my bed."

His tone had become soft and seductive. Her heart leaped exultantly. "I know," she began helplessly. "I am not sure how to get past you."

He put his knee on the bed, as if to press her down and cover her body with his. "I am not sure I would let you flee, even if you wanted to," he murmured. "And I think you do not want to flee. You could have done so at any time."

Amelia bit her lip hard, because he was right. But even as their gazes locked, even as she knew he was going to kiss her, the same questions that had afflicted her last night arose. Could she really give him her body when she wanted to give him her love? What about her morals? What about the children? And what about her own future?

She freed her arm, which had been trapped between them, and cupped his jaw. "Will you ever let me help you? Will you ever tell me the truth?"

He closed his eyes and sighed. A shudder went through him as he turned his head and kissed the center of her palm, hard. She also shuddered, incipient waves of pleasure washing through her. "I don't remember.... I don't care. I only care about this, that you are here with me now." He kissed her palm again before placing it on his collarbone, beneath his wet shirt. His skin was damp and hot, but not as hot as his eyes, which were searing.

She slid her hand lower, over the slab of one chest muscle, his nipple instantly hard and taut beneath her hand. And she recalled touching him everywhere, in the shameless throes of passion, ten years ago. His other knee came down on the bed and he straddled her. Simon bent, eyes closing, and he feathered his mouth over her jaw.

She sighed. "Do you always sleep with a loaded pistol by your bed?"

He lifted his head and looked at her. "It is an old habit, Amelia. Some habits die hard."

She reached for his face again. "Some old habits never die."

His eyes blazed and he claimed her mouth with his.

Amelia cried out as his mouth opened hers, settling his body on hers. She wrapped him in her arms, kissing him back urgently. But even as she kissed him and he kissed her, she kept thinking, this was an affair, not a marriage. What would happen to the children when it ended?

What would happen to her?

He lifted his face, breaking the kiss, and cupped her face in his hands. "What is it?"

She opened her mouth and then stopped herself from blurting out her feelings, *I love you.* Instead she managed to say, "I want you, Simon, very much. I care about you, very much."

His gaze roamed hers, his face anguished. "But it is not to be. It is not right. The children come first. And you deserve more than a few hours in my bed."

She nodded and she felt tears moistening her eyes. God, she deserved more and she wanted more…. Why didn't he offer her more?

He suddenly kissed her again, fiercely. Then he leaped up from the bed. "Lucille is still crying. Please attend her, Amelia." His back was to her.

For one moment, Amelia didn't move. Why did this feel like a terrible ending? She did not want anything to end, she wanted everything to begin!

"Amelia," he snapped.

She somehow scrambled from the bed and hurried from the room. He was right—Lucille was wailing. She must be colicky, she thought. And her worry for the infant finally pushed her need for Grenville back where it belonged, into the recesses of her heart and mind. Amelia rushed to Mrs. Murdock's door and knocked. She was told to immediately enter.

"Oh, this is the worst case of colic that she has had," the governess wailed.

"It will pass," Amelia said, aware that Mrs. Murdock was staring at her disheveled hair and flushed cheeks. She took the baby from her and began to pace the room, while rocking her and singing to her. She glanced at the governess, wondering if the secret she and Grenville shared was out.

It took some time, but eventually, Lucille quieted and fell asleep.

Amelia held her closely, thinking about Simon. What was she going to do? He was in danger—and she was dangerously in love.

And then she looked up.

Simon stood on the threshold of the nursery, clad in a simple caftan now. And he was staring at her and the baby.

Lucille had fallen asleep. It didn't matter. Amelia approached. "Do you want to hold her?" she asked, praying he would accept.

But he shook his head. His gaze hooded and dark, impossible to read, he bowed his head and left.

Amelia held the baby and watched him go.

CHAPTER ELEVEN

LLOYD HAD JUST INFORMED HER that she had a caller. It was Lucas.

Amelia hesitated, and not because she knew that they would have an argument over her position in Simon's household. She was the housekeeper. Where on earth would they converse?

"Miss Greystone, his lordship is out for the afternoon."

She smiled at Simon's butler. "Are you suggesting I entertain my brother in one of his rooms?"

"You were the mistress of Greystone Manor until recently. Had Lady Grenville not passed, you would not have taken up the position that you have. If you wish to entertain Mr. Greystone, I would suggest you use the pink room. It is rarely used and I do not think his lordship would mind." He gave her a significant look.

Her heart thrummed. She was fairly certain that Mrs. Murdock suspected that she had been in Simon's arms last night. Had the governess already spread such a rumor? What else could that look have meant?

Her cheeks heating, she debated having Lucas come to visit her in the kitchens, where she and Lloyd were discussing the matter of his visit. But that might only serve to inflame her brother. And he would be right to object to her employment, she thought, because last night she had almost succumbed to temptation.

"Very well." She removed her apron. "But I am not going to entertain him, Lloyd. It is not my place to do so. We will not need any refreshments. I am sure this call will be short." When she saw that he was poised to object, she patted his shoulder. "My brother is a busy man and I am a busy housekeeper."

Amelia left the kitchens, her stride brisk. She knew exactly how the conversation was going to go, and she knew she was going to have to proceed with the utmost caution. She did not want Lucas to suspect that she had fallen in love with Simon—if she had ever stopped loving him—or that their passions were running rampant. If he ever guessed the truth, he would remove her from Lambert Hall, no matter how she objected.

She smiled widely as she entered the foyer, although that felt entirely artificial. Lucas was impatiently waiting, studying the various oils on the walls. He turned as she appeared on the hall's threshold.

Lucas was as dashing as ever, even plainly dressed. He wore a simple and unadorned dark brown coat with a black-velvet collar and cuffs, a gold vest beneath it. His golden hair was drawn into a queue. But he was tall and handsome, his presence powerful and commanding. In spite of the dilemma she was in, she loved him. He would always be the brother she could count upon.

He did not smile back at her. Bicorne hat in hand, he strode to her. "Hello, Amelia. Imagine my surprise when I received your letter upon arriving at Cavendish Square last night." His gray eyes flashed with ire.

She looped her arm in his firmly, and planted an equally firm kiss on his cheek. "I am thrilled that you are back in town. I have missed you." She started to lead him into the west wing.

"Do not even attempt to manipulate me! You are Grenville's housekeeper?" He was incredulous.

He knew her far too well, she thought nervously, somehow maintaining a smile. "When I realized how his children needed me, there was no possible way I could refuse. And the boys are doing so well, Lucas."

He studied her grimly as Amelia led him into the small salon with pale pink walls, white ceilings and gilded trim. She released him to shut the door behind them.

"Are you in one piece?" he demanded.

She whirled, her heart slamming, but she spoke mildly. "What does that mean?"

"It means that I have not forgotten that, ten years ago, he flirted with you outrageously. It means I have not forgotten that you were madly in love." His stare was unwavering. "It was one thing to help with his children after the funeral, Amelia, but this is out of all bounds."

She noticed that he had circles under his eyes. "That was ten years ago. I was sixteen years old, Lucas. Now I am a grown and intelligent woman. You know that I am a woman of compassion. His children are doing so much better now and I am happy to take some credit for that."

"And how is Grenville doing?" he asked pointedly.

She prayed she did not flush. "He remains afflicted by his loss." She paused, suddenly wanting to ask Lucas what he thought about Simon's odd behavior. But then he would suspect even more than he did now! She quickly decided to change the subject. "When did you get back? While your shoes are hardly dusty, you seem tired."

"I got back in the middle of the night, Amelia. I haven't slept in days, frankly, and I could not sleep after I read your letter," he said tersely.

She forgot about defending her position to him. "Were

you where I think you were?" Had he been in France, helping unfortunate families emigrate?

His gray gaze narrowed. "I was at the mine."

They both knew that was a lie. "Lucas!" She rushed to him and took his hands in hers. "I have seen Julianne. She has told me how horrible it is in France now. It isn't safe for you to set foot on the soil there. If you are ever caught, you will be put in prison, with little hope of ever getting out!"

"If I am caught, I will be sent directly to *le Razor*." He was blunt.

She cried out. "I am begging you—I know you are a man of honor and a patriot, but please give up your wartime activities!"

He took her shoulders. "Do not ask the impossible of me, Amelia. And do not change the topic! It is you I am worried about. I saw the way you and Grenville looked at one another before the funeral."

She froze. "I beg your pardon?"

"He could not look away from you—nor could you look away from him!" Lucas cried.

And now, Amelia knew she flushed. "I think you are mistaken," she said.

He gave her a disbelieving look. "How did he convince you to become employed by him? Or should I guess? Once a rake, always a rake!"

She slipped free of his grasp. "If you are suggesting that he made advances in order to gain my employment, you are wrong." She was actually telling the truth, still, she felt as if she were lying. "Grenville is not a rake! You probably do not know that after the funeral, I went to St. Just Hall to help with the children. He was in a ghastly state, Lucas. He was locked in his rooms, instead of caring for his sons. The children needed me desperately then, just as they need me now."

"Why? Is he still locked in his rooms?"

She tensed. Lucas was rarely angry, and never mocking. "That is hardly fair."

"Falling for him another time will be unfair, Amelia. He is grieving for his wife," he warned.

She knew better than to tell him otherwise. And she would ignore his first barb. "There is more. The infant isn't his daughter. When he asked me to manage his household, he confirmed the gossip I had heard. Lucille was fathered by Thomas Southland. Oh, Lucas!" She went to him and took his hand. "He won't even look at her, and we don't know if Southland will ever come for her. That little girl needs me, as well!"

He sighed and put his arm around her. "I have heard the gossip, but I dismissed it." His stare was searching. "So you are comforting the children—and while caring for them, you have become far too attached, haven't you?"

"I love those boys," she whispered. "I love Lucille. Of course I do."

"And Grenville? Who is comforting him?"

She flushed again. "I will confess, I am also concerned about his welfare, and I am happy to offer him some small comfort, too, if I can."

"Amelia, we are close. I only have to look at you to know that you remain infatuated with him."

She choked. How would she deny it?

"Is he treating you with respect?" he demanded fiercely.

And finally, she could be entirely truthful with him. "He is being very respectful, Lucas."

His eyes widened. He finally said, "I believe you."

"Good." She somehow smiled. It was shaky. "We are being very careful not to let the past affect the present. We are trying very hard to maintain the roles we have taken as housekeeper and employer."

His gaze narrowed. "Does that mean you have discussed your past affair?"

She did not want to lie. "Of course we have. I never said that this situation isn't somewhat awkward. But his children come first—we are agreed upon that."

He sighed. "You sound so controlled, Amelia, and so sensible—which is what I would expect of you in any other circumstance. I actually like Grenville. I respect him. But right now, my instinct tells me not to trust him—not where you are concerned."

Would she ever stop blushing? How could Lucas be so astute?

He grimaced. "And the worst part is that I know you so well. You may be a grown woman, inordinately sensible most of the time, but I also know that you remain as naive as you once were. And no one is as loyal. Compassion can be misleading. Can you look me in the eye and tell me that you have no genuine feelings for him? That you are merely his housekeeper?"

She wrung her hands. She finally said, "Of course I still care, Lucas. I am not a shallow woman, to give her heart away briefly and then to selfishly take it back."

"Then I am afraid for you."

"Don't be. I am a strong woman and I am not a fool. I took up this position to help his children."

"But you are also helping him."

She met his gaze and nodded. "Yes. But before you berate me another time, have you forgotten how moral I am?"

He hesitated and she suddenly knew he was thinking

about how she had forgotten her morals ten years ago. "I know you would never deliberately act in any way that is dishonest or immoral. But you are in an unenviable position, Amelia. It must be impossible to forget the past you shared, being around him all of the time. I am afraid you might secretly dream of a future you cannot have."

She shook her head, but a terrible pang went through her. "I harbor no illusions." Even as she spoke, she recalled his kiss last night, and wondering why he did not offer her far more than an affair.

"Good." He pulled up an ottoman and sat down. "But I continue to have reservations about your being here."

"I can't leave those boys or that little girl." She sat down in a gilded chair.

"Or him?" His gray gaze was searching. When she decided not to answer, he said, "And what if Southland comes?"

"If Southland comes, I will try to be happy for Lucille, because she belongs with her natural father, but it will break my heart."

He took her hand and clasped it. "I probably should not give you my opinion, but I do not think Southland will come."

She started, hopeful. "You know him?"

"I ran into him at a weekend party in the north, about a year ago. He is a bachelor and a rogue. Of course, that was some time past, so maybe he has changed." He shrugged, clearly not believing that.

She was so relieved.

"Amelia, you need children of your own."

His declaration jerked her attention back to him. Simon had said the very same thing. "You may be right," she said, very carefully, "but I am nearly middle-aged. And I have a reputation, Lucas, as a committed spinster."

"If you give me permission, I will work on finding you a serious match."

She froze, and all she could think of was Simon. Suddenly, almost every memory she had raced wildly through her mind.

"Amelia?"

She somehow forced Simon's dark image away. Should she try to find a suitor? Oh, the position she was in was so untenable. She would love to have children of her own. But Simon and his children needed her. "I will have to think about it." Partly to change the subject, but mostly out of concern, she said, "Have you seen Jack recently?"

The last time she had seen Jack had been in February, when he had appeared briefly at the manor, lingering only for two days. He had not given her any explanations; as a smuggler, he was always at sea, on the run or in hiding. She had encouraged him to go to London to see Julianne, who had recently eloped. He had said he would do his best. But Julianne had seen him exactly once, in early March. He hadn't seen his newborn niece yet.

Lucas looked away. "Yes, I have. I saw him a few weeks ago."

"I am becoming worried about him." She lowered her voice. "Is he still running the blockade?"

"From time to time, when it suits him." Lucas did not seem very pleased.

"He never comes home. He hasn't seen Jaquelyn yet. That is not like Jack. As reckless as he is, as much as he loves the sea—" and he loved the challenge of outwitting the British navy even more "— he is a family man, in his own way. He adores Julianne."

"Like you, Jack is in one piece. If he is lucky, he will

survive the war. I think the less you know, the better," Lucas said. "Why don't we leave it at the fact that he remains a free man?"

"You should stop him from running the blockade."

"I've tried. You know our brother. He thrives on danger and he thinks he is immortal."

"I miss him. I am hoping he will come to town. If he does, make certain he calls on me."

Lucas hesitated. He leaned close. "He won't come to town, Amelia. It's too dangerous." When she stared in confusion, he said reluctantly, "There is a bounty on his head."

It took her a moment to comprehend Lucas. She cried out. "The authorities have put out a warrant for his arrest?"

"It is even worse than that. There is a movement under way to suspend the writ of habeus corpus. If Pitt succeeds in getting such a suspension made into law and Jack is ever apprehended, he might never again see the light of day."

Amelia leaped to her feet. "Such a law will never pass! It is a basic freedom, Lucas, a basic right to know what you are being accused of. Such a suspension would mean that almost anyone could be thrown in prison, for any reason, without ever being charged!"

"Yes, that is exactly what would happen. And we would not be very different from France, then, would we?" He also stood. "Except Jack is wanted for treason. That is a hanging offense."

She took his arm. "You are connected. Warlock is connected. Why can't you have the bounty removed?" If Jack were caught, he could hang!

"Warlock has said he would help Jack—but only if Jack helps him."

"What does that mean?" she cried.

"It means our uncle can be heartless. It means he wants Jack in his command."

Amelia paced. Could Warlock be so despicable? Jack was his nephew! "Is Warlock holding something over you, too?"

Lucas approached. "No, Amelia. I am helping those poor souls flee France because I believe in real freedom, the kind that allows a man to speak out for or against his government, without fearing for his life—and those of his family."

She hugged him. "I am sorry I asked. I am so frightened for Jack and I am afraid for you, too." And as she held Lucas, she thought about Simon, whom she was even more frightened for. She looked up at him. "There is more. I am also worried about Grenville, but not because he has lost his wife."

He tensed visibly, setting her back, his expression hard. "What do you mean?"

"I am beginning to think that he is as involved in the war as you are!"

Lucas's expression never changed—which surprised her. "Grenville, an agent of some kind?" He was incredulous. "Why would you think such a thing?"

"He has nightmares, Lucas, in which he speaks French and screams about blood and death. He keeps a loaded pistol in his desk downstairs, and another one beside his bed. One night a shutter came loose. He ran to the door, holding a gun, as if he expected to confront French soldiers!" she cried. "Last night I was telling the boys a bedtime story. I heard him shouting in his rooms. I thought he was in trouble and when I went inside, he pointed a gun at me!"

Lucas took her arm, his grasp firm. "I cannot believe

you would barge into his rooms. Clearly, you were not hurt!"

"What do you think?" she demanded.

"I think he is an odd beast, period. Everyone knows he is a recluse who prefers the barren northern reaches of this country to town. I have even heard gossip that he is somewhat unhinged. Perhaps he is losing his mind with grief?"

She stared, in disbelief. Why would Lucas suggest such a thing?

"Or perhaps he is being blackmailed, or some such thing." He shrugged. "But I have never heard Grenville utter a political opinion. I doubt he is any more a patriot than the livery boy down the street."

Amelia slowly shook her head. "Why are you trying to tell me that he is some melancholy madman? I heard him cry out for someone named Danton. Julianne told me about Georges Danton and his execution. I am beginning to think Simon was in France, and that he knew Danton—that they were friends!"

"That is an incredible leap to make!" Lucas exclaimed. "If you want to comfort Grenville, Amelia, that is one thing. He is surely grieving for his wife. But to come to such wild conclusions, that is another. Leave well enough alone." He suddenly looked past her.

Amelia felt her nape tingle and she slowly turned.

Simon stood in the doorway, smiling politely at them. She did not know how long he had been standing there.

"Good day, Greystone. I was wondering when you would call," he said calmly.

"Grenville." Lucas bowed his head, and then he gave Amelia a warning glance. No look could have been clearer: she was wrong. She was not to believe what she was thinking, and that was that. She was taken aback.

Simon sauntered into the room. "Would you care for a glass of wine? I believe it is about that time," he said. He turned blandly to Amelia. "Miss Greystone? Please have Lloyd bring a bottle of my best claret."

Amelia looked back and forth between both men, almost fearing a battle. But she realized that no battle was going to occur. Simon wasn't exactly looking at Lucas— and Lucas wasn't glancing at him directly, either.

"I have come to inquire after my sister," Lucas said.

"Yes, I imagined you would do so."

Amelia backed out, stunned.

Lucas and Simon knew one another—far better than they had ever let on.

WHEN AMELIA HAD LEFT, Simon went to the door and opened it, to make certain she was not eavesdropping. But she was gone. Grimly, he closed the door and turned to face Lucas. Greystone stared coldly at him in return.

Simon recalled the last time he had had a conversation with him. They had shared a drink last summer, when he had briefly been in the country. Then, they had spoken only of events in France, and how it impacted Britain. In fact, he felt almost certain that they had never had a personal exchange in the three years or so that they had been secret allies in the war effort and under Warlock's command.

"She is going to uncover you," Lucas said.

"I heard. She has been regaling you with stories of my odd behavior." He meant to be indifferent and he shrugged. But Amelia was the most determined woman he knew, and he was becoming afraid that she was not going to give up the tack she was on. His behavior wasn't helping. He cringed whenever he recalled pointing a gun at her temple last night.

"She is suspicious."

"Yes, she is," Simon said as mildly. He wasn't surprised that Greystone had called on his sister. He had expected such a call, sooner or later, just as he had expected Greystone to object to Amelia being his housekeeper. "Your sister is rather inquisitive and she is very clever."

Lucas strode to him. "You have lost all common sense, to bring her into your household. But frankly, Grenville, right now I do not care if she discovers what you are up to. I care that you have put her in danger by bringing her into your home." His gray eyes blazed.

Simon remained outwardly calm. But Lucas had just voiced his own fears. "How so?"

"How so?" he exploded. "Last summer, the radicals here in town tried to use Amelia against Julianne," Simon started. Lucas continued fiercely. "Julianne was asked to spy for the Jacobins. When she refused, Amelia and our mother were threatened. That is why Garrett remains with them at all times!"

"I did not know," Simon said slowly. But he felt himself flush. Hadn't he known all along that it was better to stay away from Amelia, and that to bring her close could only put her in jeopardy? Lucas would be even more agitated if he knew just how much danger Simon was placing her in. But he said, "You should calm down. I asked her to take this position for the sake of my children. My enemies can't possibly know that we have any relationship outside that of employer and housekeeper. They cannot know that they could use her against me if they wished."

Lucas flushed. "Ah, yes, now we get to the reason I am livid. What exactly is your relationship if not that of housekeeper and employer?"

"She is my neighbor, and we are friends."

"Funny—Amelia never once mentioned that you are friends! Haven't you forgotten the most relevant point?" Lucas mocked.

He was taken aback, but he did not let his surprise show. But Lucas had been just as protective of Amelia ten years ago, when he had forbidden Simon from calling on her. And maybe it was time to be rather candid with Amelia's brother now. "Greystone, we have never discussed what happened a decade ago."

"No, we haven't. When Warlock introduced us a few years back, there was no point. So many years had passed that discussing the past seemed irrelevant and inflammatory. The war was my sole focus, but, then, I did not know your wife would die and you would reel Amelia back into your life."

"You are making it sound as if my intentions are dishonorable. They are not."

"Amelia is an innocent, in spite of her age," Lucas flashed. "She will always give everyone the benefit of the doubt—even you. To make matters worse, you have lost your wife and you are grieving. She feels sorry for you, never mind your callous disregard for her feelings ten years ago! And I know you will use that to your advantage. I am warning you—lay one hand on her, and I will be the one to bring you down."

Simon tensed. "You are a patriot. You would never betray me to my enemies."

"Really? Touch her and you will find that I am your worst enemy."

And Simon realized that he meant it. "I brought Amelia into my home to take care of my children—not to abuse her. I have regrets, Lucas. I am sorry I pursued Amelia as I did, ten years ago." He would not tell him that he could not regret the time they had spent together. "But even then, I respected Amelia far too much to take advantage of her. I certainly respect her too much now." But as he spoke, his heart drummed. Last night, he had been a heartbeat away from making love to her. He had been recalling having her in his bed, beneath his body, ever since.

Lucas snarled, "You broke her heart."

His tension spiraled. "As I said, I have regrets. Amelia and I have discussed the past and agreed to put it behind us. I am very concerned for my children, Greystone. I did not ask her to take this position impulsively. I thought about it at great length. With Lady Grenville gone, I needed someone I could trust to care for my children, both when I am in the country and when I am not. And if one day I do not return, at least I will die knowing that Amelia is here, doing what is in my children's best interests."

"That was a pretty speech," Lucas said. "Since when is a man of your stature 'friends' with his housekeeper? And since when can a pair of lovers ignore the history they shared?"

Lucas would be furious if he knew that they had not been able to put the past behind them, not at all. "It is an unusual arrangement," Simon said. "Can you at least admit that she is wonderful with children, and that my children sorely need her? That I am right to trust their futures with her?"

"She needs children of her own," Lucas said flatly. "And I am going to begin looking for a husband for her immediately."

Simon was shocked and then dismayed. Greystone thought to find her a husband?

"Oh, I see that does not sit well with you!"

"No." He managed a smile. "I happen to agree with you, Greystone. She deserves a family of her own." But all he could think of was his children. What about William and John? What about Lucille?

And how would he manage, without her?

"Really?" Lucas approached. "I want your word, Grenville, that you will not touch her. I want your word that you will keep her safe."

Simon realized he hesitated. In that moment, all he could think of was how it had felt to have Amelia in his arms last night. All he could remember was the terrible, maddening urgency, the utter desperation he had felt. In her arms, there was no war, and death did not shadow him.

"You cannot give me your oath?" Lucas gasped.

He flushed. "My intentions are honorable." And he knew he must not let another moment of insane passion overwhelm them. Amelia deserved more than he could ever give her. "So, yes, I am giving you my word. I will treat Amelia with the respect she deserves." But even as he spoke, he trembled, because somewhere deep inside, he hated making such an oath. But his next promise came from his very soul. "I will keep her safe, Greystone. I swear. I would die to keep her safe."

"Good." Lucas turned as a knock sounded on the door and Lloyd appeared with the bar cart. Amelia stood behind him, pale, her eyes wide and bright. She looked back and forth between both men.

"I'm afraid I am not staying," Lucas said. "Enjoy your claret, Grenville. Amelia, walk me out."

She inhaled. "I see no blood has been drawn. I am grateful for that." She glanced worriedly at Simon.

"I have no intention of fighting with your brother,"

Simon said tersely. Softening his tone, he said, "Why
don't you see him out."

Giving him a last worried glance, Amelia turned.
Simon watched Amelia and her brother leave. Then he
poured a glass of wine and downed it. His first oath felt
like a lie. His second one felt like a premonition.

THE SALON DOOR LOCKED, Simon faced himself in the
Venetian mirror that was hanging over a small, marble
table with gilded legs. It was almost midnight. He continued buttoning up the black-velvet coat he had just put
on, staring at his pale reflection. He had whitened his
skin with asbestos, a chalklike product favored by many
noblewomen, and he had lightly rouged his lips. He was
also wearing a bright reddish-gold wig.

He looked very outlandish, rather effeminate, and not
at all like the Earl of St. Just. He was fairly certain that
his disguise would pass muster, at least at first glance.

As for getting out of his home without discovery,
Amelia was upstairs, keeping sentinel on the boys. He
had claimed that he believed John had had a fever earlier in the evening. She had told him he was imagining
it, but he had insisted that he thought his younger son
was becoming ill. He had told her that it would put his
mind at peace if she would stay with the boys for a while
that night, just to make certain John was not becoming
sick. When she had seemed doubtful, he had told her
he would read in the library—and he had promised to
stay out of her way.

He finished buttoning up the black coat and he smiled
grimly at his eccentric reflection. Amelia would not
leave John's side, he was certain, for several more hours,
allowing him to escape the house in disguise and unde-

tected. When he returned, he would leave his disguise in the stables.

The plan was not perfect, but it would do.

Satisfied, he glanced at the bronze clock on the mantle of the fireplace. He was going to be late. He was supposed to meet Marcel at midnight, and he would not be there in ten minutes. But that was the point. He had no intention of being the first to arrive at the tavern.

Simon snuffed out the three candles that had been burning, and slipped out of the library and into the dark hallway. He did not carry a taper, and he had made certain to extinguish all the lights when he had gone in earlier.

A horse was saddled and waiting for him in the stables, the groom sworn to secrecy.

Simon strode down the hall. The entry was also unlit, but he had no intention of going out the front door. He would exit through the terrace doors of the ballroom, as he had done a few days ago at dawn. The stables could also be reached from the gardens outside.

But he had to cross the entry hall, and he did so swiftly and soundlessly. He had just entered the west wing when he felt the hairs on his nape prickle.

And he felt someone else's presence.

Simon turned slightly, searching the darkness of the entry hall and froze. Amelia stood at the opposite end, a tray in her hands, with a single taper set on it.

He could see her perfectly, as he was in the shadows and she was illuminated, but she could not see him— not yet.

"Who is it?" she gasped, setting the tray down abruptly and lifting the taper high.

What was she doing downstairs? He turned to go, but just before he did, their eyes met.

She cried out. Ducking his head, he ran down the hallway, but he did not hear her following. Simon rushed outside in disbelief. Amelia had not only seen him, he was certain that she had recognized him!

As he strode across the gardens, he looked back at the house. The ballroom remained in blackness. When he did not see the light of a single candle appear, some small relief began. She wasn't following him.

Maybe, just maybe, she thought him an intruder. He cursed as he reached the stables. He was going to have to invent a plausible excuse for leaving at midnight in disguise, in case she had recognized him.

The groom rushed forward with his horse, pretending not to notice his absurd and effeminate ensemble. Simon thanked him and leaped astride. Then he trotted swiftly from the stable yard. As he entered the drive in front of the house, he saw a light burning in one window by the front door. He had not a doubt that Amelia stood there, watching him. He cursed again.

She was so damned nosy!

He spurred the gelding he was riding into a canter and loped down the drive. She was also impossibly brave. Damn it!

London was mostly in blackness as he left Lambert Hall behind. The great houses lining the square were cast in shadow. As he hurried through Mayfair, finally leaving the stately mansions and townhomes behind, he debated the stories he could tell her. The groom had wondered if he was going on the town to pursue boys, he was certain, but Amelia would never believe that. He supposed he could tell her he had gone out to meet a mistress. But he would still need an excuse for such an elaborate disguise.

She would be hurt, he knew, if he convinced her he had a lover. Simon cursed again.

Thirty minutes later, he reached the inn where he was meeting his contact. A moon had emerged from the clouds drifting across the night sky, along with a scattering of dull stars. A stable boy had come out of the inn's stables and he handed his gelding to the boy, giving him a shilling. The boy gaped at the handsome sum. Simon said, "Keep my mount out front. I may only be a moment or two, or I may be an hour."

"Yes, my lord," the boy said quickly.

"Where is the back entrance?"

The boy directed him around the side of the main building. "Right there, my lord, but it leads to the kitchens."

"Good lad." Simon gave him another shilling and strode swiftly toward the back door. He had no intention of going in the front, where Marcel would see him before he saw Marcel.

He forgot about Amelia now. He forgot about his sons. Now, it was only the dangerous game of meeting an adversary that could be the death of him if he did not outwit him at every twist and turn.

Pots were clattering and dishes clanking as he entered the kitchens, which were almost cleaned for the evening. No one did more than glance at him cursorily as he strode through. The hall outside was small, narrow and poorly lit. As he traversed it, he could hear the raucous sounds of the inebriated patrons in the public room.

He paused in the shadows of the hall on the threshold of the common room, scanning the crowd. Perhaps two-dozen men were present, with five or six barmaids and prostitutes. He did not bother to look at any of the women, and he dismissed all but four of the men.

But those four men present were gentlemen of some sort. He stared at a heavy, gray-haired man who was drinking rum or whiskey and pinching a voluptuous, barely clad barmaid. The man was clearly drunk. Simon dismissed him instantly.

Another gent, in a pale blue coat and a white wig, also seemed deeply in his cups. Simon glanced at the third gentleman, who was playing cards very intently with the fourth man. He studied them for some time, but both men were engrossed in the poker game they were playing and neither looked up even once.

He looked back at the heavyset, gray-haired man with the barmaid. He was most definitely drunk, to the point of falling over.

And Simon felt that he was being watched. He jerked his gaze back to the man in the white wig and the pale blue coat. The man was drinking his ale, but Simon was almost certain he had caught him staring.

He stepped back into the shadows, his gaze unwavering as the man turned his back mostly to him, to watch the gents playing poker. As he did so, he noticed the man's pale complexion and his hooked nose. Suddenly he froze, in shock.

Was that Edmund Duke?

Duke was Windham's clerk.

He inhaled, certain he was staring at Duke—who was every bit as disguised as he was.

Windham was the War Secretary. There was a mole in the War Office. Paget had said that the mole worked closely with Windham.

Could Duke be the mole? Was Duke Marcel?

Or was Duke one of Warlock's men? Had Warlock sent Duke to spy on him?

Simon did not know. But he turned and rushed down

the hall and through the kitchens and outside. "Boy! Bring my horse!" he shouted.

And a second later, he was galloping away, covered in sweat.

CHAPTER TWELVE

AMELIA WAS AS STILL as a statue. She wasn't sure when she had crept into his rooms, but it had been shortly after he had left the house. In disguise. She did not think she had done more than breathe ever since.

And her mind had not stopped racing, not even for a moment.

She shivered, hugging the wool throw to her body. Why had Simon left the house in such an elaborate disguise? My God, she had barely recognized him!

The chair she sat in faced the front door of his apartments—the door he must eventually enter. A fire blazed in the hearth to her left, but otherwise the sitting room—and his bedchamber—were in darkness. But there was a gilded clock with a white face on the mantel. If she turned her head ever so slightly, she could make out the time.

It was just shy of half past one in the morning.

For the past hour, she had been replaying his behavior in her mind. She kept thinking about the fact that he was never in residence with his family, and that while he claimed to often be in the north, no one had ever really known where he was—not even Lady Grenville.

She was so afraid he was playing war games.

Hadn't Julianne told her that there were French spies in the city? Was Simon trying to enter those circles?

He was well-known—but tonight, no one would recognize him!

She prayed that there was another reason he had left the house as he had. She reminded herself that he seemed utterly indifferent to the war. If he was a part of Warlock's circle of spies, then he was a consummate actor—and it would explain so much. The nightmares, his references to death, his crying out for Georges Danton...

She felt tears rising in her eyes. Oh, why, Simon, why? She wanted to cry. He had changed so much, he was so dark and anguished, and he was afraid of something or someone. If he were spying for his country, and she would be a fool not to believe the most likely possibility, then he was most definitely in some danger.

They are coming for me.

She would never forgot that harsh, terrified declaration, made in the midst of a nightmare.

Amelia finally moved. Using her sleeve, she wiped her eyes. She was putting the cart before the horse. She supposed there was a slim chance he was in disguise for some other reason—that he was visiting a bawdy house or a gaming hall. As the Earl of St. Just, there might be unsavory places he wished to be, yet he wouldn't want to be recognized in them. But she doubted Simon would avail himself of a prostitute; she didn't think he gambled. And she had checked the drawer in his desk. The gun was gone. He had taken it with him.

Would he take a pistol with him to a gambling hall? She hardly thought so!

And she knew that John wasn't coming down with a cold. She had not thought he was sick, no matter Simon's insisting otherwise. Simon had set her up, obviously. His worries about his son had been a ruse to keep her upstairs and out of his way, so he could escape into the night.

She trembled with anger. But mostly, there was fear. How could he put the children in such jeopardy?

Last year, radicals had threatened to harm her and Momma if Julianne did not do as they wished. There was no honor amongst men, not in war. If Simon was dabbling in war and revolution, his children's lives were endangered. She couldn't imagine what he was doing, out at this hour, in such a disguise. But she intended to find out. She had every right to confront him when he returned. The children were her responsibility, too!

If he was simply gambling the night away, then he would have to be honest with her. And she knew he wasn't with another woman, not even a prostitute. He wouldn't do that to her....

Amelia realized her ankles were becoming numb. She tucked them under her. Soon she would go down to the library, just to make certain he was not back and hiding in his usual retreat. The one thing she would not do was sleep. But he had only been gone for an hour. She doubted he would be back for some time.

And then, to her surprise, she heard the floorboards in the hall creak. Amelia tensed, straining to see, staring at the closed door.

Simon could not be returning already, could he?

Now, she wished she had taken the gun he kept beside his bed. Her heart hammering, she became utterly still as she heard someone pause outside his sitting room. She heard the knob turn. The door creaked. It opened and a man stepped into the room.

Instantly, she recognized Simon.

He was not in disguise. His hair was loose, brushing his shoulders. The black coat was gone. There was no strawberry-blond wig, either, no white complexion. He closed the door and started across the parlor, not having seen her.

Amelia's heart thundered wildly. There was no relief; her tension had never been higher. "Simon."

He halted abruptly and turned toward her, his eyes wide in the dark.

"You haven't been gone for very long," she said. She doubted her legs would work, so she did not even try to get up. Breathing was difficult enough. Dread consumed her.

A long, terrible pause ensued. "I take it you are waiting up for me?"

How calm he sounded. Using the arms of the chair, Amelia somehow stood. Her ankles prickled. Her heart was pounding even harder now. "I did not expect you back so late—or should I say, so early."

He slowly smiled, but his gaze slipped suggestively down her body. "Amelia, do you think it wise to confront me in my rooms?"

"You are not frightening me. Or rather, I am already frightened, but I know you well. I realize that you think to unnerve me by looking at me that way."

"I think you should reconsider our having this discussion now," he returned as evenly.

"Where have you been, Simon? What happened to your wig?"

"You are behaving like a wife—not a housekeeper. I do not believe I have any intention of reporting to you." He was firm.

"I am worried about your children."

"My children have nothing to do with this."

"To the contrary, if they are in any danger, then I

must know!" Her tone rose. She heard how sharp it had become.

He slowly smiled again. "I go out for a drink, and you conclude that my children are in danger? Come, Amelia, are you using them now so you can spy upon me?"

She wanted to slap him. "Do not dare turn this around!" she cried. "I saw you go out and you also saw me. I saw your elaborate disguise. Where is that red wig, Simon? Where is the black coat?"

"Very well," he said harshly. "I went out tonight. I went to a gaming hall for a drink. I was in disguise, Amelia, because I did not feel like having a dozen of my peers about whom I don't give a damn pretending that they care about Lady Grenville's death!"

"I want to believe you," she cried, "but you took your pistol with you. I checked your desk!" She felt tears rising. It was an accusation.

"Highwaymen roam the streets of London at this late hour," he snapped. "I am not going to argue with you. I went out for a drink. I went out in disguise, but for the purpose I stated—and nothing more. Whatever you are thinking, I suggest you stop."

She finally marched over to him. She took her thumb and rubbed off a patch of white from his cheek, which he had clearly failed to remove. "Did you use asbestos? How clever!"

He seized her wrist. "Have you noticed that we are alone in my rooms and it is dark and late?"

Her pulse leaped. "What are you doing, Simon? Where have you been? Why did you leave this house in disguise? Why did you think to divert me with your insistence that John was ill? Are you some kind of spy?" Panic filled her breast.

His gaze locked with hers, darkening. "I am not reporting my every movement, Amelia, not to you, not to anyone, not now or ever. I suggest you accept what I have thus far said, before I become truly angry." He released her.

"When did you become close to Warlock? You did not even speak of him ten years ago! I recall that you told me you had Warlock look out for the boys while you were in the north. But were you in the north, really, Simon?" Tears fell.

"You need to leave my bedroom and go to your bed and forget this night ever happened." An edge had crept into his tone. But his gaze was unwavering upon her face.

"You rouged your lips—you looked like a fool! You would never go out that way—not unless you had to," she cried desperately.

He released her abruptly. "It is late. I am tired. You are tired. We should not be having this conversation now, and certainly not here." Giving her a dark look, he walked past her and into his bedchamber. "Good night."

He hadn't turned to look at her as he dismissed her. In more dismay, Amelia followed him partway to the threshold of his bedroom. Then she froze, because he had shrugged off his lawn shirt. His upper body was hard and lean, a mass of sculpted muscle.

Her heart slammed. Her mouth went dry. She loved him so—that was why she was so terrified. And she desired him. "I want to help," she whispered.

He glanced briefly at her. "If you keep standing there, we both know where you will wind up."

She realized she was staring at his bulging arms and hard chest. She jerked her gaze to his face. "You owe me an explanation. Not because we are friends. Not because we are employer and housekeeper. But because

I love your sons and Lucille, and it is my duty to keep
them safe. How can I keep them safe, Simon, if you are
in danger?"

"I am not in danger." He sat down on the velvet bench
at the end of the bed and removed one boot and then
another.

Amelia knew she should leave. He was disrobing,
and she thought he might go so far as to do so entirely
in front of her, in order to get her to flee. But she was
not going anywhere until he confessed the truth—and
he hadn't gone out for a drink, she was certain.

He pulled off one stocking, then another, and sat up,
facing her. His brows rose. "I am going to disrobe."

She could not swallow now. His chest was bare. So
were his calves and feet. How could she not recall their
encounter in his rooms at St. Just Hall, after the funeral?
"You would not go so far."

He stood, his gaze moving down her bodice. "You
are impossible, Amelia. And that is why I brought you
into my household. You are perhaps the most determined
woman I know."

She decided to ignore the muscles rippling in his arms
and rib cage, if she could. "Then you know I will not
give this up, Simon. I have every right to know what you
are doing in the middle of the night. Enough is enough.
Tonight you must confess. Your behavior has been too
odd—and you know it."

He reached out and tucked a tendril of hair behind
her ear. "As I said, impossible."

She refused to stop, even though her heart slammed.
"Do not think to seduce me. You have the children to
think of. If you are engaging in dangerous activities,
then by association they are in danger, too."

"I would never put my children wittingly in danger, Amelia." His tone was harder now.

"Then what are you doing? What can you be thinking?" she cried.

"I am thinking," he said slowly, "that I am mostly undressed, it is very late and there is nothing I would rather do than stop this conversation by taking you to my bed."

She trembled. "Simon!"

"Has it ever occurred to you that it is best if you do not know every detail of my life?" He reached out and slid his hand over her jaw, and then down her neck.

Desire fanned into huge flames. "Don't. This is too important. Were you in any danger tonight?"

Did he hesitate? "Not the kind of danger you are thinking of. The only danger is your being here with me." And he smiled, his gaze heavy.

"What does that mean? I know you are trying to cover up your activities, Simon! Are you being pursued? How can I take care of your children if I don't know what you are involved in?"

He rubbed his thumb over her neck, and then lower, toward her cleavage. "I fail to follow your logic, Amelia. How does my going out for a drink affect the welfare of my children?"

His touch was impossibly arousing. But Amelia did not attempt to pull away. "You have no intention of telling me what you were really doing tonight, do you? I am putting the children first, Simon, but you are putting yourself first."

His eyes flickered. "You are right. Just now, I am not thinking of the children, and just now, I am not putting their needs first."

Her heart slammed as he grasped her shoulders and leaned toward her. She wanted to tell him not to kiss her—this was too important. She had to learn the truth! But she had been waiting for this moment. She had been waiting for his kiss.

His grasp tightened and he smiled; then his mouth closed over hers.

Amelia closed her eyes, forgetting everything. And as his mouth moved over hers, again and again, with determination, with urgency, someone moaned. She realized it was herself.

Instinctively, she stepped closer. His shoulders were hot and bare beneath her hands. It was hard to think now. He wrapped his arms around her and too late she was in his embrace, acutely aware that he was shirtless. As the kiss deepened, she slid her hands over his chest.

Simon moaned, and she thrilled at the sound. Amelia finally kissed him back, hot and hard and passionately, her fingers sliding down his back.

He groaned and let her go, breathing hard and raggedly. "I swore to Lucas I would respect you!"

She shook her head, briefly incapable of speech. Her mind was spinning, her body on fire. How long could they go on this way?

"Amelia—you must leave." He was final.

Her mind began to function. She inhaled, shuddering from a wave of desire, but she did not start across the room. "Where did you go tonight, Simon?" she finally managed to ask. "Please."

His chest still rising and falling, he stepped even farther back. "Do you ever give up and quit? You do not want to know, Amelia."

She tensed, and not just at the warning note in his tone. Was he about to admit that he hadn't been out for a drink? "Last night you pointed a gun at me, Simon!

Tonight you went out armed, in a deliberate disguise. What should I think?" She hugged herself.

He stared for a long moment, his broad chest rising and falling. "You have leaped to all the wrong conclusions," he finally said. "Yes, I am afflicted with dark moods. Has it ever occurred to you that I never recovered from my brother's death?"

She stared closely, because she did not know what he would say next. She did not quite believe him.

"You already know I despised my wife. And everyone knows I am a recluse. Why do you wildly assume that I am some kind of patriot, as Bedford apparently was? I don't give a damn about our country, Amelia. I don't give a damn about the war." His eyes were dark and flashing. "Warlock is an acquaintance, not my master!"

"Then where were you?" she cried. "And don't tell me you were having a drink in that strange disguise!"

"I was with a woman."

She started. It took her a moment to even comprehend him. "That is absurd. You would never bother with a prostitute, and such an explanation does not account for your disguise." But even as she spoke, she could imagine a gentleman disguising himself in order to visit a bawdy house.

His brows lifted and he stared.

Amelia became uneasy. "Simon?"

He turned his back on her. He walked over to the armoire facing his bed and removed a caftan from it. It was navy blue, pin-striped, and embroidered with gold. "Did I say I was with a prostitute?"

He shut the door somewhat heavily, and it slammed. Simon faced her, his expression twisted. "I have never been with a prostitute."

He was lying, Amelia thought, oddly frantic. He had

not just had a tryst with a lover! But an image assailed
her of Simon in some lush woman's arms. She forced it
away. "I don't believe you."

"I had no intention of confessing. I am sorry if you
are hurt."

She could barely breathe. He could not be telling her
the truth, could he? Simon wanted her. They had a romantic connection. They shared a raging attraction. "If
you went to a lover, why bother with such a disguise?"

He hesitated. "Elizabeth is not yet cold in her grave,
Amelia. How would it look, if the ton knew I was rushing off to a mistress now?"

So he had a mistress? Was it even possible?

But wasn't this better than his being a spy?

"Hurting you is not my intention," he said firmly.

She heard herself whisper, "You want me."

"Yes, I do. But it is forbidden, is it not? We agreed that
an affair is out of the question. We agreed that the children come first—we agreed to be employer and housekeeper. So what am I to do?"

A terrible pain began. Simon had gone to another
woman? Was it possible?

Simon had a lover.

"I am sorry, Amelia. I am very sorry. Why were you
spying on me?" he cried. "Why couldn't you leave well
enough alone?"

She hugged herself, moisture gathering in her eyes.
She was beginning to feel ill. "I want to keep the children safe."

"My children need you. I need you. I need you here,
in this house, managing it and everyone within it as
only you can do!" His stare was intense and searching.

Amelia somehow shook her head. "I cannot believe
you would go to someone else."

His face hardened. "Nor can I.... Please go now."

His voice was thick, as if he had tears rising, too. Amelia hurried past him, suddenly imagining him in another woman's arms. And she realized that she was devastated.

He suddenly caught up to her from behind, taking her arm and halting her. "Amelia! I am sorry. My intention has never been to hurt you. You deserve so much more than I can ever give you!"

What did that even mean? She pulled away, shaking. Shouldn't she have expected this? He had broken her heart ten years ago, and if she allowed herself to think about what he was telling her now, surely her heart would break all over again.

"I care about you," he said roughly. "Very much. And I want you to know that."

"If you cared about me, we would not be having this conversation."

He did not speak. She stumbled as she turned to leave. But at the door she paused, clinging to it. How could this be happening?

"Do you hate me now?" he whispered.

Incapable of speaking, Amelia fled.

TEARS IN HER EYES, Amelia smiled at Lucille, who lay in a cradle in the kitchen, as the staff began cleaning the dishes left over from that morning's breakfast. Pots banged and pans clanged, the water ran and the boy, Fred, was whistling. It was a busy, happy morning. Her fat fists clenched, Lucille beamed back at Amelia.

"She thinks you are her mother," Jane said, walking by with a pile of dirty plates.

Amelia felt her heart lurch with anguish. She walked over to a kitchen window and opened it. Birdsong joined the cacophony in the kitchens. A sweet breeze entered, as well.

"Has his lordship heard from her father?" Mrs. Murdock asked, raising her voice over the din. The nurse was seated in a chair by the central table, knitting tiny socks for the baby. Jane scrubbed the wood top with soap and water.

"No, he has not," Amelia answered. She could hardly breathe. She hadn't slept at all last night; she had tossed and turned, fighting tears, in disbelief and in heartache. Simon had taken a mistress. A part of her simply did not believe it, even now! But he had confessed, he had insisted, and she had caught him in the act of sneaking in and out of his house. And his explanation made sense!

She knew she should be relieved that he wasn't a spy, but she was ill. He had broken her heart a second time. How foolish could she be?

"He must be traveling," Mrs. Murdock said. "Otherwise he would at least reply to the letter."

"She is so pretty, surely he will decide to claim her once he sees her," Jane said.

"Yes, I think he must be out of town," Amelia said. She knew how lackluster her tone was. She quickly smiled and went over to the stove. "Fred, I do not think I have ever seen as clean an oven."

The freckled lad smiled at her. "I can do more, Miss Greystone, or I can clean the fireplace."

"The stove is fine, and we have chimney sweeps for that." Amelia patted his red head.

"Is anything wrong, Miss Greystone?" Mrs. Murdock asked.

Amelia kept smiling and turned to face the nurse, who had stopped knitting and was regarding her expectantly. Aware of needing the baby for comfort, she went to Lucille. "I am fine," she said, fussing over the baby.

"You seem wan today," Mrs. Murdock said.

Amelia smiled at Lucille again. "I doubt I even know what wan means," she said as Lucille grabbed her finger and seized it.

But as she did, the kitchen suddenly became shockingly silent, except for the birdsong from outdoors. All conversation ceased.

Amelia tensed. She looked up and saw Simon on the threshold of the room.

She was shocked. As far as she knew, he had never once set foot in the kitchens.

But he had stepped inside now. He stood on the threshold, staring at her. When their eyes met, he nodded politely. Everyone else in the room was studiously pretending not to have seen him.

Amelia felt her heart drop. She turned to Lucille, adjusting her collar and sleeves. What was he doing? She was most definitely panicked.

Lucille flailed her arms, grinning. Amelia tried to quiet her, wondering if he would go away. When she straightened, she knew he stood beside her. Fury began. She carefully gave Lucille her pacifier.

"Are you ignoring me?" Simon asked.

Last night, he had been with his lover. If he was to be believed! It was a moment before she could speak, and finally, she looked at him. "Of course not, my lord. Is there a problem? Did you wish for another course? Or perhaps the eggs were overcooked, or the ham burned?"

"You did not set foot in the dining room today."

"I have been preoccupied this morning." She realized her tone had been tart. "Lucille has been rather fussy," she added.

He was silent.

Amelia suddenly realized that Simon had sought her out—and in doing so, had been brought face-to-face with Lucille. Impulsively, she picked up the baby and faced him. "But she is doing well now, as you can see."

He looked at her. Then he looked at Lucille for the very first time. "She resembles Lady Grenville."

"Yes, we all think so. She will be a beautiful child." Amelia rocked her gently.

His stare intensified. "I wish to speak with you. Would you care to come into the library?"

She recalled the entire episode from the night before. "I am very busy this morning. Can it wait?"

His expression hardened. "No, Miss Greystone, it cannot."

"Very well." Not looking at him, Lucille in her arms, she started across the kitchens. He followed.

"What are you doing?"

"I am adjourning to the library, my lord."

"Can you please hand over the child?"

"I prefer not to," she said, but she clutched Lucille so tightly that the baby wailed.

Simon jumped.

Amelia sighed, suddenly near tears. Mrs. Murdock was on her feet, at once anxious and surprised, and she handed the infant to her. "I will be right back," she said, but whether she spoke to the nurse or the child, she did not know. Then she faced Simon, who was waiting for her, appearing entirely displeased.

He nodded at her and she marched ahead of him, out of the kitchens, and toward the library. He followed in silence. And when she entered the room, he closed both doors behind them.

She said, "Is that necessary?"

"I see I am being punished for my bad judgment."
His stare was searching.

"Children are punished."

"Reprimanded, then."

"If you wish to consort with your mistress, that is
not my affair."

"But it is affecting our friendship."

"What do you want, Grenville?" She trembled. "Do
you want my forgiveness? Understanding?" Do you like
her more than you like me? she almost asked.

He was grim. "I do not know what I want…. But I
cannot stand having hurt you, Amelia. Surely you know
that."

She suddenly stared into his eyes. Hadn't Julianne
worried that Simon was playing her all over again? "I
have always trusted you," she said truthfully, "but I am
beginning to believe that you are not trustworthy."

He winced. "I am not."

She was stunned.

He turned away. "I am very sorry you had to find out
what you did. Amelia? Please attend my children and
leave me to my affairs."

He was asking her to stay out of his business. "I believe I have learned my lesson," she said, but even as she
spoke, she thought about the rest of his strange behavior. Why did he expect marauders to come to his front
door in the middle of the night? Why did he sleep with
a gun beside his bed? Did he know Georges Danton?
Why did he dream of blood and death?

And then she realized she was doing precisely the
opposite of what he had asked. She dismissed her questions.

"I cannot believe you are surrendering so instantly,"
he said.

She shrugged. "My concern is the children. If they are not in harm's way, then I am pleased." But she wanted to cry.

He was as grim. "On that note, I began to go through my mail this morning from yesterday. I have heard from Southland."

She froze. "What does he intend to do?"

"He says he will call on me this week, but has not indicated if he will take Lucille or not."

Amelia felt her knees buckle. She was exhausted and anguished, and she feared collapsing.

Simon swept his arm around her. "You are pale. Are you going to faint?"

For one moment, she clung. He was strong and powerful, and in his arms she felt cherished and safe.

But it was a lie.

She let him go. "No. Is that all?" She managed to sound brisk.

"Have I lost my friend?" he asked.

She decided not to answer, and she went to the door.

"Amelia," he said, causing her to halt. "There is one more thing. You are to forget that you ever saw me leaving this house last night, much less in a disguise."

She half turned to look at him. He added, "And you are to share my confession with no one."

Of course he would not want new gossip added to the old. Somehow Amelia nodded. "I happen to be discreet," she said. And when he stared so unwaveringly that her heart leaped, she hurried away.

CHAPTER THIRTEEN

AMELIA HAD JUST RECEIVED the most welcome news—her sister and Lady D'Archand had called! Her spirits had remained impossibly low all morning. Not only did she have Simon's affair to brood about, she was worried that Southland would appear at any moment and take Lucille away from them.

Taking off her apron, she thanked Lloyd for the news. "Would you please make up some refreshments for us?" she asked breathlessly. She no longer cared that she was just the housekeeper. She wished to entertain her sister. Besides, Julianne was a countess, and she could hardly be put in the kitchen. She had never needed her sister and her dear friend more.

It was early afternoon. Simon had gone out before lunch, declaring that he would be dining with some associates. Amelia had refused to even look at him, and he had finally turned and left. The boys had taken their lunch in the classroom, and now they were both on horseback with their riding master. Julianne's timing could not have been better.

Amelia rushed into the large, formal red-and-gold salon where Lloyd had escorted the women. As she went inside, she passed a brown trunk in the front hall and she wondered if Simon was leaving. Her heart lurching, she paused on the threshold of the opulent room.

Neither woman had taken a seat, and they both turned and smiled as one.

She forgot about being hurt and anguished. "I am so happy to see you both," she cried.

Julianne's eyes widened. "Are you all right?"

Amelia did not answer, hugging Julianne first. Simon's treachery hurt her so! She turned to Nadine, fighting sudden tears. And as she was embraced in return, she caught their reflections in the mirror hanging on one red wall.

Nadine was a petite but stunning brunette, resplendently dressed in a royal-blue gown and some small sapphires. Julianne was wearing crimson and rubies. Both women wore their natural hair, but Nadine had her long tresses curled and pulled to one side with blue ribbons, while Julianne wore an elaborate red-and-gold headdress with white lace. Both women were smiling, and obviously in good spirits.

Amelia, on the other hand, was wearing a dove-gray cotton dress that fit very much like a potato sack. She was pale and wan. She wore no jewelry, and her hair was in a single, unflattering braid.

No wonder Simon preferred someone else, she thought, inhaling.

"I was so delighted to hear that you are in town," Nadine said, smiling. "But I was surprised when I had learned that you had taken a position in St. Just's household!" She gazed closely at her, clearly wondering what was wrong.

Amelia glanced at Julianne, who gave her an innocent look. She realized that her sister had yet to say a thing. Finding composure, she took Nadine's hand and clasped it tightly. "I have known Grenville for years. He has been my neighbor ever since I can recall. We even had a flirtation once, long ago. When I went to his wife's funeral, it was obvious that his children were in desperate need. I could not turn my back on them."

Julianne made a sound.

Nadine glanced at her and asked, "And how are the children managing?" Her look was bright and interested, but she would never ask about the so-called flirtation and Amelia knew it.

"They are doing very well. In fact, I would love you to meet the boys if they return early enough from their riding lesson. And you must meet Lucille." And to her horror, she felt her smile falter. The pain kept bubbling up in her heart. Simon had betrayed her—again. Yet she was foolish enough to have trusted him a second time.

Julianne patted her shoulder. "Is Lucille all right? Has something happened?"

She swallowed. "Southland has finally contacted us. He will call this week. Whether he will take her or not, he hasn't said."

Julianne looked worriedly at her. "I know you have fallen in love with her, but it would be for the best if her father claimed her."

"I know," Amelia managed to say, and more anguish went through her. The house would not be the same without Lucille in it.

"I would love to see the infant," Nadine said. "Even though I doubt I will ever have children of my own, I so adore them."

Amelia glanced at her friend. They had become close during the winter. Nadine had been a constant visitor at Greystone Manor.

Once, she had been engaged to Bedford—they had been friends since childhood. Now she and Julianne were the best of friends, and Bedford was like a brother to her. She had only arrived in Britain last spring—almost two years ago, she had been caught up in a riot in Paris and left for dead. She did not speak very much of the time she had spent in France, during the revolution. But she was very political and loyal to the émigrés fleeing her country. Amelia was certain she had been involved in helping her peers escape France before she had herself fled.

Nadine was open about the fact that the war had completely changed her life. She had lost her home, her mother, her friends. She had also lost all interest in marriage. She had no time for suitors.

"When you finally fall in love, you will change your mind," Julianne stated.

Nadine simply smiled, clearly not believing that she would ever fall in love. "Perhaps. But until then, I am going to enjoy being a near aunt to your daughter, and maybe to Lucille and Grenville's sons." She looked at Amelia. "Even though we are St. Just's neighbors, we have never met him. Is he in?" The D'Archand family had relocated to the St. Just parish in Cornwall.

She felt another pang. "He has left, perhaps for the day. I wouldn't know."

Julianne seized her hand. "What has he done?"

Amelia felt tears arise. "I am a fool!"

Nadine looked back and forth between them, then handed Amelia her handkerchief.

Amelia dried her eyes. "Nadine, it was more than a flirtation. When I was sixteen Simon pursued me and I fell madly in love. One day he left Cornwall—never to return."

"I am sorry," Nadine said sympathetically.

"I was truly over him. I had forgotten all about him. It was ten years ago. But when we met again at his wife's funeral, it was as if nothing had changed. His children weren't the only ones who needed me. He needed me—and I could not help myself. I had to meddle, I had to comfort him. I took this position, as awkward as it was." She wiped her eyes again.

Julianne put her arm around her. "Has he played you?" Anger laced her tone.

"Yes, he has," Amelia answered, and she broke away to sit down.

Both women sat with her. Julianne put her arm around her and Nadine took her hand. Her sister asked, fiercely, "What happened?"

"I caught him going out at midnight last night." Her heart hurt her again. "I was concerned—he was in an elaborate disguise, in fact. I was so afraid he was following in Bedford's footsteps. But when I confronted him an hour later, he confessed that he had been with his lover. Julianne, what am I going to do?"

Julianne had dropped her arm. "He went out in disguise?"

"Why would he disguise himself to meet a mistress?" Nadine asked.

Amelia looked back and forth between them. Both were wide-eyed and concerned.

"And he was only gone for an hour?" Julianne asked.

"All told, I would say an hour and fifteen minutes or so," Amelia said, beginning to comprehend what both of her friends were thinking. She added tersely, "He took a gun and he was hardly recognizable—he chalked his entire face."

Julianne stood up. "He claimed he was with a lover—or a woman of ill repute?"

Amelia also stood. "He said he has a lover, Julianne.

He was firm—he does not care for and has never been with a prostitute."

Julianne began shaking her head. "I might believe him if he had said he had gone to a prostitute. No man would linger with that kind of woman. But a lover? Are you telling me he disguised himself, took a gun and ran off in the middle of the night to spend a few minutes with a lover?"

"Maybe he is a poor lover?" Nadine interjected, with some humor.

"He is not a poor lover," Amelia said, without thinking.

They stared at her.

Amelia felt herself blush.

"He did not go off to meet a lover," Julianne stated. "Not for a half an hour, not in disguise, not with a gun."

"Perhaps you should tell me what is really going on," Nadine added firmly.

When Julianne and Nadine left, Amelia returned to the salon, closing both doors behind her. Alone, she walked over to the sofa and collapsed upon it.

And once there, she could not move. She was emotionally exhausted.

How could she have believed, even for a moment, that Simon had gone to another woman?

She stretched out, shoes and all, and tears finally spilled. Of course Simon hadn't gone to a mistress last night. Julianne and Nadine were right. Even if he feared gossip, he would never get up such an elaborate disguise, and he would not have returned so swiftly. She recalled being in his arms. If he had been with another woman, she would have smelled some perfume or fragrance!

He was in danger after all.

She had reiterated all of her suspicions to both women; she had detailed all of his strange behavior. Nadine's reaction had been frightening. She had become paler and paler the longer Amelia spoke.

"He knew Danton," she had said tersely. "I feel certain. Danton was only recently executed, that is why he was dreaming of him."

Amelia had been so frightened.

She was frightened now.

He must be in terrible jeopardy, if he would tell her such a monstrous lie—if he would choose to hurt her instead of telling her the truth.

And she knew what she had to do. As he wasn't going to be honest with her, she was going to have to uncover the truth herself—even if it meant spying on him. If she were not so exhausted just then, she would begin immediately with a thorough search of his desk and library.

But Rome wasn't built in a day.

She had full run of his house. She would have many opportunities to go through his desk, his library and his private apartments. Amelia closed her eyes.

On the one hand, she was relieved. On the other, she was so frightened....

But now, she had two confidantes. Nadine had told her that she remained in touch with a great many "friends" in France. She was going to make some very clandestine inquiries, without using names, without putting Simon in any more danger than he was already in. Bedford had claimed that he did not know anything about Simon, but Julianne was going to press him.

And just as Amelia was drifting off, a knock sounded on the salon doors. She somehow managed to fight off the heavy stupor of her fatigue, sitting up and sighing. "Yes?"

Lloyd opened the door. "I am so sorry to interrupt, Miss Greystone, but you have another caller. Mr. Thomas Treyton is here to see you."

Fear arose.

"Miss Greystone?"

Tom Treyton had once been a friend of the family's—and a suitor of Julianne's. He had been to Greystone Manor a hundred times over the years. But he had been a radical, even before the revolution. And recently, he had not only sympathized with the Jacobins, he had been actively working for them on behalf of the French republic. Amelia knew this because, once upon a time, Julianne had been working with him to help the French defeat their country. Tom was so actively involved in the war that he had even been arrested by the British authorities last summer. For old time's sake, Julianne had begged Bedford to help arrange his release. She had feared he would hang as a traitor.

Amelia wanted to send him away now. She was tired and frightened—she wasn't certain she could manage this development. For Julianne was no longer friendly with Tom. Even though she had arranged his release, she had mentioned that he had become so dangerously political, she considered him an enemy.

But of course, that had been months ago.

Why was Tom calling? Had he changed his leanings? Was this a social call? Amelia knew she must invite him in and find out if he was still an old friend—or a new enemy.

"Send him in, please," she said.

Tom entered the room. Amelia came forward, smiling. "Lloyd, thank you. And you may close the door." She took Tom's hand in hers. "This is such a pleasant surprise!" But her heart was thundering as their gazes met.

Tom was Julianne's age, four years younger than her. He was of average height, boyishly attractive and blond. He wore a white wig, a camel-velvet coat and tan breeches. "Hello, Amelia. I heard you had taken up here as Grenville's housekeeper."

She was taken aback because he seemed amused. Or was she imagining that? "Hello, Tom. It has been ages. I am glad to see you. When I saw St. Just's children at the funeral, my heart went out to them. Shortly thereafter, Grenville availed himself upon me."

"I can imagine you as a housekeeper—I do not mean to be insulting, but you have always managed Greystone Manor in the most excellent way," he said lightly. "And of course, you have known Grenville for years."

She felt some alarm. Surely he did not know of that long-ago affair, did he? "He has been my neighbor since I was a small child. How are you, Tom? Are you practicing in London now?" Tom was a barrister.

"We do not get many calls from accused smugglers here in town," he laughed. "So I still practice at home. However, I have become very fond of town. There is so much to see and do. And you? Do you enjoy being in town? I always thought you more inclined to a life in the country."

She wondered how long the small chitchat would last. "I love the country—I miss home—but I also love town. Not that I have had a moment to go out, except to see Julianne, as I am so terribly busy with this house." The moment she spoke, she wished she hadn't.

He smiled. "And how is the countess?"

She stiffened. "She is fine. I hope you do not hold grudges, Tom. Julianne is happily wed."

"Yes, she loves his lordship, and they have a child."

He shrugged. "I was very fond of her once. I am happy for her."

Amelia hoped he was telling the truth.

"How is your mother? Have you seen your brothers? I take it they are well?"

"Momma certainly likes town. Garrett takes her for a drive about the best neighborhoods or through the park every day." She hesitated. "Both of my brothers are well." She decided not to elaborate.

"And Grenville? I imagine he is grieving for the loss of his wife. You are brave, Amelia, to have taken on such a situation."

"This is a difficult time," she said, aware that they were moving on to dangerous terrain.

"He must appreciate your efforts on his behalf and that of his family," Tom mused. "Do you bake the children those corn muffins you used to make?"

"There is a cook, and I have not given him the recipe yet." She was becoming uneasy.

"Then you should give it to him. His boys will adore you for it."

Suddenly she could not take the casual conversation for another moment. "Why have you called? Is there something I can do for you?"

"We are neighbors, in a way. I wanted to make certain you were getting on. They do say Grenville is rather difficult. Don't they?"

"I wouldn't know," she said tersely.

"Well, Amelia, everyone knows he was estranged from his wife. I have even heard that he walks in his sleep. Have you caught him out and about at odd hours— acting strangely?" He laughed, as if amused and merely gossiping.

Her heart lurched with alarm. She was certain he was

questioning her seriously now. "Of course not." She was suddenly angry. "Are you still radically inclined, Tom?"

His eyes widened, but his smile never wavered. "I am not unprincipled, Amelia. I hardly change my spots, as did Julianne."

No attack could have been as obvious. "Julianne is very principled. She believes in liberty for all mankind— not just for the poor and the oppressed."

"Since when have you become political?"

She ignored that. "I take it you support France, even though she is at war with our country?"

"I take it you have become a royalist—like your sister?" He wasn't smiling now. "I can imagine the discussions you and Grenville have…. If there are discussions?"

She gasped. "What does that mean?"

"I was there ten years ago, Amelia, in case you have forgotten? Julianne and I were friends when you were being courted by Grenville."

She was shaken. She had forgotten! "I do not know why you are bringing such a subject up. It is very ungentlemanly of you."

"Ah, so where there is smoke, there is fire."

"What does that mean?" she cried.

"Have you ever met Henri Jourdan?" he asked, unsmiling.

She did not have a clue as to who he was talking about. But she sensed she must be very careful about how she answered him. "I have been gracious enough to overlook your falling-out with my sister. But you have come into my house in a very provocative manner. I have no interest in continuing this intercourse. Good day, Tom."

"Jourdan has called on St. Just, surely?"

"Good day." Amelia strode to the door and flung it open, shaken but hiding it. "Lloyd! Please escort Mr. Treyton out." She faced Tom. "Please, do not make me bar you from this house."

Tom smirked. "And why would you do that?" He saluted then, sauntering past her. "I think I can let myself out."

Amelia stared after him as Lloyd appeared, following Treyton to the door. Only when the door had closed behind Treyton did she grasp her hands and sink into the closest chair.

What had that encounter been about?

Who was Henri Jourdan?

But she had to trust her instincts now. Tom was the enemy, and somehow he was hunting Simon.

It was very late, and Simon had yet to return.

In his library, Amelia paced. That afternoon, he had sent a note, stating that he would not be back in time for supper, and that he might not be back to say good-night to the boys, either. There had been no explanation, and the boys had been put to bed hours ago.

She had made up her mind to spy upon him, if that was what it took to discover the truth about his activities. But she was loath to begin searching through his private effects. It felt like a violation of her morals, as well as a violation of his privacy. Still, in the past hour, she had gone through all the drawers in his desk. She hadn't found anything alarming—except for the fact that the pistol was gone.

He had left the house before noon. Why did he think it necessary to go out in broad daylight with a loaded gun?

When he returned, Amelia meant to confront him until she got to the truth.

But her fear and worry were exhausting her. She suddenly sat down at his desk, slumping over the leather top there.

"So you are waiting up for me, again?"

She flinched, leaping to her feet. Simon stood in the doorway in his navy blue coat, smiling slightly at her.

She trembled. "Yes, I am waiting up for you."

His gaze moved over her figure. The trunk she had seen in the front hall had been for her. It was filled with clothing her sister had purchased for her. She had decided earlier that she might as well surrender to her sister's will and see what she had actually bought for her, as she was tired of looking like a washerwoman or a domestic housemaid. Amelia had changed into a rose brocade dress with a heart-shaped neckline and three-quarter sleeves. He looked up. "This is a pleasant surprise, Amelia…. I like the gown."

There was no mistaking the admiring look in his eyes. But surely she hadn't put on one of the gowns Julianne had sent on his behalf? "Julianne left me a small wardrobe." She felt herself blushing. "I was tired of looking like a washerwoman."

His smile was broader now, his tone softer. "You could never look like a washerwoman. You are lovely," he said.

She was gripping the edge of his desk. "Thank you," she said unevenly. "Are you attempting to divert me?"

"Do you need diversion?" He finally moved into the room, leaving the door open. "I can't imagine why you are here, much less why you are at my desk, but somehow I do not think I am forgiven for my wanton behavior the other night."

She wet her lips. "There was no wanton behavior."

He started and she said, "We both know you did not go out last night to be with a lover."

"I am not going to argue with you. But if you wish to believe in me, you are making a mistake." But he had halted a few feet from the desk, and he appeared distinctly wary.

"You must be in terrible danger, to tell such a lie."

"Has something happened today that I don't know about?" He spoke calmly. "Last night, you certainly believed my confession—and it was the truth, by the way."

She decided not to go through the logic which had led her to her conclusions. "I was threatened today— here in this house."

Simon's eyes widened. "What!"

"I was threatened by a radical, Simon, and he was clearly interested in you."

Simon's mouth closed but he blanched. And he came forward with hard strides. Amelia did not move; he rounded the desk and seized her wrist. "What happened?"

"Do you remember Tom Treyton?"

"The name is somewhat familiar—"

She interrupted. "His father is a country squire. He is a solicitor with a practice in Penzance. He was also a friend of Julianne's, and of my family's. I know firsthand from Julianne that he has been here in London, trying to subvert the war effort. Last summer he was arrested, and Julianne feared he would be charged with treason. She persuaded Bedford to work on his behalf and he was released. He called on me this afternoon. But it was you he wished to speak about."

"What did he want to know?"

"He asked me if I knew someone named Henri Jourdan," she said.

Simon blanched.

"I am becoming frightened," Amelia cried. "Simon, who is Jourdan? What are you really doing here in town? What were you doing last night?"

He inhaled harshly. "What did you say, Amelia? What did you tell him?"

"I did not even answer him, I sent him from the house!"

Their gazes locked and she saw fear in Simon's eyes. "If you are ever asked again, Jourdan is my cousin. He resides here from time to time, but is currently out of town!" He turned away from her and paced.

She ran after him and seized his arm. He faced her. "If I must lie for you, I will gladly do so, but don't I have the right to know what is going on?"

"I would tell you everything if I could," he cried raggedly. He grasped her shoulders. "I should have never brought you to London!"

"I want to be here! I love William and John—I love Lucille—they need me!" She felt the tears filling her eyes. She almost blurted, I love you—and you need me, too! "Are we in danger, Simon?"

His grip tightened. "I am determined to keep you safe. I am determined to keep the children safe. I am doing my best...." He trailed off.

Amelia did not know what to do. He was obviously overcome with anguish. "I am good at keeping secrets." She clasped his cheek, which was slightly rough.

His gaze locked with hers. "You do not need to be burdened with my secrets, Amelia, and you may trust me on that."

She could not understand why he wouldn't tell her what he was dealing with. "Are you involved in the war? Perhaps the way Lucas is, perhaps the way Bedford was?"

He began shaking his head. "From now on, Garrett will escort you everywhere you go, even into my own gardens!"

"Who is Jourdan?" she tried again.

"He is my cousin, from France," he said firmly, but he hesitated before answering.

She was surprised. "You have French relations?"

He wet his lip. "Most are dead."

She studied him desperately. "Will we be receiving him?"

"Amelia, do not press me! Damn it! I cannot answer any questions. But know this. I am going to keep you safe," he said huskily.

His eyes were shimmering with tears. He added, "I am going to keep the children safe—even Lucille, for as long as she is with us."

Her heart swelled with love. "I know." She clasped his jaw again.

And he took her hand and turned it over and kissed it with shocking passion. And then he kissed it again, and again. "What would I do without you? What would I do without your faith? How can you trust me?" He paused and stared into her eyes. "I did lie, Amelia. There was no one else last night. How could there be anyone else—when it is you that I want, you whom I admire?"

Relief consumed her—and desire flamed. "I know. Simon… I will always trust you. It is as natural to me as breathing."

He cried out. And then he swept her hard into his arms, and she turned her face up for his kiss. It was fierce and hungry, it was consuming. As wildly, Amelia kissed him back.

It was Simon who broke away, after an endless, heated moment. "I am not going to be able to restrain myself," he said harshly, "not now, not tonight."

"And I will not let you," Amelia cried. "I am too frightened—and I care for you too much."

He went still, breathing hard. For one moment, Amelia was afraid that she had said the wrong thing. But then he pulled her into his arms, kissing her and whirling her around toward the sofa as he did so. Without breaking the kiss, he shoved the library door closed. Amelia clung as he laid her down on the sofa.

He paused beside her, one knee on the sofa. "You deserve more than I can give you."

"I want whatever you can give me." Amelia took his hand and slid it over her bare collarbone.

His eyes blazed. "Amelia, I have already hurt you, and if there will be regrets—"

"There will not be regrets." And as she spoke, she opened his shirt, exposing his hard chest and muscular belly.

Her dress already unbuttoned, he froze, their gazes locked. Amelia laid her palm on his ribs, and gave up. She closed her eyes, tears of need arising, moaning as she slid her hand across his abdomen and down his pelvis. His skin was like velvet, except it was burning hot.

He claimed her lips feverishly as she delved even lower, and when she touched him, feeling his hard, hot length, the urgency became unbearable. She cried out, soblike.

Simon gasped and jerked down her bodice, his mouth on her neck, her breasts. Frantically Amelia ripped off his jacket, then helped him tear down his breeches. Her skirts were somehow up about her waist and Simon smiled at her, his eyes burning and black. She wanted to tell him to hurry. She wanted to tell him that she loved him. Instead, staring into his eyes, very faint now, she reached down between them and guided him toward her. He gasped and then he was abruptly filling her....

Amelia threw her arms around him and wept.

CHAPTER FOURTEEN

AMELIA THOUGHT SHE FELT Simon brush his mouth over her temple. She was surely dreaming, wasn't she? Confusion began as she slowly awoke. And suddenly she realized that she was in his arms—and that they were in bed. The mattress shifted as he got up.

She was instantly awake. Last night they had made love, over and over again.

A delirious joy began. Amelia blinked, because they were in her bedroom, and it was still dark outside. Simon was gathering up his clothes and dressing.

She remembered making love on the sofa in the library, their passion finally exploding. It had been breathtaking and miraculous, at once. Nothing in her life had ever felt as right.

They had stolen upstairs afterward, into her bedroom. They had made love again—and again. Each time had been fierce, frantic and thrilling.

She gripped the covers, consumed with the depth of her love. She had never loved anyone this way before, she thought helplessly. She knew she had never stopped loving Simon—nor would she ever do so. Yet with the profound joy there was despair.

He was in trouble. Her suspicions had been right, apparently, but he hadn't admitted anything! The only thing she knew with any certainty was that he was afraid, and that he felt it necessary to keep her and the children safe. But what or who were they in danger from?

"Simon?" she whispered as his clothing rustled.

He sat down on the side of the bed, touching her face, his shirt half buttoned. "I did not want to awaken you. Good morning." He smiled.

Her heart turned over, hard. His smile was so tender, so caring—and she recalled his intense and heated looks last night. "It's all right. Are you trying to sneak away?" she asked, with some uncertainty, but trying to sound casual. Surely he did not mean to steal away from her, not after the extent of his passion last night!

His eyes widened. "Yes, I am intent on stealing from your chamber—but not because I want to leave you. I am trying to protect you. I don't want anyone to know that we have spent the night together. I do not want your reputation blemished."

She couldn't believe that she had had some doubt. But uncertainty remained. "I thought you might have wanted to escape me."

"Why would I want to flee from you?" And he seemed genuinely bewildered.

"Because you are ashamed, because you feel guilty, because you have regrets..." she said.

For one moment, he stared. Then he said softly, "Are you ashamed? Do you have regrets?"

"I know we had decided not to allow this to happen, but I cannot regret the night we just shared. It was the best night of my life."

His eyes darkened. "Do you really mean it?"

"I mean it!" she cried.

He leaned closer and slid his hand into her hair, around her nape. "What happened last night means more

to me than you can possibly know." His tone was rough
with emotion. "I just wish—" He stopped.

The love in her chest swelled. She touched his face.
"What do you wish? Do you have regrets?" He hadn't
answered her and she was acutely aware of it.

"Yes, I do." Their gazes held. "You deserve more than
this. We both know you are not meant to be a mistress.
You deserve a home and family of your own, not a clandestine affair. I hired you as my housekeeper, but now
you are in my bed!" Before she could protest, he said,
"You deserve all the splendor life has to offer. Instead,
I have immersed you in the most sordid aspects of my
life, Amelia. I swore to myself I would never do such
a thing, yet that is exactly what I have accomplished."

She did not quite understand him. And she was dismayed. "So you are sorry about what happened?"

"I am not sorry that we made love," he said. He hesitated. "But I regret ruining you, Amelia, for that is what
I have done."

He had taken her virginity, and he didn't seem about
to offer marriage. She wasn't sure what to think, feel or
say. And it wasn't quite true, but she said, "I am twenty-
six. I haven't thought about marriage in years. I do not
care that we are lovers, and not man and wife. I care
about you, Simon, obviously. Therefore I want to be involved in your life, both when times are good and when
times are difficult."

He stared for a long moment. "I remain amazed by
your loyalty, Amelia, for I have done nothing to deserve
it. Why? Why are you so moved to help me?"

She could not tell him that she loved him. "We have
a connection," she said softly.

"Yes, we do. We had it ten years ago, and apparently
time has not eroded it." But he did not smile.

And Amelia felt as uncertain as she had once been, when she had been a girl of sixteen. "I am not sure the passage of time will ever affect it."

"I am a selfish bastard, aren't I? I feel as if I am using you. And I certainly know better." He suddenly pulled her into his arms and held her, hard.

It was an outburst of affection, Amelia realized as she embraced him in return. But she did not understand why he didn't offer her marriage. Surely he cared for her. He had said he needed her. His children needed a mother. And he was a widower—so what was holding him back?

She realized she was afraid that he simply didn't want to marry her. Worse, it was now obvious that she wanted even more than an affair from him. As he had pointed out, she was hardly meant to be a mistress.

"I had better go," he suddenly said softly. "It will be five soon, and the staff will begin to arise."

"I am the only one up before six," she said, suddenly bewildered and even hurt. But consuming love remained. She knew it would never fade—not for her.

He kissed her cheek and stood. "We can speak later. Amelia… If you decide you have regrets, you must be brave and tell me."

Amelia somehow smiled, hugging the covers to her chest, and watched him leave. Then she leaned back against the pillows. She was so deeply in love, but the confusion remained. She was suddenly afraid that she would not be very adept in the role of mistress. She was suddenly afraid of being hurt by Simon all over again.

But she did not want to lose him. Wasn't this better than nothing?

Besides, he was in danger—and apparently the children were in danger, too. She would not back out of their friendship, and she did not want to end their love affair, either. In fact, she missed him already!

And she suddenly threw the covers aside. She knew she would never fall back asleep. She would begin her day early.

AMELIA WONDERED IF SHE would be able to stop thinking about the night she had just shared with Simon as she went downstairs, a half an hour later. Aware that no one would be up yet—except for Simon—she glanced at the library as she entered the central hall. The door remained open and she smiled, recalling how they had escaped that room last night, having barely reconstructed their clothing, and pretending that naught was amiss. They had sauntered from the room slowly, then made a mad dash for the stairs. Choking on laughter, they had rushed up to her room.

The library was empty—apparently Simon was still upstairs—and impulsively, she went inside to tidy up the sofa where they had first made love.

As she rearranged the pillows, joy overcoming her previous doubts, there was a flash of movement outside. Amelia glanced up at the window. The sun had risen, and the morning was bright with its first light. Roses were blooming. And then she realized that a man was standing outside of the window!

Amelia froze in fear—and then she ran to Simon's desk, seizing the drawer where he kept the gun. She pulled it open, took the pistol and turned. As she raised it, the man pressed his face to the window.

She choked in shock.

Amelia, he mouthed.

It was Jack, her long-lost brother!

Jack, who had a bounty on his head.

Amelia pointed toward the west wing of the house, and ran from the library. She pushed open the doors to the first salon—the opulent red-and-gold room—and then closed them. She realized she was still holding Simon's pistol as she raced across the salon and opened the terrace doors. Jack rushed inside, grinning at her.

Before she could reprimand him, he reached for her. He plucked the pistol from her hand and swept her into a hard embrace and whirled her around until she was breathless.

"The gun is loaded," she choked, afraid it would go off.

He laughed with disdain and set her down, putting the gun on a small table. "Since when do you carry weapons?"

She stared at her brother, who looked like the smuggler he was—or a pirate. His face was bronzed from the wind and the sea, he wore a plain brown coat over a lawn shirt that was open to the chest, his golden hair was loose, and he wore Hessian boots with his breeches, not shoes and stockings. He also wore a waist belt with a pouch and holster, in which she could clearly see a carbine pistol. "Since when do you?" she cried.

"Aren't you pleased to see me?" He grinned. And before she could respond, one tawny brow lifted. "Hmm, you do not look like a housekeeper, or, come to think of it, like my sensible older sister."

Amelia felt herself blush. She was dressed in a lovely pale pink silk gown, in a rose print, which was hardly suitable for a housekeeper. She had pinned up half of her hair. The rest she had brushed and was hanging loose. Worse, she happened to know that she looked particularly radiant today. Simon, of course, was responsible for that.

Jack was an unrepentant ladies' man and she was afraid he would suspect what she had been up to last night. "I am thrilled to see you and you know it," she said. "Lucas told me about the bounty, Jack."

He did not seem perturbed. "Do not lecture me now. Why are you all dressed up at five in the morning?"

"Julianne sent me the clothes. Frankly, I have been working myself to the bone, taking care of Grenville's poor children. I became tired of seeing my reflection in the mirror and looking like a fishmonger's wife."

"And how are Grenville's children, Amelia? Come to think of it, how is Grenville?"

She tensed. "Lucas and I have already had this out. He has come to terms with my taking on the position as Grenville's housekeeper. His children have lost their mother, Jack. And the infant, Lucille, why, she isn't even his child, so she currently has no one."

"She has you."

"Yes, she does."

He sighed. "I got into town last night. Lucas has told me everything—including that you are very involved in Grenville's household. Amelia, I have not forgotten that he broke your heart, even if it was many years ago. I remember hearing you crying in your bedchamber. I remember wanting to hunt him down and kill him! I was shocked when Lucas told me that you were his house-keeper. And now, well, I can't help remarking that you have never looked better—or lovelier."

She felt her cheeks heat. "It is the dress!"

He stared searchingly.

She folded her arms defensively. She had pulled the wool over Lucas's eyes, but Jack would be harder to fool. "Have you seen Jaquelyn yet?" she asked, referring to Julianne's daughter.

"You are changing the subject. Where is Grenville, anyway? As much as I shouldn't let him see me, I want to have a word with him."

She was alarmed. Jack had a temper. He had meant it when he had just stated that, a decade ago, he had wanted to kill Simon. He would not be calm and rational in this regard as Lucas had been, she was certain. "He is probably asleep. I do not think it wise for me to wake him up."

His eyes widened. "My God, were you even considering doing such a thing? Of course you can't barge in on him—or can you? What is going on here, anyway?"

He was suspicious of her relationship, she realized, with some panic. "You are wrong. I was not even thinking of going upstairs to awaken him. It would be entirely inappropriate, obviously."

"That dress is inappropriate. So is your position as his housekeeper."

"I told Lucas and I will tell you. I cannot abandon his children now. They are becoming very accustomed to having me run their home. I see to their meals, review their studies and tell them bedtime stories!"

"Really?" He made a mocking sound. "I am going to remain here until Grenville comes downstairs. I wish a word with him."

"Jack, you cannot afford to have him see you." Amelia was horrified. Jack meant to interview Simon and decide if their relationship was appropriate or not—she was certain.

"Grenville hardly frightens me, Amelia," he said, with vast arrogance. "I have been eluding two navies ever since the blockade was declared. I think I can elude Grenville and his cronies, if he ever decided to turn me in!"

"You are lucky, Jack, but I am afraid you don't know it."

He eyed her. "Don't be afraid for me."

She went to him and touched his arm. "Of course I am afraid for you." She lowered her voice. "How many times have you been off the French coast, unloading embargoed goods, with the British navy on the horizon? How many times, Jack?"

He stared at her, a funny expression on his face. "I don't want you to worry about me. I have the oddest feeling you are preoccupied enough now."

"My God, I was right! You drop anchor to unload, with British sloops almost in striking distance!"

"How amusing would it be if they weren't on the hunt?"

She felt like striking him, hard. "This is not a frivolous game, damn it. If you are ever apprehended, they will charge you with treason, Jack. I am worried to death about you being caught by our navy, just as I am worried to death about Lucas being caught on French soil, by the French authorities!"

Jack suddenly pulled her close. "And I love you, too." He released her. "Frankly, I worry about Lucas, as well. He should stop aiding the émigrés, Amelia. Terror truly reigns in France. There is no concept of mercy now, or of justice. Anyone even associated with a suspected traitor is sent to the guillotine, and that means women and children are dying senselessly, every single day. If Lucas is caught on French soil, there will not be a trial. His fate will be the mob or the Blade."

She was sickened. "I was not certain he was still working with émigrés in France."

"He is." Jack was blunt. "I have even heard the rumor that your friend Nadine D'Archand is involved in aiding the émigré community there. I hope that is not the case. If she wishes to help her compatriots, she can help them here, once they have safely landed on our shores. Lucas should do the same."

She was surprised. "Nadine is very political, but she has never given any indication that she is doing anything at all to help émigrés flee France. You must be wrong."

"I hope so," he said.

Amelia stared at him for a moment. "Maybe you can help me, Jack. I am worried about Grenville."

He started. "So I am right. There is more here than meets the eye. You are hardly his housekeeper, if you are so worried about him!"

"We are friends!" she cried. "He is in danger and the children might be in danger, too—he has admitted as much. But he won't admit to anything else. I think he might be a spy!"

Jack took her arm and pulled her close. "Lucas told me that you were suspicious of him." His stare was piercing. "What do you mean, he admitted he is in danger?"

"He referred to keeping the children safe. But when I directly asked him if he is a spy, or some such thing, he hedged, and changed the subject."

Something flickered in Jack's eyes. "You should stay out of this, Amelia. I do not want you involved in the war, not even on its periphery."

"I am already involved, because of you and Lucas, and now Simon," she said tersely.

"So it is Simon! I knew it—you are glowing because you are in love with him all over again," he accused.

She pulled away. "Yes, I love him, Jack. Just as I love his children. He is in trouble. Can you help me find out why?"

His face was hard and tight. "If I didn't know how

prim and proper you are—how sensible—I would ask if you are having an affair!"

She flushed. "What a rude comment to make!"

He rushed on, as if he hadn't heard her, "But I know you, Amelia, and you would never become a man's mistress. Thank God for that! Why has Lucas allowed you to stay on here? Why don't you go with Momma and stay with Julianne? If Simon is in danger, then so are you."

"I am not abandoning him and his children," she cried. "So you also think that he is in danger?"

He said carefully, "I don't know." He stared grimly, and she could feel his mind racing. She wished she knew his thoughts. "Has he indicated that he is leaving town?" he finally asked.

She shook her head. "No, he has not said a word about leaving town. Why? If he leaves, does that mean he is going to France—as Lucas does?"

"No, it does not. It could mean anything."

"He is rarely in town—that is what I have heard!" She worried that Simon meant to soon leave—yet he hadn't said a word. "Did Lucas tell you all the reasons why I am so worried?"

"He mentioned something about odd behavior, nightmares, some ramblings," Jack said.

She stiffened. Lucas and Jack had had a lengthy conversation about Simon—she was certain.

Jack grimaced. "Damn it. I did not plan on staying in town for another day. But I am going to see what I can find out. You have made me curious. I cannot imagine why Grenville would feel that there is danger here in town—whether his activities are related to the war or not."

"Thank you, Jack," she said. And she hugged him, hard.

IT WAS VERY DIFFICULT to concentrate on the task at hand, Simon thought grimly.

It was not even ten that morning. Simon was at his desk in the library, ostensibly dealing with some estate accounts. But in truth, he was trying to decide how to deal with Marcel. Jourdan had just received another summons—the drop-off location for messages was a small shop on Pall Mall. Either he had to come up with a foolproof disguise or he was going to have to send someone in his stead to meet Jourdan's contact. Both options were far too risky. Just then, he preferred the latter choice of sending intelligence to Marcel through a courier he could trust.

But as he brooded upon how best to proceed—and time was not on his side—he had been hard-pressed to keep his attention on the subject of his intrigues. Amelia was haunting him.

There was no small amount of guilt. She was a good, upright, moral gentlewoman, and he had taken advantage of her affection for him and the attraction they shared. It was simply unacceptable. But he could not regret the night they had shared. She had said that it had been the best night of her life; it had certainly been the best night of his.

There was also so much pleasure, so much joy. She had done more than warm his bed, she warmed his heart, even now. She was everything he was not. She was good and kind, honest and warm, compassionate and selfless. He knew he was not going to be able to give her up, not as a friend and not as a lover.

And that just highlighted their differences; he was entirely selfish.

Of course, sooner or later he was going to be sent back to France, and that would end the affair. He couldn't imagine what excuse he would give to her then. But he would never frighten her with the truth.

For he recalled the way she had looked at him, time and again. Was Amelia in love with him? He thought so—he hoped so!

He shoved the ledgers he was supposedly reviewing aside. Amelia was astute and tenacious. She suspected that he was a spy. How was he going to convince her otherwise? He did not want her burdened with the truth. He did not want her living in fear for him.

He would be the one to live in fear—for them all.

A knock sounded on his door, which was open. Lloyd stood there—and so did Sebastian Warlock.

Absolute displeasure began. Simon stood up stiffly as Lloyd said, "Mr. Warlock insisted, my lord. I apologize for the interruption, but he said you would not turn him away, not even at this hour."

A new tension riddled him now. Simon smiled coldly. "Thank you, Lloyd. Please close the door. And we are not to be disturbed."

Warlock sauntered inside as Lloyd backed out, closing the ebony door. "Hello, Grenville. Am I interrupting?"

"I dislike surprises," Simon said. "But of course, you are always welcome." And they both knew that was a lie.

Warlock seemed amused. Clad in a black-velvet coat and tan breeches, he took a chair before the desk. "You haven't sent me a report. How did your meeting with Jourdan's contact go?"

Almost furious now, Simon took his own seat. He hated being controlled, as if a puppet on a string! "He did not show up," he lied.

"Really?" Warlock's brows lifted. "Hmm, that is two times in a row. I am beginning to grow suspicious."

Simon felt his heart lurch, but he was careful not to change a single facial muscle. He certainly wasn't going to tell the spymaster that Marcel was Edmund Duke—and the mole.

Or had Duke been sent to spy on his meeting with Marcel—by Warlock?

Was it possible?

God, anything was possible in these times of war and revolution! "Are you sure you did not apprehend my contact?" Simon asked, sounding wry. "For that is the obvious conclusion to draw."

Warlock crossed his legs. "I will have to chat with my friends in the Alien Office. I do hope we are not interfering with one another. Miscommunication is so bothersome."

Before he had finished speaking, there was another knock on the door.

Simon tensed. He had told Lloyd not to interrupt, and he knew who was at his door. And even as he thought about Amelia, the door opened and she poked her head in, smiling. "Simon, I was wondering," she began. But she saw Warlock and stopped.

His heart lurched wildly, with so many soaring, jumbled emotions that the only thing he was certain of was his raging desire. He wanted to sweep her into his arms again and make wild love to her. But he could hardly do such a thing, so he stared, marveling at how beautiful she was. But even as he did so, he was acutely aware of Warlock, who had stood up and was glancing with interest at him and then at Amelia.

Simon was afraid he looked entirely smitten.

Her smile faltered as she turned to her uncle. "Oh, dear. I did not realize you had a caller." She smiled again.

"I am sorry, I have disturbed you.... Sebastian, this is a pleasant surprise!" She was flushed.

Warlock ambled over to her and took her hand and kissed it. "I am so pleased to see you, Amelia. I was hoping to have a chance to speak with you after Grenville and I finished our affairs. How are you?"

Simon did not want them conversing—not at all! But she said, "I am well enough, thank you. You seem well, sir."

Simon stepped around his desk, joining them. "Amelia, good morning. Is there a problem with the children?"

She flushed again and did not meet his gaze. "I had a question, but it can wait." She smiled at Warlock. "I look forward to our conversation." She glanced aside and hurried out, closing the door as she did so.

She had appeared so guilty, Simon thought.

"Amelia has never looked better," Warlock mused. "Yet she is a housekeeper."

She hadn't appeared like any housekeeper he knew, Simon thought. She had looked like the mistress of the house. "She adores my children—and Lucille," Simon said sharply. There was a warning in his tone.

"I am sure that she does. Just as I am sure you were in great need of a suitable housekeeper, given the state of your personal affairs. Can we get back to more pressing matters? Have you arranged another rendezvous?"

"I am working on it," Simon said. "But time is running out. The French took Menin and Courtrai a week ago, which means the Allied invasion of Flanders is surely about to begin. I am hoping to meet with Jourdan's contact by tomorrow at the latest. What can I give him?"

"Coburg will attempt to retake both cities, with forty thousand men."

Simon did not allow his expression to change. Was Warlock lying? Bedford believed that Coburg had mustered sixty thousand troops—although his belief was based on gossip.

"Are you certain?" Simon asked, very calmly. "I must give Marcel a genuine number, otherwise they will take my head."

"I am very certain. I would not compromise your value as an agent, Grenville. Surely you know that?"

Simon knew no such thing.

Warlock added, "You are my most valuable asset. You are in the perfect position. The French believe you are their agent, when you actually belong to me." He smiled, but it did not reach his eyes. "I am not sure when I will want you to return to France. In fact, the more I think about it, the more I realize how useful you are here in town, feeding the information I choose to Marcel and the other Jacobins here in town, and thus to *le Comité* and Robespierre."

"How pleased I am to hear that," Simon managed to say, but his heart was thundering. Was it possible he wouldn't have to go back? He prayed that would be the case.

"You are useless to me if you are uncovered, much less captured and thrown back into a French prison."

As Simon thought how heartless Warlock was, a thump sounded outside the library door—as if someone standing there had dropped something. Simon froze. Amelia. Warlock strode to the door and swung it wide—and Amelia fell forward, into the room.

Warlock stepped aside, appearing disgusted, and she stumbled. Simon lurched forward and caught her, preventing her from falling.

In his arms, she looked up at him, her eyes huge, her face ashen.

She had heard them, Simon thought, stricken.

"Well, well. It appears that spying runs in the family," Warlock said.

CHAPTER FIFTEEN

AMELIA CLUNG TO SIMON, beyond shock.

He gripped her arms tightly, staring down at her, his face taut with tension. Dismay darkened his eyes.

Simon was a spy—as she had suspected. But he wasn't just a spy—he was a double agent. Yet there was so much more....

"I am ashamed of you, Amelia," she heard Warlock say. "To spy upon your own family, to bite the veritable hand that feeds you." He was mocking.

"Simon," she said. But before she could beg him to deny everything—before she could ask him if he had been in prison—a warning look entered his eyes. He shook his head, very slightly.

Her heart continued to thunder and it was deafening. He had been in prison. She suddenly felt faint and sick.

Warlock closed the door. Amelia heard him walk up to her and a new tension began. Simon released her and slowly, with dread, she somehow turned and faced her uncle.

"Why were you spying on us?" Warlock asked coldly.

Before she could respond, Simon stepped between them. "You cannot speak to her in such a manner. I will handle this."

"I am afraid that is not possible," Warlock said. "Not because she is my niece. This is a matter relating to national affairs, this is a matter of state."

Amelia shuddered. "I did not mean to spy."

Simon whirled as Warlock made a scoffing sound. Her uncle said, "Of course you did. You were purposefully standing outside the door, with your ear pressed upon it. I happen to know you are not the radical your sister was. So why would you spy upon Grenville?"

"You do not have to answer him," Simon said.

Amelia was frightened. Her uncle had never appeared as cold or as powerful—or as ruthless. But Simon was frightening her, as well.

He was an agent, and not just for Pitt. He was playing some kind of terrible game, because the French believed him to be one of their own. No wonder he lived in constant fear, for she knew what his fate would be if he were ever caught.

She began to shake. He had been in prison, in France. Was that why he had changed? Was that why he had nightmares? Was that the reason for the haunted look in his eyes?

Warlock was waiting for her to answer. She said carefully, "There are three small children in this house. It has been clear to me for some time that something is wrong—that Simon is in trouble or in danger. I must protect the children. Your relationship with Simon has raised so many questions. So, yes, I decided to eavesdrop."

"Not a wise decision," Warlock said. "I take it my other niece did not speak glowingly of me?"

She inhaled. "You made Bedford's life hell, Sebastian. You even made Julianne's life hell—yes, she told me, you wanted her to spy on Dominic! How could you ask your own niece to do such a thing?"

"I want to win this war. I want to prevent the revolution from coming to our shores. And to accomplish those goals, I will do what I have to do—even if it means asking my own flesh and blood to engage in an unsavory task or two." And Warlock's dark eyes blazed. "So call me a bastard if you will, but someone has to win this damned war and someone has to keep this country safe."

She looked helplessly at Simon. He stepped toward her, and for one moment, she thought he was going to put his arm around her. As if remembering that he must not do such a thing, he dropped his arm.

"She will keep this to herself, I am certain," Simon said.

"Will she? For how long?" Warlock was caustic. "How much did you hear, Amelia?"

She hesitated.

"I thought so," Warlock said flatly.

Amelia shivered. "I would never betray Simon! I would never tell anyone what I have learned."

Warlock was entirely skeptical. "Not even your sister? Or Lucas?"

She flushed. Could Lucas help Simon? "Are you advising me not to speak of this to anyone—not even Julianne or my brothers?"

Warlock said, "The fewer who know, the better. I am not advising anything. I am telling you to keep this matter to yourself. I am asking for your word."

She shivered. How could she give it? She knew Lucas would help Simon if she asked him.

"I know how loyal you are, Amelia," he added softly. "I remember you as a small child, when your father left you, almost twenty years ago. You became a matriarch at the age of seven. I know you will do anything for those you love. In fact, I believe you think it your duty to do so—as it became your duty when you were such a small child."

Warlock was speaking the truth. But Amelia doubted they had exchanged more than a dozen words in the past five or six years. He hardly knew her now. "Then I am flattered."

"I am not trying to flatter you. I am trying to explain to you that we are all on the same side of a war. You, Simon and I have the same interests and aims. And while your brothers and even Julianne are on our side, the less who know the truth about Simon, the better."

"I understand," Amelia said.

"You haven't given me your word," Warlock pointed out, too lightly.

She felt herself flush. How could she promise not to go to Lucas? She trusted her brother. He was on her side. She did not trust her uncle.

Simon looked at her. "He is right."

"She will not give me her word," Warlock said to Simon, speaking as if Amelia were not in the room. "You know as well as I do that if our enemies ever realize how close she is to you, they will do whatever they must to get her to break."

Amelia was frightened. She had never seen this side of Simon before—or of Warlock. "What do you mean — they will break me?" she cried.

"No," Simon said swiftly. "Amelia is my housekeeper. No one will ever think otherwise, and no one will ever think she knows anything of value."

Amelia looked at Simon—who was grim and unhappy— and then at her uncle. He wore an almost identical expression. And suddenly she realized that she might be in danger, too.

"Send her back to Greystone Manor," Warlock said. "And that is not a suggestion. I want her gone by tomorrow morning." His face hard, he turned abruptly and walked out, not bothering with a goodbye.

Amelia collapsed in the closest chair. Simon strode to the door and slammed it closed. He faced her. "Damn it, Amelia, you have gone too far!"

"I am not returning to Greystone Manor—he does not control our lives!"

"He controls mine!" Simon shouted.

Amelia flinched.

Simon knelt beside her. "And he is right. You cannot tell anyone about me. You are in danger now, because of me."

She took his hand. "Then we will face the danger together."

"No. I knew it was wrong to ask you to be my housekeeper, just as I knew I shouldn't bring you here—or take you to bed! When will you see that I am an insufferable and selfish bastard?"

She clasped his face. "You are a hero and I love you."

He inhaled. "You are deluded!"

She shook her head and kissed him briefly.

He pulled away. "He knows that we are lovers, Amelia. I have no doubt. If he can discern that, then my enemies will as well, and they will go after you, Amelia, to hurt me...." He trailed off.

He was in anguish. Amelia slid to the floor and pulled him into her arms. "We will face this together," she said.

He took her face in his hands. "I will do whatever I have to do to keep you and the children safe."

"I know," she whispered, meaning it.

He kissed her—like a dying man.

HIS HEART CONTINUED to thunder. Holding Amelia very tightly, still fully dressed, only his breeches undone, his jacket on the floor, Simon rolled to his side. But he kept her securely in his arms as he did so.

He had never needed anyone as he did Amelia, he somehow thought. How he wished he could make an honest woman of her, and take her and the children far away.

She was gasping for breath. She snuggled against him, her cheek on his chest, and Simon pulled her skirts and underskirts down. Had he loved her as much ten years ago? He could not recall. He knew he had been smitten then, but it was so much more now.

They were in her bedchamber, the door locked. "Are you all right?" he asked unevenly, when he could finally speak. He had been in such a mad rush to make love to her. "Amelia, were you pleased?"

She smiled up at him, perspiration on her temple. "Was I that quiet?"

He smiled back then. He had clasped his hand to her mouth when she had climaxed—it was the middle of the day. "You exercised admirable restraint," he whispered.

"It was wonderful, Simon," she whispered, and she laid her cheek on his chest again.

He stroked her hair, the euphoria beginning to recede. As it did, he recalled Warlock's orders that he send Amelia away and everything else that had just transpired in the library. His heart sank.

Did Amelia know everything?

What would she think of him when she finally realized the extent of what he was doing?

She glanced up at him. "We should not linger, Simon, although part of me does not care if we are caught like this."

"I care!" he said fervently. "No one can know that we

are lovers, Amelia. No one." God, she was in so much
danger. And it was entirely his fault.

"Were you ever going to tell me the truth?" she asked,
her gaze searching.

"How much did you hear?" Suddenly he hoped that
she had only heard that he was a spy for Warlock—he
prayed she did not know any more, for entirely selfish
reasons.

"I heard everything, Simon. You have been spying
for us—but the French think you are spying for them!"
In his arms, he felt her shudder.

He looked up at the ceiling. When would she realize
what the double game he played really meant? Because
when she realized what he was capable of, she would
finally lose her faith. Amelia slipped out of his arms
and sat up. Sickened, he sat up, too. He began to but-
ton his breeches.

"You have been in France," she said.

It was a careful accusation. "Yes." He did not look
at her.

"For how long? Is that why you were never at home
with your children, with Elizabeth? Is that why no one
ever really knew where you were and how to reach you?"

"For the most part, I have been living in Paris for the
past two years, clerking in the city government. There
I am known as Henri Jourdan—who was my cousin,
by the way, before he was executed along with most of
Lyons and the rest of my French relations." He finally
glanced at her.

"I am sorry." She was ashen. She took his hand. "How
did you ever get into such intrigues, Simon, when you
have children who need you? Are you a patriot, then?"

He pulled it away. She was finally judging him. "I
had many reasons for accepting Warlock's proposition,

three years ago when he first approached me, and patriotism was only one of them." He stared. "Most of my reasons were selfish."

"I do not believe that."

"My reasons were selfish," he repeated.

"You love your children," she said firmly. "I cannot imagine you giving up fatherhood the way that you did!"

"I was never a good father." How calm he sounded. "I had been staying away to avoid Elizabeth because that pleased me—never mind that my sons needed me. I rationalized that she was an excellent mother, so my presence did not matter." He shrugged. But his heart pounded painfully. "Warlock presented me with an opportunity that offered me an excuse to remain in continued exile from my family. Why wouldn't I accept it?"

Tears filled her eyes and she took his hand again. "I wish you had had a good marriage, Simon. I am beginning to think that if you had, you would have never gone to France and we would not be here, worrying about French agents learning of your affairs—or worse."

"You really mean it!" he exclaimed. Her selfless virtue would never cease to amaze him.

"Of course I do. Simon, how much danger are you in? Is it the French that you fear?"

He knew he must not answer her truthfully. He did not want her even more frightened. "Right now, I am not in any danger, Amelia, as Jourdan is entirely trusted."

Her gaze was piercing. "They put you in prison."

His heart sank.

"I heard Warlock say that it would not serve him well if you were captured and sent back to prison."

He inhaled. She was too clever to be misled.

"Do not patronize me. We are in this together and I am not a fool. I refuse to be left in the dark."

"No, you are not a fool, Amelia. Yes, they imprisoned me."

She was so still, so calm. "What happened?"

"It doesn't matter."

"It matters—it matters to me. So please, tell me why
you were imprisoned in France. Did they realize you
were an Englishman?"

He wet his lips, his mind racing. He would omit parts
of the truth, but he would never tell Amelia a lie, even if
she had just given him the perfect lie to tell. He found
his voice and cleared it. "No, they did not discover that
I was an Englishman. They continue to believe that I am
my cousin, Jourdan. I made a terrible mistake, Amelia.
Last November, I returned to London to see my sons—
because it was William's birthday. I only stayed in town
for two days. But the moment I disembarked in Brest, I
knew I was being followed. Within three weeks, I was
apprehended and accused of treason, and thrown into a
prison in Paris." Suddenly his voice broke. He recalled
that cell in absolute detail, and he could not continue.

A crowd of thousands filled the square.

He grasped the iron bars of his cell, staring outside,
filled with revulsion and fear.

Behind him, he heard footsteps. He tensed. Were they
coming for him?

The crowds roared…again. *Le Razor* had just taken
another victim….

And the stench of blood was everywhere.

Somehow he said, "It was play them or go to the
guillotine. I had to convince them that I really was
Jourdan—and that I would go to London and visit my
cousin, St. Just, and attain the information necessary
for them to win the war." He could not face her now.

Amelia pulled him into her arms, his face against her

breasts. As if he were a child, she kissed the top of his head. "It's all right now. You are here with me, with the children. You will never go back there again and you do not have to speak about it. You did what you had to do to live, Simon. I understand."

Did she? He wanted nothing more than for her to understand, but he didn't believe that she did, not for a moment. He knew he had to pull himself together. He was precariously undone.

He sat up and reversed their positions, sliding his arm around her. "I don't want you to worry. I don't want you involved. You are to forget everything you have learned today, Amelia."

"I am more worried now than I was before," she said harshly. "And I intend to help you, Simon, not hide like an ostrich with its head in the sand."

"Warlock is helping me. No one is as brilliant."

"You don't trust him entirely—and neither do I."

He refused to lie so he said, "Warlock is right about one thing. You and the children should return to Cornwall, before someone else discovers our relationship and thinks to use you against me."

Her eyes widened. "I am not going anywhere. I am not leaving you here. We will fight this battle together."

His heart swelled with love. "I am fighting this battle alone."

"No, I won't let you. When will you attempt to meet with the French agent again?"

"I will hardly share such details with you!" he cried, aghast.

"But there will be a meeting, won't there? I heard you and Warlock, Simon. You are supposed to tell them about our troops, aren't you? Isn't that what Warlock said?"

He felt the blood draining from his face. "Amelia, you are to forget everything you heard!"

"How can I? You are going to meet some French spy here in the city, and if he realizes you are not who you say you are, he might kill you!"

He pulled her close. "My contact has no reason to be suspicious. You are worrying needlessly now. I have been playing spy games like this for over two years, Amelia, and I am adept at this kind of deception."

"I am so afraid," she whispered. "And I want to help, in any way that I can."

"You have already helped. At least I know the children are in good hands." He managed a smile, not adding, *no matter what happens to me.* "Amelia? You do not know how much your loyalty means to me."

She suddenly smiled, and as she did, Lucille wailed from down the hall. "You will always have my loyalty—and my love." She slid from the bed, smoothed down her skirts, and then went to the mirror above her bureau.

He trembled, filled with an answering love and so much gratitude, watching her as she fixed her hair. She was the most courageous and determined woman he had ever known, and he admitted to himself just how deeply he loved her. He did not know how he would survive if anything ever happened to her. Somehow, he must keep her and the children safe.

Lucille was still crying. Amelia smiled at him and hurried from the room.

Simon got up slowly, retrieving his rumpled jacket from the floor. Sooner or later he would probably have to meet with Marcel. For now, he would send the information Warlock had relayed via a courier. Dread filled him. He prayed that Coburg had only mustered forty thousand troops for the Allied invasion of Flanders. But that number seemed frighteningly weak.

Warlock was clever and he needed Simon; surely it was too soon for him to throw Simon to the wolves. He shook his jacket out and slipped it on, aware that the infant had stopped crying. He walked over to the mirror and retied his hair in a queue. He remained pale—except for two bright spots of color on his cheeks, and the shockingly bright light in his eyes. His heart was racing. He tucked his shirt into his breeches more securely. Reality had returned—with a vengeance.

Warlock was right when he had said that Amelia knew too much now. There was no way she could remain in his household, not with him there, not when they were lovers.

Especially when he could not keep his hands off of her, not even in the middle of the day.

He was going to have to send her away—he was going to have to give her up in order to ensure her welfare and safety.

His heart aching, Simon fixed the bed and went to the door, peering out. The corridor was empty, so he swiftly stepped out of her bedchamber and hurried down the hall. But as he approached the nursery, he slowed. He glanced inside—and saw Amelia standing in the center of the room, rocking Lucille in her arms.

His heart thudded wildly and he halted. He wasn't sure he had ever seen such a beautiful sight. He was acutely aware that Amelia needed her own child—and that he wished he could father that child for her.

And then Amelia saw him and smiled warmly.

He knew he should not go inside that chamber. Lucille was not his child and Amelia was not his wife. The sight of them there was a terrible illusion. But his feet would not obey his mind. He drifted closer, across the threshold toward them. "May I come in?"

"Of course," Amelia said.

And Simon walked over to her, their eyes meeting. Then he paused and looked down at Lucille. The baby beamed. He slid his arm around Amelia, and realized he was smiling back.

SIMON WENT OUT right after lunch the following day. And the moment he left, Amelia took off her apron, fled the kitchens, retrieved a light shawl, and rushed from the house. She hadn't told anyone where she was going or when she would be back. Warlock would be furious if he knew she meant to ask her brother for help. Going to visit Lucas at Warlock's Cavendish Square house, where her brother was staying, was terribly risky. But Sebastian was not in residence currently, and she needed to speak to Lucas immediately. She did not really think Warlock would have her watched. Still, she walked across Mayfair, all the way to his Cavendish Square house, instead of using Simon's gig.

Now she used the door knocker, out of breath from the long, rapid walk. Sweat trickled down her temples and between her breasts. It was already a perfect spring day, at once warm and sunny. But her heart was filled with dread and dismay, when there should be joy and love. Simon was in so much trouble.

She did not even know if Lucas was in town, she thought desperately, using the knocker again.

A maid finally answered the door and told her that Mr. Greystone was in the parlor with a guest. "He says he is not to be disturbed, madam," she added worriedly.

Amelia stepped past her. "Mr. Greystone is my brother. I will let myself in."

The maid left, not particularly happy. Amelia hurried to a pair of closed doors and heard the rumble of voices from within. She had to make certain that Warlock was not with Lucas, never mind that the maid hadn't mentioned the master of the house. She pressed her ear to the wood and started. Nadine d'Archand was Lucas's guest!

Amelia opened the door abruptly. Lucas and Nadine were seated on the sofa, engrossed in what appeared to be a very serious conversation. Nadine was saying, "They should arrive on the fifteenth, weather permitting. The forecast is for fair seas. Can we—" She stopped, having glimpsed Amelia.

Lucas turned and got to his feet, smiling slightly.

And Amelia felt certain that her brother and her friend were conspiring, although she did not know exactly what they had been discussing. "Am I interrupting?" She recalled Jack's insistence that Nadine was still very involved in aiding those men and women fleeing France.

"You could never interrupt," Lucas said. But his gray gaze was sharp and piercing as he studied her—he knew she was upset.

Nadine picked up her reticule. "I am running late anyway. Hello, Amelia." She kissed her on each cheek. "I see you are enjoying the wardrobe Julianne sent you?" Her tone was teasing.

Amelia was wearing a beautiful canary-yellow dress. "If I am interrupting," Amelia began, glancing back and forth between them.

"You are not interrupting. I was just getting ready to leave." Nadine smiled at Lucas. "I appreciate your advice." She turned to Amelia. "Your brother was giving me some suggestions regarding an investment we might make in a mine not far from our new home in St. Just."

Amelia simply smiled. She did not believe Nadine,

not at all. When the other woman had left, she closed the door and looked at Lucas. "Is she a spy, too?"

"What?" Lucas chuckled.

"Then is she helping bring French families here?"

His smile faded. "She is a woman, Amelia, a noble-woman trying to restore her life with limited means. I was advising her financially."

Amelia knew it was not true. If anyone needed financial advice, it would be Nadine's father. "Of course you were. Is Jack still here?"

His gaze sharpened. "He is in town, and we will leave it at that."

She folded her arms. "It's not safe for him here?"

"No, it's not." Lucas went to her and took her arm in his. "You're distraught—and not because of Nadine or Jack."

"I was right. Simon is a spy, Lucas, and he is in danger."

Lucas blanched. But his expression was a distinctly unhappy, not surprised.

"Lucas, I am begging you for your help."

"Damn it, Amelia, why can't you leave well enough alone?"

"Why aren't you surprised that Simon is a spy? My God, you already knew!"

He sighed. "Of course I knew. Warlock's circle is small, Amelia. We all know one another."

She trembled. "Do you also know that Simon is posing as a Frenchman—and that the French think he is loyal to them?"

And finally, his eyes widened in surprise.

"I see you didn't know that! Did you know that he was in prison in France? And that if the French ever suspect him of treachery, he might wind up there again?" She was suddenly enraged. "He is supposed to meet with some Frenchman here in town and give him valuable information about our troops! I am terrified for him!"

Lucas pulled her close. "You know too much. I am sorry, Amelia, so sorry that it has come to this."

She twisted away. "Forget about me! How can Simon get out of the war? Damn it, Lucas, he has children to think of!"

"Warlock won't let him out. I imagine he will soon go back to France, where he can continue to uncover the intelligence we need to win the war."

"But that is why the French have sent him here! And Warlock was clear—he is pleased to feed all kinds of information back to the French through Simon! Can't you see that Simon is in an impossible predicament? He is in impossible danger!"

Lucas breathed hard. "Damn it. You are committed to him now!"

"I am more than committed. We are lovers, Lucas, and I am not turning my back on him." She glared.

Lucas flushed, clearly incredulous.

She stared defiantly. But as angry as she was, she was even more desperate. "We need your help, Lucas. Simon doesn't want to do this—I am certain! How can we protect him from his enemies? How can he get out of these war games? Bedford got out!"

Lucas's stare hardened. "You have become his mistress. So you are not good enough to become his wife?"

She cried out. "That is not fair!" But hadn't she wondered almost the exact same thing?

"Do not speak to me of fairness. You are a wonderful woman, you would be a wonderful wife—you are not a trollop. He happens to be a widower. He is going to marry you, Amelia." He was furious.

"Lucas, I cannot marry him—not under these circumstances." She was lying to her brother now, because she would marry Simon in an instant. "The first order of business is to find a way to extricate Simon from these intrigues." She added, "The next time he meets with someone they are calling Marcel, he might never come home!" She choked as she finally revealed her greatest fear—that Simon could wind up dead the very next time he met his French contact.

"Grenville will hardly be taken by surprise, Amelia. He is as clever and as dangerous as his enemies, you may trust me on that."

She sat down, shaken. "I pray you are right. Will you help him—will you help us?"

Lucas came and sat beside her. "Of course I will—but I am very displeased with your affair."

"I love him." She shrugged helplessly. "And I am hardly a child."

He took her hand and held it tightly. "If you were happy, I might feel differently."

"When I am with Simon, and we are at home, as if the war does not exist, I am ecstatic. I am happy—but I am terrified for Simon—I am afraid for his life. Lucas, I never stopped loving him."

He sighed. "I think I have known that, all along." Surrendering, he squeezed her hand. "You do realize I intend to make certain that Grenville holds you in the highest regard?"

"He does," she said firmly.

"I didn't know he was imprisoned. That worries me, because it means he was already suspect when he was still in France. It means suspicion must remain. I imagine he is being carefully watched by his French friends."

"You are not making me feel better."

"I will have to think about this. He can't simply walk away from his French masters. The one thing I have learned during the course of this war is that the French republicans are as mad as rabid dogs. You are either with them or you are not. Enemies of the Republic are given one fate, and that is the guillotine. He would have to disappear, Amelia, in order to escape their vengeance, should they ever learn he is one of us."

She shuddered. "He has children."

"Entire families have fled France and are in hiding here in Britain," he said.

"Do you think it possible for the Earl of St. Just to simply take his children and disappear?"

"I think it would be far more difficult for someone of St. Just's stature," he said.

She groaned. "Then what will we do?"

"We may not be able to do anything. You seem to be forgetting that if Grenville decided to get out of the game, Warlock would be his enemy, too. Warlock would never give up a valuable agent like Grenville— not willingly—not until he is no longer of value to him."

She felt tears finally arise. "I just don't know how long Simon can keep his French liaison convinced of his loyalty," she whispered. "I am worried he is on a terribly slippery slope."

Lucas simply stared.

"What is it?"

"I meant it when I said that Grenville is clever and dangerous."

She became chilled. "And what is your point?"

"This war has made men like myself—and like Grenville—chameleons. We have become leopards adept at changing our spots. We have learned how to do whatever we must in order to survive."

"You are making me uneasy."

"You never told me how Grenville became an agent for the French."

Her heart thundered. "He did what he had to in order to survive," she said slowly. "He had a choice—become one of them or go to the guillotine."

Lucas made a harsh sound. "Amelia—would Grenville ever betray his country?"

She shot to her feet. "Of course not!"

Lucas studied her. "Not even to save his own life—or yours—or his children's?"

And suddenly Amelia was at a loss and she could not answer him. Because Simon would do anything he had to do to protect her and the children. He had said so—and she believed him.

"I thought so," Lucas said.

CHAPTER SIXTEEN

LUCAS HAD INSISTED THAT SHE take his carriage home. He had a driver, and Amelia sat in the open curricle in the backseat, curled up in the corner. Her mind was racing uselessly. She was exhausted from the emotional turmoil she had been swept up in, ever since she had eavesdropped on Warlock and Simon yesterday.

It was almost supper time. She could not wait until the evening meal was over, and the children had been put to bed. All she wanted to do just then was crawl into Simon's arms, close her eyes and let him hold her tightly.

Her driver cried out.

Amelia gasped, her eyes flying open as the curricle she was riding in swerved hard to the curb. A large black coach was passing by them and it had come dangerously close. She clung to the seat as one of the curricle's wheels hit the curb. Shocked, Amelia turned to stare after the black coach, expecting it to continue its mad rush by them. Instead, the coach's two-horse team turned sharply in front of them, causing Lucas's carriage horse to scream in alarm as it reared up to avoid crashing into the other team. The black coach braked in front of her curricle, positioned in such a manner that they were prevented from going forward.

Amelia was disbelieving—was the other driver insane? Or intoxicated? They had almost had a terrible collision! "Is our horse all right?" she cried.

"He's fine," the driver gasped, "but we are lucky, madam, we did not crash into this coach."

Amelia was standing now, and holding on to a safety strap for support. The team of black geldings in the coach's traces seemed unnerved, but otherwise fine. Before she could ask if there was anyone in the coach— and if anyone was hurt—its door was flung open. A man descended rapidly in a whirl of dark clothes, and was striding toward her.

"Sir?" Amelia began, confused. His face was set, and suddenly he was opening her own door and seizing her arm. Amelia cried out as she was pulled bodily from the curricle.

And as she was pushed toward the other coach, she realized what was happening. She was being abducted. Amelia screamed, trying to pull free of the stranger as her driver shouted in protest. "Unhand her!"

But it was too late and Amelia was already thrust up into the dark interior of the other coach.

As she fell hard and face-first onto the seat there, the man shoved the coach door closed behind her. Instantly the coach moved forward.

She had been abducted.

Fear immobilized her, but briefly. And Amelia realized she was not alone.

She started to sit up, and as she did, a strong hand closed around her waist, helping her.

More fear assailed her. Amelia pulled free, sitting up instantly and pressing backward into her seat. And her gaze locked with Warlock's.

"You are fortunate," he said softly, "that it is I who wishes a word with you and not the enemy."

She gasped. "How could you do such a thing?" But as she stared at her uncle, she realized that he was right.

She was in danger now, because she was Simon's lover and she knew too much. French agents could abduct her, just as her uncle had.

"I asked you to give me your word, Amelia, and you refused to do so." He shrugged, his expression bland. "It hardly takes genius to know you would run to Lucas the first moment you could do so. But at least I trust him."

She was gasping for breath and trembling wildly. "You frightened me!" But what did that mean? Was he implying that he did not trust her—or Simon?

"Good, because you should be frightened. You should be on your way to Cornwall, in fact."

She was beginning to regain some composure—and she was furious. "I am not leaving Simon, damn it."

His brows lifted. "Then you will stay here at your own risk—and now you comprehend just how risky it is to remain here."

"You are certainly making your point, Sebastian. In the future, I will be more careful and travel with Garrett at my side. But if you have staged a false abduction to impress me, then you have wasted your time!"

"A wise decision, to keep a bodyguard, but I did not stage an abduction just to frighten you. I told you to keep everything you have learned in confidence. You disobeyed me, and there is always a price to be paid for disobedience, Amelia."

She stared, taken aback and uncertain of how she should respond. Should she fear her own uncle? He had come to the family's aid twenty years ago, but two decades had passed since then and the country was at war—and war changed everyone. She knew that first-hand.

She finally said, low and carefully, "I have done no

harm. As you said, Lucas is trustworthy. Simon is in trouble, and maybe Lucas can help."

"I can help, Amelia. It is to me you should have turned." He was calm.

She was not about to tell him that she did not trust him, and perhaps, that she feared him. "Yes, you can help. I want you to let Simon out, Warlock. He has been in your intrigues long enough. He has a family to think of, especially now that his wife is gone. He is being ripped apart by these terrible deceptions. He needs to be a father to his children, not be one of your spies."

"Even if I decided to let him out, to use your term, his French masters would hardly be so agreeable. They are expecting Grenville to provide them with valuable intelligence, Amelia. The reach of the Terror is vast. It has come to our shores. Grenville must dance to their tune, otherwise he will pay a dear price for his treachery."

She shivered. "We could go into hiding. We could disappear."

"He cannot give up an earldom, Amelia."

"Then what is the answer?" she cried. "Or is the real answer that you won't give him up?"

"Grenville remains terribly valuable to me, more so than ever, in fact. Come, Amelia, you are highly intelligent. Surely you know that Grenville is perfectly placed to do the worst damage to France? You remain a patriot, do you not?"

She hissed, "I will not sacrifice Simon to the damned war!"

"And I hope you do not have to. Grenville has been playing a dangerous game for several years. If he can continue to do so successfully—and there are men like him who have done so successfully for many years—he will survive. Do you really wish to help him? I have no doubt that it would ease his mind if you took the children and went to Cornwall."

Had she become a distraction—a dangerous one? But she knew Simon needed her close by! She was consumed with dismay. There was no end in sight to these horrible war games. She simply could not imagine going around and around like this, bowing to one master and then another for years and years, and wondering every time Simon went out into the night, if he would ever return. "Simon needs me. I cannot leave him now. So do not ask me to do so again."

"I thought that would be your reply." He seemed slightly amused.

She shook her head grimly. "I will do my best to be a help to him—not a hindrance or a distraction. But you must assure me of one thing. Assure me that you will not send Simon back to France, not now, not ever."

"You may rest assured that right now, I prefer him to be where he is. But I can make no promises, Amelia. None of my men have spoken with Robespierre, but he has."

She clenched her fists, horrified. Had Simon become that deeply involved in the French republican government? "I won't allow him to go back. It is too dangerous. They already imprisoned him once! He would never survive another prison term."

"Unfortunately, he will do as I say." He was calm. "But I will certainly take what you are saying into consideration."

She shook her head, feeling powerless. "You are heartless, Sebastian."

"If I had a heart, I would probably be dead, as would most of my men." He shrugged.

"I am your niece! I love him!" she cried.

"Yes, that is obvious—too obvious. You cannot allow his enemies to realize that you are lovers, Amelia. Because if his deception is ever uncovered, Grenville is in jeopardy, as are you and the children."

She turned to gaze out of the window at the passing buildings, tears arising. She hated Warlock now. She hated the war.

"I am not the enemy. I want nothing more than to attain a happy ending for us all."

He spoke softly, and Amelia looked at him, wondering if she had misheard.

"But I have found that there are few happy endings to be had, outside of fairy tales and novels. I look forward to the day when Grenville can return to his life as an earl and a father, when I have no further need for him, when this damned war is over. But I am a realist, Amelia, not a dreamer, and my attention is on the present and the immediate future. You need to be a realist, as well. You need to keep your romantic expectations in check. These are not romantic times."

She hugged herself and stared out of the window again. He was trying to tell her that the odds were not in her favor, she realized with a sinking sensation. He was saying that she would not be happily settled in the country with Simon and the children one day.

"I brought you here for a reason."

She jerked, meeting his gaze with dread.

"In this time of war and revolution, there is no reason that you cannot do your part, too."

She stiffened. She knew she was not going to like his suggestions.

His gaze was sharp, his smile casual. "You are living with Grenville now. And you know him well—better, perhaps, than anyone."

She did not like this new tangent. "I know him very well."

"He seems entirely fond of you."

She tensed. "We are friends."

"Good. Friends and lovers, it is truly perfect."

Her tension grew. "You do not sound mocking."

"I am not being mocking. If you are going to remain here in town, then you may as well be useful. And you can be very useful, Amelia, by listening carefully to what Grenville says and how he says it—by watching him with care and reporting all of this back to me."

She was aghast. "I am not spying on Simon!"

"Why not? If he is doing what he claims, then there is nothing untoward that you could possibly reveal, is there?"

She inhaled. "What does that mean?"

"I believe you know exactly what I am saying." He added, "Grenville has convinced his French masters that he is one of them—and that is no easy task. So I must wonder, is he one of them or is he one of us?" The bland indifference was gone. Warlock's dark eyes burned.

She cried out. Hadn't Lucas questioned Simon's loyalties, as well? "He would never betray us. He would never betray our country."

"War is a monster that devours men whole," Warlock said harshly. "I know—firsthand. Sometimes it takes their bodies, at other times, it takes their souls. So the question becomes, who has Grenville's soul?"

"I will never spy on him." Amelia trembled.

"Not even to save him from the French?" Their gazes locked. "Not even to save him from himself? Not even to simply...save him?"

Amelia stared through her tears, incapable of looking away.

SIMON'S BODY BEGAN TO SPASM as Amelia moved her mouth over him. "Amelia," he gasped, seizing her arms.

Amelia allowed him to drag her up his body. He wrapped her in his arms and thrust upward, deeply, into her. Astride him, she held him close as their bodies fused with both desperation and love. She knew that every time they made love, it could be the last time. She had never been as bold, as aggressive, as frantic, as she had just been.

He cried out wildly, but she followed him a moment later with her own climax.

She floated in that state of euphoria she was becoming familiar with, still in his arms, her body draped over his. "You did not have to do that," he whispered roughly.

She tightened her grasp, her cheek nestled against his chest, the pleasure fading rapidly. There was no following sense of satiation. Instead tension began. Every moment of that day rushed back to her, in vivid detail. Lucas had questioned Simon's loyalty. And her uncle wanted her to spy on him....

"Are you all right?" he whispered, kissing her temple and moving her to the bed, beside him. He kept her in the circle of his arms.

What were they going to do? What was she going to do? How could they keep the children safe? She kissed his chest and looked up, aware of the need to cry. "Being with you is always wonderful, Simon."

"Then why do you look so sad?" His gaze was concerned and searching.

She reached for the covers and pulled them up, suddenly cold. "Would you ever consider running away with me and the children?"

His eyes widened. "If I thought, for a moment, that

we could run and hide without being discovered, yes, I would consider it."

She studied him in dismay. "Why would it be so hard to hide?"

"I am a gentleman with means. You are a lady. Our presence would be easily remarked, no matter where we went." He sat up and so did she. "Is that what you want to do?"

"If that is what it would take to keep us all safe—and together—then, yes, that is what I want to do."

He began shaking his head. "And what about your brothers? Could you really run away without telling them where you are going? What about Julianne? Your mother? She would not be able to come with us—she could so easily give us away."

Amelia sank back against the pillows. She hadn't thought any of this through. "So that is it, then? We will stay here, like this, until the war ends—or until my uncle sends you back to France?"

His face darkened. "Amelia, I have never regretted anything more than I regret bringing you into my sordid life."

"You are the joy in my life," she cried.

"No, I am the reason you walk about with fear in your eyes." He got up abruptly. "How could I have thought, even for a moment, that you would not learn the truth about me?"

"I am glad I learned the truth, so we are in this predicament together." She tried not to stare. The fire in the hearth was low, but a half a dozen candles were lit, illuminating the bedchamber. She hadn't ever seen Simon walk about so immodestly before. He had always been careful to avert his back to her, and quickly reach for his clothes. She watched him go over to the chair where his caftan lay, her heart racing with renewed desire. He was all lean, hard muscle, as superb as a Greek athlete from bygone times. She pulled her knees up to her chest and hugged them.

He glanced at her, catching her staring, before he turned and shrugged the silk garment on.

She must not be distracted. "Are you going out tonight?"

He did not face her. "No."

"I know you are going to go out to meet Marcel sooner or later," she began, with great care.

He interrupted rudely. "I am not discussing this with you."

He had not gone out last night, or the night before. Had he met Marcel during the day, then? If that were the case, she would be relieved. Did she dare ask?

And it crossed her mind that if she had been spying on him as Warlock had asked, she would know the answers to her questions. She would also know that the danger they were in hadn't changed; that there wasn't a new threat. On the other hand, if he had yet to meet Marcel, anything could happen at that rendezvous.

"Would you tell me if we were in any new danger?" she finally asked.

He slowly turned to look at her, his expression hard to read. He finally said, "We are not in any more danger, not that I know of. I hate this, Amelia. I hate that you could be in danger now, too!"

"I know you do. Simon, this is not your fault!"

"It is entirely my fault. But you should know that I am very careful, Amelia, to cover my trail," he said harshly. "I have no intention of leading anyone back to this house. I have been very careful, for some time, to stay one step ahead of all my masters."

He meant to outwit Warlock as well as the Jacobins, she thought with more dread. "I really don't care about myself. It is the children I am thinking of."

"I realize that. However, I care about you as I do the children, and that is why I am playing this game so slowly and so carefully."

He was playing "slowly." The word felt odd. It was a statement Warlock would certainly be interested in. "Even if the children were in Cornwall, if you were ever discovered, Simon, they would still be in danger."

He grimaced and did not answer, which was answer enough.

She blurted, "Do you trust my uncle?"

His glance was razor sharp. "That is a loaded question, I think."

"Do you?"

He did not approach, keeping to the other side of the bedroom. "Sometimes I do—without a doubt. At other times, no, I do not."

Aware of what she was doing, she felt terrible—guilty and treacherous, at once. "But he is a patriot, Simon. We are all on the same side."

He stared.

She got out of the bed, taking a sheet with her, which she kept wrapped around her. His gaze slammed over her. She approached. "We are all on the same side, aren't we?" she whispered.

"Is this an interrogation?"

Her heart thundered. "No. Why don't you trust him? Because for some reason, I don't trust him entirely, either."

He stared at the full curve of her breast, then lifted his eyes. "He has one overriding ambition—winning the war."

"But you share that ambition."

He seized her hand, as she held the sheet to her chest. "My greatest ambition is keeping my sons safe."

He tugged at her hand. She released the sheet and he watched it fall. Then his gaze locked with hers. "Are you spying on me now? Did Warlock put you up to this?" He was cold.

She somehow shook her head no. But she had just learned the answer to both Lucas's and Warlock's questions. Winning the war was not Simon's first ambition; keeping his children safe was.

Which meant that he would do anything to protect them—and she was glad!

"Answer me, Amelia," he said harshly, his grasp on her wrist tightening.

"I would never spy on you," she whispered. And it was a lie—because she had just done that—and they both knew it.

His eyes were blazing. She thought he was going to release her and walk away. But he jerked her close, anchoring her against his body, kissing her hard.

THE WEATHER COULDN'T HAVE BEEN more perfect, Simon thought. The downpour was torrential, the night cloudy and dark, making it almost impossible to see. He was hurrying down an alleyway behind the cobbler's shop on Darby Lane, heavily disguised, his wig bright red, his skin covered with asbestos. Because the weather was so inclement, he wore a hooded cloak.

But he was filled with tension. He was about to meet Marcel, who might very well recognize him. And he had the oddest sensation that he was being watched when he had left the house. However, he had been careful crossing town, and he knew he hadn't been followed.

At the end of the alley, he saw two men, also in hooded cloaks, standing beneath the overhanging roof of the adjacent building, out of the rain.

His heart thundered. There had been no way to continue avoiding a meeting with Marcel. Simon had sent intelligence twice the week before by courier, but Marcel had demanded they meet in person. So he had finally agreed to the rendezvous, but he had insisted it be after dark and outside, in an unlit alley. He hadn't known it would rain. God was surely on his side tonight.

But that did not reduce his fear.

As he led his sodden horse down the alley, images flashed in his mind—Amelia as she writhed in ecstasy beneath him, Amelia as she read a story to the boys, Amelia smiling in the entryway as the boys raced in to greet her, Amelia holding Lucille and feeding her from a bottle. His heart ached now. His boys adored her, as did Lucille. He adored her.

But the war had tainted their love.... She was jumping through Warlock's hoops now.

He was trying not to feel betrayed. No one knew better than he how manipulative and powerful Warlock was.

"Finally," an Englishman said, stepping to the edge of the invisible line between his shelter and the pouring rain. "We have been waiting, Jourdan."

Simon shoved his personal feelings aside. The Englishman's hood had fallen back, revealing vaguely familiar features: curly, dark blond hair, pale skin, blue eyes. Simon tensed. He was certain he had met this man, once upon a time.

He halted before the overhang, remaining in the rain, his hood covering his forehead and the sides of his face, his collar up and concealing his jaw and chin. "It was hell, getting across town," he said, speaking with a French accent.

"You have been avoiding us," the blond gentleman said, his eyes flashing. "Not that I blame you."

No attack could have been as clear, but Simon merely smiled. "I dance to no one's tune, except for my own, and when we meet, as now, it is on my terms. But I do apologize for keeping you waiting in the rain. To whom do I have the pleasure of speaking?"

"Treyton," he said, "Tom Treyton."

Simon felt his heart cease beating, before it quickly resumed its pace.

Tom Treyton was smiling, coldly—belligerently. "How is your dear cousin, Jourdan? The cousin who was to welcome you with open arms into his home?"

Simon regained his composure. "St. Just recently lost his wife. I did not feel it proper to intrude upon a household in mourning, although I called upon him to tender my condolences. He was very civil." Had Treyton been watching Lambert Hall?

Treyton seemed skeptical, one dark brow slashing upward. "Surely you met on some common ground? After all, you are cousins, and while he has lost his wife, you have lost your parents, your brothers and sisters and your French cousins."

Simon instinctively did not like this tangent, as he was not sure where Treyton meant to lead. "I did not wish to burden him with my own losses," he said, referring to the massacre of the entire Jourdan family in Lyons.

"Of course not. Hmm, I just realized he is your only remaining family."

Simon tensed, wondering what Treyton was driving at. But the man standing behind Tom stepped forward.

He was tall and thin, with very white skin and shockingly pale blue eyes. Edmund Duke's gaze locked with Simon's.

Simon's tension escalated. He was there to meet Marcel, whom he had assumed was Duke. Very carefully, Simon inclined his head, breaking eye contact. "Bonjour, Marcel."

"We meet at last," the French spy said, in perfect English. Duke was certainly facing him now, but he did not seem to recognize Simon.

Simon looked up.

Duke's eyes flashed with rage. "Two days ago," he said, "Coburg took Tourconing."

That had been on May 17, Simon thought uneasily. He had heard of the news yesterday. "He was driven back to Tournai," he said.

"Coburg had sixty thousand troops!" he exclaimed.

Simon stared in dismay, with one coherent thought—Warlock had played him. Warlock had insisted that the Allies would only field forty thousand men. Damn him!

But he remained calm and contained. He said flatly, "Then my sources were wrong."

"Yes, your sources were wrong, and you have hardly proved your value to us or your loyalty," Duke said coldly. "Who gave you the information, Jourdan?"

"My cousin, of course."

"Ah, so he does not trust you, either."

"No one builds Rome in a day," he said, thinking of Amelia. "I cannot befriend St. Just overnight, even if we are cousins. And we do not know that he gave me misinformation. He may have believed that his facts were correct."

Duke studied him. Simon flinched but did not look

away. "If you are suspect, if they are using you to play us, then you have no value to me, to Lafleur, to France."

"I am not under suspicion. I have barely arrived in town. I have yet to establish the network I need in order to give you the kind of information that will help you to win the war."

"St. Just is friends with Sebastian Warlock and Dominic Paget. He moves in Tory circles. Get into them, Jourdan, and give us what we want—before General Pichegru attacks the Allies."

He kept an impassive expression. "I will do my best."

Duke made a harsh sound. "You do not want me to tell Lafleur that you are entirely useless."

Inwardly, he recoiled. "I need time."

"You do not have time. Pichegru will attack Tournai in days." Duke added suddenly, his eyes burning, "I have heard that one cell remains vacant at La Prison de la Luxembourg. It is Number 403."

Simon froze. 403 had been his cell.

And suddenly the alleyway reeked of blood. Suddenly he could hear the crowds screaming, *"À la guillotine!" Thump.*

He blinked and realized that he was sweating as he stood there in the cold rain, and that Duke had strode away. He watched Duke mount his hack and trot past them and out of the alleyway, not bothering to look his way another time. Slowly, with dread, he faced Treyton. No threat could have been as clear, he thought.

Tom smiled at him. "You do not want to become useless to us, Jourdan, and you may trust me on that." Treyton walked over to his horse, untied the reins and led it forward into the downpour. He mounted and paused beside Simon. "Give my regards to St. Just—and to his lovely children."

"Leave my cousin and his children out of this," he heard himself say harshly.

"Hmm, it is as I thought—they are your only family now and you are taken with them." Tom saluted him and broke into a gallop.

Simon watched him ride out of the alley, in growing horror.

CHAPTER SEVENTEEN

AMELIA SMILED DOWN AT LUCILLE, who lay in her cradle, beaming happily back at her. She reached down and the baby grabbed her finger and gurgled. Love swelled within her breast.

But it did not vanquish the anguish that resided there.

Somehow, she kept smiling at Lucille, as tears filled her eyes. Simon had gone out last night, directly after supper. It had been raining torrentially, and no one in their right mind would go out in such weather. But he hadn't had a choice and she knew it.

She had caught him on the stairs, and his face had been stark-white, chalked with asbestos. His lips had been rouged. He had already donned a cloak, but the hood had been carelessly pulled up, and she had seen his crimson wig.

She had begged him not to go.

He had refused to consider her plea. Instead, he had told her not to wait up, and he had continued down the stairs. She had remained frozen in fear on the steps. The front door hadn't slammed, indicating that he had gone out a terrace door. She had finally sunk down on one of the steps, hugging herself and crying.

And he had not come to her bed last night.

Since their affair had begun, he made love to her every night, staying with her until dawn. He was obviously so very angry with her; he had been immersed in his newspaper during breakfast and hadn't glanced up at her once.

"At least he is safe," she whispered to Lucille. She wondered if she should try to explain that she hadn't spied on him. She hadn't relayed a single word he had said to Warlock. She wasn't sure that would make a difference; she had been manipulating him to discover where his loyalties actually lay.

"Miss Greystone!" Mrs. Murdock cried.

Amelia whirled as the nurse came rushing into the nursery. "What is it?" she asked, alarmed by Mrs. Murdock's expression.

"Mr. Southland is here!"

Amelia felt her heart lurch so terribly that for one moment she could not breathe. "It's not even eleven o'clock." She could barely think straight. Southland had come for Lucille. "Is he taking her?"

"I don't know. His lordship has taken him into the library, and he has closed the doors."

"Oh, God," Amelia cried. Her heart continued to pound. She had the urge to take the baby and run away. In that moment, she knew she loved Lucille as if she were her own child.

What was she going to do? She stared at Mrs. Murdock. "How did he seem? What does he look like?"

"He seemed anxious, Miss Greystone. He is a big, handsome fellow."

Amelia looked at Lucille, who continued to gurgle happily, staring up at the revolving coasters hanging above the crib. Southland was her father; he had every right to take her, care for her and love her. It simply hurt so much. "His lordship did not instruct you to bring Lucille down?"

"No, he did not. Oh, I am going to miss her so!" Tears filled the governess's eyes.

Amelia promptly picked up Lucille and held her close. She still couldn't breathe properly. She loved her so. But she had to do what was right. Southland deserved the opportunity to claim his child. "Can you accompany me downstairs?" She heard how hoarse her own tone was.

They went downstairs slowly, Amelia filled with dread and holding the baby tightly. In the front hall, she gave Lucille to Mrs. Murdock, afraid she might never hold her again. "Take her for a moment. I wish to meet Southland. Why don't you wait in the pink room?"

Mrs. Murdock nodded and walked to the salon. Amelia watched her and the baby for a long moment, struggling for composure. Then, inhaling, she strode into the east wing and knocked firmly on the library door.

"Come in," Simon called.

She stepped inside and knew that Simon had been expecting her. He was seated at his desk, but he arose, his expression utterly impassive. Southland had been seated in a chair before the desk, his back to the door. He also stood, turning.

"Mr. Southland, this is my housekeeper, Miss Greystone. She has taken a personal interest in Lucille," Simon said, a question in his eyes.

She met his gaze, somehow sending him a wan smile. But he knew how she felt about the baby; he knew she was so reluctant to give her up. Then she smiled brightly at Lucille's father. "Good morning, sir."

"As I was explaining to his lordship, I cannot thank him—and you—enough for all you have done," Southland said.

Amelia studied him now. He was a tall man in a light brown wig, wearing a green jacket that matched his eyes.

She could imagine that he was a pleasant fellow and he was certainly a gentleman. But his gaze was filled with worry, and he did not smile now.

"Lucille has been a welcome addition to this household," Amelia said roughly. "We all love her very much."

From the corner of her eyes, she noticed that Simon did not move. His expression was impossible to read. She added pointedly, "We have been expecting you for some time." She wanted to know why it had taken him a good six weeks to come and see his child.

He shoved his hands in the pockets of his pale breeches. "I would have come sooner, but I was traveling…and I could not decide what to do."

Simon stepped out from behind his desk and said smoothly, "Southland was just telling me that he did not know about the child until he received my letter."

Southland flushed.

Simon added, "Apparently the affair ended in the fall."

His color rising, Southland looked as if he wished to escape the library—as if he wished to escape Simon. But of course he did. He had cuckolded the Earl of St. Just.

"We have a great deal in common, then—as I did not know about the child until recently, either." Simon's smile was cold and it came and went.

Southland faced him. "I am so very sorry, my lord, that I have put you in this position!"

"I told you, Lady Grenville had my permission to have her affairs." He shrugged.

Amelia looked between them with growing anger. She did not care for any rivalry that might exist between both men. But she could comprehend why it had taken Southland so long to call. He must have dreaded facing

Simon. "What about the baby? What about Lucille and her future?"

Southland faced her, still flushed. "I would like to see her," he said. "If I may?" He glanced nervously at Simon.

So did Amelia. She expected Southland to state that he had come to claim his daughter, but it wasn't clear if that was the case. They had to know what Southland intended. But Simon was silent, not asking any questions of Southland.

He glanced at her. Her heart sank as their gazes met. Silently she tried to tell him that she did not want Lucille to go. He looked away. "Of course you may hold Lucille. She is your child."

"Thank you, my lord."

"I will get her," Amelia said, quite ill now. She hurried from the room, and in the pink-and-white salon, she approached Mrs. Murdock.

"What is happening?" the governess cried, handing her the baby. Lucille had fallen asleep.

"I don't know. He is very young, and he seems more interested in placating Grenville for having had an affair with his wife than he does in meeting Lucille!" Amelia rocked her, hushing her, as her lids drifted a bit. Dread and dismay were making her sick. Her heart already felt broken.

Mrs. Murdock touched her arm gently. "No wonder he didn't come till now—he must have been deathly afraid of his lordship!"

Amelia smiled grimly and left the salon. She understood why Southland had procrastinated, but if he was capable of cuckolding Grenville, then surely he could face him and claim his daughter! There was no excuse for such procrastination.

Both men were standing in the library, waiting for

her, Simon with his hands on his hips. Southland was pale and he appeared nervous.

Amelia marched over to Southland. "She is asleep." She refrained from offering his daughter to him to hold.

His eyes widened. "She is such a little angel!" he exclaimed. And finally, he smiled.

Amelia's heart sank. It was as she had thought. Southland had taken one look at his daughter and fallen completely in love. "Here," she whispered, choking. She meant to give him his daughter to hold.

He backed away, alarmed. "Maybe it is best if I don't hold her!"

Amelia blinked through her tears at him. "Why not?" She inhaled. "Mr. Southland. I must be direct. Aren't you here to take her home with you?"

"I don't know!" he cried, his gaze moist. "I just don't know! How can I take her home? I am a bachelor of twenty-two. I live alone, with a single manservant. I am not ready to have a family. I am not even ready to wed!"

Amelia began to have hope. Incredulously, she glanced at Simon. Their gazes met, his eyes flickering as they did.

Southland added, near tears, "Of course, my parents could take her. They have an entire staff. But I haven't even told them about her. Miss Greystone, I simply don't know what to do. I am torn—I am afraid!"

Amelia looked at Simon. "Please," she said.

He came forward decisively then. "She is welcome to remain here, Southland."

Southland faced him, his eyes wide with some disbelief. "You would keep her?"

"She is welcome to remain here," Simon repeated flatly. "I would not turn my wife's bastard away—God rest her departed soul. But if you walk away now, you will not be invited back. She either goes with you or she stays here—as a Grenville."

Amelia's heart soared. This was why she loved and admired Simon so—he was so noble and so generous—he was so kind!

Southland nodded, seeming torn between relief and despair. "I believe that it is best that she stays with you, my lord, because you can give her the life I cannot." He faced Amelia. "It is better if I don't hold her. It is better if she doesn't awaken—if she doesn't see me."

Amelia remained in disbelief. They were going to keep Lucille.

"You should go," Simon said to Southland. He came to stand closely beside Amelia, as if feeling protective of her and the child.

"Yes, I should." He hesitated, staring at Lucille.

Amelia hugged her, afraid he was going to change his mind. But then he smiled grimly, moisture in his eyes, and dashed from the room.

Amelia sagged, Lucille in her arms.

Simon steadied her, grasping her elbow. "He would be disastrous as a father. He is much too young, with no means to care for his child—and no real interest in doing so."

"Simon, thank you," Amelia cried.

And his mask slipped away. Warmth and concern filled his eyes. "I know how much you love her, Amelia."

She began to cry. "And I love you, Simon, so much."

His face hardened. "But you questioned my loyalties."

"Yes, I did. But you would not act any differently than I would, if it came to making a choice that involved saving the children."

"You did not let me finish. You were right to question my loyalties. I would betray my country if I had to." He slid his arm around her. "You know me too well…. Yet you love me anyway."

"I love you because of all I know!"

"I know you mean that now. But I pray that the day doesn't come when you feel very differently."

"I will never feel differently," she whispered, loving him so much that it hurt. "Simon, I haven't said anything to Warlock."

He was grave. "If there is something he wants you to tell him, you will do so, sooner or later, whether you wish to or not."

"I will never betray you." She was final.

"No, you wouldn't—not knowingly." He put his arm around her and kissed her cheek, then nuzzled her jaw. "I missed you last night."

Desire fisted. Love swelled. "I missed you, too."

And Lucille yawned and began to awaken.

AMELIA REMOVED HER APRON, standing in the kitchen by the center island, surveying a perfectly roasted pork loin. "That looks wonderful, Cook," she said, meaning it. "You have truly outdone yourself."

The chef beamed, thanking her and covering the sterling platter with a silver cover. Amelia smiled at Jane and Maggie, her spirits high. Ever since Southland had left that morning, leaving Lucille behind, she had felt as if a huge weight had been lifted from her shoulders. Just then, life felt almost perfect—she almost felt that they had become one big, happy family.

Simon had made it clear that he meant to raise Lucille as his own child. She had never been as relieved or more grateful. The moment Southland had left, Lucille had been returned to the nursery, and she and Simon had made love with shocking urgency and passion on

the library desk. Amelia had never loved him more and
she had told him so—repeatedly. He had made love to
her as if he loved her in return—and she knew he did.
He had held her afterward as if he was afraid she was a
ghost or an illusion that would disappear at any moment.

"I am happy you are happy," he had said.

Love and joy churned within her chest. Tonight, after
supper, she would read to the boys as she routinely did.
But this evening, she meant to include Simon—she
would insist that he join them. She could imagine him
seated in the chair adjacent to her own, before the fire, as
she read to the boys in their beds. She would even bring
Lucille's basinet into the boys' room so she could share
in the experience. And once the boys and Lucille were
all safely asleep, she would go to her own bedchamber
and await Simon....

And she wondered if the day would ever come where
they would be a real family. All Simon had to do was
adopt Lucille. All he had to do was make her his wife.

Some of the pleasure faded. Simon had yet to tell her
that he loved her. On the other hand, his actions spoke
volumes. But he hadn't ever mentioned the future, or
shown any interest in marrying again. And that worried her! On the other hand, he was not in any position
to ask anyone to be his wife.

A pan rattled, jerking her out of her fanciful musing.
She glanced at her pocket watch. Simon had been out
all afternoon and he had yet to return. Supper would be
served at seven o'clock, as always, and it was a quarter
to the hour. He hadn't sent word that he would be late,
so she expected him at any moment.

She sobered, worried. The glow she had carried with
her all day began to rapidly dull. He hadn't bothered to
tell her he was going out for the afternoon, but he was

hardly in the habit of reporting his movements to her. And their life was hardly perfect. They weren't a real family, nor was she certain that he would ever ask her to be his wife. More importantly, Simon lived in the dark, dangerous world of espionage, with the constant threat of being uncovered by his enemies, and the danger of the retribution that might follow.

Fred was entering the kitchens and Amelia glanced at him as she hung her apron on a wall peg. "Has his lordship returned yet?"

"No, Miss Greystone, he has not."

More anxiety churned. Amelia left the kitchens, glancing into the dining room as she did every night. The table was perfectly set with crystal, china and linens. White and yellow roses formed the centerpiece.

And suddenly she saw Simon seated at the table's head, in the bronze-velvet coat he had been wearing that day, the two boys seated on his left in their blue dinner jackets. And she glimpsed herself seated on his right, wearing her new rose-damask dress....

She stiffened, surprised by her wishful thinking, and then she was angry with herself. What was wrong with her? There was a time and a place for everything. Until Simon was freed from his services as a spy, she must put her own dreams aside.

Amelia left the dining room, hurrying into the front hall. It was five to seven. She approached the front door where a liveried doorman stood, and glanced out of the tall arched window beside it. His coach was not coming down the drive; it was not parked to the right either, by the stables.

"Miss Greystone!"

Amelia whirled at the sharp cry, as Mrs. Murdock came stumbling down the stairs. Panic had been evident in her tone, and she was ashen. "Mrs. Murdock? Is someone hurt?"

"Miss Greystone—I can't find her!" Mrs. Murdock ran across the hall to her.

Amelia felt her heart lurch. "Whom can't you find?"

Panting, Mrs. Murdock said, "The baby is gone! I have looked everywhere! I left her asleep in her cradle, but she isn't there—she has been stolen, Miss Greystone, stolen from her very bed!"

Amelia stared in confusion and disbelief. Lucille was gone? Lucille was stolen? She did not believe it! "Mrs. Murdock, surely the boys have taken her into their rooms!"

"I have checked everywhere." Mrs. Murdock began to weep. "Lucille is gone!"

And as the comprehension began, so did the horror.

SIMON SAT BACK GRIMLY in his coach as it moved through his Mayfair neighborhood. His efforts that afternoon to uncover information that would appease his French masters had been an utter waste. He had called on Bedford, Greystone and Penrose, in that order. But he had not been able to ferret out information that might help Pichegru when he attacked the Allied position in Flanders.

His temples ached and he rubbed them. Two days had already passed since he had met up with Marcel and Treyton. His time was running out. From the moment he received any intelligence, it took at least twenty-four hours to get that information to the French on the battle lines, depending mostly on the weather, but also on the network of couriers inside France. The French would move on Tournai at any moment. He was desperate.

Marcel's threat had been very clear—his old cell in the Parisian prison awaited him, if he failed to provide the French with the intelligence they needed. And as sick as that threat made him—he knew he would never survive another term in prison—it was Tom Treyton who haunted him now.

"Give my regards to St. Just—and to his lovely children."

That bastard had dared to threaten his children. Simon abruptly opened a window, feeling sick.

Treyton had decided to use the children as leverage. And that made Treyton his worst enemy.

Not for the first time, Simon debated arranging a private meeting with him. And he knew if he did that, Treyton would not leave that meeting alive....

Amelia's image flashed in his mind. She thought him noble—but he was ruthlessly considering murdering a man in cold blood.

She said she understood that he would do anything to protect the children, but she didn't understand at all.

And she would not love him if she understood.

One day, the truth would be revealed, and she would be appalled by the man he had become.

And when that day came, she would walk away from him, horrified. He stared out of his window blindly, wondering if he would be able to survive a life without Amelia in it. He wondered if his children would survive.

He knew the answer, so for now Treyton would live, and he would attempt to dance madly to their tune. And he still had one bit of intelligence that he could use, if there was no other choice. He could tell Duke that a number of men, including Warlock, knew he was Marcel, and that he was being played....

He felt sicker now. But it was too soon to play his best and last hand. And it would be his last hand, because once he betrayed Warlock—and his country—in such a way, there would be no going back.

His carriage had halted, he realized. Simon felt warmth begin to steal through him as his door was opened. He couldn't wait to walk inside his home, greet his sons, see Amelia and pretend, if only for a while, that their life was an ordinary one.

He stepped out of his coach, smiling at the footman. But as he did, he glanced warily around. Earlier, he had been suspicious of another coach, some two blocks behind him. He had wondered if he was being followed, but then the coach had turned off the main street.

No one seemed to be lurking about the stables or the gardens now, spying on him. He was even looking forward to a glimpse of Lucille, and then, of course, there was Amelia... He wished he could find a pretense to have her dine with them.

The front door of his home flew open and Amelia came running out of the house. He took one look at her pale, frightened face, and knew that the serpent had struck them, at last.

His heart seemed to drop to the ground beneath his feet. The force was sickening. He rushed toward her. "Amelia?"

She reached him and cried breathlessly, "Lucille is gone. She has been abducted." And she began to tremble helplessly, tears spilling, seizing his arms.

For one moment, Simon did not believe it. And then he knew that it was the baby they had chosen to use against him....

AMELIA HUGGED HERSELF, fighting tears, listening carefully as Simon interviewed the last housemaid, an hour and a half later. But Bess had seen nothing and no one.

In fact, not a single servant had seen a stranger in the house that evening, much less someone leaving with Lucille, and the entire staff had been accounted for. It was as if the baby had vanished into thin air!

Her heart cracked apart in anguish another time. She was terrified for the child, whom she very much considered her daughter. But no one would hurt an innocent baby, would they? Oh, God, it was cold and raining out. What if she was cold? Hungry?

"Thank you, Bess, for your help," Simon was saying. "If you happen to recall something, anything, whether you believe it to be related to Lucille's disappearance or not, you must tell me right away," Simon said calmly. "Someone entered this house. He or she might have left a clue somewhere. We will continue searching the premises for some sign."

The weeping maid nodded, turning to leave. Lloyd stood stiffly by the door to the gold room where Simon had been conducting the interviews, Mrs. Murdock with him. "Sir, I will begin another search of the entire house and grounds."

"No one is to leave these premises, not without my permission," Simon said. But he couldn't look at her, and Amelia was aware of it. His spying had brought this down on them!

As Bess ran out, Lucas came striding in, unannounced.

"Lucas!" Amelia rushed into his arms, momentarily relieved—if anyone could save the day, it was her heroic brother. "Thank God you have come to help!"

Lucas held her tightly, but only briefly. "Grenville sent word. My God—Lucille is missing?"

Amelia nodded. "We are desperate to find her! Simon

has interviewed the entire staff, but no one has heard or seen anything."

Simon stepped forward. "Lloyd, bring a bottle of claret and three glasses. Mrs. Murdock, please check on the boys."

As both servants left, Simon closed the pair of rose-wood doors behind them. "Babies don't disappear," he said, facing them grimly. "But whoever took her, he or she has hidden their trail."

"No, babies do not simply disappear. And it isn't easy walking into a house like this unremarked. Could some-one have been paid off to remain silent?" Lucas's gaze was narrow.

"That seems likely," Simon said grimly. "But no one is confessing to his or her complicity in this affair."

Amelia gasped. "You mean that someone did see something—perhaps he or she even saw Lucille being taken—but they are being paid to remain silent?" She was shocked and furious, too.

"It is beginning to appear that way," Simon said grimly.

Amelia clenched her fists. "Why?"

But Simon did not hear her—either that, or he was ignoring her. He faced Lucas. "Lucille was last seen in her crib at half past six. She was asleep. When Mrs. Murdock went to feed her at seven, the crib was empty."

The two men stared at one another.

"I can't help if I don't know what is really going on," Lucas finally said.

Amelia stiffened, staring at her brother and Simon. Simon glanced at her. "Why don't you leave us?"

Fury erupted. "I am not going anywhere! I have every right to know what has happened to Lucille. Do you think I am a fool? We simply assumed your enemies would target the boys. But, then, almost no one knows that Lucille isn't your daughter. Damn it, Simon! Why did they take her?" she cried. "Why? What do they want?"

He took her by both elbows. "Amelia, you must trust me, now. The less you know, the better."

"How dare you!" She wrenched away, striking him across the face. His eyes widened, and even as she knew she shouldn't have struck him, she shouted, "I am done, Simon, done! I will not let you shut me out of this! They have taken Lucille. They have taken my beautiful baby—because of your spy games! It is cold and raining out. She may be wet—she may be hungry—she could get sick! Why did they take her? What will they do to her? Will we ever get her back...alive?" She started to sob.

It was Lucas who pulled her close. "We will do our best to find her, Amelia, but your becoming hysterical won't help."

She looked up at him through her tears, the anger receding, replaced by raw fear. "Why did they take her?" she managed to ask, looking only at Simon.

He hesitated, then said thickly, "She is leverage, Amelia. They need information from me immediately, and they have ensured that I must do as they wish."

"If you have information, give it to them!" she cried, seized with hope. "Do you have the information they want?"

"It isn't as simple as you might think," he began.

"No!" She wrenched free of Lucas. "You would betray your country for the boys—but not for Lucille?" She was incredulous and furious, at once. "You give them what they want to hear, Simon. I mean it. You will make certain they give us Lucille back!"

Simon breathed hard.

Lucas said to him, "Do you have what they want?" He was very serious.

Simon turned to him. "No."

Amelia cried out, fists clenched again. "Then make something up," she screamed.

He flinched, ashen now. "I should have known this was coming. They threatened the children, quite explicitly, just hours ago."

Lucas's eyes widened.

"This is my fault!" Simon suddenly turned to Amelia. "Does that make you feel better? This is my worst nightmare come true!"

She inhaled. "No, it does not make me feel better! I want Lucille back. And I want this to end." She was panting.

He stared. "I will do what I have to do to get her back," he finally said.

Amelia had a frisson of fear.

"Do not walk into their noose." Lucas seized his arm. "That won't help anything."

Simon shook him off and approached Amelia, who was frozen. She desperately wanted Lucille back, but it had sounded as if Simon might sacrifice himself for the baby. "What are you planning?" she asked.

He kissed her hard and briefly. "I am doing what I must to bring Lucille home. And when she is home, you will take her and the boys to Cornwall."

Amelia became alarmed. "And you will come with us?"

He suddenly smiled, but it was both amused and sad—it was resigned. "I doubt that," he said.

And he was striding toward the door.

"Simon! What are you going to do?" Amelia cried in fear.

But he did not answer her; he left.

SIMON PACED THE LOBBY of the prestigious and very exclusive St. James Club. Two doormen stood by the front entrance, ignoring him, and several gentlemen were seated about the spacious wood-paneled lobby, awaiting their guests.

Edmund Duke entered the lobby, removing his sodden black cloak. Duke instantly saw Simon; their gazes locked.

Handing his clock to a servant by the coat closet, Duke said something, then started purposefully toward Simon, a benign smile on his face. Simon simply waited.

Duke paused before him. "Your note was a surprise. Good evening, my lord."

"Good evening, Mr. Duke," Simon said. And as he spoke, alarm filled Duke's eyes.

Simon knew he had realized his tone of voice was identical to Jourdan's. He was undoubtedly wondering if Jourdan and St. Just could be one and the same man.

Simon had probably met Duke three times in the past three years, when he had been invited to meetings at the War Office. He had never been formally introduced. Duke had ushered the War Secretary's guests in on two occasions before leaving; on the third, he had served drinks and had been present for some time before being dismissed from the room.

"I imagine that my invitation was a surprise. I do not believe we were ever properly introduced," Simon said. "However, my cousin has spoken a bit about you."

Duke's bland smile vanished. "I beg your pardon?"

"Jourdan has enjoyed meeting you, Mr. Duke. Or should I say, Monsieur Marcel?"

Duke paled. "What do you want?"

"Return Lucille. Go home, Marcel, and tell Lafleur you have been uncovered and you are being thoroughly played."

Duke's pale blue eyes flashed. Clearly, his mind was racing. "Jourdan could not have done this."

"I am not sure how you were uncovered—Warlock has known for some time. As do others. As do I." Somehow, Simon smiled. "Return my child—or live in constant fear of my reprisal." He turned to go; Duke seized his arm.

"Where is Jourdan?"

Simon did not hesitate. "Jourdan is dead."

Duke's eyes widened. Simon smiled and left.

CHAPTER EIGHTEEN

"MISS GREYSTONE! MISS Greystone! The baby is back!"

Amelia was with the boys in their bedroom, although neither John nor William showed any signs of sleep. Momma was also present, immersed in her embroidery. Overcome by fear for Lucille, and afraid of what Simon must do to gain her return, she had hoped to be distracted by the boys.

Amelia's heart seemed to vanish; somehow, she stood up. The young housemaid, Bess, stood in the doorway, her eyes wide, smiling.

Amelia was afraid to believe Bess. Simon had left the house only three hours ago, to do God only knew what. It was raining again, and he had yet to return.

"Where is she?" she cried in disbelief, praying that she was not in the midst of a dream.

"In the kitchens," Bess returned breathlessly.

Amelia gasped, hope surging. She turned incredulously to the boys, who were as wide-eyed as she was. "Come! Your sister is home. Oh, Momma. This is wonderful news! Hurry!" And the joy began.

In a group, they raced from the room and down the hall, John and William in the lead. "Is she all right? Have you seen her?" Amelia demanded, following both boys.

"She was fussing, but the moment Mrs. Murdock gave her a bottle, she was fine," Bess said, smiling. "Oh, Miss Greystone, we were all so worried about her!"

They continued in a mad rush down the stairs, Amelia stumbling in her haste. "Who returned her?"

"There was a knock on the kitchen door, Miss Greystone, and when Cook opened it, a big man with a hood pulled over his head simply shoved the babe at him. Then he turned and left, departing in a waiting carriage."

Simon had somehow attained Lucille's return. Her heart thundered. The boys raced ahead of them, through the entry hall and past the dining room. Amelia lifted her skirts, breaking into a run.

And the first thing she saw was that the entire staff had congregated in the kitchens, standing in a circle around the center table, where the baby must be. Her view was blocked, but then William and John rushed past two servants, shouting for their sister. And as the men stepped aside, Amelia saw Lucille.

She was in Mrs. Murdock's arms, nursing happily from a bottle, wrapped in a white blanket.

"Lucille, where have you been?" William scolded gently, pausing by Mrs. Murdock.

John stood on tiptoe and kissed her cheek and beamed.

Lucille paused from drinking greedily to smile at her brothers.

Amelia realized her vision was blurring. She had been so afraid for the baby! She hurried past Jane and Maggie, wanting nothing more than to hold her, and Mrs. Murdock met her gaze, her own eyes moist. "She seems fine, Miss Greystone, just fine."

Suddenly speechless, Amelia simply nodded. Mrs. Murdock gently handed the baby to her, without disturbing her. Amelia held her closely, overcome with relief. Momma clasped her shoulder comfortingly. "Thank the lord," she said.

Lucille was home. Briefly, Amelia could not speak.

"Will we ever know who took her—or why?" Mrs. Murdock asked softly. "Was there a ransom?"

Amelia started. The staff must be terribly curious. Obviously no one knew of Simon's wartime activities, so it would be natural to assume that Lucille had been taken for a ransom. "I do not know the details yet," Amelia said. She and Simon must discuss how to best manage the staff.

Her heart lurched with dismay. She had accused him of endangering Lucille, and she had even slapped him. But he had endangered Lucille—just as he had put the entire family in danger. "Is his lordship back?"

"He has not returned," Lloyd said gravely. "He left on horseback."

Amelia tensed. The rain was tapering off, and she hoped Simon had the common sense to get in from the inclement weather. How had he attained Lucille's release? She trembled. Did she really want to know?

"I am going to take Lucille upstairs. She seems dry, but I think I will change her anyway. William? John? It is past your bedtime." Amelia smiled.

A short time later, Lucille was soundly asleep in her crib, Momma had retired for the evening and the boys were settled in their beds. Amelia suddenly realized that she was so exhausted her knees were weak and she felt faint. It had been a trying day, and a trying night. As she shut the door, her smile vanished. She could hardly rest now, as one question was haunting her. Where was Simon?

Obviously she was not going to bed until she knew he had returned, safe and sound. An acute fear began. How had he obtained Lucille's release? Surely he was all right. But why wasn't he home?

She told herself not to think the worst. He would walk in the front door at any moment. Of course, she had a fence to mend. Had she really hurled all those accusations as she had? Just now, with Lucille safely in her crib, she was filled with regrets.

But she had only spoken the truth.

She leaned against the wall, brushing stray hair out of her eyes, knowing she must apologize when Simon returned. More fear stabbed through her. She wondered if she should send a note to Lucas, asking him if he had seen Simon since that afternoon or if he knew where he was.

And then she heard his footsteps. Amelia turned and saw him coming up the stairs at the opposite end of the hall.

His glance locked with hers but he did not falter. He went into his suite of rooms.

She sagged with relief. But he had not uttered a word of greeting, and he had seemed as exhausted as she was, in every possible way.

The war was coming between them, she thought in dismay. Amelia lifted her blue-silk skirts and hurried determinedly down the hall, but her heart pounded with dread. Now, she had nothing but regret for her earlier behavior. She paused to knock briskly on his door; he had left it slightly ajar.

A moment later he appeared there, opening it more widely. He had removed his dark jacket, but his shirt was damp, and his breeches were sodden, his boots muddy and damp. His hair was soaking wet. His regard was impassive, meeting hers.

"Thank God you are back. I have been worried," Amelia said.

He ran a hand through his damp hair, which was

loose, and stepped aside. Amelia entered the sitting room. "Are you all right?" she asked cautiously.

"Are you?" he returned evenly.

She trembled. "Simon, I love you. I am sorry I accused you as I did—"

He cut her off. "You were right."

She inhaled. "I had no right to rail at you as I did, and I struck you! I am so sorry. Will you forgive me?"

"You had every right, both to rail and to strike me, so there is nothing to forgive." He suddenly closed the door and began removing his shirt. "I beg your pardon. I am very wet and it is unseasonably cool tonight."

He was being so formal. Amelia rushed forward, helping him out of his shirt. "You will catch a terrible ague like this."

He did not respond, walking past her. He poured two cognacs and handed her one.

Amelia set it down. She went into his bedroom, but did not have to go to the armoire—his valet had laid out a caftan for him. She took it back into the salon, where he stood shirtless, sipping his cognac and watching her over its rim. "Please put this on, before you become ill."

He set his drink down and shrugged on the navy jacquard robe. "How can you possibly care?"

"Didn't you hear me? I love you, Simon—"

He interrupted her again. "I should have never brought you here. I should have insisted you stay with the children in Cornwall, where, at least, there was some modicum of distance between you and my enemies."

"Please don't blame yourself for what happened to Lucille. She is all right!" Amelia cried desperately.

"If I am not to blame, who is?" he asked sharply. "We both know I have put this entire household in jeopardy."

She walked over to him and took his hands in hers

and held them to her chest. "No one has a crystal ball, Simon. When you first agreed to spy for your country, you could not anticipate how dangerous your activities would become. You could not know that one day, you would have to spy for our enemies in order to survive. It is heroic and patriotic, to do what you have done." She tried to smile and failed.

"But?" he demanded harshly.

She knew what she wanted to say—what she must say—but she said instead, delaying, "You are a hero. You are a patriot, Simon."

"I am a coward. I am a traitor," he said harshly.

She gasped. "What did you just do?"

He pulled free of her. "Trust me, you do not want to know."

She was incapable of drawing a normal breath now, as he paced, drink in hand, sipping from it. What had he done? Were they still in danger? "Simon, these war games must end. Tell Warlock you are done. Tell him you must put your family first," she finally said, her heart racing with desperation. "We cannot go on this way."

"Warlock? He is not going to be very pleased with me. But it is not Warlock I am worried about," he said, his stare direct. "Warlock will not use my children against me—he actually has a conscience. But they have already done so once, and why wouldn't they do so again?"

He was referring to his French spymasters, she thought. "Are you saying that you will never be free of the French? That they will manipulate you through your children?"

"Didn't they just do precisely that?" He was mocking.

"Simon! There has to be a way out."

"If there is a way out, Amelia, I have yet to discover

it," he said tiredly. "In fact, my value to Lafleur has undoubtedly just risen."

Amelia stared. He had been shouting the name Lafleur in his nightmares, and she recalled the fact vividly.
Now, she knew the name of one of his French contacts.
She shuddered. She truly didn't want to know about Lafleur, did she? And what had Simon just meant? What
had he done to make the French value him even more
than before, as one of their agents?

Simon had finished the brandy. He was staring un-
seeingly at the dark fireplace. His expression had never
been as ravaged.

Tears arising, Amelia went to him and wrapped him
in her arms. "If you cannot get out, then we will manage together, somehow."

He trembled. "I am so sorry, Amelia," he said.

"Shh," she returned. "You have nothing to be sorry
for. Lucille is home, the children are safe. We will figure out how to end these affairs, Simon, although perhaps not tonight."

He made a mirthless sound, reversing their positions
and wrapping his arms around her. "I do not believe I
have ever told you how much I love you," he said softly.

She froze. He had never declared his love for her before.

Simon smiled lopsidedly and kissed her. "I would be a
madman without you," he said. And he kissed her again.

SIMON SAT AT HIS DESK in the library, staring at the brief
missive he had received at breakfast. Warlock was on his
way to speak to him and the matter was urgent.

His tension was almost impossible to bear. Warlock
knew what he had done yesterday, of course—nothing
happened in London that affected the British war effort

that the spymaster did not know about. Why else would
Warlock be calling the very day after Lucille's abduction
and return—the very day after he had compromised the
British war effort?

His temples throbbed. He had spent another sleepless night. After making love to Amelia, he had held
her while she fell asleep, wondering at her loyalty and
tenacity—wondering when her feelings for him would
change. And once she was soundly asleep, he had gone
to check on the sleeping boys, and then Lucille. And as
he had stared down at Southland's daughter, he had realized that her welfare had become very important to him.

Lucille felt like the daughter he wished to have with
Amelia—but never would.

Afterward, he had wandered about the house, finally
going into the library, where he had stayed till dawn,
reading some articles about the war. The news was stunning. General Coburg and the Duke of York, who was
leading the British Allied contingent, had decided to go
on the defensive now. Could this war even be won? One
side would capture a garrison or a town, and then the
other would recapture it. So far, the spring had been a
series of victories followed by defeats. He did not care
for the Allies going on the defensive so soon.

"Hello, Simon."

Simon leaped to his feet, not having heard Warlock
come to the open door. "You seem surprised, Simon. I
did send a note," Warlock drawled.

"Close the door," Simon said curtly. "What happened
to my butler?"

Sebastian smiled and obeyed. "I told him I knew my
way through the house—rather forcefully. Do not be too
hard on him. He is a good man."

"What do you want?" Simon asked darkly.

His brows lifted. "Why aren't you in better spirits? You got the child back."

Simon snorted, without mirth. "I take it you have spies in my household?" How else would Warlock know of Lucille's abduction and return?

"I considered it," Warlock said smoothly, sprawling out in a chair before Simon's desk. "In fact, I asked Amelia to spy on you, but she loves you and she refused."

He choked. "She should be left out of this damned war!"

"And how the hell can you accomplish that, when she is here, in your home? Lucas called on me. He was very concerned about the baby's abduction. He asked for my help. And that is an example of the kind of loyalty I am prone to reward." His stare narrowed.

Simon sat down behind his desk, perspiring. "You don't care about my children or anyone else's. I had no intention of discussing this with you."

"I do not know why so many think me so heartless. I do care about the innocent—it is why I am in this damned war to begin with." His eyes flashed in a rare moment of genuine passion. "And you could have come to me. I immediately suspected who had taken Lucille, and I quickly learned that I was right. But of course, you took matters into your own hands. Duke has fled the country, by the way."

Simon stared. "I had to give him up."

"You are very impressive, Simon. When did you discover the truth about Duke?"

"Shortly after my return to London."

"Of course. You needed an ace up your sleeve. In any case, I am thrilled that the child is home—and unharmed."

Simon actually believed him. There was no relief. "What are you going to do?"

"To you?" Sebastian smiled. "Simon, from every downturn, there is an upturn. A phoenix can always arise from the ashes. And these ashes are very, very intriguing."

Simon crossed his arms, with no small amount of trepidation. He would not charge him with treason? He wet his lips and said, "I don't care about any damned phoenix. Find someone else to play your dirty games. I want out, Sebastian. I am tired. I am done. I want to live an ordinary life with my children and Amelia. I told Duke that Jourdan is dead. I don't know if he believed me, but if that were the case, Jourdan could not continue on for Lafleur and *le Comité*."

"Simon—Jourdan is not dead. Not only is he alive and well and sitting before me, he is perfectly placed. He has just given the French absolute proof of his loyalty, proof of his value, his worth. No moment could be more opportune. I have already set in motion a plan for Jourdan to return to Paris, where he will be welcomed as a hero. Of course, you must avoid Duke now—if he is there. I have heard that he has fled to Spain, however. And once you are back in the Commune, you can begin to report on the opposition to Robespierre, which is growing." Warlock smiled. "As I said, you are perfectly placed and perfectly trusted."

Simon stood up. "You are mad to even think of sending me back. They imprisoned me once. One false step and I am a dead man."

"But you are adept at taking the right steps." Warlock stood and said seriously, "You are my best agent, Simon. You always land on your feet, like a cat with nine lives. You do not give yourself the credit you deserve.

I know of no one who could have talked his way out of the prison—and *la guillotine*—as you did. It was brilliant. I have complete faith in you now."

Simon had never felt more despair; he was clawed with it. "And you trust me?"

"I don't have to trust you, Simon, I simply have to stay a half step ahead of you."

The sense of hopelessness was consuming. "And if I refuse?"

"How can you refuse?" Warlock smiled. "I know what you did yesterday, Simon. Some might call your disclosures to Duke an act of treason."

Simon inhaled. "You bastard. You are threatening me."

"I prefer to think of it as simple persuasion."

SOMETHING WAS WRONG with Simon, Amelia thought. Supper was almost over, but Simon hadn't touched any of his plates—she doubted he'd taken a single bite of food. The few times she had glanced into the dining room, the boys had been chattering away, but Simon had seemed lost in thought.

Of course, he was filled with guilt over Lucille's abduction and Amelia knew it. But his dark mood had been worse today than last night. She knew him so well. Something had happened, and she was terribly afraid to find out what that something was.

Amelia came into the dining room, wearing a bright smile. "William, John, you may be excused. Please go upstairs and get ready for bed. I will be up in a bit to read and say good-night." As she smiled at the boys, she was aware of Simon staring intently at her. A flush began, prickling at her nape and her breasts.

Last night, his lovemaking had been frenzied and fe-

verish. She glanced at him. His gaze was so direct. She
felt herself blush. She knew when he needed her, when
his thoughts were illicit and sensual.

When the boys were gone, she smiled a little and said,
"May I sit down?" Two servants were clearing the table.

"You may always sit down and you do not need to
ask," he said abruptly.

Amelia glanced nervously at the two servants, but
neither looked at her as they carried the trays with the
dessert dishes from the room. She took William's chair,
on his right. "Of course I need to ask, Simon."

He shocked her by cupping her jaw with his hand.
"Warlock has asked me to return to Paris."

She cried out.

He grimaced, dropped his hand and moved his wine-
glass to the place mat which remained in front of her.
"He insists. I do not think I can dissuade him," he said.

Amelia ignored the glass of wine. "You cannot go
back," she gasped, stricken. "I need you, Simon—the
children need you. You are their father—the head of
this household!"

She was leaning on the table and he covered her hands
with his. "I cannot refuse him, Amelia. And maybe it is
for the best. I am well placed amongst the French now.
You will be safer when I am gone."

She choked. "You cannot go back!"

His grasp tightened. "I am not being given a choice."

Tears began to interfere with her vision. "You were
imprisoned already, Simon. It is too dangerous. You cannot go back. What is wrong with Warlock! Damn him!
Why didn't you refuse?" Amelia realized she was crying. "Please, if you really love me, refuse. Refuse to go.
He cannot force you."

He was silent for a moment, staring in anguish at her.

"But he can, Amelia. He could charge me with treason if I do not do as he says."

And Amelia felt all the blood drain from her head and face. She reached for the table, afraid that she might faint. What had Simon done?

"My orders are clear, Amelia. I have been given a month's reprieve. I am bound for France at the end of June." He stood, taking her with him. "I think we should relish the time we have left."

AMELIA DID NOT KNOW how she could so acutely feel the passage of every hour, of every minute, of every second. Five days had passed since Lucille had been returned to them and Warlock had ordered Simon to return to France. But it felt like five seconds. They had one month left before Simon must depart for France to spy for his country—perhaps never to return.

She was sick with fear, seated in the pink salon across from her sister. Julianne had called, determined to be with her during her ordeal. Amelia had confessed everything to her, needing her sister as never before. As they took tea, the boys were immersed in their lessons, and Julianne's daughter, Jaquelyn, was in the nursery with Lucille. Simon was in his library, and she had seen him take the week's newspapers with him. She knew his attention was on the war.

Julianne reached across the table where they were sipping tea, taking her hand. "This is so unfair," Julianne whispered. "I know better than anyone what you are going through. But I only had a day in which to anticipate Dom's departure for France, in which to live in a state of fear and dread."

"You lived in a constant state of fear and dread from the moment he left until the moment he returned," Amelia said. How well she recalled her sister's own ordeal. "But Dominic did return to you, in the end. I am terrified for Simon, Julianne! What if he doesn't return? What if the French catch him spying on them? What if he is sent to the guillotine?"

"Simon will return to you as well, Amelia. He is so clever and so resilient. He loves you so." Julianne was firm.

"He shouldn't have to leave in the first place!" Amelia exclaimed. She flushed angrily. The one thing she hadn't told Julianne was why Simon hadn't been able to refuse their uncle. "We were just finding happiness when Lucille was abducted. We were just becoming a family…and now, Warlock snaps his fingers, and for love of country and king, we must all suffer the consequences of his dictums!"

Julianne was silent for a moment. "What aren't you telling me, Amelia? Warlock must be holding something over Simon, to have him leap to obey his every command."

She pulled her hand away. She did not want to lie to her dear sister. "He is entirely ruthless. I went to see him yesterday, to beg him to change his mind. He said he had no choice in this matter. There is always a choice!" Amelia cried.

"How is Simon managing?" Julianne asked, after a pause.

Amelia inhaled. "I am so worried about him. Simon is deeply scarred by his time in France, and especially by having been incarcerated there. He still has nightmares! He dreams of the time he spent in prison and of the innocent lives claimed by the guillotine—he dreams of death. He never speaks openly of it. But I have heard enough to understand how terribly affected he has been.

I am afraid that even if he survives, he will return to me an entirely different man."

Julianne squeezed her hand. "You must think positively, Amelia. And you must take every moment Warlock has given you, and live it as if there is no tomorrow. In fact, I should go and you should interrupt Simon and remind him of why he loves you so."

Amelia smiled sadly at her sister. Maybe she would do exactly as Julianne was suggesting. It would hardly be the first time she had seduced Simon in the middle of the day. Their afternoon trysts were becoming more frequent now. She knew he was as desperate as she was. They were racing the clock, but it was a losing battle.

Julianne stood. "Let's get the children. And maybe Warlock will change his mind," she said. "This war is always filled with unexpected twists and turns. Maybe the Allies will triumph on the battlefield this month, making Simon's return unnecessary."

Amelia sighed, as the war seemed to seesaw back and forth between both armies. It was impossible to tell who was going to triumph in the end. As she stood up, she suddenly heard someone rapidly approaching. She recognized the sound—the footsteps belonged to Lloyd, yet he never rushed. She stiffened with some incipient alarm as he ran into the room.

"Something is amiss, Miss Greystone. Your uncle has just barged into the house, demanding to know where his lordship is. I told him that his lordship is in the library. I am sorry, Miss Greystone!"

"It is all right." But she felt her heart lurch.

Why would Warlock behave in such a manner? Amelia glanced at Julianne, even more alarmed, and lifted her skirts and ran from the room, followed by both her sister and Lloyd.

The library door was wide open, and as Amelia rushed to the threshold, she saw Simon standing behind his desk, facing Warlock. Simon seemed stunned.

Terribly frightened now, Amelia whirled. "Lloyd, leave us, please," she cried. When he was gone, she shared a look with her sister, and rushed into the library, as well. "What has happened?"

Simon glanced at her, his eyes wide with shock.

Warlock turned to Amelia and Julianne. "A warrant has been issued for Simon's arrest."

Amelia cried out in disbelief. Was this a jest? Simon barely looked at her. "The charges?" he asked Warlock hoarsely.

Warlock hesitated, his regard unwavering upon Simon. "Treason."

Amelia gasped. She looked back and forth between both men, and suddenly realized that this was no mistake. Someone other than Warlock had learned of the double game Simon was playing. So much dread began. "Can we stop this, somehow?"

Warlock glanced at her. "The warrant has been issued, Amelia. We cannot stop the authorities from descending upon this house and removing Simon from it."

She seized the edge of the desk to keep from reeling. "Simon?" What were they going to do?

Simon inhaled and looked at her. Their gazes met.

Amelia did not know what his unwavering regard meant. But her own mind had gone strangely blank. The British authorities were going to arrest Simon; they were going to charge him with treason. The British authorities were going to send Simon back to prison.

Oh, my God, he would never survive another term of incarceration.

Warlock broke the tension. "You do not have time

on your side. If you wish to avoid detention, you must leave London now."

Simon had to flee, Amelia thought, stricken.

"I need to say goodbye to the children," he said harshly.

"Then do so now," Warlock flashed. "But hurry, and do not alarm them. We will claim you are out later, when they come looking for you. I have already sent for Lucas. He will help you flee."

Simon nodded, his face a dark mask of determination, and then he looked at Amelia. "I know you will take care of the children," he said.

She seized his arm. He was leaving her. "Where are you going to go?" she heard herself ask hoarsely. "When will you be able to return? When will we see each other again?"

"I don't know," he said roughly.

How could this be happening? How could their lives be imploding this way? She turned to Warlock, desperately. "Can we go with him? The children need their father—and I need him!" But even as she spoke, she knew the answer.

"Simon—you must hurry," Warlock said with urgency.

"Amelia!" Simon took her shoulders. "I should not ask this, but I am going to ask you to wait for me," he said roughly. "Will you wait for me, Amelia?"

Of course she would wait, she thought, crying. But Simon could be in hiding for years. And then she knew she could not wait without a promise for the future. "No! Simon... Marry me now, before you flee."

CHAPTER NINETEEN

HIS EYES BRIGHT WITH UNSHED TEARS, he lowered his gaze to her hand. "With this ring, I take you to be my lawful and wedded wife," Simon said softly. He slid the gold band onto her finger. "Until death do us part."

Outside the small, fifteenth-century church, the rain had stopped. The stained-glass windows no longer rattled, and a bird began to chirp. A ray of sunlight entered the room. Amelia faced Simon, her heart filled with both anguish and joy. She was about to become Simon's wife—and then he would leave her.

Lucas stood beside her. He had brought the rings. Warlock had suggested they attempt to marry in one of London's many small parish churches as Simon fled town. Amelia did not know how Simon and Lucas had arranged the brief, highly unorthodox ceremony, but she suspected a great deal of funds had changed hands.

The reverend was nodding at her, in encouragement.

Amelia stared back at Simon, and said hoarsely, "I take you, Simon, to be my lawful and wedded husband, until death do us part."

"By the powers vested in me by God and the Church of England, I now pronounce you man and wife," the reverend said. And bowing his head over the Bible he held, he began to read a blessing aloud to them.

Amelia did not hear a single word he said. She and

Simon were married, and in another moment, he and Lucas would ride away.

What if she never saw him again?

How could this be happening?

"Reverend." Lucas firmly interrupted, stepping forward. "We have to go. Thank you, sir."

Amelia didn't even see the exchange. Tears were blinding her. She was aware of Simon putting his arm around her and walking her down the nave of the old church. Her low heels clicked on the stone floors. He pushed open the heavy wood-and-iron door, the hinges moaning, and they stepped into the small sodden garden outside. Red roses sparkled with drops of water, as did a huge hydrangea bush.

Amelia shivered, suddenly freezing. Her coach was parked on the street beyond the church's front gates. Two horses were tied to its rear fender. Small bags were strapped to the saddles.

Could she survive without Simon? He was the love of her life!

Simon pulled her into his arms. "I wonder if that ceremony was even valid?" But he did not smile at her.

She wished she could laugh about the ten-minute service. She wondered if she would ever laugh—or smile—again. "I don't care if it is valid or not. In the eyes of God, we are man and wife." She began to cry.

"Don't. Amelia, this is a time of war. We cannot control our destinies. We can only respond to fate the best that we can."

"Damn whoever betrayed you, Simon! You are a patriot, and now, you must flee the country as an outlaw!"

He pulled her close and held her, hard. "Remind the children of how much I love them." He looked down at her. "Never forget how much I love you."

She couldn't stand the pain of their impending separation. Her heart was crushed with anguish. "I know you are coming back to us. I know it!" she cried.

"Warlock will lobby Windham until the charges are dropped." Simon was firm. But doubt was reflected in his eyes.

"I love you so much."

He held her, hard, and they both knew that their embrace might be the last time they were in one another's arms.

He somehow let her go. She stepped back, but she held his hands. "Write to us when you can."

"If I can get word to you, I will. Amelia—I want you to return to Cornwall. You will be safer there." He suddenly glanced past her.

Amelia half turned and saw Lucas hurrying from the small stone church, his face grim, urgency flashing in his eyes. It was time.

Frantic, she faced him. "I love you. I always have. I will never stop."

His grasp on her hands briefly tightened, and then he released her.

"We have to go. I want to be as far from the city as possible when night falls," Lucas said sharply, reaching them. Then, to Amelia, he said more kindly, "I will take good care of him. Do not worry."

She nodded, incapable of speech or movement.

Simon looked at her. His regard was sharp, lingering.

And then he and Lucas were striding purposefully to their horses, untying the reins, and leaping astride. Amelia covered her mouth with her hand, her heart lurching in pain, as Simon lifted his hand in farewell, glancing at her one final time. Then he whirled his mount, as did

Lucas, and the two trotted down the street. They vanished around a corner.

Amelia just stood there, staring after them, crying for a long time.

THE DOORMAN, GEORGE, held the front door open for her. Amelia couldn't smile at him. She had wept openly and unabashedly the entire carriage ride home.

Simon was gone.

Julianne rushed into the hall, surprising her. "Oh, Amelia!"

Amelia nodded at the doorman and met her sister in the center of the hall. "It is done," she said raggedly. She took off her gloves, revealing the simple, unadorned gold wedding band.

Julianne stared, her gaze filled with worry, and then she hugged her. "And Simon?" she whispered.

"He and Lucas rode away…. They would not tell me where they are going." She heard her voice break.

Julianne slid her arm around her. "We will repair this, Amelia. I have already spoken to Dom. He will lobby Windham immediately for a rescission of the charges. He is furious, by the way!"

"I never told you the entire truth, Julianne." She took her sister's arm and pulled her into the nearby salon. "Simon was spying for the French as well as for us. He may very well be guilty of the charges."

Julianne gasped, turning pale.

"I am so afraid I will never see him again!" She inhaled, pain stabbing through her breast. "But Simon is right. This is war. We cannot control fate. Fate controls us." She struggled for composure. "I must be strong. Simon is gone. I pray that, one day, he will be able to return, but in the meanwhile, there are three small children in this house, and they need me."

Julianne seized her hand. "What are you going to tell them? And what will you tell the staff?"

Amelia had spent the past half hour indulging herself in her own grief, in her tears, and she hadn't had a chance to think about what she must do. It was tempting to tell the boys that their father had gone to visit his northern estates, at least for now. And she could tell the staff the very same thing.

But there was a warrant out for Simon's arrest. Could such news be kept secret indefinitely?

She thought about the boys again. William was only eight, but he was mature beyond his years. On the other hand, he had just lost his mother. "My instincts tell me that William must know the truth, sooner or later."

"What if we can bring Simon home soon? In a matter of weeks or months?" Julianne asked.

"What if he is gone for years?" Amelia responded. Her heart throbbed with pain at the thought.

Julianne squeezed her hand.

An insistent knocking sounded on the front door.

She tensed in alarm. "I have to think about this," she told her sister as footsteps sounded in the front hall. It sounded as if a number of men had marched into the house.

Amelia shared a glance with her sister; Julianne was as alarmed. Then she ran to the threshold of the salon, her sister behind her. Amelia faltered.

A uniformed officer of the guard stood in the front hall, with two other soldiers and Lloyd.

"Miss Greystone," the butler said, coming forward, his eyes wide. "The captain is looking for his lordship. Do you know where he is?"

Somehow she lifted her chin and squared her shoulders, smiling as she walked to the waiting officer. His blue gaze was sharp, meeting hers.

Amelia extended her hand. "I am Miss Greystone, the housekeeper." She would not reveal that she and Simon had just been married—it might raise too many questions and lead to the truth that he had fled town. "I'm afraid that Lord Grenville is out, but we are expecting him back for supper."

The officer bowed. "I am Captain Johnson, Miss Greystone. May I have a word privately?"

Amelia nodded. "This is my sister, the Countess of Bedford. Do you mind if she joins us?"

The young, blond captain started. Of course, such a family connection was highly unusual for a housekeeper. "Of course not," he said.

Amelia led the captain and Julianne back into the salon. She closed both doors behind them and managed another smile as she faced the captain. "How can I be of help, sir?" she asked calmly.

He produced a rolled document, tied with a dark velvet ribbon. "I'm afraid, Miss Greystone, that I have a warrant for Lord Grenville's arrest."

Amelia simply stared. Inwardly, she curdled. "May I see the document, sir?"

"Of course." He untied the ribbon, unrolled the page and handed it to her.

Amelia looked at it. It was hard to read the writing on the page, as her vision was blurring. She felt her sister come to stand beside her, and Julianne said, "It is an arrest warrant. Simon is being charged with treason."

Amelia inhaled. "This is absurd, sir."

"I am very sorry to bring you such tidings," Captain Johnson said. "I am merely following my orders,

Miss Greystone. And my orders are to arrest his lord-ship tonight."

"I see," she managed, rather foolishly.

"Where would it be convenient for me and my men to await Lord Grenville's return?"

"You may wait here," Amelia said.

"WHAT DO YOU THINK, Signor Barelli?" Amelia asked impatiently.

It was midmorning, a week later. She stood in the classroom with her hands on her hips, as the tutor fin-ished reading her notes. She had spent almost an en-tire week revising the boys' curriculum. William loved languages and excelled at them. He should be spend-ing more time on that subject, and less on mathemat-ics, which he abhorred and struggled with. John was fascinated with all manner of science, from the nature of insects to the motion of a ball and the position of the stars. Why not immerse him in an introductory course on biology? Or astrology?

"I think that this is a highly, er, unusual schedule, Miss Greystone," the Italian schoolmaster said. "Mas-ter William barely received a passing grade on his last arithmetic examination. He should spend more time on mathematics, and less on French, Italian, German and Latin. He already excels in the languages. And why add Russian to his curriculum?"

"He has asked me if he could begin to study Russian, and current political discourse suggests that the Russians will become more important to Britain and the world, not less. Why not allow William to study the language?" She spoke firmly, but she smiled. "I have little doubt that, if his lordship were in residence, he would allow me to revise their studies as I have chosen."

Signor Barelli pushed her notes aside and stood, his gaze filled with sympathy. "Dare I ask, Miss Greystone, has there been any word?"

Her heart flooded with the grief that never completely dissipated. She had not been able to hide the fact that a warrant had been issued for Simon's arrest. When the authorities had come to the house intending to arrest Simon and he had not been home, Captain Johnson had decided to wait for his appearance. That hadn't raised eyebrows. But when Simon had failed to return, the captain had insisted on searching the entire house thoroughly. The search had taken two and a half hours, and it had disrupted everyone.

William and John had wanted to know why soldiers were in the house. Amelia was a firm believer in the truth, but not in these circumstances. She told the boys that the soldiers were looking for their father—but that it was a terrible misunderstanding, one that she was already attempting to clear up.

She had managed to keep the entire truth from the boys. William had asked why the soldiers wanted to speak with his father, and she had told him that they believed he had important information about the war. She didn't want them to worry, and she had done her best to make light of the matter. Both boys had been convinced that this episode would quickly pass. But there was no deceiving the rest of the household.

Amelia had assembled the entire household the following morning at dawn, excluding the boys, who remained asleep. She had told everyone about the charges, and that they were a terrible mistake that would be sorted out eventually. The staff had been shocked to learn that Simon was being charged with treason—and that he was suspected of spying for the French republicans. She had

looked each and every man and woman in the eye, and
told them that she expected their faith and loyalty. "If
anyone here does not believe in his lordship's innocence,
I expect you to step forward now. You will be dismissed,
but with a week's wages and good references."

No one had stepped forward.

When both Lloyd and Mrs. Murdock had approached
her individually, professing their outrage over the
charges, it was clear to her that they both believed in
Simon's innocence. As the rest of the staff looked up to
them both for direction, Amelia was relieved. Any ma-
lignant gossip below stairs would be quickly laid to rest.

And then there was Momma. In an entirely lucid
moment, she wanted to know where Simon had gone
and when he was returning to them. Amelia had almost
collapsed in tears. And now she had to lie to her own
mother. For she was afraid that, when her wits were addled, Momma might innocently disclose the truth. "He
has gone to his northern estates, Momma," she had whispered, praying God would forgive her. "He will surely
return to us soon."

Meanwhile, Dominic was directly petitioning the War
Secretary to have the charges against Simon dropped.
If Windham would not change his mind, he planned to
speak directly with the Prince Regent, whom he knew
rather well.

Warlock had also devised a petition, which he had
already sent to the War Office. It hadn't been answered
yet. Amelia hadn't expected him to be helpful, but he
was irate over the injustice being done to one of his men.
However, he also said that Windham seemed to be taking the news of Simon's betrayal very personally. That
did not bode well.

Now Amelia faced the tutor, pain stabbing through

her breast. "There has been no word, Signor, and I am sure it is safe for his lordship to send word." Captain Johnson had called again. She knew he was hoping to catch Simon at the house, on the off chance that he would return to visit. Johnson had warned her that if she was aiding and abetting a fugitive, she could face charges, as well. Amelia had decided not to reply to such a comment, obviously meant to wear her down.

"Can I count on you to begin the changes to the curriculum that I have suggested?" she added, smiling at Signor Barelli.

"Of course." He bowed.

Amelia quickly left the classroom, fingering her wedding band, which she wore on a chain around her neck. It would be wonderful to shout out to the world that she was now Lady Grenville, but she knew she could not. Simon had fled the law, and if she confessed to eloping with him beforehand, it would obviously make her an accessory to his escape.

Amelia strode down the hall, passing open door after open door. She had decided to thoroughly clean the entire house, and windows were wide open, beds were stripped, rugs were rolled up, furniture was being dusted and cleaned, the floors waxed and polished.

The "summer" cleaning would be finished in a week or so. The house would never look better, once she was done. Next week, she intended to attack the kitchens and begin a massive reorganization of the pantries, cleaning every nook and cranny to be found. After that, she was to discuss the state of the gardens with the head gardener. She wanted to plant a maze behind the house, reminiscent of the maze at St. Just Hall in Cornwall.

She faltered. A poignant memory assailed her, of hid-

ing breathlessly in the maze as Simon hunted for her.
When he had found her, they had nearly made love....

She shook herself free of the long-ago past. While
Simon was gone, she would do her best to manage his
home and his estates. Repairs would be made when necessary. There would be restorations and refurbishments.
When he came home, he would see that she had kept his
estate for him in the best possible condition....

But when would that be? He had been gone for eight
days. It felt like eight years!

Amelia hurried directly to the library, where she had
an appointment. As she had thought, she was late.

A rustically dressed gentleman stood there, hat in
hand, and he bowed when he saw her.

He was a steward from one of Simon's largest northern estates, and she had written to him, asking him to
come to London to meet Simon. She doubted he would
have come to town if summoned by a mere housekeeper.
"Good day, Mr. Harold," she said cheerfully, espying
a large ledger on the desk. "I am Miss Greystone, and
I am acting on his lordship's behalf. As you may have
heard, he is out of town."

The steward was a middle-aged man in a gray wig
and a brown-velvet jacket. He blinked at her. "I was summoned here by his lordship, Miss Greystone. I received
a letter directly from him."

She smiled again. "Actually, I wrote that letter, as his
lordship cannot currently oversee his estates, and the
duty had fallen upon me—just as the duty of caring for
his children and his home has fallen upon me."

He blinked again. "I had heard some gossip about his
lordship, but I dismissed it. Surely it isn't true?"

"There has been a misunderstanding," she said firmly.
She closed the library door. "A warrant has been issued

for his arrest, and I imagine that is why his lordship left town so suddenly, without explanation." She faced Mr. Harold and smiled again. "I have no doubt that when the charges are dropped, he will return. In the meanwhile, I intend to make sure his estates are being run as effectively as they were before his departure."

The steward fidgeted. "Miss Greystone, I have always dealt directly with his lordship—or I have been left to my own devices."

She went to the desk and gestured at a chair facing it. Mr. Harold simply stared, so she ordered, "Sit down, Mr. Harold. Or should I summon my brother-in-law, the Count of Bedford? Surely he will convince you to be cooperative. We must all do our duties, with his lordship absent."

Mr. Harold immediately sat down.

Amelia smiled and took Simon's seat behind the desk. She opened the ledger. "We are going to go over all the accounts. And we will start with your weekly expenses."

Mr. Harold nodded.

Dublin, Ireland, July 29, 1794

THE LAST FEW RAYS OF SUNLIGHT slipped into the small hotel room. Simon hunched over the writing tablet, seated at a tiny desk, dipping his quill and writing frantically to outrace the fading daylight. The room was already dark with shadow.

"The sun is about to set, so I must end this missive now. Not a day goes by that I do not anticipate our joyful reunion. My heart remains with you and the children, Amelia, as always. Yours truly, Simon."

He briefly closed his eyes, as deeper shadows consumed the narrow room. He could hear the sounds of children playing outside in the street below his window. There was laughter and happy shouts. Then he heard a woman calling to them. His heart clenched with anguish.

In his mind's eye, he saw Amelia hurrying through his house, calling for the boys. They came running eagerly out of the classroom and she was smiling....

He missed his children so. He missed his wife.

Simon inhaled, opening his eyes. He had never imagined that they would have the opportunity to wed, and it amazed him still that she was his wife. Would he ever be allowed to return home? Would he ever see her again? Hold her? Make love to her?

Of course, there had been no word from her. What had she told the boys? Were they all right? How was Lucille?

His chest was constricted. He still clutched the quill, so he relaxed his fingers and laid it carefully down. He did not want to break it; he only had one spare left.

He had been in Ireland for almost two months, and his finances were becoming precarious. He could hardly go to the bank and identify himself and await funds from his accounts in England. However, he and Lucas had discussed all of his plans, including his need for funds, when Lucas had left him in Carlisle. He had opened an account at a Dublin bank in the name of Tim O'Malley. Eventually Warlock would arrange for a transfer of funds. He hoped the transfer would happen soon.

He shoved his chair back rudely from the tiny table, which was more the size of a dinner tray. The abrupt action caused his letter to fall to the floor. Suddenly furious and frustrated, he stood.

The letter wasn't dry yet as he retrieved it, but he didn't care. He turned, opened the room's single bureau and shoved the damp letter inside. Dozens of other letters were already there. He could write to her as much as he desired, and he wrote to her every single day. But he couldn't post a single letter. It was too damned dangerous.

His heart aching, he closed the drawer and lit the candle that was on top of the bureau. Then he poured wine from an open bottle into a tin mug, and he caught a glimpse of his reflection in the rusting, chipped mirror hanging over the bureau on the wall.

He only shaved once a week now. There was gray in his beard and white streaks at his temples. His hair was loose, and well past his shoulders. He desperately needed a haircut.

He wore a poor man's cotton shirt, without any adornment. His hands were free of rings. He did not wear a belt. His breeches had a hole in one knee.

No one would assume him to be anything but a down-and-out Irishman.

He took the mug and went to the window, pushing it as widely open as possible. He was hoping for a glimpse of the two boys who so often played stickball in the street. One was red-haired and William's age, the other a bit younger and blond. But it was dusk now, and the boys were gone.

He decided he would spend another evening at the small pub on the corner below the inn. While he spoke to no one—he didn't dare—he craved the human company.

Someone knocked on his door.

Simon tensed, putting his mug down and taking a dagger from beneath the single pillow on his narrow bed. He was barefoot, and he took two soundless steps to the door. He leaned against it, listening.

Someone knocked again. "O'Malley. O'Malley! It's me, Peter."

He relaxed slightly, slipping the dagger into his shirt-sleeve. After he unbolted the door, he opened it a fraction of an inch and saw Peter, a freckled lad of about eighteen, but his attention was on the narrow hall behind him. It was empty.

He finally relaxed entirely and opened the door so he could face the boy.

"Ye said ye wanted news of the war." Peter grinned eagerly. "And I got news, sir!"

Simon gave him a coin. Peter brought him the *Times* once or twice every week, and he had instructed him to bring him any exceptional war news as well, for which he would be paid. The French had scored a massive victory in Flanders at the end of June, in the Battle of Fleurus, humiliating the Austrian army. Since then, the French had consolidated their armies along the Sambre-et-Meuse, and General Pichegru had gone as far as Antwerp, defying the armies of the Prince of Orange and the Duke of York. General Schérer had successfully besieged Landrecies and was advancing on Valenciennes. The war was not going well.

"From that smile, I would say it is grand news indeed." Simon did not smile.

"It is worthy of another shilling, sir, at the least!"

Simon leaned his shoulder against the doorjamb and waited.

Peter looked disappointed. Then he blurted, "They arrested Robespierre!"

Simon straightened, certain he had misheard. "What?"

"He was arrested, sir, and so were his closest supporters, maybe two days ago!"

His heart was thundering. The face of the Terror had been arrested.

Acutely aware that he could have been in Paris just then, and the city was surely in chaos, Simon took a shilling out of his pocket and handed it to the lad, still in disbelief. "What will they plan? Now what will they do? What is happening in Paris?"

"The Convention has taken power, sir, and the government has been sent to the Blade. They were all executed, every one of them, even Robespierre!"

And Simon stood there, shocked.

The Reign of Terror was truly over.

AMELIA WAS IN DISBELIEF. Robespierre was dead.

He had been executed by the Terror—his own terrible policies had been used against him.

Amelia closed the newspaper, her hands shaking. "Thank God Simon didn't go back to Paris," she whispered to Julianne and Nadine. They sat together in a salon in Julianne's house.

The three women stared at one another, all wide-eyed. Robespierre's closest allies had been executed with him, as had seventy-one members of the city government in the following days. Had Simon taken up his old position in the Commune, he could have been amongst the dead....

"This is wonderful news!" Nadine said. "Maybe now, at last, there will be sanity in government and normalcy in Paris. Maybe now, at last, the killing will stop."

Amelia barely heard her friend. She closed her eyes, and for one moment, she felt that she was with Simon. She could see him standing in a small room, in dark shadows, a single taper burning. Then the image was gone.

He had left town fifty-eight days ago. There hadn't been any word, as it was too dangerous for him to write.

Lucas had told her that he was most definitely out of
the country, but he wouldn't say where. Did it mean he
was in the north, in Scotland? Could he be in Ireland?
Surely he hadn't gone to Europe, not with the chaos of
the ongoing wars there.

"Are you all right, Amelia?" Julianne asked.

Amelia faced her, trying to smile. "I wonder if he has
heard." If Simon ever came home, he would no longer
have to fear the deadly serpent. If he ever came home,
he would be free of fear of retribution and vengeance.
He would be able to say "no" to Warlock, he would be
able to walk away from all of these war games, knowing his children were safe....

"News like this travels like wildfire," Nadine said. "I
am sure he has heard. We must celebrate."

Amelia wished she felt like celebrating, but she
missed Simon too much. She watched as Nadine went to
the side bar and poured three glasses of sherry. Anguish
pierced her. If only she could send a letter to Simon.

"Maybe this war will soon end," Julianne said.

Amelia looked at her. "Julianne, he would remain an
outlaw. As long as those charges are hanging over him,
nothing changes for us."

The doors to the salon burst open, revealing the Count
of Bedford. Julianne leaped up, surprised. "Dom?"

He slowly smiled at them. "Have you heard the
news?"

"Yes, we have," Julianne said. "Robespierre is dead,
damn him to hell. The Terror is over."

Dominic's smile changed and he walked over to Amelia. "No, that is not the news I am referring to."

Amelia tensed, with sudden hope. Why was Dominic looking at her that way—with a smile in his eyes?
Why did he look so satisfied?

He held out a scroll. "This, my dear sister-in-law, is a royal pardon for Grenville."

Amelia reeled.

"I imagine that Simon is on his way home, even as we speak."

IT WAS EARLY MORNING. William clung to the window-sill beside the front door, while John galloped around the hall on a stick with a horse's head attached to it. Momma sat in one of the thronelike chairs against the wall, happily embroidering. Amelia was giddy and faint with hope, expectation and joy.

She was almost afraid that she was dreaming. But Warlock had confirmed the news and Lucas had already left to retrieve Simon, within an hour of Bedford's achieving the royal pardon.

"It's Papa!" William cried.

Amelia ran to the window, as John galloped over, screaming, "Papa! Papa!"

And sure enough, two horsemen were cantering into the driveway, and she recognized her brother and Simon.

Amelia ran to the front door, which was already being held open, her mother following. William and John were faster than she was, and they beat her down the front steps. Simon pulled his mount to a halt before the house, leaping off of it before it was standing entirely still. His hair loosely pulled back, his clothes and boots muddy, he ran toward them.

Amelia stopped, letting the boys leap into their father's arms first. She started to cry. Simon was thin and pale and his hair was so long, but he was home. Her beloved husband was home.

And as he embraced both boys at once, he looked over their heads at her. He was crying.

Amelia came slowly down the steps. Her heart thrummed.

Simon straightened, releasing the boys.

She hesitated—and he swiftly, purposefully came forward. Amelia was swept into his hard embrace and held there.

"I have missed you so," he said roughly.

She looked up, taking his beautiful face in her hands. "Thank God you are home! I have missed you, too, Simon, impossibly!"

He suddenly smiled, his eyes lightening with happiness, and he swooped her closer and kissed her for a long, long time.

"Ewwww," John cried.

"Shh. Father loves her, can't you tell?" William returned.

"Boys, we must give them their privacy," Momma said sternly.

Amelia heard them all, but she took Simon's shoulders and allowed the kiss to go on and on until she couldn't breathe, until her knees were buckling, until she absolutely had to take him upstairs and tear off his clothes—and be a proper wife.

Simon finally came up for air, looking very pleased. "Some things haven't changed," he said softly.

"You, my lord, shall pay quite the price for such a lengthy absence," she managed to flirt, rather breathlessly.

He grinned. "I hope so...wife."

Amelia started. "I have told no one yet." She lifted the chain with her wedding ring from beneath the collar of her dress.

Simon took her shoulders and turned her around. Realizing what he meant to do, Amelia stood very still as he undid the chain, her heart thundering. She was so overcome with love and joy and desire that she could hardly stand it.

He turned her back to face the boys, Momma, Lucas and the coachman and footmen, smiling. Then he grinned at her and she held out her hand. He slid the band onto her fourth finger.

"Papa?" William gasped.

Simon turned. "We have an announcement to make. Amelia and I were married on June 3. Amelia is the Countess of St. Just."

Both boys blinked. Momma started, while the staff looked as surprised. Lucas, of course, simply smiled. And then John ran to her and threw himself at her, hugging her hard, with a screech. William approached, more slowly, but with a smile.

"Can I call you Mama?" John asked, grinning up at her.

"Of course you can," Amelia said, stroking his hair. Her heart surged with too much emotion to bear.

"Should I call you Mother?" William asked, very seriously. He looked first at Amelia and then at his father.

Simon deferred to Amelia.

She put her arm around him. "You may call me whatever you like—whatever feels right."

William stared, beginning to blush. "I am pleased, Miss, er, Mother, that you have married my father."

Amelia laughed and hugged him. And then it was her mother's turn. Momma was crying a mother's tears of joy.

"Oh, darling, I always knew he loved you!" she cried, hugging her, and Amelia had the odd feeling that her mother was recalling the long-ago past, when Simon had so recklessly courted her when she was just a sixteen-year-old girl.

But the present consumed her now. Laughing, she turned and looped her arm in Simon's. She had never been so happy; there had never been so much joy.

He was tugging her toward the house, a definite glint in his eyes. "Why isn't Lucille here to greet me, as well?"

She laughed again. "She was sleeping, the last I looked, but we can wake her up."

"Good," he said, rather ruggedly. "Because we are going to celebrate—as a family."

John clapped his hands. "Can we go to the gypsy circus?"

"I do not see why not," Simon said, smiling. And still smiling, he gave Momma a kiss on her cheek. She blushed.

"We could go up the river on my yacht," William said eagerly.

"First, we are going into the house, where we are going to allow your father to rest after a long and maybe difficult trip. And then we shall make all of our plans," Amelia said. And as they walked past the doormen, they bowed their heads and murmured, "My lord, my lady."

Amelia faltered and turned to gape at both doormen, but they simply grinned at her.

And as Mrs. Murdock came into the front hall with Lucille, Lloyd appeared from the kitchens. John shouted, "Papa has married Miss Greystone! She is my momma now!"

"She is the Countess of St. Just," William declared proudly.

Mrs. Murdock cried out, and even Lloyd started.

Amelia gestured and the nurse came forward, handing the baby over to Simon. Lucille gurgled at him and he smiled down at her.

"Congratulations," Mrs. Murdock whispered.

"Lady Grenville, shall I bring tea and pastries?" Lloyd asked.

Amelia inhaled, taking a good look around her. John was galloping about the front hall on his stick pony, William was admiring Lucille, while Simon had given her his finger to tug on. Mrs. Murdock was beaming at the sight of father and daughter, and Lucas had just entered the hall, escorting their mother. He sent her a warm smile. "Well, Lady Grenville?" her brother teased.

Simon turned, rocking Lucille now. "Lady Grenville?"

Amelia looked at them all. They were her wonderful, beloved family, and Simon was home for good. "Yes, Lloyd, do bring refreshments," she said.

Lloyd bowed and left the room.

And across the children's heads, Simon Grenville looked at her, and for the first time in a decade, the anguish was receding from his eyes. Instead, something bright and joyous was brimming there. "I am home, Amelia, and this time, I am home to stay."

She went to him. The war wasn't over—but it was finally over for them. "Finally," she whispered, as he slowly embraced her. "Finally."

* * * * *

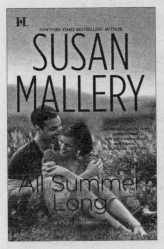

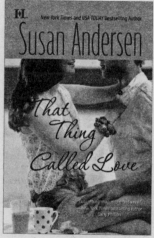

REQUEST YOUR FREE BOOKS!

2 FREE NOVELS
FROM THE ROMANCE COLLECTION
PLUS 2 FREE GIFTS!

YES! Please send me 2 FREE novels from the Romance Collection and my 2 FREE gifts (gifts are worth about $10). After receiving them, if I don't wish to receive any more books, I can return the shipping statement marked "cancel." If I don't cancel, I will receive 4 brand-new novels every month and be billed just $5.99 per book in the U.S. or $6.49 per book in Canada. That's a saving of at least 25% off the cover price. It's quite a bargain! Shipping and handling is just 50¢ per book in the U.S. and 75¢ per book in Canada.* I understand that accepting the 2 free books and gifts places me under no obligation to buy anything. I can always return a shipment and cancel at any time. Even if I never buy another book, the two free books and gifts are mine to keep forever.

194/394 MDN FELQ

Name _____ (PLEASE PRINT)

Address _____ Apt. #

City _____ State/Prov. _____ Zip/Postal Code

Signature (if under 18, a parent or guardian must sign)

Mail to the **Reader Service:**
IN U.S.A.: P.O. Box 1867, Buffalo, NY 14240-1867
IN CANADA: P.O. Box 609, Fort Erie, Ontario L2A 5X3

Not valid for current subscribers to the Romance Collection
or the Romance/Suspense Collection.

Want to try two free books from another line?
Call 1-800-873-8635 or visit www.ReaderService.com.

* Terms and prices subject to change without notice. Prices do not include applicable taxes. Sales tax applicable in N.Y. Canadian residents will be charged applicable taxes. Offer not valid in Quebec. This offer is limited to one order per household. All orders subject to credit approval. Credit or debit balances in a customer's account(s) may be offset by any other outstanding balance owed by or to the customer. Please allow 4 to 6 weeks for delivery. Offer available while quantities last.

Your Privacy—The Reader Service is committed to protecting your privacy. Our Privacy Policy is available online at www.ReaderService.com or upon request from the Reader Service.

We make a portion of our mailing list available to reputable third parties that offer products we believe may interest you. If you prefer that we not exchange your name with third parties, or if you wish to clarify or modify your communication preferences, please visit us at www.ReaderService.com/consumerschoice or write to us at Reader Service Preference Service, P.O. Box 9062, Buffalo, NY 14269. Include your complete name and address.

ROM11

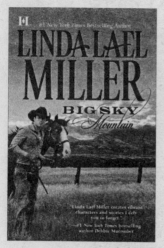

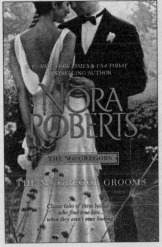

BRENDA JOYCE

77655	SEDUCTION	___ $7.99 U.S.	___ $9.99 CAN.
77551	DEADLY VOWS	___ $7.99 U.S.	___ $9.99 CAN.
77547	DEADLY KISSES	___ $7.99 U.S.	___ $9.99 CAN.
77541	DEADLY ILLUSIONS	___ $7.99 U.S.	___ $9.99 CAN.
77507	THE MASQUERADE	___ $7.99 U.S.	___ $9.99 CAN.
77460	AN IMPOSSIBLE ATTRACTION	___ $7.99 U.S.	___ $9.99 CAN.
77442	THE PROMISE	___ $7.99 U.S.	___ $9.99 CAN.
77346	DARK VICTORY	___ $7.99 U.S.	___ $7.99 CAN.
77334	DARK EMBRACE	___ $7.99 U.S.	___ $7.99 CAN.
77275	A DANGEROUS LOVE	___ $7.99 U.S.	___ $7.99 CAN.
77219	DARK RIVAL	___ $7.99 U.S.	___ $9.50 CAN.

(limited quantities available)

TOTAL AMOUNT	$ _____
POSTAGE & HANDLING	$ _____
($1.00 FOR 1 BOOK, 50¢ for each additional)	
APPLICABLE TAXES*	$ _____
TOTAL PAYABLE	$ _____

(check or money order—please do not send cash)

To order, complete this form and send it, along with a check or money order for the total above, payable to Harlequin HQN, to: **In the U.S.:** 3010 Walden Avenue, P.O. Box 9077, Buffalo, NY 14269-9077; **In Canada:** P.O. Box 636, Fort Erie, Ontario, L2A 5X3.

Name: _____
Address: _____ City: _____
State/Prov.: _____ Zip/Postal Code: _____
Account Number (if applicable): _____

075 CSAS

*New York residents remit applicable sales taxes.
*Canadian residents remit applicable GST and provincial taxes.

HARLEQUIN® HQN™
www.Harlequin.com

PHBJ0812BL